"WHAT IS THIS?" JACK ASKED.

Rosaline did not pull away, for she wanted him to see it clearly, wanted her husband to understand that, although he may possess her body and her dowry and her future tonight, he did not possess her emotions. "Look for yourself," she said.

The locket released easily beneath his touch. Inside, it revealed the miniature self-portrait of the artist Rosaline Cheevers had loved. And still loved.

For several seconds Jack contemplated the memento before his fingers twisted the chain.

Fearing that he would snap it loose. Rosaline bit her lip and squeezed her eyes shut in an effort not to jerk free, for she knew that a physical battle with Jack Darlington would be a futile effort. She surmised that her wearing of the locket on her wedding day had struck a blow to his pride.

Gradually, as if forced, Jack's hand relaxed and released the locket. Pressing his mouth against her ear, he said, "Keep it then. Wear your locket even while you lie with me. I suppose it's only fair."

DANGEROUS GAMES   (0-7860-0270-0, $4.99)
by Amanda Scott

When Nicholas Barrington, eldest son of the Earl of Ulcombe, first met Melissa Seacort, the desperation he sensed beneath her well-bred beauty haunted him. He didn't realize how desperate Melissa really was . . . until he found her again at a Newmarket gambling club—being auctioned off by her father to the highest bidder. So, Nick bought himself a wife. With a villain hot on their heels, and a fortune and their lives at stake, they would gamble everything on the most dangerous game of all: love.

A TOUCH OF PARADISE   (0-7860-0271-9, $4.99)
by Alexa Smart

As a confidence man and scam runner in 1880s America, Malcolm Northrup has amassed a fortune. Now, posing as the eminent Sir John Abbot—scholar, and possible discoverer of the lost continent of Atlantis—he's taking his act on the road with a lecture tour, seeking funds for a scientific experiment he has no intention of making. But scholar Halia Davenport is determined to accompany Malcolm on his "expedition" . . . even if she must kidnap him!

RED PETALS

Debra Hamilton

Zebra Books
Kensington Publishing Corp.

http://www.zebrabooks.com

ZEBRA BOOKS are published by

Kensington Publishing Corp.
850 Third Avenue
New York, NY 10022

First Printing: December, 1997
10 9 8 7 6 5 4 3 2 1

Printed in the United States of America

Chapter One

Orkney Islands, Scotland, 1864

Cloud and sunlight shifted in such swift, ever changing patterns over the green landscape that Jack Darlington felt as if he were peering at it through the broken lens of the kaleidoscope he had stolen when he was five.

What an uproar *that* theft had caused! Jack still remembered the cursed shouts and clawing hands, the startled horses and careening coaches. He remembered how fast he had run, too, darting through ginger beer sellers and hurdy-gurdy men before burrowing into the musty racks of a second hand clothing shop. It had been the first of many such episodes, the inauspicious beginning of a way of life.

With a rueful acceptance of his own destiny, Jack smiled in a manner that had turned countless feminine heads, then braced his legs against the wind and studied the land, this new home of his, with eyes that instinctively, through many years of necessity, assessed everything for its value. He had chosen this island, he supposed, because it matched something in his own nature that was equally remote, equally unpredictable—perhaps even a little ominous to those who weren't intimately acquainted with it.

"Mr. Jack! Mr. Jack!"

Turning at the sound of the reedy voice, Jack watched a boy negotiate the stony, upward path. The lad's small legs resembled two matchsticks anchored to the ground by a pair of oversized black boots. His clothes swallowed him up; the sleeves to his jacket hung below his palms and a woolen cap drooped like a bird's nest over one dark brown eye. Six months had passed, and despite Mrs. Wiggins's surfeit of meat pies and vanilla custards, Rajad seemed not to have gained a sparrow's weight. Jack had no idea how old the boy was, but he guessed six or seven.

The waif sidled up to him, so frail and insubstantial that the wind might have carried him away. In his usual grave and deferential manner, Rajad stretched out a fragile hand, bowed and offered Jack a crumpled letter. "For you, Mr. Jack," he said.

"Thank you, Rajad. Have you been helping Mrs. Wiggins up at the house?"

The boy nodded solemnly.

"How many fish did you catch this morning?"

A thin, brown thumb and forefinger created the shape of a zero.

"None? Rajad! Too bad. Perhaps I should go with you tomorrow and show you how to cast properly."

The boy, somewhat like a shadow, preferred to be close but unobtrusive. While Jack tore open the envelope, Rajad quietly sank cross-legged onto the ground, his skinny arms folded. He gazed up in awe at the fierce, blue eyes that seemed to reflect all the colors of the sky.

Jack scanned the contents of the letter, his expression flickering with reaction. The news related the conclusion of a rather unconventional business transaction, but the timing had been moved forward. It seemed there was now some urgency to the matter.

With a long, thoughtful frown, Jack refolded the paper and slid it into his pocket.

"Well, Rajad," he murmured with his eyes fixed, unseeing, upon the racing silver clouds, "it seems I'm to have a wife before long."

In a rapid untangling of limbs, the child leapt up from the ground, and with mouth agape, stared at Jack with a mixture of uncertainty and fear.

"Will you like such an arrangement, do you think, Rajad?" Jack asked calmly, folding his arms across his chest. "Will you like having a lady about the house?"

Rajad hadn't the confidence to risk censure by being honest, so he simply continued to regard the man with a horrified stare.

Chuckling, Jack touched the top of the boy's head, straightening the crooked cap. He wondered at the boy's reaction. Not so long ago in the perilous streets of Calcutta, he had found Rajad, an ill-treated, unwanted wisp of humanity, a lad so wizened and starved that his mere survival had defied belief. After filing papers with an indifferent Indian government office, Jack had brought the boy home on a steamship. Upon their arrival, his housekeeper, Mrs. Wiggins, had asked Jack why on earth he had decided to raise a nameless heathen waif. Ignoring her appalled expression, Jack had muttered an evasive and very careless answer. "I haven't the slightest idea, Mrs. Wiggins, except that the lad reminds me of someone I used to know."

Now, knowing that the boy feared any change in the daily routine that had been rather inexpertly established for him, Jack smiled reassuringly and patted Rajad's shoulder. "The lady will be very kind, I'm sure. I'll tell her you don't like to be scrubbed behind the ears or forced to eat porridge. I'll tell her that you have a fondness for fishing and a positive aversion to wearing socks. Deal?"

After a moment of consideration, the boy nodded, even while doubt still lurked in the hollowed features of his small brown face.

"Let's walk home, shall we?" Jack invited.

In his birdlike, deliberate manner, Rajad began picking his way over the tumbled rocks, the black shoes meticulously avoiding sun sparkled puddles left by a recent shower. Jack followed, strolling easily over the wind gashed lowlands, his long legs—used to running, vaulting, riding—consuming the distance with hearty ease. While he walked, his eyes fastened upon a distant building nestled in the wrinkled cleft between a pair of craggy green hills.

Long and low, with a thickly thatched roof, the house was truly born of the Orkney earth, its walls constructed of the same mellow grey and brown flagstone quarried from the sea cliffs. The sun veered past the clouds and flitted over the series of tiny leaded windows, so that the facade of the house appeared diamond studded, a jewel fallen amid a casket of emerald green. Unfortunately, its front door was flanked by only a few pathetic specimens of rowan and hazel, for with the constant onslaught of wind and salt, trees did not thrive on the island.

But Jack had built a high stone wall around the back of the house and created a sheltered garden where angelica and alpine flourished. He had planted every cutting himself, nurtured the fledgling plants until they had become hardy and needed only an occasional helping hand with the creeping weeds and thistles. And yet, had anyone asked who had done the gardening, who had dug and watered the plants, whose hands had tended them, Jack probably would have simply shrugged and claimed not to have known.

He paused on the rocky path and scanned his property: the whitewashed byre, the wrinkled fields, and the shaggy chocolate colored ponies he had bought from nearby Shetland. It was the first piece of land, the first home, he had ever owned. The house was not pretentious, and had been neglected for the most part until now. But it suited him and he valued it far more than he was inclined to let anyone know; Jack had learned early in life never to reveal his love of anything—except perhaps, danger.

Every now and then it bothered him that he hadn't come by the house honestly. But then, strictly speaking, he hadn't come by much of anything honestly in the thirty-three hard, perilous years of his life.

Now, having reached his prime through some miracle of divine benevolence, Jack was at last ready, if reluctant, to take a wife, a woman who could oversee the house during his many absences, a woman who would be waiting for him with scented hands and a soft, undemanding voice. But in the same way that fate had always skated capriciously through the best laid plans of his life, it seemed that Jack Darlington was not to acquire *her* honestly either.

He and the boy stood together. From their vantage point, they could see over the mellow stone wall into the green garden.

Breaking his silence, his voice almost swept away by the wind, Rajad tugged at Jack's sleeve and asked tentatively, "Lady's name?"

"What? Oh, the lady I'm to marry, you mean?" Jack ran a hand through his black hair. "Rosaline, I believe. Her name is Rosaline. Pretty, isn't it? Like a flower."

The boy considered, then slowly moved his head up and down with no particular enthusiasm.

Jack smiled with both a rueful self-mockery and hard, inward satisfaction. "She's the honorable Rosaline Cheevers–the daughter of a baron, if you can believe my luck. The lady doesn't have a particularly large dowry, but she does have respectable breeding. According to her father's letter, I'm stealing her from another man."

A former thief himself, a scavenger amid the rubbish piles of Calcutta's most desperate slums, Rajad accepted the comment with perfect equanimity.

"Of course, the lady doesn't *know* she's been stolen," Jack went on. "It seems the announcement of that piece of news—which she'll probably find appalling–is being put off until the last possible minute. You see, her father doesn't care to suffer any more female histrionics than he has to."

Jack raised a brow. "Where's your lucky piece, Rajad?" he asked with a frown, referring to the polished tiger tooth that usually hung on a chain around the child's neck.

The boy looked startled, then distressed, until through some sleight of hand, Jack produced the dangling charm and held it out.

The lad snatched it back with wondering eyes, an elfin smile tugging at his mouth.

Jack strolled on, speaking offhandedly. "The lady's father says she's docile, for the most part, and more intelligent than some men would prefer. But we don't want a dull-witted woman to manage our home, do we, Rajad? We want her smart enough to untangle fishing lines and tie lures, don't we?"

The boy did not smile again, but his expression softened to a conciliatory thoughtfulness.

As they trod through the high, purple heather to reach the rutted drive, Jack studied his house again. He doubted that his prospective bride would care for the wild, inaccessible Orkney, which meant 'island of the wild boar people' according to Celtic legend. Uttering such thoughts aloud, he said, "How do you think Rosaline will like our Boar Isle, Rajad? She's from a big city, you know, one called Edinburgh."

The boy shook his head and looked doubtful.

"I suppose if she doesn't enjoy walking and riding and gardening, then she'll have to learn to like them." Jack's jaw tightened, and he added, "Just as she'll have to learn to like–or tolerate–my difficult demands. And my bad temper, I suppose. Yes, and above all, my need for personal privacy. Isn't that right, Rajad?"

The boy nodded.

"Marriage is a bargain of sorts, after all," Jack went on, philosophizing for his own amusement, "and the honorable Rosaline Cheevers will have to learn to make compromises. In exchange, I'll be generous with her, give her whatever she requires to run my household smoothly and with grace." Jack had decided he wanted grace in his life rather badly.

He ran a hand over his jaw, wondering how the constraints of marriage would suit him, how his own hard edges would affect the lady. Perhaps, if the two of them got on well together, something more satisfying than a cool, convenient arrangement could develop. Perhaps they could eventually enjoy an amiable partnership. He hoped the woman would not come to expect more than that, for he knew himself to be incapable of providing more—not only incapable but unwilling.

He had fallen in love once, was still in love, and did not intend to love a second time.

Jack unlatched the wooden gate that led to his garden and breathed in the scents of the green life which flourished there, so different than the smoke and filth of London which always seemed to cling to his nostrils. When he was a lad, they had called him Jackdaw because by the age of seven, he had been able to dart in and out of chimneys and nooks, mimic gentry, and pick pockets faster than anyone in Piccadilly. Eventually, finding it more propitious to have a name, he had become Jack Darlington, and now, a few decades later, he could honestly—or not so honestly, depending upon one's viewpoint—call himself the master of a small laird's estate.

Jackdaw, he reflected, that tough little cutpurse with no identity, had come a long way. And yet, for all his hard-won, if not strictly scrupulous gains, he was still discontented.

For a moment, Jack stared up at the shifting sky and pondered the source of his dissatisfaction, his curious yearning for more, realizing it was something intangible, glimpsed occasionally in the last flicker of a sunset, heard in the echo of an unfamiliar voice, and felt very briefly, every now and then, when he awoke from a particularly sensual dream. Yes, he wanted something that seemed just out of his usual skillful reach. Jack had hoped this island house would satisfy that mysterious yearning, but instead, the yearning tugged more persistently than ever at his heart. It had nothing to do with Julie anymore, he realized. No, Julie had become scarcely more than a painful memory, a ghost that he still hoped, but did not really expect, to find again.

Entering through the front door of the house, Jack removed his tweed jacket and tossed it on the coatrack, his eyes scanning the lime washed walls and low raftered ceilings, the huge stone hearths and heavy carved furniture, the well-woven if slightly thread-bare rugs. Two hundred years old, the house smelt of tanned leather and candle wax, of turpentine and old wood overlaid with salt from the sea. It was restful, mellow, inviting. And yet, still, it lacked something—much in the same indefinable way, Jack surmised, as he did.

He heard a snigger, and without glancing up at the steep wooden stair, said sternly, ''Antonio, if you treat the top of the bannister as a crow's nest one more time, I'll thrash you. And remove my jackknife from your waistband, if you please, before I skin you with it.''

The gleam of dark eyes, the flash of an agile, sneaky hand were the only signs of the miscreant he addressed. But the boy, who Jack was beginning to believe was incorrigible, obeyed.

Jack had encountered this particular little thief, Antonio, in the streets of Rome stealing a pocket watch from an English tourist. When the police had threatened to imprison him for the crime—far from his first—Jack had intervened. Without entirely understanding his own motives, he had taken the lad home with him. And so, happily or not, Antonio was ensconced here in this house along with Rajad, who was now curled up in a green parlor chair mending—or trying to mend—an old fishing rod.

From time to time, Jack asked himself why he had been moved to charity not once, but twice. He wasn't certain, exactly, except that giving the pair of unfortunate boys a decent place to live seemed to atone in some small measure for all the other less noble things he had done in his life. Of course, his new wife would have to take the lads in hand and make something of them—gentlemen, preferably, since Jack had set out to be one himself. He had neither the time, patience—or in the case of Rajad—the understanding to accomplish it himself. Besides, women were supposed to be good at mopping up drippy noses and soothing fragile little hearts, weren't they?

"Mr. Darlington, sir, your dinner is ready to be served."

His housekeeper, Mrs. Wiggins, stood in the doorway of the dining room awaiting his word. She had been with him several years, done her best to please him on the rare occasions he remained at home.

"I've worked up quite an appetite, Mrs. Wiggins," he said cordially and, proceeding to the sideboard, leaned down to smell the aromas steaming up from the covered dishes. She had learned quite well to make the Scottish dish of *haggis,* as well as the *finnan haddie,* which was haddock hung up the chimney and smoked over a peat fire. "Delicious, as always," he added.

Noting that her face appeared more weary than ever, older than its sixty years, he waved her aside. "We've never stood on ceremony, have we, Mrs. Wiggins?"

"Why, no, Mr. Darlington."

"I know you would prefer that we behave more formally toward each other, now that I have this house. You want me to act like the proper gentleman while you bow and scrape like a proper servant. Well, let's pretend to be respectable tomorrow night, all right? For now, I'll serve myself, and you go along and put up your feet."

The housekeeper, small in the shadow of his towering height, hesitated and twisted her plump red hands. "Mr. Darlington, sir, I beg your pardon, but how are we ever to teach proper manners, proper *order,* to those heathen—er—children, if we don't create some semblance of propriety? Structure is what they need."

"A good thrashing is what one of them needs," he drawled, helping himself to wild fowl and parsleyed potatoes in spite of her continued hovering. "The other . . . well, truth to tell, I haven't a clue what Rajad needs."

"Neither do I," she sighed. "But that Antonio! Good heavens. He scribbled rude words on the wall in his room again. The third time."

"What rude words?"

Two spots of color splotched Mrs. Wiggins's cheeks and she blustered indignantly, "Oh, Mr. Darlington, you surely don't expect me to *repeat* them?"

His mouth twitched. "Not if you don't care to. I hoped to be entertained, that's all—but not at your expense, of course, dear Mrs. Wiggins."

She released a breath of relief. "I thought perhaps the little scoundrel should go without his supper tonight, for punishment, sir, if you agree."

Jack stilled, the gravy ladle poised in his hand. His eyes, an uncommon dark blue, hardened to a flintier shade, and his voice deepened markedly. "He'll not go without food, Mrs. Wiggins. Not tonight. Not ever. Is that understood?"

She nodded, shifting her feet nervously. "Yes, sir."

Taking a currant roll from a covered basket, Jack put it on his bread plate, and his low, dangerous tone softened into what his housekeeper understood to be a sort of apology. "I realize the boy has very nearly been the death of you, Mrs. Wiggins. I'll have a talk with him tonight. If he can be found."

"Yes, sir. If he can be found." Mrs. Wiggins looked as if she wished very much that he could not. Ever.

"At any rate," Jack continued, seating himself at the long table laid with old pewter and patched linen. "You'll have help soon. I'm leaving tomorrow for Edinburgh in order to . . ." He broke off abruptly, almost having said, "to pick up a wife." Thinking that a bit too casual, he amended, "To meet the lady who is to be my wife."

"Your *wife?*" Mrs. Wiggins repeated, first in bemusement, then in astonishment that the impossible, the miraculous, had actually, finally, happened. Her smile indicated that the very idea delighted her beyond words.

"Yes. We'll marry there, and then I'll bring her home. You'll no doubt be surprised to know she's the daughter of a baron— quite a catch for a man of uncertain beginnings like myself, eh?"

"A real lady, sir?" Mrs. Wiggins asked with breathless wonder.

"Very real. Shortly afterward, once she's settled in, I'll have to begin traveling again."

"Another trip to Algeria, sir?" the servant asked carefully, breaching her own rules of decorum and Jack's unpredictable touchiness in order to satisfy her curiosity, or to simply talk, since her life was as lonely as his.

"No," Jack answered, his voice tightening just a fraction. "Not to Algeria. To Egypt."

Mrs. Wiggins had been pouring a good Burgundy into his glass and, at the unexpectedness of his announcement, spilt several dark red drops on the table. The very sound of the word "Egypt" on his tongue was like a most bitter venom.

Unsteadily, she continued to pour, and when her irrepressible inquisitiveness overcame her fear of Jack, her voice quavered. "To look for Miss Julie, sir?"

With a studied calm, Jack laid down his fork, finished chewing the bite of bread in his mouth and swallowed. Then, quite succinctly, in a low tone, with eyes that could either melt a heart or knife it, he advised, "Don't utter Julie's name again, Mrs. Wiggins. Please. Not to me or anyone else." He picked up his fork again. "That will be all for tonight, thank you."

Chapter Two

His brush trailed paint over the point of an almost white shoulder, then highlighted the curve of a bent neck. The model wore a string of pearls, their color and texture blending with her flesh, and the brush outlined each bead before copying the whisper of ivory lace draping her arms. Her hair was dark, mink colored, and the hothouse rose nestled in its piled curls was red, the color of her lips. Her pose, like her nature, was demure. But her eyes gave the artist his greatest challenge, for they were dark and introspective, a reflection of a deep thinking mind.

Rosaline.

Any artist would want to spend his life studying her profile, contemplating those rare, deep eyes, wondering how one who was barely twenty-six could command the self-possession of a woman twice that age. She was not beautiful by any means, but claimed the sort of unusual features artists loved to paint. And she was so pure, so . . . *good.*

Abandoning his brush, the artist went to her, bending with soulful passion over the white shoulder, his lips touching its rounded point. The spicy fragrance of the roses nestled in the folds of her bodice filled his nostrils and moved him to an unbearably sensuous fever.

Rosaline did not pull away, but laid her head to one side languorously, letting the lace shawl droop lower over her arm. With her lips parted, she allowed the artist his liberty, shivering with it. She touched his jaw, then the strands of his long, golden hair while he kept his lips pressed to her neck. How sensitive to mood he was, she thought. How attuned he was to the beauty around him, to the nuances of color and sound. Like her, he loved to ponder faraway places and dream of sailing there. Such dreaming made Rosaline grow hot with images of a world she had never visited, one that revolved far outside the cloistered realm in which she lived. And the artist with his feather light hands, poetic words and pretty manners had touched within her some brilliantly colored chord with pinned wings that struggled to be free.

Rosaline did not flinch when the artist's hand slid down to her breast above the lace, nor did she resist when he pushed her gently back upon the scarlet chaise lounge.

"Rosaline," the artist whispered. His fingers moved as if they painted her portrait, not on canvas now, but on his memory. "Come to Italy with me," he pleaded. "You'll be the model for a dozen of my paintings. Three dozen."

"Yes, David," she breathed. "We have only to ask my father."

"We'll see Venice and Smyrna, all the places we've talked about, dreamed about."

"Yes, David."

"And at night," he said, his fingers still tracing, molding, insinuating, "we'll sit on a terrace and read aloud to each other, sip wine, dream of a new destination."

"Oh, yes." Usually Rosaline could only escape the monotonous routine of her life in secret, in her mind, savoring a few stolen moments when she lay immersed in the scented water of the tub or when she sat in the sunshine and read a book.

Now, she had found a fellow spirit who actually *understood,* who could share—

Suddenly, the door to the little conservatory shuddered open. "What in blazes is *this?!*"

Rosaline struggled up, her usual aplomb abandoning her completely at the sight of her father's furious expression. Her mortification prompted her to clap both hands across her naked bosom while the poor, startled artist fell backward against his paint tray, the bottles of turpentine and linseed oil crashing in amber pools all over the flagstones.

Lord Bardo stood like an enraged lion before them, his cheeks aquiver beneath his side whiskers, his eyes bulging behind their spectacles, his mouth drawn down. "You devious little libertine!" he bellowed, addressing David while the painter scrambled to his feet. "I never would have thought you man enough, and certainly not *impertinent* enough to take advantage of an innocent woman in her own home beneath the very eyes of her father. Eminent portrait painter or not, you're out! *Now!* Your things will be sent to you."

To his credit, the artist attempted to protest, to accept blame while defending his motives. But Lord Bardo, veteran of the Crimea, intrepid explorer and ruthless politician, threatened to fetch his sword and run the artist through.

Highly offended but convinced of Lord Bardo's sincerity, David shouted a few assurances to Rosaline while her father forcefully ushered him to the door, threw him to the ground, and slammed the door shut.

"Rosaline!" Lord Bardo barked, wheeling about, turning his ire upon his daughter now. "I find myself almost speechless with disappointment. It did not seem to me that you were resisting that fool's advances."

Rosaline had regained her cool grace and now rearranged the wisp of shawl over her shoulders. With composure she answered, "No, Father, I suppose I was not."

"Am I given to understand, then, that you welcomed them?"
She met her father's eyes, which missed little of what went

on around them, and whose pale, grey shrewdness had helped earn him a high position in the Foreign Office. His eyes were particularly good at detecting insincerity, but, as it was never Rosaline's way to be anything but scrupulously honest, she admitted slowly, "Yes, I believe I did."

"Why?" he blurted, as if unable to formulate even the thinnest reason.

She picked up the artist's brush from the floor and sighed. "Because he is like me, Father."

"*Like* you?" Lord Bardo snorted, glancing at the half-finished portrait where all but the face and shoulders were a hasty sketch. "What would possess you to say such a thing? You have more nobility, more good breeding than he could ever dream of having, despite his so called artistic fame."

"David and I *think* alike," she said steadily, watching her father for his reaction, knowing he was not without an occasional flash of empathy.

But Lord Bardo had not reached the hierarchy of British political structure without a great deal of hardheadedness, and he regarded his daughter with a speculative gaze. While he thought about his answer, the humidity of the conservatory coaxed perspiration to the bridge of his nose and he carefully wiped it away with a handkerchief.

"I have raised you to be a practical woman, Rosaline," he said finally in the disappointed voice he always used when he wished to shame her. "And a sensible woman. As I've always told you, flights of fancy cloud good judgment. Of course, were you a young *man* indulging himself with a light o' love before settling down, that would be acceptable, even expected. But you are not."

"Indeed," she murmured.

"You're a young woman who needs a husband to give you stability. In fact, you need a man who is strong-minded enough not to fall beneath the tyranny of your own quiet independence." Lord Bardo shifted his feet, his heel grinding against the broken glass of the turpentine jar, the red petals strewn on the ground. "That artist fellow has no more stability or sub-stance than a damned butterfly. He would abandon you in a month. Or, if not, there'd come a time when you'd grow tired of discussing poetry with him and watching him paint—or seduce—women in every European port. You'd want some-thing more, Rosaline. Something more *basic*."

Rosaline's independence bristled. She resented her father's desire to keep her chained to his huge echoing house whose domestic needs swallowed her up. She had devoted her life to him and his elderly sisters, dutifully meeting their needs. She was a good, practical, modest daughter, they all said, with cool, capable hands that always knew what to do. A competent nurse and hostess. The perfect—if sadly plain—wife for some fortu-nate man.

Rosaline had always maintained a pleasant relationship with her father, as close as both their reserved natures allowed. But Lord Bardo had been away much of the time, and she had always felt there was a side of him she didn't fully know.

With care she said, "You're not forbidding me to see David again, I hope. To marry him if I choose?"

Sir Bardo's answer was immediate. "That is precisely what I'm doing."

"Then I'll not accept it. You've brought me up to think for myself, and I shall certainly do so in this regard." She folded her arms across her chest.

"No, you won't."

"And why not?"

"Because I've promised you to another man, that's why."

Rosaline stared at him, shocked. "I beg your pardon?"

"We spoke of it a few months ago. You told me that since you had found no acceptable suitors and were approaching spinsterhood, you would not be averse to my ... arranging something for you. Those were your exact words, as I recall. You wept at my feet as you spoke about your loneliness and lack of hope."

Rosaline searched for reasonable words to counter her previous outburst of emotion. Her agreement to accept an "arrangement" had come at a weak moment when she had felt desperate to escape the demands of Sir Bardo's elderly sisters, their dozen wheezing spaniels, and the old Edinburgh house. She wanted her own home, her own children, and had despaired of ever getting them. She had gone down on her knees before her father and wept, insisting that gentlemen rarely looked at her twice. She had given up finding a kindred soul, a man who could understand that beneath Rosaline Cheevers's practicality, beneath her cool exterior, there lay a deep fire and a soaring imagination—and possibly something more, although precisely what, she wasn't certain. David, at least, had woken her to the possibility that she could experience something more.

Rosaline did not often use devious feminine tactics to fight against what was regrettably a man's world. But glancing at her father in his formidable Bond Street suit and wing-tipped collar, she lowered her eyes to David's paintbox and thoughtfully touched a forefinger to the alizarin crimson. She knew that propriety and reputation were of great importance to Lord Bardo. Therefore, perhaps they were the easiest means of reaching him.

With the perfect amount of humility, Rosaline murmured, "I think it best, Father, that I . . . marry David."

Lord Bardo suddenly regarded her with wary eyes. "What are you saying?"

"I'm saying that, under the circumstances, I fear marriage would be the wisest course." Rosaline's head bowed. "Since . . . well, since David has . . . compromised me."

Her sire's head snapped back. *"Compromised* you?"

"Yes."

"Do you mean . . ." he hesitated. Even his experience with countless mistresses had not equipped Lord Bardo to speak bluntly with his daughter on sexual matters. "Do you mean to say, Rosaline, that the fellow . . . that *this* . . ." he swept a hand toward the chaise lounge, "has happened before? Gone to . . . greater lengths?"

She kept her eyes cast down. Although unused to deceit, she was determined not to have her chance at freedom snatched away. In a properly ashamed voice, she breathed, "Yes."

Lord Bardo exploded. "Has the artist gone so far? I shall kill him! Good God, I should never have believed it—not of you, Rosaline, with your cool head. Of course, I'm certain it was all *his* fault. He's well-seasoned with women, no doubt, used to frivolous seductions. Why, I'll see him run out of Edinburgh before the day's out! And you, my dear girl, shall have to be taken care of expediently. Most expediently."

The situation had not progressed at all in the way she had intended, and Rosaline stiffened, her fingers squeezing the oily tube of David's paint. "Father," she said, her usual cool grace cracking like ice beneath a skater as she tried to salvage the situation. "I shall not let you decide matters for me in this way. I have never gone against your wishes, but have been the best daughter I know how, taking over Mother's duties at her death when I was barely nine. I'm no longer a girl, and it's an insult to my integrity to be *told* what to do, to give up the man I love simply because he's unconventional and because *you* do not care for him."

"Rosaline," Lord Bardo spoke in a reasonable tone and reached to take the tube of paint from her fingers, drawing her away from the portrait as if to draw her away from its artist. "Need I remind you that a daughter is under her father's care? Need I remind you that a gently bred girl has no alternative but to either stay at home and care for elderly relatives or to marry well? You know that a poor marriage—one that wouldn't provide the things you need—would be disastrous. For all intents and purposes, it would be forever undissolvable, as well. You *do* realize that, of course."

"I only want the freedom to make my own decision as to marriage, Father!" she cried. "And David touches something in me that . . ."

"Dear Rosaline," Lord Bardo interrupted hastily, with a sudden embarrassed twinkle in his eye. "You mustn't confuse

. . . *urges* with an abiding love." He cleared his throat, uncomfortable speaking of such matters, but thinking they needed to be said. "You'll do the right thing because you've always done the right thing."

"Surely there's more to a woman's life than that," she returned bitterly.

"Now, now." Lord Bardo patted her shoulder in an awkward attempt to comfort a daughter who suddenly seemed to have grown too self-reliant for her own good, too complicated for his usual efforts at fatherly guidance. With gruff warmth, he said, "Do your old papa a favor and run along to the house. Wash your face and tidy up. There's a good girl. Trust me to do what's best. I'm going to send a letter along right now that will settle your future for you. A letter that will, in fact, tie up your life quite nicely."

As her father had always known she would, Rosaline eventually came to her senses. Lord Bardo had made it a point to call upon her sterling sense of honor, reminding her that, since she had asked him months ago to arrange a suitable marriage for her, there was now a gentleman in the Orkneys preparing to come and claim his bride. He further pointed out, brutally, one rainy day in his library that her artist lover had made no attempt whatsoever to see her again.

"It has been three days and he has sent no message, Rosaline, nor has he come pounding on the door demanding to speak with you, which a determined man would do. Had you married him and found yourself in dire straits someday, you see now that you would not have been able to count on him. He has no fortitude. But this other man, the one I've chosen . . ."

"I don't care to hear any more about *him* presently, Father," Rosaline interrupted, hiding her devastation. She could scarcely ignore David's abandonment. Every day she had watched anxiously from her window, trusting him to reappear, to come back for her. She concluded now, with bitter suspicion, that her father had intercepted the artist's messages. David couldn't have possibly forgotten her, gone away without her to Smyrna or Greece. Could he?

"Don't you care to discuss your prospective husband, Rosaline?" Lord Bardo inquired gently. "Ask more questions about him?"

Keeping her tears in check, Rosaline turned away and crossed the dim, book-lined space that never seemed adequately lit. She had made her decision. If she could not have David, she supposed she'd just as well take the only chance at marriage left open to her. Nevertheless, she spoke sharply, "You have already told me that this Jack Darlington is acceptable, Father, the owner of an estate in the Orkneys, and of strong character. You have given me a physical description, assuring me he's suitably attractive. Therefore, I cannot doubt that he is."

"It is not like you to be hard, Rosaline."

"Isn't it?"

"You'll present yourself to him agreeably?" Lord Bardo was suddenly concerned.

Rosaline pivoted to face him. She studied his thin, tawny hair streaked with grey, the sagging flesh of his jowls, and his eyes, which did not seem as sharp as they once were. "Haven't I always presented myself agreeably to every guest you've invited to this house?" she demanded.

"You needn't take that stiff tone with me, Rosaline. And this isn't just another guest, but your husband-to-be."

"I won't discredit you, if that's what you're worried about," she snapped, cutting him off as she proceeded through the door.

"No, I suppose you won't," Lord Bardo said, hearing her heels click briskly across the hardwood. "You never have."

The old man sighed, wondering, not for the first time, how he would replace her, how he and his sisters would manage without the woman who always knew precisely the way each of them liked their beefsteak cooked, their tea served, their clothes pressed. Yes, Rosaline kept the wheels of two damp old houses turning comfortably, spending her days smoothing out every tiny domestic care.

And yet, Lord Bardo knew it was not a satisfying life for his daughter.

Regrettably, Rosaline was not pretty. Lord Bardo studied the framed miniature of his daughter propped in its silver frame upon his desk. She was too tall, with unusual features that did not even border on beauty, and an intellect that would frighten most men away. She spent an inordinate amount of time reading inappropriate books—philosophy, travel, religion—when she was not idling in the fussy little herb garden she had created and cherished like a child. And yet, to her credit, Rosaline rarely complained. Therefore, her tears of self-pity a few months ago had wrenched Lord Bardo, and he had set out to make a life for her, to find her a home and family of her own since she could not seem to find them for herself.

Grunting, Lord Bardo settled back in the worn, brown leather of his chair and rested his hands beneath his flabby jowls. Staring at the pair of crossed swords on the wall, he frowned thoughtfully. Yes, he had secured Rosaline's future for her, but he had secured it in a way that had been equally beneficial to his own interests—to his own career. To Britain.

He would sacrifice his life for Britain.

But would he sacrifice his own daughter?

Sighing, Lord Bardo closed his eyes and pondered the question.

As scheduled, Jack Darlington arrived late that afternoon during a downpour, his coat glistening with rain, his curly-brimmed beaver hat dripping as he stepped inside the house.

After a hearty welcome, Lord Bardo ushered him into the chilly drawing room with its creaking floors and smoky fireplace. While offering Darlington a seat in the most comfortable chair, the old man eyed him consideringly.

Upon seeing Jack after a long interim, Lord Bardo always

found himself a little taken aback, having forgotten each time just how disturbing Darlington's presence was. Jack's charm could not be described precisely, but the fellow could stand in the shadows of a room alone, say nothing, and still command the attention of every one around. There was an indefinable quality of power about him which Lord Bardo suspected came from Jack's having melted into the streets of too many dangerous places. The man had seen the darkest side of misery and violence and emerged from them outwardly unscathed. Moreover, Lord Bardo knew Darlington had done many unscrupulous things in his life—some of them for money, some for advancement, some for simple survival. And yet, oddly, when it came down to trust, Jack was the sort of man a fellow would want to have beside him in the heat of battle. Yes, despite his questionable past and the slight air of danger that seemed to hover just behind Jack Darlington's wide shoulders, there were few men Lord Bardo respected more.

He pointed again to a chair beside the window and invited Darlington, who still stood restively, to sit down. "You look well, Jack, damned elegant, in fact. Very British, not dark as an Arab as you were at our last visit together."

"The Orkney sun is mild," came the taciturn reply.

A maid bustled in pushing the tea trolley, positioned it close to Jack's chair and, after giving him a blushing glance, retreated with more sway in her hips than usual. The smell of tea and lemon combined with the musty odor of the panelled room, its heavy rugs and damp window frames. Jack's shrewd eyes scanned the room. The colors were brown and drab, the ceiling high, the rugs good but thin with age. He noted the fineness of the white porcelain cups, the gleaming polish of the silver service, and the starched, meticulously embroidered napkins. The furnishings might be shabby with age, but someone had made certain that the serving of tea was a pleasant ritual for guests.

"Help yourself, Jack," Lord Bardo said. "Normally, Rosaline would come in and pour, but I feel it best that we speak privately first.''

Jack brushed the raindrops from his black broadcloth cuffs and raised a rueful brow. ''Ah, I presume you want to work out the particulars of the transaction now, before I've met the bride?''

The older man made a face, the folds on either side of his mouth deepening. ''Must we term it in such a way, Jack?''

''I believe we must, Lord Bardo.''

''Always watching your back, aren't you?''

Jack smiled without revealing a glimpse of his white teeth. ''I've found a man can considerably increase his life span that way.''

''Yes. Yes, I'm sure you have.'' The older man, equally accustomed both to hard bargaining and delicate negotiating, wandered restively about the room, pulling out a pipe and tobacco, taking time to light it. The sounds of hooves and wheels on wet cobbles filled the room, mingled with the crackle of the fire in the grate, which, despite its brightness, could not take the chill away.

''Shall I brief you on conditions in Egypt?'' Lord Bardo asked finally, a cloud of blue smoke wreathing his head. ''I received quite a lengthy report from the Foreign Office just yesterday.''

''I'm always eager to know what I've let myself in for,'' Jack returned, reaching for the trolley to sample one of the scones brushed with butter.

Lord Bardo frowned, his eyes looking more faded than usual as he spoke. ''To put it mildly, Egypt is on the brink of turmoil. The sultan has borrowed heavily from England, and is in danger of being overthrown. British investors are growing nervous.''

''And?'' Jack asked calmly.

''There's a fellow called Arabi Bey stirring up trouble among the Egyptian people and threatening to depose the sultan. Unfortunately, he has a fanatical following and commands considerable respect from both the rich and the poor citizens—a dangerous combination, as you know.''

Had Lord Bardo not not been gazing out at the figures hurrying along the rainy street, he might have seen Jack's face tighten at the mention of Arabi Bey; he might have seen his fingers close over the leather arm of the overstuffed chair. But unaware of Darlington's tension, the aristocrat continued in a conversational tone, briefing the man who was to perform yet another delicate service for the Foreign Office.

"At any rate," he said, "this Arabi Bey will have to be stopped some way or other, at some point. Those details, of course, will be worked out when you arrive in Egypt. You'll be glad to know that there's been a change in your status . . ."

Jack lifted a brow. "My status?"

"Yes." Lord Bardo was pleased to impart the information. "This time we're giving you a position that's not only quite enviably high up in the Foreign Office, but very respectable, even visible. For the first time, you'll be an official member of the staff."

"Indeed?" Jack's surprise was evident, his tone wry.

Lord Bardo regarded him ruefully. "I hope you've not grown so fond of your usual clandestine assignments that the dull position of attaché will have no charm."

Jack smiled. "Oddly, Lord Bardo, respectability has begun to appeal to me."

"In light of the fact that you're to marry my daughter, I can't say I regret to hear it." Lord Bardo helped himself to a dish of sugared nuts from the trolley. "I would even encourage you to take Rosaline with you to Egypt, let her entertain British society in Alexandria and Cairo, enhance your social position there for the sake of appearance."

"You want me to take a gently bred woman with me to Egypt?" Jack did not bother to hide his surprise.

"It's important that you maintain the appearance of an ordinary attaché in the diplomatic service. As you expressed a desire to return to Egypt—God knows why—you should find this post the easiest we have ever given you. Although, admittedly, it may well require more . . . finesse than the other assignments.''

Jack did not reply immediately. It was his way never to answer with haste. He broke another scone in half and watched the steam rise from its center. ''If I'm to be promoted,'' he said carefully, ''and I assume from what you've said that I *am . . .*''

''Of course, of course.''

''Then, isn't there the possibility that, when your daughter and I are making social rounds in Cairo, some inquisitive officer's wife might look into my background? The matrons of British society are quite careful to do that, I understand, so as not to include in their circle the . . .'' Jack quirked his mouth, ''wrong sort of people.''

Lord Bardo, being a member of that circle, knew that he had just been insulted—subtly but with no malice. Smiling, he poured himself tea in one of the porcelain cups Rosaline always inspected so assiduously for cracks. ''We've taken care to alter your identity, of course, Jack. Not too drastically, but enough, we think, to suffice.''

Darlington's face altered with lazy amusement. ''Who might I be? Or am I not allowed to know yet?''

''You'll keep your own name. But we've changed your records, given you a . . .'' Lord Bardo hesitated, not wanting to offend. ''A respectable past. You now hail from a remote village in the north of Scotland, one that no one will be particularly interested in. You're the second son of a vicar. After a few years of schooling, you signed on with a merchant ship, then joined the Foreign Office.''

Jack raised his brow. ''A vicar's son, Lord Bardo?'' Laughing, he added, ''Someone in your office has a sense of humor, obviously. What does your daughter know of this—and me?''

Lord Bardo took up a stance beside the mantle and contemplated his pipe. ''Rosaline knows nothing at all except that you own an estate in the Orkneys and are connected with my office.

She's always understood that there's some secrecy involved in my work with the Foreign Office. I don't think she'll be bothered to learn that her husband is likewise required to keep certain things under his hat. So, however you choose to explain your change in identity—provided you desire to at all—is up to you. You may tell Rosaline as much or as little about your past as you wish."

Jack grinned. "No doubt she'd be appalled to hear the real story. Perhaps I'll start anew. Tell her I really am the son of that upstanding little bookbinder in the North and forget the rest. Otherwise, she might be afraid to be alone with me after dark."

"I believe Rosaline could accept the truth. I'm proud to say I've raised a daughter who's trustworthy and loyal."

Idly, Jack examined the pattern of green ivy embroidered on his napkin. His voice was suggestive. "But not as trustworthy and loyal as you would like her to be, perhaps, Lord Bardo?"

The older man cleared his throat uncomfortably. "Well, yes, as to *that*. Quite a shock to me, I must tell you. Completely out of character for Rosaline. And I can only surmise that the artist fellow was exceedingly . . . persuasive."

"No doubt." Jack leaned back in his chair. Steepling his long hands, he contemplated their shape for several moments before speaking. "When you contacted me by letter last winter, you asked if I would be interested in matrimony. I answered that I might consider it, for an exchange of favors. Recalling that I had mentioned a need for a suitable lady to run my home, you wrote about your daughter. You said you wanted a husband who would treat her with courtesy and respect. I agreed to do that. Do you still trust that I will?"

"Of course," Lord Bardo replied quickly, but warily, as if he were walking beneath a bridge and expecting it to fall.

"And as a show of mutual good faith, you suggested that, as a future son-in-law, I might expect a promotion?"

"Correct. A promotion which I have just given you—the authorization from the Foreign Office is in my desk."

"Yes. But I was given to assume," Jack said soberly, concealing a private amusement over his host's unease, "that the wife-to-be was—well, forgive me for being so indelicate as to raise the subject—but isn't there now a question of purity?"

Lord Bardo sipped his tea hastily, wetting the whiskers about his mouth and blustering, "Yes, well, as to that, there does seem to be some uncertainty . . ."

"Uncertainty?" Jack interrupted casually, with the same cool ease he might use when discussing the rainy weather.

Lord Bardo fidgeted. "Yes. That is, I wrote you requesting expediency, but the truth is I'm not quite sure there's a real need for any. However, to be perfectly safe, I believe the marriage should take place without delay."

As if in deep thought, Jack stared at the worn Turkey carpet. He could have simply asked Lord Bardo whether he would be getting a virgin on his wedding night. Instead, for his own ulterior purpose, Jack drew out the game of words and said, "Are you telling me that I'm not only getting a wife whose heart belongs to another man, but one whose body—just possibly—belongs to him as well?"

Lord Bardo coughed and went to pour himself another cup of tea. He was growing testy, and although he didn't care for sugar, he found himself taking up the silver tongs. "Absolutely *not*. At least I don't think so. The dalliance was surely nothing more than a moment of madness. Rosaline was clearly taken advantage of. The artist is a libertine, and she is a gently bred lady."

"Nevertheless," Jack persisted, managing to look pained. "Aside from your daughter's emotional attachment to the artist and her reason for the—er—slip in self-control, there *could* be consequences, couldn't there? In eight months or so, is there a chance I'll have to play father to this artist's child?"

Lord Bardo set down his cup. The interview had suddenly taken a bad turn. Although Jack had never broken his word before, Lord Bardo was beginning to fear that he might do so now. Darlington had certainly not lived a conventional life—

a *moral* life—but Lord Bardo supposed there were limits to
his forbearance. Some men were particular about women and,
suspecting that Jack had no dearth of them clamoring for his
attention, one couldn't blame him for being reluctant to take
on a soiled wife and—possibly—her illegitimate child.

"It's just that she won't *tell* me," Lord Bardo complained.
"Which, of course, tends to make me rather more suspicious.
And I couldn't bear to call in a physician and have him well—
I've heard such examinations can be quite brutal, traumatic to
young women who haven't . . ."

"I see," Jack cut in, staring at his intertwined fingers as if
deep in thought.

Fearing that Jack was on the verge of reneging on the marriage, Lord Bardo hastened to salvage the situation. "Perhaps
I could make arrangements to have your pay raised, Jack. Yes,
indeed, I daresay the Office could be persuaded to do that, if
I were to put a bit of pressure to bear. With a raise in pay, you
could afford better accommodations in Egypt, a few luxuries.
Would that suffice?"

"Well," Jack considered, stretching out his legs and frowning with a studied indecision. Honestly, he didn't care a whit
whether Miss Rosaline Cheevers was deflowered or not, carrying a child or not. Such ripe feminine states had been a
normal, if tragic, part of his everyday experiences growing up.
Back then, in the streets of London's East End, he didn't believe
he had ever known a virgin over the age of eleven or twelve.
Except one, perhaps.

"An increase in pay?" he murmured now, still studying the
mesh of his fingers. "Yes. I believe that would be fair. Especially if there's a child to be cared for, a bit of extra cash would
come in handy." Then, deciding to put the older man out of
his misery, Jack drew in his long legs and stood up, holding
out a hand. He had grown tired of the play, and most important-
ly, had achieved what he had set out to accomplish in the first
place. "I believe we can consider the transaction complete."

With visible relief, Lord Bardo clasped the firm, fine fingered had offered him. Jovially, he said, "Congratulations, then. And I look forward to welcoming you as a member of the family."

"May I be introduced to your daughter now, do you think?" Jack's eyes twinkled darkly. "I find myself rather curious to know how a vicar's son is to get along with the daughter of a diplomat."

Vastly relieved, Lord Bardo released a breath. "Yes. Yes, indeed, Jack. You shall meet Rosaline immediately. But don't expect—well, I shall let you judge my daughter and her attributes for yourself."

Chapter Three

Lord Bardo had told Rosaline that he did not think she would be disappointed with the physical appearance of her groom-to-be. Of course, when she considered the attributes her father might assume attractive to a young woman, Rosaline was not particularly reassured.

The worst part was, she found she did not care as much as she should. She could think only of David. She wondered where he traveled, whom he painted. What would her life have been like if he had had the courage to spirit her away into "his disreputable creative world" as her Aunt Columbine had so scandalously hissed?

To Rosaline's delight, her father had been wrong when he claimed David had made no attempt to contact her. Only an hour ago, just after Jack Darlington's arrival, a messenger had rapped at the kitchen door with a small, paper bound package. Nestled in the folds of silver tissue, the artist had sent a miniature of himself in the form of a locket on a chain. A golden snippet of his hair was curled inside, along with a scrap of paper that read, "Until we meet again, my love—if ever."

Ecstatic that he had not entirely forsaken her after all, Rosaline had clutched the necklace to her bosom, then fled upstairs and slipped the chain around her neck. After a few moments cradling the locket in her hand, she had sighed, knowing she would have to accept the reality of her situation.

To have run off with David, irresponsibly or not, was the only thing she had ever truly wanted to do in all her life. But it had not happened, and was not likely to ever happen. Rosaline knew she had to put the notion away.

And yet, for a few sweet moments, she had clung to the memory of David like she had clung to the locket, for it was the very last vestige of a pleasant, if impractical, dream.

Now she was to go down and meet another man, a *stranger,* into whose care her father had consigned her for the rest of her life. When they married, Jack Darlington would have legal control of all the money and possessions she brought with her, legal control of any children they might have, legal control of her body. Of course, he would provide a home for her in return.

Rosaline wondered what sort of home it would be. Since Mr. Darlington reportedly traveled a great deal, she would at least have a certain amount of freedom in his absence, she supposed, freedom to dine when she pleased, retire when she pleased, enjoy the solitude she craved. Rosaline took comfort in that, unable to imagine that the quiet household of an Orkney squire could be nearly as demanding as the one—or two, counting her aunts' house next door—she managed now.

Wanting to make a favorable first impression, Rosaline put skillful last touches on her toilet. She was not pretty, of course, not fortunate to have been born with the fair hair and blue eyes that were all the rage, but she prided herself upon her neat grooming. She rubbed beeswax onto her tidy nails, dabbed heliotrope on her skin and, feeling a trifle wicked, dipped a piece of crimson silk in red wine and rubbed it on her cheeks to give them a bloom.

She wore a pale rose in her hair, fashionably tucked in the coils at the back, and a sensible heather colored silk gown trimmed in beige lace. Her father had bought her a silver bracelet in Constantinople, and she removed it from her jewel box and slid it over her wrist. She was tall, but had always held herself unashamedly straight, and if she suffered from the sin of pride at all, it stemmed from her noble lineage. Although no longer landed, her family was one of the oldest in Scotland.

She tucked David's locket inside her bodice, out of sight, then reconsidering, allowed it to rest conspicuously over the heather silk. The looking glass declared her presentable, at least, if not a gentleman's dream.

Steeling herself for the awkward meeting with her prospective husband, she proceeded downstairs, knowing the Orkney squire would be scrutinizing her just as thoroughly as she would be scrutinizing him. Even though she felt outwardly composed, Rosaline hesitated near the door of the drawing room, her heart beating much faster than normal, her ears attuned to catch the sound of Jack Darlington's voice, wondering what its timbre and inflection would reveal about his character. With a shock, Rosaline realized it was a voice she would be hearing for the rest of her life, in its best and worst moods, in its capacity as husband, companion, and lover.

But Mr. Darlington did not oblige her by speaking. Her father was talking instead, extolling Rosaline's virtues point by point. Lord Bardo seemed to be making certain that the prospective bridegroom knew Rosaline possessed all the accomplishments of a well-brought-up young lady, that she had a shrewd head for knowing whether or not she was being cheated by tradesmen, had a knack for growing herbs, a talent for managing servants, and above all, a highborn grace.

Smoothing her skirts one last time, Rosaline raised her head a notch and affected the capable demeanor attributed to her. Then she entered the room without announcing herself, only to stop abruptly.

Her intended stood near the window. The gray light of the rainy afternoon shone behind his head and the shadow of a lamp fell across the angular planes of his face. Although elegantly attired, his features were not elegant at all—at least not in a refined sense. At first glance, the gentleman appeared forbiddingly saturnine—or, perhaps, Rosaline thought, it was only the dim light and shadow that gave Jack Darlington's face such harshness.

She fancied, ridiculously, that he had known she had hesitated behind the door, for his eyes seemed to have fastened upon her face even before she walked into the room. He was already standing deferently, in expectation. He moved his head a fraction, out of shadow, so that his face was completely revealed. How rough-cast and austere it was. His hair was nearly black, straight, thick and recently barbered. His body was tautly strung together.

He was not what Rosaline had expected. Not at all.

She stared at him in confusion. She had expected her father to chose a dour, pinched, perhaps even puritanical laird who lived a quiet, orderly life and toiled mundanely in the fields of his estate. She had expected someone awkward and ruddy faced, wearing country tweeds.

She had not expected this man, standing so quietly and yet so compellingly. He seemed to be waiting for her to finish her examination—favorably or not—and come to grips with it so she could speak.

Jack Darlington was admittedly the sort of fellow, Rosaline thought, who would delight any bride-to-be with his unclassical handsomeness. But Rosaline, plain herself, was disturbed by his good looks, even dismayed by them.

All at once, she realized she had been *hoping* for a plain bridegroom, one as plain as she. Not a man of this caliber. She sensed immediately that Jack Darlington was not the sort who would be easily overridden or persuaded against his desires. If his appearance was any reflection of his character, he was a man of granite will and sensual appetites, a man, quite simply, who was too much for her.

Only a few seconds had passed, and yet many impressions had collided in Rosaline's mind to form a whole if not yet completely verified picture of Jack Darlington. She guessed

that he had finished his initial judgment of her as well. His
eyes had flickered over her once, very thoroughly—but only
once—as if his powers of perception were either extraordinarily
keen or as if, after all, he found her too uninspiring to warrant
further perusal.

That he might have found her terribly lacking in looks disconcerted Rosaline. But she did not allow her anxiety to show,
nor she hoped, her defensiveness. She nodded politely and
allowed him to step forward and take her hand.

"Miss Cheevers," he said in a low voice, putting his lips
in back of her knuckles and scarcely brushing them. "I'm
honored to make your acquaintance."

"And I yours," she responded cooly, realizing that he had
not been raised amid drawing rooms and strict convention, for
he had failed to wait for her father to make the introduction.

"Rosaline," her sire said now, watching the pair nervously
as if fearing one, or both, would take a violent dislike to the
other and bolt. "Have you had your tea?"

"No, Father."

"Perhaps you'd like to sit over there, then, near Mr. Darlington, and pour yourself a cup? He has been telling me about his
home in the Orkneys. It sounds intriguing."

She seated herself rigidly in an old winged back chair whose
springs squeaked with mortifying loudness as she put her weight
upon them. Aware of her fiancé's discerning, unwavering gaze,
Rosaline blushed. She hated the fact that she colored easily.
At least her hands were steady upon the silver tea service so
that, when she placed the strainer over the cup and poured, not
one drop spattered onto the saucer. How odd, she thought, to
be sitting next to a stranger who, in a quiet ceremony next
week, would become her husband.

A moment of awkwardness ensued as silence settled over
the room fraught with tension. Only Jack Darlington seemed
calm. Unable to meet his eyes, Rosaline stared at the floor,
noticing his long legs stretched out, one knee raised, the other
straight.

He seemed to be waiting for her to open the conversation, and when she did not, observed her for several seconds, then said abruptly, "Your father tells me you enjoy gardening, Miss Cheevers."

"Oh, y-yes. Yes, I do."

"What do you grow?"

She hesitated. "Well, I grow irises and roses and hyacinths. And herbs. There's a lovely old oak in the center of them all. It shades the roses a bit too much, but I haven't the heart to prune the branches."

"Do you have a particular fondness for trees, then?"

Slightly taken aback by the question, and by the man's intense regard, Rosaline echoed, "Trees, Mr. Darlington?" Her back seemed uncomfortably straight. "Why, of course I like trees. I should think everyone does."

"Your father and I were just discussing the fact that there aren't any trees in the Orkneys. I hope you won't be disappointed when you arrive and find it stark."

"There are no trees at all?" she said faintly.

"Practically none."

"Why? Does no one plant any?"

Watching her long, white hands as they raised the cup to her lips with a noticeable quiver, Jack hid a smile and replied, "The wind and salt of the island kill them. It's a wild place, barren and cold."

Rosaline met his gaze, finding it difficult to hold. For some reason, her usually calm brown eyes were unable to match his hard blue ones. She wondered if Jack Darlington were testing her in some way, if he intended to present the worse side of her prospective home to see if she would be frightened off.

Stiltedly, she said, "I daresay I'm not so shallow as to allow my happiness with a place to be determined by the number of trees, Mr. Darlington. Or by any other thing that cannot be helped or changed. You will not find me frivolous or complaining. I'm not a girl any longer, after all." Her voice was steady, she thought, and horribly prim. Why had she said such a thing?

Why did she feel the need to be defensive about her shortcomings as a prospective bride?

To her astonishment, Jack Darlington smiled. Rosaline admitted that his smile was his best attribute—and he possessed his share of fine ones. The amused expression dispelled the harshness of his face.

"I'm happy to hear you say that, Miss Cheevers," he said with a sudden drawing room politeness that did not quite match the odd, slightly wicked twinkle in his eyes. "Your straightforwardness is refreshing. I myself am straightforward, most of the time."

Lord Bardo cleared his throat, sensing some undercurrent but failing to understand it. "We were just discussing Jack's impending journey to Egypt, Rosaline. I believe you are to go with him."

Rosaline glanced at Mr. Darlington, then at her father, then at Mr. Darlington again, incredulous. "Did you say Egypt?"

"Indeed, I did."

She felt frightened, then thrilled. How odd, how ironic, that she was to travel to an exotic country after all, even if it was not to be in David's company. "Is it really true?" she asked, a trifle breathless.

"Indeed it is, Miss Cheevers," Jack replied. "We'll spend a month or two in the Orkneys first, to enable you to become acquainted with your new home, then set sail for Alexandria." He lifted a brow. "That is, *if* you care to go."

"Of course I do," she assured him readily, a hand to her throat. "How long will we be staying there?"

Jack glanced at Lord Bardo. "That depends upon my work. As yet, the length of the assignment is indefinite."

Rosaline leaned so far forward in her chair that the napkin slipped off her lap. Realizing her unladylike eagerness, she straightened so that her whalebone stays rested a precise two inches from the chair back and then spoke with her usual sedateness. "I've read Miss Nightingale's account of her Egyptian travels, Mr. Darlington. She called Cairo the rose of cities, the garden of the desert, the pearl of Moorish architecture. Do you know she sailed down the Nile? She encountered all sorts of curious people and strange customs on her journey. I can't imagine anything so exciting.''

Satisfied with his daughter's enthusiasm, Lord Bardo winked and commented, ''Rosaline has inherited my taste for travel, I believe, Jack.''

''It would seem so.''

''But isn't the country rather unsettled at the moment?'' Rosaline asked. ''Will Cairo be dangerous?''

''The politics are more unsettled than the population,'' Lord Bardo said. ''There's a large British community in Cairo made up of investors, diplomats, and their wives. Socially, you'll feel right at home, no doubt.''

Rosaline began to savor the thought of the adventure, envisioning palms and minarets and sand. The room grew quiet, the deep ticking of the dour, old grandfather clock marking the moments.

Lord Bardo puffed on his pipe and watched his daughter shrewdly through a curl of blue smoke. ''So you have no reservations at all about the trip, Rosaline?'' he asked after a moment.

''No, Father. You've assured me that it's safe. I'm delighted at the prospect. Will we be traveling by steamship?''

''Yes,'' Jack answered, giving Lord Bardo a ruefully satisfied glance. ''And we're to have the very best accommodations when we arrive. Compliments of the Foreign Office.''

''Really? Will we have a house of our own, then?''

''Yes,'' Lord Bardo drawled with a clearing of his throat and a ruefulness she did not quite understand. ''A rather fine one, I should think. And, by the way, I happen to know of several excellent British physicians in Cairo, Rosaline, should you happen to find yourself in a—er—delicate condition.''

For a moment, Rosaline thought she had misheard her father. She stared at him, her eyes wide, her movements suspended. The air seemed to thin around her. Blood roared in her ears.

She had been stirring sugar in her tea, and it took all her will power not to rattle the teaspoon against the porcelain. She clenched the spoon until her knuckles whitened. Had her father really said, "delicate condition"? How did he dare? How could her own sire have mentioned a subject so exceedingly private, so *undiscussable?* More horrifying still, Lord Bardo had mentioned it in front of Jack Darlington, who was apparently expected—although the thought of it alarmed her—to *put* her in such a condition.

Color came swiftly to Rosaline's frozen face. She avoided the pair of penetrating blue eyes across the room, looking instead at her father, pinning him with a withering glance. As she regarded him, she realized that Lord Bardo had implied that she might be in such a state *now. Carrying David's child.*

What an outrage! Why had her father embarrassed her? Did he mean to punish her for not confirming her behavior with David one way or another? Or was this some misguided attempt at kindness, his way of letting her know the topic had been broached and neatly settled, just in case she found herself in difficulties seven or eight months from now?

With a sickening certainty, Rosaline sensed that the possibility had already been discussed between her father and Jack Darlington. Obviously, for some gallant reason, Mr. Darlington had agreed to take her as his wife in spite of her alleged wantonness. Rosaline had deceived her father as a way to force his hand and allow her to marry David; it had never occurred to her that his speculations, his suspicions, would be shared with her prospective bridegroom. Dear God. What must Mr. Darlington *think* of her? A fallen woman, wayward, the mother-to-be of an illegitimate child. Lord Bardo must surely have offered him money to take her in such a plight, to secure the future of another man's child. And to think none of it was even remotely true. . . .

Rosaline's mouth felt dry, and her body hot with mortification. It was an effort to maintain her rigid posture. For once, her stock of socially appropriate words completely failed her.

She could neither adroitly change the subject nor clarify it. So she simply remained mute, her whole face as bright as a red flag. By her silence, she must seem guilty as accused.

She rose to her feet, thinking to fly from the room. But if she were to lose her composure and run out, facing Jack Darlington again would be doubly difficult. Rosaline hesitated, rooted in place. Still clutching the teaspoon, she desperately searched for some gracious way to regain her dignity.

"The rain seems to be letting up," Jack Darlington remarked in an off-handed way, coming to his feet and speaking to her kindly. "Perhaps you would be good enough to take a stroll with me, Miss Cheevers, and show me the sights of Edinburgh? A walk down Grassmarket maybe? We can see the Castle from that vantage point, can't we? I'm not too clear on its history. Perhaps you could elaborate on the high points?"

He was talking mundanely for her benefit, Rosaline knew, and between his understanding and the strain of the situation, she felt foolish tears prickle behind her eyelids. Horrible. She never cried.

With a gesture of his hand, Jack had caught the attention of a housemaid, and a moment later draped a cloak about Rosaline's shoulders. She stood stiffly, her throat so constricted it made her confounding muteness worse. Putting a hand to her eyes, she bowed her head and struggled with angry tears.

"Didn't I see you wearing a locket a moment ago, Miss Cheevers?" Jack asked, touching her shoulder. "A particularly fine one set with five or six amethysts?" He made a business of bending to search the floor for it, looking anywhere but at her face to spare her. "Did it become hooked in the cloak perhaps? Lord Bardo, can you check beneath your daughter's chair?"

And because he had provided a distraction for her through the locket, had provided something ordinary for her to say, to do, Rosaline mustered her wits and pretended to join in the hunt as well, able to keep her flushed and tear streaked face averted for the several minutes it took her complexion to return to its normal color.

"Ah, here it is," Jack declared. As if from thin air, he produced David's necklace and let it dangle from his fingers.

Rosaline stood rigid, letting Jack fasten David's memento about her neck again, thinking how ironic it was that her husband-to-be was returning her lover's locket to its resting place against her breast. She wondered how the solid, difficult clasp could have failed, and murmured stiltedly, "I'm so grateful . . . so clumsy of me to lose it. Where did you find it?"

"Where, Miss Cheevers?" Jack asked smoothly. "Why, there, beside your shoe. You must have been standing on it."

"Yes. Yes, I must have." She drew away now that the chain was refastened, uncomfortable with Jack Darlington's touch, his proximity. She felt certain she had *not* been standing on the locket, but was hardly in a position to contradict him.

"Shall we go now?" He regarded her gravely, but his eyes twinkled. How sharp they must be, she thought, to have counted the precise number of amethysts in the necklace from his distant vantage point. The stones were very small, scarcely more than chips.

Before Rosaline knew quite how it happened, Jack Darlington had donned his buff colored hat, suede gloves, his light caped coat of the same rich hue, and escorted her into the rainy air outside. He made their exit particularly smooth, tucking her hand beneath his elbow. When a black coach and six clattered past, hooves and wheels sending up sprays of cold water, he guided her neatly to one side, so that his own boots and coat received the splattering.

The coolness of the drizzle beaded her cheeks and brought Rosaline's senses sharply into focus again. On the streets businessmen in black frock coats hastened to various destinations, along with well-dressed women wearing pattens and huge veiled bonnets. Most of the ladies carried baskets on their arms; a few led children who seemed determined to splash through each puddle. On the corner, a hokey pokey man hawked flavored ices from his wooden cart, and next to him, a woman wearing a ragged tartan shawl displayed a pair of finches for sale.

Rosaline hoped desperately that the diversion on the busy cobbled thoroughfare would distract Mr. Darlington from the abominable subject Lord Bardo had raised in the parlor. Jack strolled along beside her, his long step slow so as not to tax hers. His manner was not tense at all, but at ease, as if he had found her personal crisis a moment ago less than earth shattering, a matter to take in stride, lightly even, now that he had rescued her from it.

After they walked a block or so, he asked her casually, "Do you always carry a teaspoon with you when you go out, Miss Cheevers?"

Startled, Rosaline glanced at him, then at her left hand. As if it were the hilt of a dagger, the silver teaspoon was still clenched in her fingers.

"Oh! Good heavens," she stammered, embarrassed. She fumbled with her cloak, located the pocket and slipped the offending bit of silverware inside it. "Oh, my . . . you must think me a scatterbrained fool, Mr. Darlington."

"On the contrary," he answered, producing a pair of brown kid gloves—her own—from his deep coat pocket. He held them out to her. "I spirited you outside before you had time to put on your gloves. If you hadn't been so rushed, you would have noticed the spoon. My fault entirely."

She took them, murmuring her thanks while drawing them over her shaking fingers. What an impression she must be making on this self-assured man! He seemed imperturbed, but he must surely be reconsidering his promise to take her for his wife.

They passed a coffee shop whose rich fragrances hung upon the damp air. A moment later, both glanced up to admire the facade of an old Tudor inn, whose windows sported flower boxes brimming with wet purple pansies. From the upper story rooms, an assortment of laundry hung dripping from poles, having been caught in the rain.

"Tell me about your life here in the city, Miss Cheevers," Jack invited, his reflection briefly caught with hers, in the shiny bow window of a bookseller's shop. "What do you do with yourself?"

"Do with myself?" she repeated, distracted. She drew the hood of her cloak over her now damp, bedraggled hair, and sniffed, the tip of her nose already numb with cold. "Why, I take care of my father's house, of course. And oversee the house of my two elderly aunts next door."

"And do you enjoy the domestic duties? Do they content you?"

She hesitated, watching her wet shoes as she tried to match the rhythm of his step. "I don't believe it's a question of liking it or not, Mr. Darlington, but of doing what's expected of me."

"Do you always do what's expected of you?"

Rosaline thought of David, of the chance for freedom she had lost when her father had thrown him out. She thought of her father's 'arrangement' for her, and her own resigned acceptance of that arrangement—and of the man walking beside her now.

Lowering her eyes, she murmured, "Very nearly always, Mr. Darlington."

He seemed to consider her reply, but made no response as he guided her around an old man selling coconuts on the corner.

"Cocky-nit, cocky-nit!" the tattered fellow cried. "A penny the bit! Taste and try before ye buy!"

Smelling the smooth, white interior of the coconut the old man had halved and displayed, Rosaline remembered a picture she had once seen of a grove of coconut trees. Suddenly wondering what sort of bleak, barren place Jack would expect her to call home, she asked, "What a shame there are no trees on your island, Mr. Darlington. Are there no places sheltered from the wind? No places at all?"

"Not many. The few trees that manage to survive are usually stunted and bent."

"Does that mean there are no birds, as well?"

"Why? Do you have a fondness for birds?"

"Yes, as a matter of fact, I do." She managed a weak smile. "I like to hear them sing. My room looks out onto our little garden, you see, and there are always robins and larks to wake me, to keep me company while I tend my herbs in the afternoon."

"We have gulls and kittiwakes. But I'm afraid I haven't noticed anything else. And gulls aren't quite the same as larks and robins, are they?"

She shook her head, privately disappointed. "No, not quite."

They had come to have a splendid view of the Castle. Its ancient grey battlements crowned the steep, vertical hill behind the line of chimney pots in the Grassmarket. Jack paused to scan the monument, squinting slightly against the drifting veils of mist.

"Tell me about the Castle," he said.

She told him everything she knew, which was a considerable amount, since she loved to read history and had visited the ancient edifice many times. He listened attentively, asking her intelligent questions, seemingly amused by her detailed and knowledgeable description of the architecture.

"I fear I've caused you to ruin your shoes," he said when they finished their conversation, glancing down at the soft, tan kid stained dark with water.

Rosaline lifted a shoulder. "No matter. I know how to salvage them. My aunts are always forgetting to change into sensible shoes when they venture out. Truthfully, I was no less addlepated when we left the house awhile ago." She broke off and lowered her head, sorry that she had so impulsively mentioned her earlier embarrassing behavior. Now Jack Darlington would remember the reason for it.

What if he were to reopen the subject her father had so shockingly raised? As her fiancé, she supposed Jack Darlington had the right to ask her anything he pleased concerning her relationship with another man. Delicacy aside, he could demand to know the likelihood of an impending pregnancy. Rosaline would refuse to speak of such a delicate matter. She would be mortified to discuss the issue of conception, the mechanics of which she had little practical knowledge. Should she simply tell Jack Darlington bluntly, outright, that there was to be no child? At least she knew that to be true.

She twisted her hands, on the verge of blurting out the truth. But when she glanced up, Jack seemed unaware of her agonized indecision. He was watching a little black and white terrier across the street perform tricks for a group of children who cheered its antics. When the dog managed to execute a perfect flip, he grinned and asked smoothly, without looking at her flushed face, "Shall we go back now, Miss Cheevers?"

Something in his manner suggested to Rosaline that Jack Darlington had sensed her agitated thoughts, and mercifully, had decided to spare her any uncomfortable questions. He offered his arm and they walked in silence, intent upon a quick pace, since rain had begun to fall in earnest. It soaked the shoulders of their outerwear and wet their faces. Quickly, in step, they hurried past the same booksellers, the same inns, the same coconut seller they had passed on the way to the Castle. But just before the turn that would have taken them back to Lord Bardo's staid brick house, Jack steered Rosaline toward the old crone who stood huddled on the corner holding her cage of finches.

How pitiable the pair of little birds looked, crouched together with rain dripping off their feathers. Not a peep of sound came from their throats, nor did they move.

"Do they sing?" Jack asked the old woman, speaking above the drum of rain.

"Oh, o' course, sir! O' course!" she cried, jiggling the cage a bit as if to prompt the poor finches to perform.

"How much do you want for the lot?"

The ancient woman smiled at him toothlessly while assessing with an expert glance his well-cut clothes and clean shaven face. "Eight shillings," she said, ready to lower the price should he make to turn away.

Astonished, Rosaline watched while Jack removed twice that amount from his pocket and, after putting it into the old woman's knotted hand, took possession of the cage. He raised a doubtful brow at the bedraggled finches before handing the cage to Rosaline.

"Here," he said dryly. "Take them to Orkney with you—to replace the larks and sparrows you'll be leaving behind here."

Taken aback by the gesture, Rosaline hesitated. Then deciding it was proper manners to accept a present from a man who was so shortly to be her husband, she stammered her gratitude.

Jack observed her for a moment, saying nothing. His eyes disconcerted her; she wondered if she would ever be comfortable meeting them, holding them. She wondered at his sudden silence, as well, and at the firm, almost too hard grip of his hand on her elbow. The sound of the falling rain thrummed all around them, running in rivulets off the brim of Jack's hat. The sound mingled with the haunting chime of a distant cathedral bell.

"Miss Cheevers," Jack said at last, his voice gentle but grim, even a bit hesitant. He spoke slowly, as if uttering each word with care. "I fear that life with me will not be easy. I'll demand much and give little in the way of affection. This is not a love match, and we both know that. And yet, there will be compensations, I think." He touched her arm. "Do you understand?"

Blinking her eyes against the rain, Rosaline clutched the rusted handle of the birdcage and met his handsome blue gaze with equal sobriety and a strange, unexpected disappointment that she managed to conceal. "Yes, Mr. Darlington," she said with a nod. "I believe I understand."

Jack's eyes shifted to the sky, then swept the distant landscape. Curiously, almost to himself, he murmured, "It's rare that we get what we really want, isn't it? What we dream of having?"

Rosaline was surprised by his tone, by the depth of his words. They were still strangers, after all. But she understood what he meant. "I gave up daydreaming a long time ago–when I was sixteen or so," she said rather briskly, as if she didn't care, thinking of all the years she had waited for a man to court her, to love her, to tell her that she was beautiful. "It's a rather childish thing to do, after all, having one's head in the clouds. Besides, I'm too busy for that kind of dawdling."

"Are you?" Jack asked as if he doubted her.

She knew he was thinking of her relationship with David, forcing her to think of it. Yes, she had had dreams. And truthfully, she had them still.

"Ah, well," Jack said, smiling suddenly, reaching out to wipe a drop of rain from her chin. "Perhaps you're better off being practical then."

Rosaline believed at first that he was teasing her in some way. And yet, as she regarded his handsome but hard edged face, the blue eyes which seemed to be looking not at her now, but at something far away, she believed that Jack Darlington was not thinking of her dreams at all, but of his own.

Chapter Four

From the beginning, she could tell that Jack Darlington was an impatient man, if not in all things, then at least in accomplishing what he considered to be a matter already agreed upon, settled, and best gotten over with as soon as possible. And yet, with his usual idle charm, Jack tolerated delays while Rosaline arranged the tedious details of their hasty wedding.

"You select the brand of champagne," he would say with a lazy wave of his hand and a charming smile when she would ask for his opinion. "I'm sure your judgment in such matters is more educated than mine."

Rosaline began to feel as if she were the only participant in their coming union. She nursed a deep-seated fear that Jack Darlington was not even the least bit interested in her, and if that disinterest hadn't been her common experience with almost every man she had ever met—except David—she might have been crushed.

During the two weeks preceding the wedding, she rarely saw her future husband. He booked rooms in the Green Plaid Inn, only calling at Lord Bardo's house every other day, his manner relaxed, witty, but always underlaid with the peculiar impatience of a man used to physical adventures the city could not provide. Usually he spent only a couple of hours in Rosaline's company before turning his eyes restively to the window, begging her leave, and bidding her a good natured good-day. Did she bore him? She feared so, and to soothe her resentment, consoled herself by mumbling that Mr. Darlington was not a well-bred man, after all, despite his handsome smile and good clothes.

Regardless of his social status, Rosaline suspected her husband-to-be did not lack diversion in Edinburgh, and enjoyed the gentleman's clubs, taverns, or whatever else interested a worldly man who seemed at ease anywhere. Of course, she surmised that he was self-confident enough, or arrogant enough, to be unconcerned whether people approved of him or not. She sensed, too, that Jack Darlington liked the company of free-spirited women. He had given her no particular cause to suspect that he was enjoying dalliances, but Rosaline had become acquainted with sensuality—if only dimly—in David's arms and recognized the passion that simmered in Jack Darlington's eyes.

Every Tuesday and Friday afternoon, her fiancé dutifully joined her at her aunts' home, easing himself into one of the impractical little chairs that crowded their overheated, lemon scented parlor. Jack's athletic frame scarcely fit in the gilded piece of furniture, and his presence seemed out of place in an environment whose every corner was crammed with delicate bric-a-brac, potted palms, fringed ottomans, and the spaniels who were forever demanding samples of scones.

"Mr. Darlington," Rosaline's Aunt Columbine said querulously after she had cut a slice of cake and allowed the dogs to nibble it. "You haven't told us much about yourself, not much a'tall. Indeed, you always turn the conversation around to my sister and I and our concerns, as any gentleman would do. By now we've surely told you about every ailment we've ever endured—and heaven knows, there have been many. Yes, the good Lord has seen fit to give us our share of trials."

Columbine coughed delicately, and with long-suffering eyes, drew her shawl about her chest as if to ward off a threatening ague. "Indeed, as I'm always telling Violet, it's a miracle we're still *breathing.*"

Observing him from across the room, Rosaline thought with private amusement that it was a miracle *Jack* was still breathing. Perspiration gathered on his brow and trickled down to his starched white collar. She was impressed by his tireless good sportsmanship, by the convincing, sympathetic smile he offered Aunt Violet when she ordered the hovering maid to throw yet more coal on the already roaring fire. Even though he must have been dying to yank off his frock coat and throw open the windows, he continued to sip cup after cup of the scalding lemon tea they pressed upon him.

"Do tell us about your family, Mr. Darlington," Aunt Violet demanded, shifting her huge bulk and cuddling a spaniel in each arm. "Where were you born?"

Jack balanced his cup and saucer on his knee. "I was born in Golspie, Ma'am."

Aunt Columbine frowned. "Golspie? I don't believe I've ever heard of such a place. It is here in Scotland?"

"Yes. It's a small village in the north. Not a place anyone would be particularly interested in. Cold and dreary, you know, very remote, with harsh winters." He spoke the last words with a pained smile.

Rosaline listened closely, for Jack had shared little with her regarding his background. On more than one occasion, she had asked for details, but some interruption had always seemed to prevent him from giving her any particulars.

She examined him now from beneath her lashes, studied his hands as they held the teacup. He would touch her with those hands soon, after the wedding, Rosaline realized with a shock. Until now, she had forced such disturbing thoughts away; but all at once they assaulted her with such force that she had to close her eyes against them.

"And your mother, Mr. Darlington?" Aunt Columbine persisted, soothing a curly haired spaniel with her hand. "What of her?"

Jack hesitated, but only for a fraction. "I don't remember my mother, Ma'am. She died when I was born."

"Oh, such a shame for a child not to know its mother. At least Rosaline had the company of our dear Katherine for the first nine years of her life. Didn't you, Rosaline? And, of course, we have always done the best we could to compensate. Poor substitutes we are, I know. No, no, don't protest, dear Rosaline." Aunt Violet allowed a third spaniel to jump in her lap and shifted her tiny, slippered foot to rub the belly of the fourth, continuing. "And what of your father, Mr. Darlington?"

"My father?" For one or two long minutes, Jack's eyes met Rosaline's across the expanse of fringed ottomans and potted palms. He seemed to calculate for a moment, then weigh his answer, his gaze narrowing then brightening as if with private amusement. He smiled and answered easily, "My father was a vicar in Golspie. A most respected man. Unfortunately, he passed away last year. I have no living brothers or sisters, and no particular ties with my birthplace anymore. Truthfully, I'm afraid my past has been uneventful, most of it spent sailing on merchant ships to and from America before going to work for Lord Bardo and the Foreign Office."

"I wouldn't call that sort of life uneventful, Mr. Darlington," said Aunt Violet. "Staying at home with Columbine and me is uneventful. Wouldn't you agree, dear Rosaline? Poor girl. Forgoing soirees and balls, missing out on everything that is fun, all because of us. Never any beaux to speak of—except for that artist fellow . . ." She broke off at Columbine's gasp of horror and waved her hand in an agitated manner. "At any rate, thank heavens you have come to rescue her from our monotonous routine, Mr. Darlington."

After casting Rosaline an amused glance, Jack replied, "My pleasure, of course, ma'am."

Rosaline did not respond. She was still pondering that brief spark of calculation that had caused Jack's eyes to darken, then gleam a moment ago. She felt certain there was more to Jack Darlington than met the eye. On the surface, he seemed to saunter through life as if it were something to be enjoyed, to defy convention when it suited him, just as he played the gentleman when the company called for it. No doubt he used his charm to manipulate any situation that could prove in some way valuable to him. And yet, beneath his easy manner, he always seemed to be on the alert, wary, a man watching his back out of habit.

Chagrined by her own suspicions, Rosaline wondered if she could entirely trust the man she was to marry. Her turbulent thoughts must have shown on her face, for across the room, Jack regarded her with shrewd speculation. She might have given a sweet nod to reassure him, but did not, choosing instead to keep her expression closed, having decided to let him wonder at her thoughts.

"Rosaline, dear," Columbine said, interrupting her niece's disturbing reverie. "Please call the maid and order more cake. It is all gone and poor Pookie is begging for more. Mr. Darlington, you really *should* take Rosaline to Golspie after you're married. A bride likes to see where her husband was born, you know."

"Yes, do take me, Jack," Rosaline said with quiet deliberation, pinning him with her own steady eyes. She half expected to see guardedness darken her fiancé's face, but none showed. Instead, he leaned forward in his chair and gave his own untouched slice of cake to the spaniels—doubtless to please the aunts—then smiled at Rosaline with all the indulgence a bridegroom would be expected to display.

"Why, of course, Rosaline," he said quietly, just to her, as if they were playing some game of words, "I shall take you anywhere you'd like to go. Anywhere at all. You've only to ask."

* * *

Their exchange of vows two days later was accomplished as neatly and unemotionally as any transaction of business, Jack standing erect in black broadcloth beside Rosaline in white satin. After the champagne punch and the congratulatory kiss of her father, after the alarmingly intimate touch of Jack's hands upon her waist, Rosaline changed into a green serge gown and plumed hat, and feeling sudden panic at the thought of leaving the secure routine of her childhood home, ran out into her garden to gulp deep breaths of air.

An old oak, as familiar to her as any family member, spread its umbrella over tea roses and herbs. The fragrances were soft and delicious here, the sky a benign blue, the stepping stones covered in moss and sparkling with drops of an earlier mist. For long moments, Rosaline simply breathed in the essence of it all, stared at each familiar flower, committed everything to memory so that when she stood on the barren, wind-swept isle to which Jack Darlington soon would carry her, she would have comforting thoughts to savor.

Pensive, she knelt beneath the oak and gathered its fallen acorns, cradling them in her gloved hand, studying each before slipping them into the pocket of her traveling clothes. She began to collect more then, resolved to bring something of her past to Jack Darlington's house, so that, in some small way, the island might become her home, too.

"They won't grow on Orkney, you know."

Rosaline heard the cool, self-assured voice but did not turn around. Jack's tone annoyed her, and because Lord Bardo's daughter could be stubborn too, she answered. "They'll grow."

"Even if you have to will them to, eh?" Jack asked, tilting his top hat back at a more comfortable angle and strolling nearer. "I'm beginning to believe that you have a very strong will, Rosaline."

Nerves on edge, Rosaline answered with a trace of testiness. "Probably no stronger than yours, Mr. Darlington."

As if pleased with her contentiousness, Jack grinned and shoved his hands in his pockets, the brocade of his waistcoat as bright as his teeth. Idly, he propped a shoulder against the oak, and his eyes glinted an unreadable color of blue beneath the shade of his silk hat. "A garden setting suits you. Do you sit here with your poetry volumes and tomes of Greek philosophy? Your father disapproves of both, in case you didn't know, and has warned me that I am getting a wife that is too deep thinking."

"And what was your reply to him?" Rosaline asked.

"I said that I preferred deep waters to shallow."

"Do you? Why?"

He shrugged. "Because deep waters are more dangerous, of course."

His easy way of bantering made Rosaline uncomfortable and she moved a few steps away, the hem of her skirt trailing over the flagstones.

Jack picked up an acorn, idly tossed it in the air, captured it in his palm. Then, with lazy mischief in his voice, he commented, "By the way, a few minutes ago I happened to see your unfinished portrait. You know the one—it's hidden away in the conservatory behind the potted ferns, as if someone were ashamed of it. Odd, the picture doesn't convey the . . . reserve that I see in you. No, the canvas shows a much more . . . er . . . high-strung woman."

"You were snooping about the conservatory?" Rosaline could not contain her outrage.

"Snooping?" he said with his mouth half-tilted. "Not at all. I happened upon the portrait. Do you object?"

"Yes, I do," she said, resentful of his easy manner, of the fact that he had pried into her relationship with David, of his tarnishing of it. "You had no right to look at it."

Her high handed tone caused Jack's good natured banter to change to a more subtle, less benign exchange. "I believe it's a husband's prerogative to see the canvas his wife's lover has painted of her, don't you? I find it interesting that the artist saw such a different Rosaline—but then, of course," he added, "you were doubtless gazing at him differently than you gaze at me."

"You show poor manners in bringing up the subject on such a day, don't you think?" Rosaline said, angry with herself for letting his indelicacy affect her.

Jack smiled. "Have my manners been poor? My apologies. I confess I don't always know. I have hopes—not misplaced, I trust—that you will tutor me in the art of drawing room etiquette now that we're married. I've noticed that you're a stickler for decorum, very proper and modest in everything you do. I can't imagine you ever making a social blunder."

Rosaline looked away from him. "You're goading me, I believe, although I can't think why."

"I'm restless, I suppose," he said by way of apology. And then, as if testing her composure, he said with a trace of wickedness, "But sometimes contentiousness between a man and woman can serve as a substitute for passion—and we do have a sad lack of passion on our wedding day, don't you think, Rosaline?"

She knew he referred to the fact that she had pointedly turned her head away from his kiss at the end of the wedding ceremony. But how ungentlemanly of him to remind her of it now. In a cool voice she said, "My father told me you were born of common people. He told me that you were not greatly accustomed to polite society. This is becoming more apparent by the minute."

Jack answered with no abashment at all. "It's true I've spent no more hours than necessary sipping tea in the drawing rooms of self-important people. But I intend to spend more time in them now. And I intend to have you at my side to benefit from your talents in that direction."

There was provoked sarcasm in his tone, and Rosaline made a flippant gesture. "You don't need my tutelage. When it suits you, you know perfectly well how to behave."

"Thank you. I'm reassured. And flattered. Whether you wanted to or not, I believe you paid me a compliment."

His tone was teasing, not unkind, but Rosaline still refused to be softened.

Jack stepped forward and told her, "It's time to go. The coach is waiting on the street."

"I prefer to be alone for a few minutes, if you don't mind."

For a moment, Rosaline thought Jack might take her arm, and with his usual brand of easy but forceful insistence, usher her away. But after regarding her for several disquieting seconds, her bridegroom simply shrugged and said, "Come when you're ready then."

Feeling an odd sort of misery, a realization that the two of them had gotten off to a dreadful start, Rosaline watched her husband stroll away. She had seen a side of him—a somehow discomfiting side—that she hadn't known was there. Ah, well, she would have to find a way to deal with it.

She did not hate it as she feared she might, did not shudder at the first glimpse of the wild place that was to be her home. There were few trees, as Jack had warned, and yet, as compensation, majestic stone pillars reared up from a splendrous aquamarine sea. The cliffs surrounding them glowed with the colors of ochre, grey, brown and red, and the farmland, divided by hedgerows into crazy plaids, rolled over low emerald hills. Everywhere lay a view of the sea, and the wind blew its salt spray to each rocky niche of the isle. Still, the island seemed a formidable place to Rosaline, not quiet, gentle, or even welcoming, especially now, at twilight.

From her seat beside the coach window she gazed out, her hands neatly folded in her lap to give the false impression that her emotions were equally composed. Jack had said little since their arrival in Orkney, allowing her to form her first impressions without influence, his long legs sprawled in the tight space of the coach, so that Rosaline, rather than allowing his knee to brush her skirts, had to inch away.

Through her lashes she watched as he crossed his arms across his chest, leaned his head against the leather upholstery, and with no apology at all, began to doze. She studied him with eyes that would never have been so bold beneath the directness of his gaze.

Admittedly, he was physically well-favored in every way. She stared at his hands in their suede gloves, knowing they would touch her in the strange cold bed toward which they journeyed. Yes, tonight he would make her his wife in the way men enjoyed, doing it without affection, just as he had hinted he would do the day he had bought the finches. What had he said? *I'll demand much and give little in the way of affection?*

Having felt David's body pressed against her own, and David's hands explore inside her gown, Rosaline knew—fundamentally at least—how such male attentions would begin. But David's body had been slight, almost effete, a match for his sensitive artist's soul. Jack Darlington's body, beneath its fine covering of cambric and broadcloth, was surely a hard, demanding frame with a leisurely appetite.

Rosaline was surprised that Jack had not attempted to kiss her again, or hold her in his arms once they were alone in the coach. No doubt he was dissatisfied with her. And yet, dissatisfied or not, she knew he would join her in the marriage bed tonight. She sensed that Jack Darlington was not the sort of man to leave anything unfinished, not the sort of man to ignore an opportunity that may prove in some way self-gratifying.

He stirred suddenly, opened his eyes, caught her staring at him. "I hope you weren't bored with the scenery," he said with a smile.

"No need to apologize for sleeping if you're tired," she answered, refusing to be baited. "I was just . . . looking out the window."

"I see. And?"

He expected her opinion, and she gave it with no effort to

spare his feelings, knowing he would read the innuendoes. "The island is stark and barren, just as you told me it would be."

Her words were waspish, and Rosaline was suddenly and painfully aware that she and this self-possessed man were expected to make a life together. They were still strangers who, it seemed to her, did not even like each other very much. While the strain of the situation and the thought of the coming physical ordeal was beginning to stretch Rosaline's nerves to a breaking point, Jack Darlington seemed unconcerned. His composure galled her.

"See the henge monuments there," he said, hiding a yawn while he leaned to point at a jumble of blackened stones scattered over the landscape. "They're Bronze Age. You might find them interesting to explore. I'm afraid exploring and riding will have to suffice as pastimes, since there's little social activity. The farm cottages are few and far between, and the women here have little time for socializing. Still, they'll want to know you, want to be friends with the lady of the manor."

"Are none of the women gently bred then?"

"No." He gave her a rueful smile. "They're all common. Like me."

"I didn't mean to . . ."

"Yes, you did. And if you think your sense of social superiority offends me, it doesn't—I intend to put it to good use."

"It's gallant of you to inform me," she said with her chin high.

Jack laughed. "I don't think you're a pretentious woman, Rosaline, but you do take a healthy pride in your bloodlines. I think you believe—rightly perhaps," he added, "that people like me are beneath you."

"You speak as if I have no right to be proud."

"You have a right to be as proud as you wish. But if you make a point to set yourself apart from everyone here, you'll find yourself lonely before long."

Rosaline's hands tightened in her lap. She felt bleak suddenly.

Even the overheated parlor and snuffling spaniels of her aunts' home seemed dear, and the reserved company of her father much preferable to the rudeness of her bridegroom.

"I shall manage just fine," she said through tight lips, more to herself than to him, refusing to allow Jack Darlington even a glimpse of the desolation that had beset her, the dread as she noticed gray mist blurring the landscape of her new home. It was foolish to be so mawkish, she told herself, naive to have expected more than this.

Jack nodded toward the window again. "Look there, beyond the cliffs. Those are our colonies of birds. Gulls, terns, a few kittiwakes. And we have a great brown bird with white markings that the islanders call a skua."

Rosaline paused to listen to their raucous cries, the plaintive, discordant noises that seemed far removed from birdsong, or from any sound she had ever heard in Edinburgh. Suddenly, she craved reassurance, and with surprise realized that even the rough but warm embrace of Jack Darlington's arms would be welcome at such an uncertain homecoming. But he either didn't sense her desolation or was not moved enough to soothe it.

Quietly, shutting thoughts of her bridegroom out, Rosaline lifted the birdcage to her lap and, fixing her eyes upon the silent, huddled finches, concentrated upon thoughts of her old home, her cozy chintz-decorated room, the green garden. Her feelings of sudden regret must have communicated themselves to Jack, for after several moments of a keen-eyed observation, he turned his gaze from her and ceased attempts at conversation. She felt his withdrawal, and when the aged horses at last wheezed up to the house and Jack helped her down from the rented coach, his touch was cool.

In the evening light, with the salt wind whipping her clothes, Rosaline regarded Jack Darlington's home, the grey-brown stone, the quaint thatched roof, the small scale baronial design that could be found in variation scattered all over Scotland. How isolated it seemed! There was not another house in sight, no cottages or church steeples, no sounds of traffic or street sellers' cries as there had been in Edinburgh.

"I have only a housekeeper presently," Jack commented, ushering her through the weathered door. "You'll likely feel a need to enlarge the staff."

Rosaline had no time to reply, for Mrs. Wiggins, as she was introduced, came to welcome them, appearing relieved to see her employer's new wife. "How do you do, Ma'am?" she said.

"Very well, thank you."

"Is the household intact, Mrs. Wiggins?" Jack inquired, tossing his hat toward the hat stand, his aim perfect.

"As intact as always, sir," the woman replied breathlessly. "May I take your cloak and gloves, Mrs. Darlington?"

At first, unaccustomed to the name, Rosaline failed to respond. Then, with an embarrassed smile, she nodded and slipped off her outerwear.

"We'll await refreshments in the parlor," Jack told his housekeeper and, putting a firm hand at the small of Rosaline's back, guided her down a corridor and into a low ceilinged room.

The new bride looked about with chagrin and saw fishing poles with tangled lines, creels, a well-worn saddle, a bridle tossed across a stool, a tiger pelt thrown over the floor, and a monstrous dog with muddy paws who, at sight of his new mistress, crept down and slunk away.

"That's Argos," Jack remarked. He kicked a fishing creel aside with his boot and strolled to the hearth. "I'm afraid his manners need improvement."

Rosaline stood stiffly near the threshold of the room, too nervous to ease her exhausted body onto the chair that the muddy hound had just vacated. The room was utterly masculine, untidy, filled with leather and dark wood, devoid of a single flower or scrap of chintz, far from the orderly, scrupulously clean houses she had overseen since childhood. It smelled of leather and wood and hot candle wax.

Suddenly Rosaline felt like an intruder in a male retreat. She was a feminine creature who needed dainty items surrounding her, and with dismay wondered if she would ever feel at liberty to supplant the stag horns and the scrimshaw and the old woolen tartan thrown across the horsehair sofa.

Expecting perhaps to see his wife make herself at home, wander about the room and explore its contents, Jack regarded her with curiosity. Then, understanding all at once, he took hold of her hands and began to peel off the gloves she had forgotten to relinquish with her cloak. Tossing them aside, he maintained his grip on her fingers and commented mischievously, "Your hands are freezing. What is it? Do you not feel welcome here?"

Caught up in her own dismay, Rosaline shrank from his hands and from his familiarity, sensing that her bridegroom sought to prepare her for his physical attentions, despite the fact that she had scarcely had enough time to get her bearings. She pulled away from his touch and turned her back.

Another man might have forced the issue and recaptured her hands, to let her know he would not be put off, but Jack Darlington only gave his wife a knowing smile, which made her flush.

"Shall I expect a long thaw?" he asked.

His voice was not unkind, but still, Rosaline knew she had been wrong to draw away from him so rudely. It was not a good start to their already tense marriage, and she had little doubt that Jack would have his way, sooner or later, regardless of her unwillingness. Wanting to apologize but unable to form the necessary words, she glanced around the room and murmured, "Your home . . . it's lovely."

It wasn't true, of course, and sounded ridiculous even to her own ears; the slate floors, the rough plastered walls, the low beam ceilings were too rustic for loveliness.

Nevertheless, Jack accepted her attempt to make amends and gave her a smile of good humor. "I'm glad you like it."

Mrs. Wiggins entered then, her black skirts swishing frantically as she carried a tray to the scarred sideboard, pushed a collection of fishing lures aside, and set it down. When she had arranged the pots of cream and sugar, the brandy decanter and the cups and saucers, then bustled out again, Jack observed Rosaline, who was still rooted in place like a statue on a plinth.

"I've never seen you at such a loss, Rosaline. Even during the wedding ceremony—which must have been a disappointment to you, given the change in bridegroom—you managed to maintain an admirable serenity."

She clasped her cold hands together. "I don't quite know what's expected of me, that's all. And I would appreciate it if you would not refer to my former suitor."

"Very well. Now, won't you sit down?"

Avoiding the muddied chair the dog had left, she did as bade, arranging her skirts as she eased down with stiff grace upon the horsehair sofa.

When Jack brought her tea, she coiled her fingers about the cup to warm them, sipping once or twice. The silence of the room grew heavy until her bridegroom opened a large box beside the hearth, removed a slab of peat, and threw it on the fire.

"What do you do here?" she asked him, watching his silhouette against a shower of sparks, noting that his shoulders flexed as he wielded a poker, and that his neck appeared dark brown above the white of his collar. "Do you farm?"

Dusting the peat from his hands, Jack took up a pose by the hearth with one foot propped on the fender, then smiled as if he found her question humorous. "No, I leave that to men who have natures more patient than mine."

"Then how do you occupy yourself? Do you spend your time riding and exploring as you suggested I might learn to do?"

"Rarely. I haven't owned the property long and much of it is in disrepair. I've spent my time reroofing the byre, repairing the pump, replastering walls—those kinds of things. Working for the Foreign Office requires a good deal of travel and excitement, which, believe it or not, becomes tiresome after awhile. I bought this house with the notion of . . .'' he gave her a wry glance, ''playing the gentleman, you might say. At least for a few months out of the year.''

''Playing the gentleman?''

He raised a brow at her tone, which despite her efforts, could not conceal a trace of wryness. ''Well, I can never *really* be a gentleman, now can I? Having such low beginnings?'' When she did not reply, he studied her for several seconds, then leaned to tinker with the fire again. ''Do you want to know my philosophy, Rosaline? I believe life is to be enjoyed, its pleasures stolen. Unfortunately, pleasure often requires money and bloodlines. I couldn't buy bloodlines, but I could buy an estate—of sorts anyway.'' He paused to cast her a rueful look. ''And I could marry—or steal, if you prefer—a gently bred wife who would nag at me to remember my manners. Of course, if she choses to retaliate, she can put me in my place any time she wants by reminding me that she is better born than I.''

Rosaline pursed her lips, toyed with the crisp edging of lace on her sleeve and murmured, ''I'll not do that. It serves no purpose.''

''Don't make any promises now—remember, you'll have to keep them for forty years or so. Haven't you thought of it? We'll be living together that long, just possibly.''

His words fell between them, hard and real, bringing brightly into focus the vows they had earlier exchanged, vows that nothing but death or a rare act of Parliament could sever. Of course, Rosaline thought, there was no law that said they must live together every day of their lives. When marriages proved unhappy, wives occasionally left husbands; husbands, more than occasionally, established residences with younger mistresses and spent the majority of their time far removed from the tedium of hearth and home.

But Rosaline, who had not yet been a bride one full day, did not care to dwell on those possibilities.

Still speaking on the same subject, Jack ran a hand over the rough wood mantle, smiled sardonically, and added, "Yes, during the next forty years, I suspect that weapons will be drawn between us, every now and then."

"Haven't they already?"

"I fear so."

The fire flared and the old, scarred clock on the mantelpiece chimed off-tune. Wanting to challenge this most self-possessed of men suddenly, even to wound him a little, Rosaline said, "Even though you pretend otherwise, your low birth is a sore subject with you, isn't it, Jack?"

His gaze sharpened at her words, and the fire behind him crackled like lightning as he answered in a hard voice. "I am ambitious, Rosaline. And men of common birth never, no matter their cleverness or hard work, receive the opportunities given to those born with titles. That particular fact of life rankles me, that's all. It always has."

The words, bitterly said, caused Rosaline to glance up at Jack. But he had turned to sip his brandy and stare at the dark, sooty painting of a horseman above the mantel so that she couldn't see his face. After several moments of an uncomfortable hush, punctuated by nothing more than the hiss of the fire, she asked, "Why did you choose such a remote place to live?"

Jack set his glass on the mantelshelf and roamed toward the window. He braced an arm against the frame and stared out at the night's blackness, then in a reflective voice said, "To be alone, I guess."

"But you are not alone. Not now. Not anymore."

He didn't answer immediately. When his silence stretched too long, Rosaline knew that he was saying to himself, "Yes, I am, I am still alone." Not for the first time, she sensed that there was an empty place inside the strong framework of Jack Darlington.

Perhaps he realized that his thoughts had been read and was reluctant to have them probed more deeply. Picking up a small box from a table, he opened its lid and removed a complicated puzzle carved from wood. He took the pieces apart and then, with his usual adroitness, fit them back together again. "Here," he said, tossing the puzzle into Rosaline's lap. "You might find the puzzle amusing. I bought it in Algeria."

She fumbled with it for several minutes but failed to fit a single piece together. Jack smiled, and the sheer male beauty of the smile made Rosaline's stomach tighten. Distracted, she muttered, "Aren't you going to show me the secret to it?"

"I think not. Knowing the secret takes all the pleasure out of it."

Uncomfortable with his contrary tone, Rosaline put the puzzle aside. "About our trip to Egypt . . . when will we set sail?"

The mention of Egypt seemed to jar him, and by the dim glow of the oil lamp, Rosaline could see the muscles in his jaw harden. He pivoted and returned to the window, his body tense and his manner strained. All at once, it seemed as if he found the walls of the room, or Rosaline's presence in it, too confining.

"Soon enough," he answered. Then, as if he regretted his abruptness, knew she could not possibly understand it, he said more softly, "Perhaps you'd like to have Mrs. Wiggins show you around the house now, before bed. In the meantime, if you don't mind, I'd like to take a stroll. Traveling by coach always makes me restless."

Nodding, feeling disquieted by his change of mood, Rosaline rose and Jack escorted her out into the vestibule while calling for his housekeeper. As he crossed the rough slate floor, he nearly stumbled over a small shape sitting cross-legged in the shadows. "Rajad! For God's sake. What the devil are you doing up at this hour?"

Thinking perhaps that he was to be chastised, the boy inched into a corner and hid his head. At the same time, a movement at the top of the stairs caught Rosaline's attention.

Another boy stood staring down at her, one leg slung over the bannister, his face sharp and sly, his manner bold. He held a knife in his hand.

"Jack!" Rosaline cried. "Wh . . ."

Ignoring her, Jack shouted, "Antonio! Lay that knife down at your feet now or you'll feel my hand on your backside before the minute is out."

After a few seconds, the strange, dark boy dropped the weapon on the floor, then pivoted and melted into the darkness of the corridor.

"Good gracious, Jack!" Rosaline cried. "Who on earth was he? And who is this other child?"

"They are Rajad and Antonio. They live here."

"Live here? But where are their mothers?" she asked in confusion.

"They haven't any."

"Haven't any mothers? But whose children are they?"

Jack settled his hat atop his head, shrugged into his greatcoat and opened the latch of the door. After considering her question a moment, he lifted a shoulder and said, "Yours, I guess."

"Mine?"

"Well, yes, in a manner of speaking, they're yours now, like it or not. As for their origins, I suppose one might call them strays."

"Strays?"

"Yes."

"I'm afraid I don't understand."

"Well, there are stray dogs, stray cats and stray children— as you would know if you had spent much time in the East End of London—but here is Mrs. Wiggins." Jack turned up the collar of his coat, opened the door to let in a blustery wind, and called over his shoulder, "Mrs. Wiggins, be good enough to explain the children to my wife, will you?"

The housekeeper looked as if she was about to protest, but with a tip of his hat, Jack shut the door before she could speak.

Quite dumfounded, Rosaline stared at Mrs. Wiggins, who stared back at her in turn. "Oh, those children! Heathens, they are, if you'll pardon my saying so, Mrs. Darlington. No manners, no sense of right or wrong, atrocious behavior from the little Italian devil. Cursing and sneaking about, always writing rude words."

The elderly woman marched up the stairs, her bundle of sheets trailing along the way, her voice, as always, breathless. "I'm sure Mr. Darlington is greatly relieved, Mrs. Darlington, knowing that you'll be taking them in hand. It's high time, indeed, if you want my opinion. Although I must say, few brides would be up to the task. Especially gently bred ones. You're a brave lady, Ma'am. Best of luck to you—both with the boys and with Mr. Jack. In case you haven't discovered it, he isn't the easiest of men."

"But, Mrs. Wiggins." Seeing that she would get no answer, Rosaline let out a breath of exasperation and threw up her hands. "My children, indeed!"

Chapter Five

Her trunks had been put in a bedchamber that showed no sign of Jack's occupation. Apparently she was to have her own room. Grateful, Rosaline shook out the crumpled garments of silk and gauze and velvet from her trunk, hung them up, then laid out her toilet articles before sinking down on a striped wing chair that had seen better days.

She was eager to speak with Jack. Why on earth had he never bothered to tell her that he was ward to a pair of young and—according to Mrs. Wiggins—ungovernable boys? The news was flabbergasting, and Rosaline felt appalled that she was expected to take not only this disorderly stone house in hand, but two unruly children as well.

She gazed through the window at the dark landscape and frowned. She wondered whether her husband intended to make another appearance tonight. Two hours had already passed and he had still not come in from his wanderings outdoors. Could it be that he was so disinterested in his new bride that the prospect of completing the marriage with her held no particular appeal?

No, Rosaline told herself, trusting her own instincts. He

would come. Sooner or later, before the night was out, Jack Darlington would make his leisurely way upstairs and perform his duty as her husband.

The more she pondered it, the more the idea of physical intimacy with a stranger—and Jack Darlington *was* a stranger—appalled Rosaline. The fear began to burgeon to alarming proportions, due in part, she knew, to her ignorance concerning the advanced mechanics of the marital act. Her aunts, not daring to risk indelicacy and speak directly on the subject, had whispered of pain and humiliation, male appetites, and above all, unbearable shame if a wife enjoyed any part of what her husband did to her. "Just endure it, dear. Just pretend it isn't happening and think of something else."

Well, then, she would endure it. Just as she would endure those odd, untamed children, just as she would see to the neglected furnishings of this house and arrange to have the staff increased. Jack Darlington had told her he wanted a gentleman's life, and as far as she was able, Rosaline would give it to him. Through the act of marriage, she had agreed to do at least that much. If nothing else, Rosaline had been raised to do her duty.

The minutes passed, tripping on toward midnight, and Rosaline paced the room, examining the limewashed walls with their dark paintings of hounds and thoroughbreds, the scarred floorboards, the canopied bed with its clean but aged counterpane whose embroidered unicorns pranced around a ragged hem. With a start, she realized that this was to be her *place,* the place where she would lie down and wake up most of the rest of her life, the place where she would take tea in the morning and cocoa at night, the place where her babies would be conceived and born. She shuddered.

She trailed her hand over the oak mantlepiece, over the secretary with its monstrous claw feet, over the ordinary, old hassock with its tattered fringe. The furnishings were plain, impersonal, without sparkle or flare. *Like me?* she asked herself, realizing that she was, after all, a bride with an absent bride-groom.

As if to answer the question, Rosaline crossed the room to the mirror, touched a pale cheek, then the back of her tightly coiled hair, and wondered if her plainness had already put off the worldly, dashing Jack Darlington who had, no doubt, squired countless beautiful women over the years.

"Don't be afraid, wee ones," she whispered to the brown finches Jack had bought her. Their cage had been placed next to the window. "We shall manage somehow." From her pocket she removed the acorns she had collected in Edinburgh and lined them up on the table next to the finches. Already she missed the gentle air and sturdy old oak of her garden.

When a sudden rap sounded on her door, she started, then, steeling herself, turned around. With her hands clasped tightly across her corseted waist, she bade her husband come in.

Jack entered like the cool, steady wind outside, still attired as he had been when he had so inconsiderately left her to cope with the shocking news of the children. His hair had been mussed by the bluster outside, and the cold air had given a ruddy tint to his lean cheeks. He held a bottle in his hand, not champagne as might be expected on a wedding night, but whiskey. She didn't approve of whiskey. Truth to tell, she didn't approve of drinking unless it was part of the civilized ritual of wine at dinner and brandy afterward.

"Did Mrs. Wiggins see that you have everything you need?" he asked, setting the whiskey and glasses next to the bed. Then, as if it were quite the most natural thing to do in her presence, he slid out of his jacket and tossed it with a swish of silk lining across the back of a chair.

At the easy gesture, which seem to proclaim his temporary ownership of the room, Rosaline's anger sharpened, and she raised her eyes to meet the blue ones regarding her quizzically across the room. "You might have told me about those chil-dren," she accused. "You might have mentioned them during the course of our courtship in Edinburgh. Or even on the journey here.''

Jack's gaze narrowed at her high-handed tone, but he did not offer a conciliatory remark. Instead, with a quiet, unrepentant directness he countered, ''I don't recall that we had a courtship. But anyway, would it have made a difference if I'd told you about the children?''

''It would have been considerate. Polite.''

''Ah, you see,'' he said, loosening his neckcloth, roaming about the room to inspect her toilet articles, her silver backed brushes, her bottles of scent. ''A day has not yet passed since our marriage, and already you are reminding me of my lack of manners. Downstairs, just a few hours ago, you swore you never would.''

''Perhaps I was hasty.''

''Perhaps.'' Jack's tone was amused, not sarcastic as hers had been. He poured a measure of whiskey into the glass and, with a cavalier lift of his hand, offered it to her.

''No thank you,'' she said, raising her chin. ''I don't drink spirits.''

''You should.''

''Why? I have no need to dull the edge of my reason.''

''It's not a bad idea, especially on a night like this. Whiskey does wonders for tense nerves and prudishness.'' He gave her a half smile. ''And you really are a confoundingly prudish woman, Rosaline.''

''You've led me to believe that is to be my role in your life,'' she said through thinned lips. ''That my good breeding is to be used to your advantage.''

Conceding, Jack raised the glass in salute, then eased down on the bed and propped his back against the headboard while leisurely sampling his drink.

''Are there to be other surprises?'' Rosaline asked after a moment, still standing in the middle of the room with her hat on, its green feather aquiver.

Unaffected by her stiffness, Jack swirled the rich colored

whiskey in the glass and contemplated it. "There are no more children, if that's what you're asking. At least . . ." He gave her midsection a meaningful glance. "None that I'm presently aware of."

Rosaline colored in the splotchy way she detested, but did not deny or confirm the implied question. She suddenly hoped Jack would think the worst of her and David, hoped he would become offended and leave her alone. But she suspected Jack Darlington was not easy to offend, too full of self-assurance and convenient indifference to chafe over anyone's insults.

She turned her back and reached to toy with the acorns on the table top. "Are we to toss words at each other all night?"

He shifted on the bed, making himself comfortable, regarding her closely through his lashes. "I would rather we didn't—although, some women seem to enjoy it, believing it lends spice to a relationship."

"I am not one of them."

"Good. I suspect you are like me in that regard. You prefer to dispense with small talk and cut to the chase." In a graceful coordination of long legs and broad shoulders, he got up and strolled toward her, stopping en route to inspect the finches, who crept warily away from him to the other end of their perch.

"Do those birds ever sing?" he asked.

"No. I rather think they dislike being caged." The words were short, not meant to encourage conversation.

"At least they don't complain," he said, watching her fidget with the acorns. "Ah, you collected thirteen acorns, I see. Too bad. It's an unlucky number." Reaching out a hand, Jack retrieved one acorn, held it for a few seconds in his palm, then slid it in the pocket of his breeches. "There. That's better, isn't it? Twelve instead of thirteen."

Aware of his closeness and made uncomfortable by it, afraid he would touch her, Rosaline made herself busy by rearranging the remaining acorns again. Nervously, she grouped them in threes, and realized that there were still thirteen. Puzzled, she counted again, certain that Jack had taken one away. "You took an acorn, didn't you?'' she asked, turning to look at him. ''You put it in your pocket?''

''One?'' he asked.

''Yes. One.''

He extended his closed fist, opened his fingers, and showed her his palm.

Astonished, Rosaline saw that not one, but two acorns rested there. ''How did you do that?'' she demanded.

His teeth flashed and he laughed, a hearty, rich sound deepened by whiskey and enjoyment. ''I'll show you some time. But not tonight.''

Rosaline assumed he had played the silly game with her in order to lighten her mood, to diminish her tension. But because she felt that Jack always sought the advantage in any situation, his amusement only served to annoy her. Not intending to flatter him, she muttered, ''You are very clever with your sleight of hand.''

''Am I, do you think?''

As if to let her judge, he put his hands on her neck and stroked, pulling the bodkin from her hat and removing the fussy confection of green felt and ostrich feathers. He touched the tight coil at the nape of her neck. ''You're uneasy with me, aren't you?'' he asked plainly, unabashedly. ''Uneasy having me near.''

''Yes.''

''As I thought. Well then,'' he declared in a quiet, pragmatic voice, ''we had better get it over with, don't you think?''

Rosaline knew, of course, what he referred to. She knew, too, why he had phrased it as if the act were a duty to be done, for she had shown no eagerness for it, had not been soft or flirtatious or welcoming on her wedding day. But, then, she reasoned, neither had her bridegroom. Still, she could not face Jack Darlington, could not do anything at all but stand rigidly beneath his hands as they took off her hat, framed her throat, then began to pull loose the prim, twisted braid at her nape.

Dry mouthed, she jerked away and took up a nervous stance

in the shadowed space beside the window. Inhaling an unsteady breath, toying with the lace at her sleeve, she hissed with a note of plaintiveness, "Must we . . . ?"

At first he did not reply, but strolled to the window and slowly raised the sash, allowing the cool air to invade the room and lift the white lace drapes like sails, bringing the smells of salt and earth into the hot space that stretched so distressfully between husband and wife. After a moment, with the air rippling his hair, Jack moved to Rosaline's side once more and spoke to her in a voice that was not unkind or impatient, but practical and firm. "Yes, Rosaline. I think we must. Because you fear me, or dread what I will do to you. If we delay, you'll only dwell on it, and grow to dread it more. Our imaginations tend to make great cowards of us if we allow them to—at least, I have always found it so."

"I doubt that you have ever been a coward," she said resentfully.

"Oh, but I have, every now and then. Any man who claims otherwise is a liar." He touched her sleeve. "Tonight will bind us together, and we need to be bound so that we can get on with the business of being married, don't you think? I won't demand much of you in our life here. I only want a gentleman's home, a gentleman's way of life—call it a fanciful wish, if you want. But I think, Rosaline, that you are quite capable of providing that for me."

Rosaline still stood with her back to him, and he reached over her shoulder to trail his fingers down her throat. She swallowed, not resisting, and yet not surrendering. Yet, when he unfastened the top buttons of her jacket, untied the scarf ends of her blouse, she recoiled.

He would not allow her to struggle, his determined mouth at her nape, the roughness of his jaw scraping the flesh of her shoulder. He removed the pins from her hair and let it fall, and the heaviness of her braid tumbled, a dark brown rope the length of her back. His fingers worked loose the three woven strands, then clutched the wavy length as if to know its texture

better, before his fingers slid again to her throat, to the skin
that curved and pulsed beneath the collar bone.

As if it were his prerogative–and it was, she supposed–he
explored her thoroughly, and she remained still. She endured
his liberties, which halted only when his fingers discovered the
locket hidden within the folds of her chemise.

Jack stilled, then drew the silver oval into the lamplight in
order to study it better. "What is this?" he asked.

Rosaline did not pull away, for she wanted him to see it
clearly, wanted her husband to understand that, although he
may possess her body and her dowry and her future tonight, he
did not possess her emotions. "Look for yourself," she
said.

The locket released easily beneath his touch. Inside, it
revealed the miniature self-portrait of the artist Rosaline Cheevers had loved. And still loved.

For several seconds Jack contemplated the memento before
his fingers twisted the chain.

Fearing that he would snap it loose, Rosaline bit her lip and
squeezed her eyes shut in an effort not to jerk free, for she
knew that a physical battle with Jack Darlington would be a
futile effort. She surmised that her wearing of the locket on
her wedding day had struck a blow to his pride.

Gradually, as if forced, Jack's hand relaxed and released the
locket. Pressing his mouth against her ear, he said, "Keep it,
then. Wear your locket even while you lie with me. I suppose
it's only fair. I have a locket too, in a manner of speaking. Not
a locket like yours—not one you can see. But it's with me just
the same."

She did not respond, did not know what to say. Jack grew
less patient then, as if there were no point in delaying, in
pretending to feel what neither felt.

He removed his shirt. She heard the impatient swish of it as
he drew it over his shoulders, then the tiny clink of the buttons
as he let the garment drop to the floor. She allowed him to
divest her of her clothes until she stood in nothing but petticoats

and chemise, her eyes fixed on the floor, her corset constricting her frightened breaths while Jack's hands released the strings.

He directed her to the bed, a tall stranger with his torso bare and lean, his body unflawed—splendid really. Rosaline wished he had extinguished the lamp, wished that she might have at least been spared the scrutiny of his eyes, if not the exploration of his hands. But he kept the wick burning, studying her body as he pushed her clothes away. Perhaps, she thought, he wished to see all that his plain gold ring had purchased today.

And then, as she lay with every muscle coiled, trying hard to think of David, Jack Darlington began the business of knowing her, claiming her, his hands moving to ease a passage before his body entered it. He knew perfectly what to do, of course, as she had suspected he would; he was no fumbling bridegroom, but smooth at obtaining his pleasure in spite of the sharp moment of discomfort she felt.

And yet, it was a discomfort Rosaline concealed through the stubborn will to do her duty by him.

He moved above her, kissed her neck, her shoulders, but not her mouth. And during the whole process, he murmured no words, only tensed once in a shuddering pleasure, strained, then relaxed with a long, hissed breath.

After that, he rolled away and laid upon his back with his hands behind his head, his breathing having returned to normal.

So this was it, Rosaline thought as she lay silently beside him. This was the thing of mystery, the thing so shameful for women to want, but the greatest pride of manhood. And without understanding the source of her knowledge, she realized that, although Jack Darlington had experienced a release of his body's excitement, he had not been satisfied with her. And that knowledge wounded Rosaline most of all. It wounded her to think that her husband had not enjoyed what his maleness had so obviously craved.

For several moments she lay still, just as her bridegroom had left her, not even bothering to pull up the sheet and cover herself. Then, very slowly, she turned her back to him and drew up her legs, watching the long, white curtains billow at the windows while cool air brushed the point of her naked hip.

She wished the silent stranger next to her would say something, anything—false or not—to make the night less strange and stark and desolate. But he did not. He only remained as still as she, staring at the ceiling.

And in those moments, Rosaline knew with an odd intuition that her bridegroom was not thinking of her at all, but of someone else—the woman, perhaps, that dwelled in his own private locket.

She moved a hand to David's memento, gripped it, held onto it just as she held onto thoughts of the artist himself. Then, very quietly, her mouth dry, she breathed a question. "Why did you marry me, Jack?"

At first he didn't reply, only releasing a long breath in the darkness. "Rosaline . . ."

"No, don't protest. Tell me why. I want to know. It's important for me to know."

He ruminated a moment. "I daresay my reasons for marrying you are no more romantic than the ones you had for marrying me. But is that a reason for us to go on holding it against each other?"

"You regret it now, don't you? Our marriage, I mean? You feel as if . . . as if your life has taken a wrong path. Or at least an unhappy one."

"How can it be a wrong path when I made the decision to take it?"

A pause ensued, marked by the snap and billow of the white drapes. Softly she said, "But people make mistakes in judgment every day. Even clever people."

"Do they?"

The wind lifted the curtains high and tumbled Jack's discarded shirt across the floor, blowing it like a foamy wave toward the bed. Rosaline watched it and breathed, "Ah, well, you're right. I suppose it does no good to ask such questions now."

And because he heard the wrenching chill of loneliness in her voice, Jack reached out a hand to clasp the smooth curve of her head. "No, Rosaline," he told her quietly. "It does no good now. It's best to get on with it the best we can."

Sometime later, Jack heard his bride stir beside him. Quietly, almost furtively, she rose from the bed, apparently believing him to be asleep and loath to wake him. The lamplight cast deep shadows over her body, over her heavy breasts and rounded hips, over her straight legs and back. Her spine was brushed by the long mink-colored hair that, an hour ago, he had clutched too hard, perhaps, in restless passion.

He saw her walk to the table and touch the acorns lined upon its surface, then gather them up before she slipped on a robe and crept out the door.

Jack raised himself upon an elbow, puzzled. Was she going outside, into the night? He went to the window, peered down, and glimpsed her tall, slight figure as she hurried into the garden below. The stone walls of the sheltered place kept most of the wind at bay, but still the sea breeze whipped the ends of her robe and her freed hair as she stood gazing up at the sky, at the star patterns winking above. He knitted his brow in thought, understanding her far better than she would have guessed. She needed solitude. Needed to be away from him.

The memory of their lovemaking caused him concern. He had made love to her hoping to evoke a response, to awaken a sensuality in her that both of them could enjoy. At least a mutual physical pleasure would have given them something to share. But she had lain beneath him passively, not protesting as he kissed her, touched her, finally thrust himself inside her body. Perhaps he had hurt her; he had tried to be alert to signals, to watch her face, prepared to stop himself if she cried out. But she had not cried out. She had not shed a single tear. It would be like her not to cry.

He watched her now as she made her way to a bare patch

of ground beside the southern wall. Kneeling down, she dug with her bare hands, making first one shallow hole, then another and another. He knew what she was doing, knew she was planting the acorns. And in that lonely, telling moment, he discovered that he both admired and pitied the new Mrs. Darlington.

Turning away, Jack returned to bed and saw the stain of blood on the sheet. Rosaline's artist had not had his way with her after all. And yet, for some inexplicable reason, she had let both Jack and Lord Bardo believe it possibile.

Sitting on the edge of the bridal bed, Jack thought about the woman he had married and wondered if he had indeed made a mistake. And then, just for a few indulgent moments, he shut out the image of Rosaline and allowed himself to remember a different face, a dark and lively face, a face more familiar to him than his own, lost but not forgotten.

The memory kept his loneliness at bay.

Chapter Six

Rosaline crept back to the house at dawn, just as the vast treeless horizon was turning apricot and violet, her body icy but her composure recovered. As she meandered through the garden with its hardy plants crouched in the shelter of the stone walls, she noted the beauty of the sky with its shifting clouds, the loveliness of the distant cliffs, and realized that her first impression of Orkney had been a false one, colored by her disconsolate mood. But this garden and the mellow stone of the house, molded from the ground itself, combined to create a place of wild and mysterious splendor.

She wasn't able to return to the bed they had shared, too disturbed by the knowledge that even while Jack had consummated the marriage, he had been thinking—just as she had been—of another form, another face. But whose face had occupied *his* brooding thoughts?

As she put a hand on the honey-colored wood of the bannister, she caught sight of movement in the parlor and leaned forward to look inside. She saw the thin, little presence called Rajad. He sat on the floor cross-legged, a fishing pole on his lap, his whole face screwed into lines of concentration as he attempted to untwist the line.

Quietly, so as not to startle him, Rosaline approached, but when the boy saw her gliding forward in her trailing robe, he let the pole clatter to the floor, then, like a startled hare going to ground, skittered behind an ottoman.

"I didn't mean to frighten you," Rosaline said softly and, realizing that he would not be coaxed out, knelt down and examined the tangled line he had abandoned. "I'm quite good at untangling, you know," she said, careful not to approach him. "My aunts are forever matting skeins of yarn—they knit shawls for their little spaniels. And the floss in my own sewing basket gets itself in the most complicated knots. It takes hours to pick out. I used to go out into my garden and sit beneath a tree to do it, letting the birds entertain me with their music while I worked."

"Speaking of dogs," she said, slanting a glance at him, hoping to entertain. "Have you heard about the one near Castle Douglas? He's a big, black dog and as friendly as can be, so friendly you can't resist leaning down to pat his head. But beware." She lowered her voice. "Your hand will go straight through him, for he's a ghost dog—a *ferlie* as we Scottish call him."

Rosaline noted that her listener had emerged from behind the ottoman, his eyes round now with curiosity. She thought she just might be able to coax him out until brisk footfalls sounded, disturbing the mood. Glancing over her shoulder, Rosaline saw Jack descend the stairs, his fine figure neatly groomed, his face shaven, his black hair still damp from bath water.

His appearance made Rosaline suddenly aware of her own disheveled looks, and she clutched her robe, shielding her body from her husband's eyes—which had already perused her with the utmost intimacy only a few hours earlier. She had never allowed anyone to see her in disarray, feeling that an untidy appearance accentuated her plainness, her square face and long neck, which she had learned at an early age to soften with an artfully placed rose, an elegant gown, a neat coiffure.

"Good morning," she murmured, dipping her head in slight confusion.

"Good morning, Rosaline," Jack returned with a relaxed, amiable smile, as if nothing humiliating had happened to her the night before, as if nothing disappointing had happened to him. "I'm pleased to see you've made yourself at home. Are you accustomed to having breakfast in your . . . night attire or shall I wait while you go and change?" A trace of humor marked his tone.

She spoke through thin lips. "I'll change, of course. But you needn't wait."

"Now, what sort of husband would allow his new bride to breakfast alone?"

In confusion, she fixed her eyes at some point above his head. "Well, under the circumstances, I thought . . ."

"Yes?" He waited for her to finish, offering no conclusion to the sentence, saying nothing to allay her uneasiness.

"I thought . . ." She paused, lifted her hands, then declared in her straightforward manner, "Well, what are people expected to say afterwards?"

Jack laughed, displaying a genuine smile that contained a good deal of rue. "A great many things, my dear. Most of which are untruths, and none of which—to our credit perhaps—were said between us."

"Lies would seem to serve little purpose."

His mouth curved. "Actually, it can do marvels for the male pride, but no doubt you would wish me to rise above that."

"I have no wish to reform you. You are the one who seems bent upon self-improvement." Rosaline continued to grip her robe, wishing Jack would come down off the first step of the stair so that she would not have to pass him so closely, so she would not have to brush past those wide, too confident shoulders. But he maintained his position, at ease himself, looking at her with a quizzical expression.

When she inched past, Jack put a hand on her sleeve. His touch evoked memories of the previous night, and instinctively, Rosaline shrank away.

Amusement flickered in Jack's blue eyes and in a bland tone he drawled, "No need to jump, dear wife. I only mean to ask if you prefer tea or chocolate for breakfast. Nothing more intimate than that."

Feeling foolish, Rosaline muttered, "Chocolate, please."

"I shall have Mrs. Wiggins prepare it. By the way, you have a rowan leaf in your hair. Did you enjoy your evening out?"

Hastily she picked out the leaf and crumpled it in her fingers so that dust drifted down. "Yes, thank you. I went out to plant the acorns."

"I suppose you couldn't have waited until daylight."

"I found the garden comforting," she said, daring to meet his eye, letting him know that she had found no comfort in his arms, in his silent, remote presence in her bed.

Jack said nothing in reply, but as she pushed past him and sailed up the stairs with her robe clutched tight, Rosaline was well aware of his speculative gaze.

When she entered the bedroom, she realized that someone had tidied it, leaving no visible evidence—no mussed bedsheets or hastily discarded clothes—to suggest the recent consummation of a marriage. But upon the smooth, white coverlet of the canopied bed lay a bouquet of heather that looked as if it had been casually tossed down.

Frowning, Rosaline picked up the bundle and put it to her nose, catching its scent. A gleam of light caught her eye, and she discovered a circlet of gold clasped around the woody stems. She drew the bauble free and admired the little bracelet, whose every well-made link was fashioned, whimsically, in the shape of a flying bird.

Sinking down on the mattress, Rosaline clutched the bracelet. It was a husband's gift to his bride, a sweet gift. She closed her eyes, feeling a sudden shame.

* * *

Jack awaited his wife in the parlor, and when she quietly descended the stairs dressed in a pale gold gown with a cameo nestled in her fichu, he lent his arm and led her into the dining room. By donning prim, impeccable clothes, he noted that Rosaline had regained her usual modesty, and her stiff, unapproachable calm. Jack smiled, thinking that such prudishness must be hell to maintain.

Detecting a trace of contrition in her eyes, Jack guessed that Rosaline had discovered his gift. He had given it to her out of guilt. After their less than satisfactory lovemaking last night, a peace offering had seemed necessary. He had purchased the bracelet in Edinburgh, intending to offer it at a more tender time, but had realized last night that perhaps there would be no tender time—at least not for a while.

And yet, with an odd, uncharacteristic yearning, Jack hoped there would be. Earlier, when he had found Rosaline sitting on the floor untangling Rajad's fishing line, seen her looking rumpled and girlish, he had felt a desire to reach out his arms and gather her close. The image of Rosaline and Rajad together had allowed him a glimpse of completeness, of a life that was well-ordered, civilized and clean—the sort of life he had wanted for himself longer than he cared to admit. Of course, he had envisioned such a life with another woman, not this stiff, proper diplomat's daughter with her cool head and unyielding body. But, Jack reflected wryly watching his wife enter the room, life had always dealt him unsettling surprises.

He seated Rosaline at the table and asked if he might fill her plate from the sideboard. She nodded, fingering her frayed napkin, and he saw that her eyes were scanning the room, taking domestic inventory, noting the unpolished pewter, the cracked dishes, the withered greenery Mrs. Wiggins had tried to arrange several days ago as a centerpiece. Yes, he thought with rue, Mrs. Jack Darlington would be well occupied setting his house in order.

After he had filled their plates with ham and muffins, Jack sat down opposite Rosaline and bade her begin, watching as she started the fascinating ritual of preparing her tea, which he suspected would be an unvarying part of their breakfasts together in the future.

When she sipped, his bracelet jingled at her wrist. Toying with it, obviously deciding she must now make some reference to it, Rosaline spoke in a faltering but very formal tone. "Thank you for the gift, Jack. It's lovely, of course. But you needn't have done it. You needn't have given me anything. I didn't expect a gift, and it was—it was unnecessary."

Jack set his coffee cup on the saucer and regarded her with a good-natured gaze, amused by her discomposure. "On the contrary. It's my understanding that a gift from a bridegroom to his bride is required."

"Yes. But . . ." Rosaline inhaled a breath and straightened, creasing and recreasing the tortured napkin in her lap. "I mean you needn't have apologized, if that's what you intended to do by giving me the bracelet. I realize that what happened last night between us was necessary, a part of . . . of the function I am expected to fulfil."

"Or put up with?" Jack shot back with one brow raised. That his wife considered an act of intimacy with him nothing more than a 'function' chafed him, and he felt a need to establish a clear understanding between them, even to wound her a little—unfairly or not—as she had just wounded him. "You do understand," he said steadily, "since we are speaking on the subject, that what happened between us last night will not be the first and only time. Unless you mean to drive me to a mistress—which I don't find particularly convenient—I will require it from time to time."

Rosaline felt color spread to her neck, and the piece of cinnamon muffin in her mouth tasted dry. "Of course," she said. She refused to meet Jack's eyes, looking fixedly at the floor and wondering if this sort of strained tit-for-tat was to be the pattern of their lives. As her husband, Jack was allowed to remind her of his rights, of course, and to claim those rights regardless of her wishes—or so she had been schooled to believe. But must she keep silent about it?

"Good," Jack said in reply, leaning back in his chair. "I'm glad we understand each other on that score."

Rosaline glanced at her husband through her lashes as he chewed his food; she watched his cleanly shaven jaws flex, his brow knit above his arched nose, and for a moment wondered at her own feelings toward him. He was handsome. Certainly any other woman would be pleased to receive Jack Darlington's attentions, to overlook his occasional insolence, to flirt with the easy, almost treacherous charm that hid another side—a dangerously secret side. What was the matter with her, then, that she could not relax enough to enjoy the enthralling company he offered, even if there was to be no affection between them?

The meal stretched on in silence, until the rattle of every cup against its saucer, the scrape of every spoon grated on her nerves. Jack's appetite was hardy; Rosaline realized with annoyance that the tension she felt was not shared by him.

Searching for something to say, she put down her fork, cleared her throat, and began. "I'd like to talk with you about the boys, if you don't mind, Jack. What do they do all day to keep themselves occupied? Shouldn't they have a tutor or attend school?"

Jack sipped his coffee and regarded her with one brow cocked. "If I could manage to find a tutor who would come to the island—and no doubt *some* impoverished young gentleman would be willing to earn thirty pounds a year—how long do you think he would last? If Antonio did not wish to be found for lessons, he would not be, and Rajad . . ." Jack paused with a sigh. "Well, Rajad is biddable enough, but difficult in his own way. He scarcely speaks."

"No doubt that is his way of getting noticed. Children do such contradictory things."

"No doubt. At any rate, there's a school four or five miles from here. But getting the two boys to the doorstep and keeping them there without testing the schoolmaster's sanity would be quite a feat, I should think.''

"But their education is essential," Rosaline argued, leaning forward. "Boys who grow up uneducated cannot be expected to earn a good living, to rise above the level of a farm laborer or sailor.''

Jack gave Rosaline a wry look, and although there wasn't the least bit of truth in what he was about to say, beyond the fact that it was a part of the false identity created for him by the Foreign Office, he felt the urge to needle her. "I was a sailor once."

"Well, yes, but I didn't mean . . ."

"To offend me?" he returned. "You didn't. I've done very little that I'm ashamed of—which is to be expected, I suppose, considering the fact that my conscience is rarely on duty."

"Perhaps it would be on duty more often if it were attended to."

Jack grinned and, reaching behind him to grab another muffin from the sideboard, tossed it in the air in a deliberate breach of manners before putting it on her plate to replace the one she had eaten. "I swear you'll receive a halo the very moment you set foot in heaven."

She let the subject pass and inquired, "Is there a pony cart on the estate I could use?"

"An old one, I believe. Where do you intend to go?"

"If I must, I shall drive the boys to and from school every day, regardless of the distance."

Jack laughed aloud. "Do you intend to tie up the hellions first?"

"I shall find a way to deal with them."

Eyeing the set of her mouth, Jack nodded in admiration. "I believe you will, Rosaline. I believe you will."

She gave him a steady look. "Why did you take the boys in, Jack? Given their difficulties, surely there are charity institutions better equipped to handle them, to understand . . ."

"I understand the boys very well," Jack cut in, stabbing

at the piece of ham on his plate. "And speaking of charity institutions, have you ever set foot inside one?"

"Not exactly—"

"Not exactly. Well, you would find a tour enlightening."

The sudden, swift change of her husband's tone caused Rosaline to glance sharply at him. Not for the first time, she sensed that Jack had more than one side to his nature, more than one secret in his past which lent him his complexity, the darkness under the bright charm. Feeling a prick of remorse, Rosaline said, "I didn't intend to sound mean-spirited, Jack. Of course I don't know the boys well yet, but I really do have their best interests at heart. By the way, will we be taking them to Egypt with us?"

"I'll leave you to decide that when the time comes. Hopefully, you'll come to know Rajad and Antonio better by then and be able to anticipate their needs better than I."

Rosaline found herself flattered by his trust in her judgment. Perhaps he would not be such a heavy-handed husband after all—at least not in all ways. Thinking suddenly of the male furnishings in the house, remembering the stag horns, the saddles, the dreadful horsehair sofa, and the barbaric tiger pelt in the parlor, she took a breath and said, "Now that we've discussed the boys, might we talk about other matters?"

"We can talk about anything you like."

"Very well. I would like to know if I have leave to change the furnishings."

Jack stopped chewing and looked bewildered. "The furnishings? Do you find something the matter with them?"

Rosaline suspected that Jack knew very well she was displeased with the decor, and that he was only pretending to be chagrined in order to annoy her.

"If I agree," he said with a twinkle in his eye, "will I find the tiger pelt banished forever to the attic?"

Embarrassed that she had allowed dislike of the pelt show, she murmured, "I thought perhaps some reupholstery, some flowers . . ."

"Anything you like." Jack waved a hand carelessly, then frowned at her. "Just so long as I don't feel like I'm walking into a boudoir every time I step inside the parlor to read my reports."

She smiled, relieved that he wasn't cross. "I promise. And, if you insist, the tiger pelt shall keep its place of honor."

"You are a diplomat," he said, thinking that Rosaline was pretty when she smiled. "Something you learned well from your father." Then, on impulse he said, "Shall we go for a stroll now that we've breakfasted? A walk along the cliffs?"

"Yes. Yes," she said eagerly, setting aside her napkin. "I'd love to see the cliffs."

A few minutes later, when they stepped out into the sunlight, Rosaline breathed deep and tilted her bonnet to shade her face. She paused to survey the property. "Your garden is really lovely, Jack. But it could use some color, don't you think?"

"What would you suggest?"

"Pink and red roses, I think."

"Are pink and red roses genteel?"

She couldn't help but smile. "There's not a more genteel flower in all the world."

"Then by all means order roses. Order them by the dozens."

Exiting through the wooden garden gate, the two of them forged a path through a sea of purple-brown heather, laughing when a hare darted down the hill and frightened a cloud of butterflies from the scrub.

"Oh!" Rosaline cried in delight.

Jack swept out on arm, satisfied at her obvious pleasure in his island. "Just look there at the landscape, at the cliffs. At the beauty of it. You don't see such things in Edinburgh, now do you?"

"No. I'm afraid one doesn't find cliffs or seals in Edinburgh. Nor shaggy ponies pulling ploughs. Oh, look there at the weather vane atop that old gabled pub at the crossroads. It's spinning like a top in the wind."

"The gales here are so strong I've often thought that vane would take flight."

"Who first settled these islands?"

"The Norse. Some of the farms you see have been tilled since that time. Even their boundaries are much the same as the original arrangement, and bear old Norse names."

"And what is the name of your property?" Rosaline asked.

Jack laughed. "I'm afraid it's not grand enough to warrant a name."

"Oh, but it *is* grand enough," she insisted. "You must think of a name for it, Jack."

"I'd only come up with something mundane like Darlington's Farm or Jack's Place. I'll let you have the honor."

Her expression serious, Rosaline turned around and viewed the house. With the wind tugging at her bonnet, she contemplated its walled garden, its wooden gate which led to a sweep of purple moors, and declared, "Arbor Gate. I think it should be called Arbor Gate."

"Doesn't an arbor suggest trees?"

"There will be trees. My acorns will grow into tall and sturdy oaks."

Jack laughed at her determined tone. They descended the hill, then climbed the tumbled rock overlooking the sea, the wind proving so strong that Rosaline had to keep both hands on her bonnet to moor it.

"Why don't you take it off?" Jack suggested. He removed his own hat, allowing his thick, black hair to be tossed. "There's no one to impress here except the seals."

"But the knot shall be pulled loose."

"Let it. I like it that way." Jack's mouth tilted and he called out, "You like to keep a tight rein on yourself, don't you, Rosaline? Why? Are you afraid to break free and run the race?"

"I don't know what you're talking about," she snapped over her shoulder, disquieted suddenly by memories of her passionate moments with David, knowing that with him, she had been on the verge of breaking free.

"I believe you know very well what I'm talking about. I'm just not sure why you're denying it. You're a puzzle I haven't had enough time to take apart and fit back together again." Jack eyed her with contemplation. "But I will, eventually."

He saw a white sea bird soar like a free spirit above his head, and could not help thinking of Julie. Briefly, he closed his eyes to let an excruciating longing wash over him. The first time he had lain with Julie, she had not been offended; she had been wild, insatiable, even unorthodox in her demands. And the women who had followed? None of them had been reluctant, none had complained afterward. Of course, Rosaline had not complained either, but her resignation had galled him.

Ahead, Rosaline walked along the path, holding her bonnet to her head with one hand and her flapping skirts with the other. On the edge of the cliffs, she spied Antonio, who seemed to be staring down at some object on the ground, so absorbed that he had not yet become aware of her approach.

She neared, and realized that the boy held a large slingshot; at his feet, a young cormorant lay injured with its wing spread out on the shale, its feathers ruffling in the wind. Rosaline rushed forward and, kneeling down, examined the beautiful creature in dismay.

Behind her, Jack's angry footsteps sounded. "Damn it, Antonio," he snapped, standing over the boy, his height casting a long shadow over the lifeless cormorant. "You know my feelings about hurting animals. To harm the sea birds is a senseless form of destruction. I've warned you before that there must be consequences for this sort of thing." Taking the slingshot from the boy's hand, he snapped it in two, then hurled the broken pieces over the cliff. "Since you've been with me, I've talked to you about the need for earning my trust. This is not the way to do it. Now, the pony you've been wanting will not be yours—not for a long while."

The boy's dark face flushed and his fists clenched at his sides. His eyes, Rosaline thought, were those of a young wolf cub, inscrutable, almost feral. But his mouth, she saw, was soft and trembling, his chin quivering as a result of Jack's stern chastisement. He was disappointed that his hope of a pony had just been stripped away. And in that moment, studying his face, Rosaline suspected the boy regarded Jack highly, craved his approval—his love perhaps—even more than he craved the pony.

"I didn't do it!" Antonio said through clenched teeth, staring hard at Jack. "I didn't harm the bird!"

"Have you given me reason to trust your word in the past, Antonio? Ever? By a single action? I defy you to name one."

For several seconds, the lad held the man's eyes, his breath coming out shallowly in anger. He seemed to be on the brink of crying out in rage, hurling himself against the man, beating his fists upon Jack's coat. He suddenly pivoted on his heel and made to run away.

Jack's hand snaked out and grabbed the boy's jacket. "No, you don't. You've not been properly introduced to Mrs. Darlington yet. You'll greet her now and be civil about it."

Held in the man's grip, Antonio stilled, but rebelliously refused either to meet Rosaline's eyes or to speak. Jack's hand tightened on his thin shoulder, and Rosaline winced, scarcely able to bear the contention between the two.

"It's a pleasure to meet you, Antonio," she said quickly. "I'll take the bird back to the house and tend it. Would you like to help me?" Reaching out, she laid gentle fingers upon his sleeve, but he jerked away from her touch and struggled to escape Jack's furious grip. Unable to stand the conflict, Rosaline put a hand on her husband's shoulder. "No, Jack—please! Let him go."

Jack hesitated; then, as if going against his better judgment, he loosened his grip and scowled when Antonio ran away dashing over the rocks and shrub like an animal escaping from a cage.

Rosaline followed the boy with her eyes, saying soberly, "I don't believe he hurt the bird, Jack. I believe he was telling the truth."

"The boy is a liar and a thief, Rosaline. He had to be in

order to survive the world I found him in. And the liars and thieves created by that world do not easily learn to be anything else.''

His tone, his very words, arrested Rosaline, and she noticed that her husband's eyes had changed, had turned flinty and grim. ''For a vicar's son from Golspie,'' she observed quietly, ''you seem well acquainted with the world of liars and thieves.''

His eyes met hers. ''What are you suggesting?''

''Nothing. But I believe there is much about Jack Darlington that he doesn't intend for me to know.''

''We all have secrets, don't we, Rosaline?'' His eyes retained their cold shade of blue, probing her own deep, brown gaze. ''Even you, I'll wager, have one or two.''

Chapter Seven

Later, watching from her window, Rosaline saw Jack stride across the fields toward the long thatched byre, his tall, well-knit form garbed in rough work clothes, his head bare. She sighed unwillingly over his handsomeness, and wondered if her life with him would ever be harmonious, for it seemed to her that such a life required a degree of trust and admiration. For some reason, she did not entirely trust Jack; and he, as far as she could tell, felt similarly.

But there was nothing to do but forge on, try to find some measure of contentment in the simple course of keeping busy. She would have to bring the boys around slowly, of course, by degrees, but she felt she must begin to tackle matters regarding the household without delay. Changing from her morning attire into a serviceable brown woolen, Rosaline marched down the stairs with her usual energy, prepared to tackle domestic calamity of any kind, searching for Mrs. Wiggins. She found her in the kitchen stirring a pudding and clucking over a dish of strawberries that lay broken on the floor.

"That Rajad!" the old woman was muttering to herself. "Like a shadow, he is, flitting around, sneaking about, rummaging through the pantry for food instead of asking me to prepare it. Oh! I beg your pardon, Mrs. Darlington,'' the housekeeper fretted, dropping the pudding spoon. "I don't mean to complain, it's just that I'm all at sixes and sevens trying to keep this household running, and it seems nothing is going right. Good heavens!'' she exclaimed as the huge hound galloped into the room and began to lick the powered sugar off the fallen strawberries. "If it's not the children underfoot, it's that monstrous dog of Mr. Jack's. Where's the broom?''

"Never mind. I'll take him in hand.'' In her no-nonsense way, Rosaline bent down to grab the brute's collar, tugging him with effort to the kitchen door. The beast planted his feet and wouldn't budge until he was dragged out inch by inch.

"Now, what else might I help you with, Mrs. Wiggins?'' Rosaline asked, dusting her hands and glancing around the kitchen, which was piled with unwashed dishes, dirty copper pots, heaps of vegetables, unplucked chickens, and fresh fish yet to be scaled and filleted.

"Oh, Mrs. Darlington, there are more things to do than I can list. But my goodness, you're a lady born and bred. You're not supposed to concern yourself with broken dishes and cakes that need icing.''

"I'm the mistress of a small but demanding estate in the Orkneys,'' Rosaline corrected, locating a clean linen apron which she tied about her gown. "An estate where the master has allowed his housekeeper to become scandalously overworked. So where is the cake that needs attention? And where might we find a strong, unflappable girl who would be willing to work here?''

The housekeeper turned a relieved gaze on Rosaline, the creases in her drawn face deepening to pleasant furrows as she smiled through misty eyes. "The cake is there—the layers still in their pans—and the icing is on the stove, warm in the saucepan. I suppose we might find a girl in Kirkwall to help.''

"Good. Tomorrow I'll send a notice to be posted near the

market. And I plan to take the boys to the local school—that is, if I can manage to catch them.''

"I shouldn't think you'd be able to, begging your pardon, of course, Ma'am. They're too wild for school, bred in the filthy alleys of strange foreign places with names that decent British folks can't even pronounce.'' Mrs. Wiggins shuddered.

Rosaline looked askance at the other woman, forced her voice into casual tones and commented, "It's a wonder Mr. Darlington doesn't take the boys in hand.''

"I've no doubt he could if he had a mind to, even if it meant thrashing that naughty Antonio every morning and night. But, for the most part, Mr. Jack lets the hellions go. Their wicked pranks and slovenly habits do not seem to shock him as they do me. Indeed, he seems most tolerant.''

Rosaline turned out the first soft, white layer of cake, positioned it on a plate, then dribbled icing redolent of vanilla over the top. "Why do you think he does that—tolerate their behavior, I mean?''

"Well, I can't precisely say. But I expect that Mr. Jack has traveled the world, and been in all sorts of odd and exotic places. Perhaps other countries aren't so proper as Britain. Do you think it possible?''

"Quite possible.''

"That unholy country called Egypt is probably just such a place. After all, Mr. Jack lost Miss Julie there—some heathen snatched her right off the streets.'' The housekeeper's voice lowered to an undertone. Clearly, she had forgotten to whom she was speaking. "Vanished, Miss Julie did, just like smoke.''

Rosaline was silent a moment, her usually steady hands trembling slightly on the knife handle as she spread icing over the crust of the cake. Without understanding how, she knew that Julie must be the woman Jack loved—the face in the locket of Jack's heart. And yet, unwilling to betray her knowledge to Mrs. Wiggins, Rosaline echoed innocently, "Miss Julie? I don't believe I know the name. Who might she be?''

The housekeeper's face reddened as she realized her blunder

and, clapping both hands to her cheeks, said in horror, "I beg your pardon, Mrs. Darlington. I believe I've spoken out of turn."

"Don't fret, Mrs. Wiggins. Did you know Miss Julie personally?"

"Yes, but only . . . for a little while." The housekeeper busied herself with the pudding, adding with a beseeching note, "But please don't ask me any more about her, Mrs. Darlington. Mr. Jack has forbidden me to speak her name."

"Indeed? Why is that, do you suppose?"

"It brings him a good deal of pain, no doubt."

"Because he loved the woman called Julie?"

"Oh, Mrs. Darlington!" the housekeeper exclaimed in a high-pitched whisper, glancing around fearfully in case her employer heard the dangerous exchange. "Please don't say such things aloud in this house."

Rosaline relented, but she continued to ponder the question with a frowning brow as she applied the final layer of icing with meticulous care before swirling it with the knife. She wondered if Jack's journey to Egypt had anything to do with Julie's disappearance. Had he specifically requested a diplomatic post in that hot, exotic country so that he could search for her again?

"Can one order furnishings in Kirkwall?" Rosaline asked Mrs. Wiggins, forcing her mind to practical matters, putting aside thoughts of the mysterious Julie, a woman who proved more disquieting, more intriguing by the moment. In spite of the fact that Rosaline's marriage to Jack Darlington was not a love match, the fact that he adored another woman nettled Rosaline in some inexplicable way, wounding her feminine pride. He was her husband, after all. With a sigh, she touched the locket tucked beneath her gown and remembered David. Justice, in its own mischievous way, she thought, often claimed the cruelest kind of irony.

Mrs. Wiggins removed the pudding from the fire. "There are furniture catalogs at the cabinet maker's," she said, answering

Rosaline's earlier question. "You could likely order anything you like from Edinburgh or London."

"Good. I'll need to order a number of things. A new sofa to replace that monstrosity in horsehair, for one. And a tea trolley—oh, and new chests of drawers for the boys—I've noticed theirs are rather rickety. By the way, where might I find Rajad this time of day, Mrs. Wiggins?"

"You might try the stream that runs beside the henge stones. He likes to fish there."

"Fish?" After a moment of contemplation, Rosaline took some pieces of lobster from the luncheon plate the housekeeper had prepared, then wrapped them in a napkin before going to the parlor for a discarded fishing pole, a red wool tartan, and her parasol. She knew a little about fishing. One summer she had stayed with her aunt and uncle in the Lake Country of England and her male cousins had taught her a technique or two. On the last day of her visit with them, she had astounded them by netting a bigger catch than they.

She found Rajad sitting along the stream bank, almost hidden in the tall, fragrant heather, his fishing hook submerged in the water but not receiving any nibbles. Rosaline did not attempt to edge too close, noting the wariness in Rajad's eyes, that shy, rabbit-like instinct to skitter beneath a hedgerow and hide. She kept her distance, neatly spreading out the tartan before easing down in a ladylike manner; then with the parasol shading her complexion from the sun, she cast her line into the water with an expert flick of one gloved wrist.

Her endeavor required an hour of patience, as dampness seeped through the seat of her gown while she waited with stoic determination. At last, with a little cry of triumph, she drew in a small but respectably sized fish, one that caused Rajad to forget his sheepishness and run forward with his creel to help secure it. Except for a polite drawing room "thank you," Rosaline made no attempt at conversation with the lad, nor did she ask him to join her on the tartan. She simply offered him the fish, packed up her things and, uttering a formal "good day,'' picked her way home over the rough green ground, smiling as she felt his dark eyes fastened to her back. She had impressed him. Next time he would come nearer.

She enjoyed the meandering walk and gathered an armload of heather she planned to arrange in the parlor vases, pausing to watch as a cloud rolled over the landscape, printing its blue pattern on the fields before tumbling out to sea again and allowing a coppery sun to shine. The rays warmed her arms, her face.

The house, Rosaline decided when she stepped inside carrying the heather, was not as crude as she had judged it to be last night; the rooms were really rather quaint. She would add a few tapestry fabrics and damask drapes, silk fringed pillows and a comfortable wing chair in the parlor. The tiger pelt and stag horns she would keep, but she intended to banish the fishing equipment to the mud room at the rear of the house. A few potted plants, a Turkey rug in jewel tones, and landscape paintings should enrich the decor, along with bowls of potpourri, vases of flowers, creweled foot stools, and her own large sewing basket with its embroidered lid.

The dog would have to stay outside—or be taught house manners, she decided, finding the monster asleep in what was presumably his favorite chair. Ignoring his reproachful eyes, she hauled him to the door, shooed him out, then retreated upstairs to wash and change.

As she paused near the threshold of her bedroom to pull off her bonnet, she caught sight of Antonio standing beside the finches, his hand thrust through the open cage door.

Her first instinct was to cry out, thinking the boy meant to harm the birds, just as he might have done the cormorant. But, with effort, Rosaline restrained her fear and silently observed Antonio's activity.

The boy's clothes and shoes were caked with beach sand, his shaggy hair tangled, and a half-eaten chunk of bread hung out of the pocket of his jacket. She tensed as she watched him wiggle his fingers inside the cage, trying to catch the terrified birds, who, in a flurry of feathers, flitted madly about in an effort to elude capture. Rosaline bit her lip, and unable to observe the unnerving drama a moment longer, stepped forward. "Would you like to help me feed the birds, Antonio?"

Caught off guard, the boy spun about, his eyes instinctively darting to the exit, which was blocked by Rosaline in her wide brown skirts.

For several seconds, the two of them stood eyeing each other, taking measure, until Rosaline, judging Antonio sufficiently curious about her purpose, crossed the room. Confident he would not bolt, she spoke with her back turned, pulling a little sack of seed from the highboy as she said, "Mr. Darlington bought the birds for me in Edinburgh. Such a thoughtful gift, don't you think? But they never sing. I can't think why. Here's the amount to feed them. Would you like to put it in the cage?"

Antonio stood rooted in place, eyeing her through his black mat of forelock, his stare that of a worldly-wise fallen angel suspicious of everyone.

"What's wrong?" she asked, her voice holding a bit of challenge. "Are you afraid of me, Antonio?"

Sneering at the mere suggestion, the boy came forward and without hesitation grabbed the feeding container from her hand before thrusting it into the bottom of the cage, spilling half the seed. He gave Rosaline a look, letting her know that although he had cooperated and fed the birds, he had conceded nothing, not warmed to her show of softness.

"Perhaps I'll let you care for the birds every day," she said when he was done, putting the bag of seed away. Listening for his response and hearing nothing, Rosaline smiled to herself. No doubt the boy was astounded over the possibility that an adult had shown faith in him. "Perhaps you can get them to sing if you whistle to them," she added. "Who knows? Young men often have a way."

Let him ponder *that,* she thought, splashing water into the basin and washing her hands, listening with an amused smile as the lad ran from the room, perhaps more frightened by her display of trust than by any act of kindness.

Satisfied with her makeshift strategies at child rearing on her first day as a mother, Rosaline began to dress for dinner, donning a lavender gown trimmed in cream silk roses, knowing the color flattered her complexion in candlelight. Without precisely understanding why, Rosaline realized that she wanted Jack to admire her. As she gazed into the mirror, her feminine vanity emerged, even while her body, instinctively and with an inward shudder, dreaded a repeat of his physical attentions. Truthfully, she regretted their chilly parting this morning on the cliffs; she wanted no further discord in their home, and to make certain that they proceeded on a smoother marital path, she decided to be particularly pleasant at dinner tonight. Could it be that she felt she had a rival? A mysterious one who had disappeared in Egypt?

While she put the final touches on her hair, Rajad materialized, hovering near the threshold, his cap falling over one eye.

"Rajad," she exclaimed. "Have you come to visit me?"

He hung back, his skinny back plastered to the wall while he stared at her hands, fascinated, watching as she inserted a silk rose deftly into the knot of hair at her nape.

"Do you wish to speak with me?" she prodded gently, making a mental note to take up the sleeves of his oversized jacket.

He nodded, his gaze still riveted upon her hair, upon the delicate, blue and jade bottles of scent lined up upon the vanity reflecting light from the window. Swallowing, he said in his shy way, "Mr. Jack wish to see you outside."

"Does he? Very well. Will you escort me there?"

She held out a scented hand, a garnet ring glittering on her finger, the fragile lace of her cuff frothing about her wrist. For an instant, the boy actually appeared to consider the idea of taking hold of her fingers before he shook his head vigorously and slipped away.

Rosaline shrugged and went out the front door. Twilight had

already begun to paint its wash of purple over the moors, and a pale sea fog drifted in shreds around the house, revealing only intermittent glimpses of Jack where he stood waiting upon the drive.

"Come and look," he said to her, motioning with his hand. "I've repaired the pony cart for you. It's ready to use any time you like. If you can catch them, you can transport those two rapscallions to school in this. I've taught Rajad how to hitch up the rig. You've only to ask and he'll make it ready for you."

Rosaline walked forward, laid a hand upon the shaggy chocolate mane of the Shetland, and smiled with pleasure. "It's just what we need to trundle over the moors. I shall enjoy a brisk morning drive every day. As we trot along, I'll teach the boys the fairy tales my aunts taught me."

"Don't be surprised if they tell you better ones," he said dryly. "Ones with far bigger goblins they'll swear they've seen themselves."

She smiled, noting that her husband was no longer in work clothes, but dressed in riding attire and a greatcoat. He would have to hurry in order to change before dinner she thought. He hadn't yet put away his horse, a tall chestnut thoroughbred tethered nearby.

"Do you know how to drive a cart?" Jack asked.

"No. But surely it can't be difficult . . ."

"Here." He showed her how to hold the wide leather ribbons, his hands brushing hers in the demonstration, his voice deep as he told her the commands the pony had been trained to obey. "Do you think you can handle him?"

"I feel like an expert already."

"Rajad," Jack called over his shoulder, and Rosaline saw with surprise that the boy had been sitting in the shadows of the house, watching. "Take the pony round to the byre and unhitch him like I taught you. Then give him oats and water and put him away for the night. Can you manage? Good lad."

The boy obeyed, timid of the shaggy beast, but feeling self-important enough with the new responsibility of caring for a horse to carry out the order.

As he led the pony away, Jack strolled to an iron ring where the thoroughbred stood tethered, and loosed the reins.

"Are you going for a ride?" Rosaline asked, bewildered, glancing down at the watch pinned to her bodice. "Dinner is to be served in a quarter hour. I've got Mrs. Wiggins on a schedule, which I hope will start the household running more smoothly—especially once I'm able to hire a village girl to help with the work in the kitchen. I . . ."

"It sounds as if you're doing a thorough job of it, Rosaline," Jack interrupted, apparently in a hurry to finish the conversation. He gathered the reins of the thoroughbred. "But I won't be having dinner here tonight. I'm leaving and not certain when I'll return."

"Leaving?" Chagrined, she stared at Jack, at his broad shoulders in the caped greatcoat, at his handsome face lined in blue by the evening light. She felt a sudden sadness, a slow quiver of alarm. "I-I'm sorry, Jack. I suppose you're angry, offended over what I said earlier on the cliffs. I'll apologize if I must. I was wrong to suggest that you were . . . were . . ." She broke off, uncomfortable repeating the unflattering words.

"A liar and a thief?" he finished.

"Yes. I-I believe that's what I implied."

Much to her surprise, Jack laughed. Then he took a step nearer so that Rosaline could smell the fine, brown wool of his greatcoat, now damp with salt mist. "I'm not so easily offended as that," he said in a voice tinged with good humor. "When I think of all the names I've been called in my life—well, being termed a liar and a thief are almost complimentary. And you're not driving me out of the house, if that's what you're thinking. Although, all things considered, I thought you might enjoy my absence for awhile."

She tensed, for the implication brought her shame. Had she driven him to seek other feminine company after only one night? She grew afraid that their marriage—so delicate and underlaid with misunderstanding—was in ruins before it had even begun. "Where are you going?" she asked.

"To London." He pulled a pair of riding gloves from his pocket and drew them on. "I've business at the Foreign Office—briefings and so on, arrangements to make regarding our journey to Egypt."

The words brought Rosaline a measure of relief. Perhaps, after all, there was no courtesan waiting for him in London with open arms—arms that might, just possibly, remind him of the intriguing Julie.

And yet, as Rosaline looked at Jack's face, at his splendid height and form, and remembered the vitality of his body as he had moved over hers, she could not help but recall that his philosophy included the belief that life was to be enjoyed, that its pleasures—if necessary—should be stolen.

As he slid his boot into the stirrup, Rosaline reached out on impulse to clutch at his sleeve.

Jack paused, searched her eyes in the darkness, then leaned to cup her face. She stood still, let him bend his head and kiss her mouth. At first the gesture was so casual as to be in no way intimate, but when Rosaline closed her eyes, he deepened the kiss, thrust his tongue between her teeth.

She let him teach, and to please him, began to respond.

"That's the way it's properly done," he murmured against her mouth. "And you enjoyed it, didn't you?"

She averted her eyes. "Yes. I believe I did, a little."

He smiled and shook his head. "We shall have to find a way to make you less civilized, for God's sake. Lady or not." Then, in a sudden change of mood, he took her hand and squeezed it. "You'll be fine alone here, won't you, Rosaline? You'll be all right without me?"

She almost told him she would not, struck by some instinctive need, some nebulous fear. But remembering her own desire for independence and Jack's need of a wife who could manage his house and his two boys and his gentleman's facade alone, she nodded with more confidence than she felt. "Go ahead to your business in London. But I warn you, you'll find your house much changed when you return.''

"The tiger pelt is not endangered again, is it?''

"No.'' She put a hand over her heart. "Upon my honor.''

Jack tipped his hat, mounted and clucked to the horse before disappearing into the night.

Behind him, Rosaline squared her shoulders, took a deep breath of the unfamiliar island air and returned to his house alone, wondering if this were to be the design of her future, the ebb and tide of her life as Jack Darlington's wife—watching his departures and awaiting his returns.

Chapter Eight

Because Rosaline was busy, time progressed with astonishing speed. She had done her best with the house, calling in a cabinet maker and upholsterer from Kirkwall, ordering Irish linens and Chinese wallpaper and marvelous English Wedgwood to be ferried from the mainland. A maid had been hired, along with a man to do the outdoor work, so that the little island estate she called Arbor Gate would run more smoothly, on the whole, than it ever had before. Of course, the establishment could have used a laundry maid, a dairy maid, two footmen, and three more helpers in the kitchen, but Rosaline was well aware that she had married a man of common means with no title, and that the dowry she had brought him was not exorbitant. Therefore, she would have to make do with basics, and that meant managing with only a few pairs of hands.

She tried her best to tame the children; Rajad was biddable enough, usually eager to please, but still secretive and half-frightened, prone to cry in silence, and often implaccably mute. Every day she drove him to school and back in the pony cart at a spanking pace of over five miles, the two of them silently enjoying the panorama of blue skies and green hills.

Antonio refused to accompany them. Rosaline was not foolish enough to try and coerce him, knowing she could not possibly uphold any threat. He could not be chased, after all, or
starved, and if she could have caught and punished him for
disobedience, Rosaline sensed that he might, at the first chance,
stow away on some ship and disappear. If so, she sensed Jack
would not easily forgive her.

She often thought of Jack, usually at night when the house
was still, cozy with fires in every fireplace, flickering gold and
warm with the light of oil lamps. She enjoyed her quiet nights
of reading and needlework, her slippered feet propped on a
footstool, Rajad playing marbles in a nearby corner, the dog
Argos sometimes—if he managed to stay in Rosaline's good
graces—curled upon a newly designated rug near the hearth.

And yet, there were times when her solitude seemed a little
wearisome, and Rosaline realized that Jack not only anchored
the house with his presence, but provided its rooms with a
vitality that Rosaline, much to her own surprise, both recognized
and missed.

He wrote to her every week, short, droll notes that revealed
nothing about his own activities, but which inquired with concern about hers and those of Arbor Gate—a name she was sure
he penned tongue-in-cheek.

When she allowed herself to ponder such thoughts, Rosaline
grew restless remembering her husband's last, somewhat
searching kiss on the drive, the texture of his wool coat beneath
her fingers, the scent of leather and horseflesh she had breathed
against the hard curve of his neck. She wondered why the
thought of her husband's well-formed mouth on the lips of
another woman plagued her with such persistence when she
was so reluctant to endure the pain of lying with him again.

Just as Rosaline was preparing for Jack's return one evening
several weeks after his departure, she received an unexpected
visitor, a gentleman who introduced himself as Mr. Lance Cardew. Complete with portmanteau and brass-bound trunk, he

stood before her fresh-faced and dapper, a smile fixed upon his thin, fine featured face.

"Good evening, Mrs. Darlington," he said with a bow and a flourish of his beaver hat. "Have I preceded Mr. Darlington? My sincere apologies. It was my understanding that he was to have arrived home from London today."

Rosaline had been setting out dishes of marzipan she had made herself, and, exceedingly pleased to have a caller at her remote estate, she invited the gentleman to come inside and warm himself by the fire. "My husband is scheduled to arrive home tomorrow," she explained, watching with satisfaction as the neatly uniformed maid appeared promptly to take Mr. Cardew's coat, hat, and ivory-handled cane. "I had a letter from him last week. Are you an acquaintance come all the way to our island to visit?"

"Not an acquaintance, no. I've been newly assigned by the Foreign Office to be his aide," he said with another half-apologetic smile. "So sorry to have arrived early."

"Don't concern yourself. You're most welcome here. Have you dined?"

"Oh, yes, Madam," Cardew said, dabbing his reddened nose with a monogrammed handkerchief. "I had supper at the inn at Kirkwall. Are you certain I shouldn't return there for the night? I didn't mean to inconvenience . . ."

"I won't hear of your venturing out again in the cold. A room will be made ready for you here. Do sit down and rest yourself," Rosaline insisted, escorting him into the parlor. "Here, close to the fire. Now, tell me again about your connection with my husband."

Mr. Cardew, with a smoothly accomplished and very proper twitch of his trouser legs, sat down on the edge of the chair and leaned forward to let the heat cast itself over his hands. "Well, as I said, I'm to be Mr. Darlington's aide. I'm assigned to accompany him to Egypt and perform all the personal and secretarial duties he might require of me there."

Rosaline nodded slightly with approval as the youthful maid

bustled in carrying a tea tray which she set down upon the polished gate-leg table at her mistress' side. Rosaline lifted the silver pot and poured the steaming brew into a rose patterned cup. She handed it to her guest and inquired, "Have you been with the Foreign Office long, Mr. Cardew?"

"For the past two years I've been in the service of a diplomat posted in France," he answered, balancing the saucer on his knee. "Upon that gentleman's retirement last week, I was reassigned by the Foreign Office to Mr. Darlington. I've traveled here directly from Paris."

He looked as if he had shopped in that fashionable city, Rosaline thought, noting the dandyish cut of his clothes, the expensive cloth, the meticulously tied neckerchief and pearl stickpin. He seemed exactly the sort of young man to be in the diplomatic service, bright, presentable, and impeccably mannered almost to the point of obsequiousness. Rosaline didn't care for obsequious men—those who fawned and flattered in order to get favors. But perhaps such a trait was necessary to a young aide ambitious to advance within the competitive political structure of the British government.

"Might I compliment you upon your home?" Cardew said, glancing around. "It's lovely. Very welcoming and warm. I always believe a home is a reflection of the lady who graces it."

"Thank you, Mr. Cardew," Rosaline said with a polite nod, suspecting that her guest sought to make a good first impression. Offering him the dish of marzipan, she said, "I detect a slight Scottish burr in your voice. Are you a native of Scotland?"

"Yes. I hail from a small hamlet called Tam."

Rosaline frowned, surprised. "Why, that's near Golspie, the village where my husband spent his childhood. If I recall my geography, the two towns are not more than five or ten miles apart."

"That's correct."

"What a coincidence. Both of you from two remote Scottish

villages not more than a stone's throw distance from each other.''

"Yes, Madam. A fortunate coincidence. It will give Mr. Darlington and I something in common right from the start, won't it?'' He made a business of selecting another sweet, delicately wiped the sugar from his fingers, then changed the subject abruptly. "The marzipan is excellent. I do believe it's better than that sold at the confectioner near the Tuilleries in Paris. Your cook is to be congratulated.''

Rosaline did not bother to say that she had made it herself, asking instead, "Have you ever been to Egypt, Mr. Cardew?''

"I'm afraid not. This shall be my first post outside of Europe.''

"Then we both have a new adventure ahead of us. I'll be accompanying my husband to Cairo.''

For some reason, the gentleman seemed disappointed by her announcement; Rosaline sensed it. Nevertheless, the evening progressed smoothly enough in Lance Cardew's company. His well-trained urbanity did not even slip when Rajad crept in like a nervous woodland creature, retreated to his usual shadowy corner, and refused to be lured to the gentleman's side for even the briefest social chat. As further credit to his tact, Mr. Cardew managed to swallow his shock awhile later when a barefoot and shirtless Antonio—holding some sort of crude spear— eyed the young aide from astride the bannister rail. Cardew even managed to smile, and, nodding in the direction of the young pirate, muttered to Rosaline, "Endearing children you have, Mrs. Darlington.''

"Aren't they?'' she said with a serene, privately amused smile as she proceeded him up the stairs to show him his room.

He obviously felt obliged to continue. "Perhaps I can become—er—better acquainted with the boys in the morning. At breakfast.''

"Oh, I don't think so, Mr. Cardew. You see, the lads usually prefer to eat outdoors.''

"Really?" he said, struggling to take the remark in stride. "What a lovely . . . custom."

"Isn't it?"

As she watched him glance nervously over his shoulder at the shadowy bannister again, Rosaline smiled to herself.

Jack looked forward to coming home. It was an odd sensation, one he had never before had the good fortune to experience, a sense of belonging somewhere, of having a little knot of people—an actual family—who depended upon him. Never mind that he wasn't close to any one of them, and that none of them really knew much about him, or had an inkling of the past, shadowy particulars of his life.

During the course of his sojourn, he had pondered over his prim, reserved but capable wife a great deal. Indeed, he had thought about her constantly while attending dinners and social functions hosted by members of the Foreign Office, imagining what an asset she would have been at his side, always saying and doing the appropriate thing, her grace and intelligence more than compensating for the lack of pink and white beauty currently so fashionable in London circles.

But most of all, he dwelled upon that glimmer of responsiveness Rosaline had displayed upon his departure from Orkney, that impulsive clutching of his arm, her almost anxious willingness to receive his kiss. Just for a moment, as Jack rode toward home now across the cold, twilit moors, he allowed himself to picture Rosaline awaiting him as an eager bride would, with a girl's brightness in her eyes, her hands outstretched instead of demurely clasped together at her waist. He pictured himself being glad she was there waiting for him—Rosaline—instead of another woman, one more elusive, passionate . . . achingly familiar.

Jack did not indulge himself long with visions of either his past romance or the idea of marital bliss, for he had been bred to expect harshness from the world more often than kindness, had learned to take enjoyment wherever he could snatch it rather than wait for it to be given. His law of survival demanded that he expect nothing free, watch his back with a vengeance, and never allow himself to trust anyone.

As Jack rode up to the house, he noticed that the windows spilled warm gold light, welcoming him. He saw that the weeds had been pulled from the sandy drive, and that the sparse patch of lawn was clipped. Dismounting, he strolled to the door, feeling an unaccustomed exuberance which increased as he threw open the portal and entered the home Rosaline called Arbor Gate.

She must have heard his horse canter up the drive, for when he entered, she was already crossing the vestibule. He stopped mid-stride, and paused as he removed the hat from his head. His eyes swept her figure, saw that she was dressed in aquamarine, the neck high at the throat and fastened with a large oval cameo, the sleeves dripping with ivory lace. The blue-green hue suited her eyes, he thought, and the cut of the gown accentuated her height. He noted that her color was high, but whether her radiance originated from his sudden presence or only seemed rosier from the wall sconces and their brightly burning candles, he couldn't say.

Upon seeing her husband, Rosaline rushed forward in an impulsive manner, then faltered, checking herself before clasping her hands at her waist in the familiar, schoolmarmish way Jack knew so well and disliked. "Hello, Jack," she said formally, but with a tentative softness to her voice.

Before he could reply, a new maid in a black uniform bustled in to take his hat and coat, and Jack noticed the vase of greenery on the huntboard, the new mirror above it, the great crystal bowls of potpourri and the thick Aubusson rug, the patina of polish on every surface.

"Jack," Rosaline said as he leaned forward, took her hand and kissed it. "We're so glad you're home. Did you have a safe journey?"

He thought that her pleasure seemed genuine, if typically

reserved. "Quite safe. There was trouble with the ferry and I was delayed a couple of hours while it was repaired, but all in all, my trip was uneventful, thank you." Jack took a closer look at Rosaline, surprised that she appeared not as he had remembered precisely, but younger, softer. Prettier. In a voice that came out more boyish than he expected, he asked, "Are you well?"

"Oh, yes. I'm very well. You'll be glad to know there have been no great disasters in your absence. The time went quickly. Indeed," she said somewhat breathlessly, "it seems as if only a week has passed instead of almost five." She answered shyly, and a moment of awkwardness followed as her eyes surveyed him in a surprised and thorough manner, as if her memory, too, had not been entirely accurate.

His wife's off-handed words caused Jack disappointment. Had he hoped to hear that her time alone had weighed heavy, that she had missed him, had looked anxiously forward to his return?

Forcing a smile, he drew a wooden top from his pocket and tossed it to Rajad, who was peeking around the corner at him. "How many fish did you catch while I was away, Rajad?"

The boy held up a thumb and forefinger to indicate zero, then said with great solemnity, "None. But the lady catch one, sir."

"The lady?" Jack regarded Rosaline with a tilted brow. "Indeed, Madam? I'm impressed, Mrs. Darlington. I had no idea your talents ran in that direction. I must say, I can scarcely picture you sitting on a muddy riverbank baiting hooks—but I'm intrigued by the idea. You'll have to repeat the performance for me."

"It was nothing, really," Rosaline murmured, uncomfortable beneath his penetrating, playful regard. "Did I mention that Rajad is going to school? He has already learned his letters, haven't you, Rajad? Perhaps tomorrow he will recite them for you, show you how clever he is."

"And Antonio?"

Rosaline shook her head. "He refused the very idea of attending school, which hardly surprised me, of course. But one afternoon, I saw him lurking about the schoolyard. I think he was curious. I'm hopeful that his curiosity will prompt him to step inside before too long."

"I could force him, if you like."

"Not yet. Let's give him awhile longer to decide to go himself. But Jack, we have a guest. Your aide arrived yesterday from Paris. He's in the parlor."

"Ah, yes. I was told he had been dispatched. Come, you can introduce me to the fellow. I'm sure you've become well acquainted by now, and that he's suitably impressed with your hospitality."

Rosaline ignored his teasing tone, and fought the urge to turn and touch him, to smooth his sleeve, to reach up and brush the dark strand of hair from his brow. How alive and real he seemed, wind-tossed and hearty from his ride over the moors, worldly from his travels. "Mr. Cardew is likable enough," she said, repressing her contradictory urges. "So anxious to please. I feel certain you'll find him acceptable. He seems to have all the qualities of a good aide, and I've seen more than a few at my father's dinner table. I suppose he shall become like one of the family now."

Jack followed her into the parlor, his eyes on the neat, shiny coil of hair at her nape, on the heavy rippling of her aquamarine skirts as she walked. His eyes missed little; out of long habit he made certain he knew everything that went on around him. And his ears, trained to hear nuances of sound that could present opportunities or save his life, caught the slight uncertainty in his wife's voice.

He wondered at it until she added over her shoulder, "And do you know that Mr. Cardew was raised in a village only a few miles from your own birthplace? A tiny, remote place, just like Golspie. Pleasant coincidence, don't you think, Jack?"

Jack paused, then murmured, "Pleasant, indeed."

* * *

Awhile later in his bedchamber, Jack untied his neckerchief and reflected upon what he knew of Mr. Lance Cardew. He did not particularly trust the young man, which, on the whole, was not uncharacteristic. Of course, on the surface the aide was affable, bright, ingratiating to a fault, but Jack was a shrewd judge of character and necessarily suspicious. He was sure Mr. Cardew did not hail from Tam, had never set foot in the place, just as Jack had never been to Golspie. Tossing his jacket across the back of a chair, he shook his head and muttered to himself, "The Foreign Office is getting a bit too careless in their assignment of identities. Must every one of Lord Bardo's employees—those with shady pasts—hail from the north of Scotland? Bloody unimaginative of those mullet heads in London."

Jack let a breath slide through his teeth, wondering where the young aide Cardew had *really* spent his early days. On the streets of East London? No. Jack rejected the idea. Cardew was too delicate looking to have endured that sort of life. But why did the Foreign Office feel the need to conceal *his* past, too?

Splashing water on his face from the basin, Jack dried himself with the scented linen towel, then shrugged away his nagging suspicions. He supposed Mr. Cardew's beginnings didn't really matter, nor did the reasons for the Foreign Office to hide them. Like Jack, many of the employees comprising the lower ranks of the Foreign Office were unscrupulous, well-acquainted with the underworld and ruthlessly ambitious, willing to do almost anything required of them in order to advance.

Jack noticed the new inlaid writing box on his desk, its bottle and pens neatly laid out, and with a frown turned his ruminations toward his wife. He was astonished by the degree of change Rosaline had wrought in the house, the atmosphere of order and warmth she had managed to convey with subtle, womanly talent. Surprisingly, she had not displaced his own things or the stamp of his occupancy, but had woven into it the creature comforts only a woman remembered, the deeply cushioned chairs, the conveniently placed newspapers, the books lying open on ottomans, the bayberry candles burning in brass sconces all the way up the stairs. Even here, in his own bedroom, a full decanter of brandy awaited, placed beside a plate of wine biscuits and a silver pot of coffee, still steaming.

Yes, he thought, in his absence Rosaline had done her best to make a home for him, create an atmosphere of gentility, and he wanted to tell her how pleased he was with her efforts. But, unused to feeling soft emotions and expressing them aloud, Jack decided it best to go to her bedroom and communicate his appreciation by making love to her. All evening he had watched her in the parlor as she had adroitly, with all the finesse of a well-bred lady, played hostess to Lance Cardew. He had watched her capable hands on the tea pot, the way her neck seemed long and graceful above its cameo and aquamarine silk, the sheen of her heavy, dark hair. She had given grace and harmony to his house, and he wanted to maintain that harmony, to hold on to the strange, fledgling sense of contentment that had eluded him before, and even now seemed to threaten to evaporate if he didn't cap it quickly. He wanted to seize it, and since he was a man accustomed to grabbing whatever he wanted with either a forceful or a cleverly quick hand, he judged that his ardent touching of Rosaline would best secure the feeling of fulfillment.

Making love was the best way he knew to express feeling. He had settled for a woman he did not love, but perhaps the genteel care she showed him substituted for the sort of violent passion he had once had, and still unwittingly craved, with Julie.

Removing a package from his traveling portmanteau, he contemplated the length of green silk inside, a fabric that had cost him a dear but unregretted price in a French couturier's shop on Bond Street.

He knocked on Rosaline's door and, receiving no answer, stepped inside. At first he thought the room empty, then noticed his wife asleep, exhausted by the look of her. She had not even taken time to unbraid and brush her hair, and he understood her well enough to know that she considered such a nightly ritual essential. She looked younger when she slept, the primness erased, the stubborn independence smoothed from her well-shaped chin. In that moment, he wanted very much to slide in beside her, smell the clean, starched scent of her clothes and hair, feel the softness of the still youthful body beneath the corset and petticoats, bring it to life with his own, more experienced flesh. But Rosaline was not the sort of woman to be awakened with kisses, he surmised, not the sort—not yet, at least—to appreciate his bold and impulsive appetites.

With a long sigh, Jack shoved the roll of silk under his arm, then turned on his heel to go, shutting the door with a rueful smile. The moment for presenting a well-intended gift had been lost again, it seemed.

Chapter Nine

Rosaline had planned a picnic on Jack's first day home, and before dawn the next morning hurried downstairs to supervise the packing of the basket.

"Wine for the men, Mrs. Wiggins," she said from her mental list while tying on an apron. "And a jug of lemonade for the children and me. Bread, cheese, strawberries, ham, mint jelly, and apple tarts. And don't forget the gingerbread and butter. Where are the napkins—the lace-edged ones that I mended yesterday? We'll need those, together with a rug to sit on. The ground will be damp."

The two women bustled about the limewashed kitchen, its every nook and corner immaculate now that Rosaline had organized it. The hanging copper pots gleamed with sunlight pouring through the tiny leaded windows, fruits and vegetables lay in bright arrangement on the work table, garlic and onion hung in bunches from the rafters, and strings of apple slices dried near the stone sink. The gingerbread had just been removed from the oven and sat in its pan, hot and honey brown, ready to be wrapped in cheesecloth and packed in the picnic basket.

Preoccupied with her tasks, Rosaline at first did not notice

Jack standing with a shoulder braced against the door jamb, his eyes taking in the homey activities, the changed appearance of his kitchen.

"Am I too early for breakfast?" he asked, causing her to start.

"Oh, Jack," she said, turning about with a bottle of wine in her hand. "Good morning. I've planned a picnic—I thought we'd breakfast by the lake. It would please Rajad. He says the fishing is best in the morning."

Rosaline took another more thorough glance at her husband, struck, as she had been last night, by his extraordinary looks. She had forgotten the way his dark hair waved back from his temples, how his eyes seemed to penetrate and yet hold secrets, and she recalled the first time she had seen him in her father's drawing room. She had been intimidated by his air of self-assurance and restrained physical power then; today, that same reaction returned to her. It made her rarely nervous hands unsteady on the gingerbread as she wrapped up the loaf, but in a deliberately airy voice she asked, "You don't mind a picnic, do you?"

Jack noticed her hands and, guessing the reason for their faltering, found himself amused. But he spared Rosaline a teasing remark, knowing she was too serious minded to take it lightly. "A picnic. What an excellent idea, Mrs. Darlington. Shall I invite that overzealous aide of mine to join us and then go gather up the boys?"

"Yes, please—although I believe Antonio has already slipped out. But I suspect the little rascal watches the comings and goings of the house, so he may follow us in his own good time. It's optimistic to expect him to sit and picnic with us, I'm afraid. Likely he'll only snatch up a plate of food and go off to eat alone."

"He's become more and more like a wild animal," Jack grumbled, moving to steal a slice of ham out from under Mrs. Wiggins's hands. "I've been too lenient."

"Perhaps," Rosaline conceded. "But let's not force him to

be sociable just yet. I'm working on several strategies to bring him around without letting him realize that he's being charmed.''

A smile played at the corners of Jack's mouth. ''Really? I'm beginning to think I married a woman who is even more clever than her father led me to believe. Am I being charmed?''

''Your wife *is* clever,'' Mrs. Wiggins cut in. ''If you don't mind my saying so, of course, Mr. Darlington. And quite capable of managing things. Most ladies of her ilk are delicate, dependent upon their men to make decisions and handle problems. But not Mrs. Darlington. A regular general she is about the house.''

Jack observed the woman who had already, in only a month, made an impact on his life. He eyed her tall, straight figure in its corset and crinoline, her set mouth and sober eyes, her proficient hands, and thought she was really quite extraordinary in a certain way. Perhaps he had not done so badly after all.

Their picnic on the lake shore was a merry one. The vantage point provided views of pasture, moor and sky, a whirl of cool hues flickering with light as the clouds galloped in a never ending path from north to south. The lake itself was a clear blue mirror rippled by the wind, and the picnic rug made a multicolored splash on the tufted green banks. The food proved savory, and Rajad ate ravenously, sitting cross-legged in the sun fishing in a contented way. Lance Cardew, as expected, was affable, out to impress everyone with his willingness to make an efficient assistant, boasting with a subtle arrogance of his experience in the diplomatic field. And even though Cardew was attired for the outdoors in casual tweeds, he still managed to appear dapper, his sleek hair shining and his shoes well polished.

In contrast, Jack was relaxed and comfortably dressed in top boots and corduroys, lounging on the bank and baiting hooks for Rajad, his smile coming more often and more genuinely than Rosaline had yet seen it. She knew he made a point to enjoy life, to wrest from it whatever he could, but today he seemed more willing to let happiness simply happen. As she sat sipping lemonade nearby, she wondered if, long ago, he had smiled so naturally for Julie.

Such dark thoughts continued to plague her, the mysterious Julie lurking often in the back of her mind. Rosaline could not fathom the reason for it, except that Jack Darlington, whether she loved him or not, whether she trusted him or not, was her husband now, and marriage engendered possessiveness. Ironically, she still thought of David with a longing ache, and wore his locket around her neck. Perhaps, she admitted, it armored her from feeling too much attraction for Jack—a circumstance which would surely only lead to heartache.

Putting such thoughts aside, she readjusted her parasol—Brussels lace over lilac silk with a rosewood handle—and listened as Lance Cardew spoke to Jack.

"So you have been to Egypt before?" the young man asked.

"Yes." Jack tossed Rajad's line into the water. "A few years ago."

"How did you find the country?"

"Full of sand and fleas."

His remark was uncharacteristically bitter, Rosaline thought; usually her husband was careful not to reveal his inward feelings during general conversation, careful to keep his responses on a surface level. But Egypt affected him differently. She had noticed it when the topic had been raised before, noted the tenseness of his body, the low-toned edge to his voice, the brief darkening of his eyes.

"It doesn't sound as if you're eager to go back, sir." Cardew ventured, having caught the undertone too.

"On the contrary. I'm counting the days."

"Really?" the young man said, puzzled by the contradictory signals. "It sounds like a dangerous post. I hear the country is in turmoil. A fellow named Arabi is trying to overthrow the government."

"He's already overthrown it—for all practical purposes, at least."

"You were briefed in London?"

"Thoroughly," Jack said as he reeled in his line.

Rosaline watched him, wondered at his attitude toward the amiable young man who had been assigned as his aide. It was clear to her that Jack had no intention of confiding in Lance Cardew. Indeed, he seemed brusquely uncommunicative on the topic of Egypt, a country in which Cardew expressed a natural interest since he was about to travel there shortly.

However, if Jack's taciturn manner offended him, Lance did not show it, and with his ingratiating smile, he turned his attention to Rosaline. "Will you try your hand at fishing today, Mrs. Darlington?" he asked.

"I believe I shall," she answered, seeing Rajad—still sitting cross-legged nearby—glance at her hopefully. She thought the boy was impressed over her previous accomplishment when the two of them had fished alone together.

His eyes suddenly twinkling, Jack handed her his pole with a flourish. "I would be honored to have you make use of it, my dear. The best place to cast is down there on that narrow sand bar. See it?"

"Yes." She eyed the location with a degree of doubt, for it would mean getting her shoes and the hem of her skirt damp, and she had wanted to look well groomed for Jack in her yellow muslin and kid boots. But, squaring her shoulders, loath to let Rajad down—and noting, most of all, the playful challenge in Jack's eyes—she conceded and stepped down the steep descent, picking her way out on the bar.

Conscious of the three pairs of male eyes upon her, she cast with a quick, forceful movement of her arm and wrist, using the technique her cousins had taught her, satisfied with the distance she achieved. The lure hit the water several yards out with a neat splash.

She could hear Lance Cardew, who was unaware that his voice carried so far over the water, address Jack on the bank.

''Mrs. Darlington is an extraordinary woman, if you'll permit me to say so, sir. Not all fluff and frills like some. I suppose a man feels fortunate to find a wife who is practical and intelligent, rather than one who exists simply to ornament a drawing room.''

Although Rosaline strained to catch her husband's reply, leaning so far backwards she almost lost her balance, his words were lost in the rush of the breeze.

It was particularly windy where she stood, and with distress she realized the large brim of her picture hat was beginning to flap madly, threatening to fly away. She attempted to anchor it while holding on to the pole, but her line bobbed suddenly and tautened with the weight of a fish. When the wind gusted and lifted the hat from her head, Rosaline lunged for it, but lost her footing in the damp sand and slid.

Ungracefully, on one hip, she landed with a splash in the shallow water.

Clamping her teeth to hush a cry of dismay, Rosaline managed to keep hold of the pole, determined in spite of her embarrassing mishap to reel in the fish. Jack was at her side immediately, ready to take over, but she would not relinquish the line, and hauled in a struggling, gleaming specimen large enough to make a meal for three. Hearing Rajad's excited cries on the bank and feeling joy at the sound, Rosaline grasped the wriggling fish and disengaged the hook from its mouth herself, holding it up triumphantly for the boy to see.

Her sense of victory quickly faded as she realized the state she was in, the way she must look to Jack. Her hat was gone and her hair was loose, whipping in long, straight wisps around her face. Her shoes were soaked and her once perfectly pressed skirts now dripped with muddy water.

She felt a hot flush creep up to splotch her neck and cheeks. She prided herself on her dignity, wore it as a shield against the plainness of her face. Now she feared she looked more than plain—ugly, perhaps.

"I'll carry you back to the rug," Jack said, moving to scoop her up in his arms.

But Rosaline pulled away, trying to manage alone. Ignoring her protest, her husband gathered her up anyway, and leaned close to her ear. "Smile, Rosaline," he whispered. "Just smile. It's really the best response at a time like this."

And Rosaline knew he understood her mortification, perhaps even knew the reason for it. Did he pity her? She wondered. She didn't want his pity, and because of that, she smiled, tentatively at first, then widely, so that by the time he sat her down on the picnic rug, the sound of her laughter rang out.

Rajad giggled happily as well, and Lance Cardew, in his ever polished way, congratulated her on her skill as an angler. "Good sport, Mrs. Darlington. I shall have to take some lessons from you."

Jack grinned too, and went to retrieve her wayward hat from the bank, handing it to her so she could cover her untidy hair and regain a measure of her confidence.

She thanked him, noticing that he was looking at her in a slightly different way than he ever had before. The change was in his eyes, she thought. As they studied her face, they seemed to flicker, just briefly, with something very close to admiration.

Much to her surprise, Antonio approached them, marched into their midst, elbowing his way rudely past Mr. Cardew until he came to an abrupt halt before Rosaline. In his arms he carried a large white gull, which flapped and squawked and struggled weakly to get free, an injury to its leg apparent.

"The bird is hurt," Antonio said with his usual belligerence, addressing no one but Rosaline. "Its leg is broken."

"Another of your victims, Antonio?" Jack said with disapproval, stepping forward, his expression changing from one of good cheer to anger. "There must be consequences this time. Your disobedience has finally exhausted my patience."

"I did nothing!" the boy cried. "Nothing!"

"Your denial won't do."

"You never believe me. You hate me!"

Jack reached out and took the gull from the boy's arms, his voice harsh. "Your self-pity does not affect me. Now go on back to the house and stay in your room. I'll deal with you later. And don't think to disobey me or I'll run you down and give you the thrashing of your life."

At Jack's command, the boy's face closed, altered itself into fierce lines of anger.

Rosaline impulsively put a hand on her husband's sleeve. "Jack . . ."

"No, Rosaline. Don't interfere in this."

His tone piqued her. He had allowed the boys to run about like savages before her arrival, and now expected her to find a way to manage them. Just as she believed she was making progress, Jack was intervening in his heavy-handed way and perhaps destroying the delicate groundwork that she had been so painstakingly laying down for them the past month.

"Very well," she said in a tight voice, turning to gather up the picnic things. "Have it your way."

Lance Cardew observed the subtly fought domestic quarrel, and, unwilling to appear obtrusive, began rolling up the rug while Rajad, always averse to contention, disappeared. As the three adults worked in silence, collecting fishing equipment and leftover food, a herd of gray clouds tumbled over the face of the sun, turning the warm day cold.

Rosaline set her mouth. Her picnic, so carefully planned to provide an opportunity for companionship between four family members who seemed to know very little about each other, was now ruined. Picking up the heavy basket herself, she began marching toward home in her muddied skirts, her shoulders squared. She felt Jack's eyes following her progress like magnets. Let him suffer my anger and silence for a day or so, she told herself. She had nothing to say to a man who acted so boorishly to a troubled child.

* * *

Rosaline did not see her husband for the remainder of the day, having been informed by a carefully expressionless Mrs. Wiggins that Mr. Darlington would be out until quite late. Squelching her frustration, Rosaline dined in the company of Lance Cardew, who seemed to feel it his duty to entertain her with stories about his sightseeing travels in France. As she listened without interest to his embroidered tales, she realized she was sorry not to have Jack sitting opposite her at the table, the candlelight playing over his dark features, his deep voice filling the room and overriding Cardew's tenor tones. She stubbornly held on to her anger over Jack's harsh behavior toward Antonio and his deliberate absence at dinner, even while feeling an inward disquiet that her attraction for her husband was beginning to grow too strong, too unmanageable for comfort.

Later that evening she sat at her vanity and unpinned her hair. It was her longstanding habit to unbind it, brush it out, then braid it again in a single plait before bedtime. A knock sounded just as she ran the brush across her scalp. Assuming the maid had brought tea, Rosaline bade her come in.

To her surprise, Jack strolled across the threshold, looking as if he had just returned from a reckless evening ride, his boots and coattails splattered with mud, his neckcloth askew, his hair wildly tumbled. He wore the air of a man who was restless, contentious, and looking for an argument. Judging by the faint smell of brandy hovering about his person, Rosaline surmised he had spent more than a few hours imbibing at the local pub.

"Your boots are muddying the carpet," she said cooly, with no welcome. She was suddenly a little afraid of him, of his maleness, of his dangerous mood, and hoped to discourage his visit with a show of chilliness. Hastily, she began to pin up her hair again, feeling it improper to allow him to see it unbound.

"So they are," he said with no concern, striding closer, tossing a large package on her vanity.

She stared at it.

"It's yours." He spoke with curt indifference, roaming about the room in that caged animal way Rosaline recognized, before finally taking up an impatient stance at the window.

Having no particular desire to open a gift that had been so summarily delivered, Rosaline plucked at the wrapping, which, when drawn away, revealed a folded length of silk—luxuriant in texture and sheen—just the color of spring grass.

"I was told it's enough to make a gown," Jack said, not glancing at her.

"It's . . . it's quite beautiful." Rosaline managed to say the words with an awkward falter. "And, yes, it will be enough to fashion a gown."

Silence fell between them before Jack took a breath, and in a quieter, calmer voice said, "I didn't mean to offend you today over Antonio. I didn't mean to be so harsh with him."

His manner was stiff, as if apology in any form did not come easily from his lips. Knowing how difficult the admission of fault had been for him, she did not rush to smooth over the incident, to allay his guilt, but said only, "I've put Antonio's injured gull in a box and tied its leg up with a strip of linen. Every few hours I feed it bits of raw fish. Perhaps it will heal."

"Perhaps." Jack shifted his feet, ran a hand through his hair, and after a moment said, "The boy will take advantage of your softness, you know."

"Really? I rather thought he was beginning to respond to it."

"He will craftily manipulate you, have you eat out of his hand. Then he will disappoint you."

"If I can get close to him," Rosaline said with heat in her voice, "I will do so even at the risk of having my feelings wounded. After all, I'm the adult and he's the child."

"Nevertheless, I don't care to let him make a fool of my wife."

"And yet you brought me here with no forewarning, Jack, and expected me to deal with him." Rosaline stood up, fighting to maintain her composure. "Why not allow me to do it the best way I know how?"

Jack clenched his jaw, loath to argue because he knew his wife was right. Surrendering—for he knew surrender was best and necessary if marital harmony was to be salvaged in this house—he said nothing more about Antonio. Staring out at the garden before changing the subject with a sudden toneless comment, he said, "We leave for Egypt in a fortnight. Can you be ready?"

He heard her quick intake of breath. "A fortnight? Why, yes, that's plenty of time. I shall be ready."

"And the boys?" Jack asked. "What is your decision regarding them?"

"They shall go with us, of course."

He glanced at her with one brow raised, his black lashes framing the blue of his eyes. "Indeed?"

"They shouldn't be left to the care of a housekeeper," she stated firmly, defending her judgment. "They need to feel included, Jack, to feel part of the family."

"They'll complicate matters there, you know."

Rosaline suspected with a vague wonder that her husband, unconsciously or not, resented the affection she showed the boys. "They'll complicate matters between us, you mean?" she challenged.

He refused to look at her, perhaps discomfitted at having been caught out. "Haven't they already?"

"You took those children in," she stated, accusing him, feeling a sharp, sudden prick of protectiveness toward the children. "They're not strays, Jack, in spite of what you say. They are not puppies to be brought home and left to their own devices. They need to have all the things boys from ordinary, loving families take for granted. They need security. More than that, they need your affection.''

Her husband's expression hardened as he countered, ''I have given them security. I've given them a place to live, food, clothing . . .''

''That is not enough.''

''It's more than I . . .'' Jack clamped his teeth on the words, on the impulsive, overly revealing admission he had almost uttered. He fixed his eyes upon Rosaline's. His own inner turmoil and the need to hide his vulnerability made his gaze intent, hard and bright. And then, regarding her in her prim dressing gown, seeing her flush with high emotion and indignation, his expression turned to speculation.

Taking a step closer, his eyes narrowed. He reached out to touch the line of her cheek. ''I took you in, as well,'' he said with quiet, almost brutal honesty. ''And do you remember what I told you before the marriage, on the day I bought the finches in Edinburgh?''

She did not pull away from his hard hands, and met his regard with directness. ''Yes, I remember. I remember very well.''

''What did I say?''

''You said that I was to expect no affection from you.''

''Precisely. I want to provide a good home for you and the boys, but that is all there is in my nature to give. The rest is suddenly proving too . . . complicated, too involved, just as I thought. More than I am willing to offer.''

The words were curt. Untrue. For even as Jack uttered them aloud, he realized in amazement, that since his return from London, he *had* wanted to give the boys and this woman more. He *had wanted* to show her his appreciation for her efforts with his home; he *had wanted* to draw out and strengthen the tenuous threads of harmony between them, that sweet, elusive taste of contentment he had experienced in a few quicksilver moments, upon his return from London last night. Indeed, when he had entered Rosaline's room a few moments ago, full of ale and lust, he had meant to sweep her into his arms and make love to her, to try and find some common understanding, some mutually agreeable ground that could establish a new beginning for them.

But by his reckless entrance, his harsh, almost taunting words, Jack knew he had spoiled any chance of a tender approach. Nevertheless, unwilling to relinquish hope, angry at her for standing up to him, wanting to master her independence, he stepped forward without preamble and seized her face between his palms. "But we should get some enjoyment out of each other, shouldn't we?" With no forethought then, determined to force her response, make her soft and pliable and a little afraid, he took her mouth with his.

To Jack, making love was an act of simple carnality, an act to be savored to the fullest, appreciated like any other sensual endeavor, emotions rarely interfering with pleasure. He sought to sweep Rosaline up in the same fire, and did not proceed slowly with her but pulled her rigid body against his, holding her with determined mastery even when she stiffened and pushed him away.

Rosaline had not meant to repel him, feeling it cowardly. But she would have liked to have been allowed time to explore her own feelings, time to encourage the budding of what she had begun to feel, weeks ago, when Jack had kissed her on the drive before his departure to London.

He would take her in a moment of confrontation, take her in a fierce, restless mood, with a kind of male dominance, as if he could force her inexperienced body to feel the same needs that fueled his more seasoned one. His roughness caused Rosaline to remember clearly the pain of the previous experience.

He pushed the dressing robe off her shoulders, and his hands followed the contours beneath her gown while his mouth tasted her neck. His hard fingers gathered her hair, stroked it, held it. She sensed a certain desperation in Jack Darlington, a longing that he hoped to satisfy in a way that would never work. Rosaline would have preferred the other side of him, the side that employed his easy charm to achieve his ends; not this side.

Perhaps, if she were to stop resisting him and yield, he would find no need to subdue her, and grow gentler in his manner. Although Rosaline resented his reminder that he had no affection to give, although she felt anger over his lack of consideration for her inexperience, she realized that the pattern of his forcefulness and her corresponding reluctance must be broken if an accord were to be achieved in their marriage.

"Go slowly, Jack," she pleaded against his ear. "Go slowly with me . . . please."

Suddenly, at her beseechment, he seemed to realize the extent of his own selfishness, or the extent of her need for tenderness. He released his hold, searched her eyes, then, with gentleness she had not felt him display before, bent his head and kissed her in a much different way.

Jack Darlington made love to her without haste. And yet, as Rosaline lay beneath his body trying to respond but finding herself too inhibited, too awkwardly modest, she sensed that Jack felt bitterly disappointed at her lack of reaction. Suddenly he gave up his languorous explorations, his attempts to rouse her, and simply satisfied his own male urge.

Later, as he moved apart from her, Jack said quietly, "I would like you to enjoy it, too."

She turned her head away. "It doesn't matter."

"It matters to me."

"Then . . . in time, perhaps."

And although she knew it was imprudent, perhaps even dangerous to call up the mysterious face which had begun to prey on her mind, Rosaline whispered a word in the darkness. "Julie."

"What did you say?" he asked, the words sharp.

"Who is Julie, Jack?"

Although no part of her touched him now, Rosaline felt her

husband's body recoil, every muscle tense as she breathed the woman's name.

"Don't speak to me of Julie again. Not ever."

She marveled at the way his voice could slice her composure like the edge of a sword; and yet, risking it again, she asked, "Why?"

"Because I have asked you not to."

"I am to receive no other explanation?"

Jack turned to face her in the darkness, and she thought she saw his eyes glitter. "No. And if you push me, if you taunt me with it, you shall regret it." He turned his face away again, stared at the ceiling, and added quietly, "And so shall I."

Chapter Ten

She had thought the journey to Cairo would throw some dark mood upon Jack, cast a brooding somberness over his handsome features, but she had been mistaken. Although his senses seemed even more keen-edged than usual, he displayed no tension as they traveled toward their faraway destination; instead, he slipped into the charming, devil-may-care persona Rosaline knew and admired so well.

As they went from port to port, she discovered that Jack Darlington knew just when to grin and to grease a palm, just when to raise a warning brow and to issue an unspoken threat, just what language to speak and where. He knew how to obtain a room in Lisbon when half the population of Portugal seemed to have flocked to the city, or how to get a first-class train ticket in Alexandria when all had been sold. He was that rare sort of man who had the ability to move and live among any sort of people, disarm or threaten them, blend in or make himself conspicuous as necessity demanded.

And during their travels, Rosaline noticed a subtle change in their relationship. It revealed itself slightly in the way Jack spoke to her when they were alone, in the way he looked at her, every now and then, across some foreign, sun-dappled room. Since the night she had breathed Julie's name in the darkness, he had not made love to her, but when they slept side by side in strange, cramped inns or in steamship berths, he did not turn a hostile back either. Instead, he adopted a sort of casual intimacy toward her, a husbandly solicitousness. Although it did not include any sexual overtures, this pleased Rosaline.

Sometimes aboard ship, he would pour a sweet red wine for her, cajole her to sip it, then lie talking quietly on fringed pillows long into the night about the customs and peoples of the countries through which they journeyed. He never spoke about himself. But they fell into a kind of pleasant marital routine which Rosaline began to treasure with a secret intensity.

Jack's manner was protective and proprietary, and as they traveled across warm, spice-scented places, none could doubt that Rosaline belonged to the tall man with the flashing, dangerous eyes. She knew he appreciated her presence, for without being asked, she took care of him too, ordering meals, laying out frock coats and trousers, sending shirts to be pressed. She managed the needs and schedules of the two boys—who were enthralled enough with their surroundings to remain reasonably obedient—by seeing them dressed each morning, put to bed each night, and fed whenever they were hungry. If they listened, she pointed out things of interest from the travel books she had bought before they had set sail.

In return, Jack did not treat her like a fragile, empty-headed doll. He allowed her to stand on her own two feet. Which Rosaline did, very capably.

As for Lance Cardew, he performed the necessary duties of an aide, but otherwise kept to himself.

When they at last arrived in Cairo, Rosaline found herself in a continuous state of awe, often running to the windows of their rented house to peer outside. They were situated on Frank Square, which contained the principal European hotels and residences of the city. The houses were all painted white, constructed of mud and topped by flat, terraced roofs, their warm, palm shaded avenues surrounded by the ancient architecture of the Moorish style which lent an Old World loveliness to every view.

The Darlington's house sported blue antique tiles, carved wood doors, lattice screens, and a delightful inner courtyard lush with banana trees, pink mimosas, and Indian figs. Upon first sight, Rosaline had loved both the house and the city, secretly imagining herself caught within the pages of *A Hundred and One Nights* as she smelled the scents of honey and spice cloaked in the balmy air once breathed by pharaohs. How intriguing it all was, so foreign to her own world, every aspect of it stirring to the senses.

"It is more lovely, far more exotic, than I dreamed," she breathed aloud at the end of their first month there, hearing Jack's footsteps behind her on the terrace. Wide-eyed, she gazed down at the streets packed with pedestrians, camels, donkeys and children, all of them vying for space in the maze of booths, barber stands, and sherbet sellers. A forest of delicate domes, minarets and mosques etched the sky, and below it lay a labyrinth of ancient tombs and shrines. Alongside the city the Nile flowed, green and mysterious. Rosaline could just glimpse a glassy piece of it from beyond the railing of their terrace. Down below the raucous sounds of foreign tongues and bawling animals created a continual din like none she had ever heard.

"So, you are enchanted with it," Jack commented, coming to stand at her shoulder the day after they arrived. His eyes, as blue and distant as the sky, surveyed the noise and confusion.

"Aren't you?" she asked, surprised.

He lifted a well-defined shoulder. "Vagabonds like me become enchanted by very little after so many years of travel."

Although his smile was easy and his manner light, Rosaline

sensed that beneath the nonchalance lay something hard. She knew that Cairo had robbed Jack Darlington of his love, and surmised that he had not forgiven it—would never forgive it.

He leaned a hip against the rail, and in a sudden brooding tone, admitted, "Egypt is the only country I've ever hated."

Rosaline observed her husband's face through her lashes as he gazed down at the bustle of humanity, at the men in turbans and skull caps, at the dark Nubian slaves, at the shrouded women in their white veils. His eyes automatically scanned and searched, just as they had been doing since the moment he had stepped onto the Egyptian soil. Yes, he searched. Rosaline had noticed. She knew that even after so many years, Jack still looked for Julie.

Impulsively, almost to herself, Rosaline whispered, "I had the oddest feeling when we left Scotland."

"Hmm?" Jack murmured, his thoughts elsewhere.

"The feeling came just before we departed from Orkney," she continued in a dreamy way. "When we were all packed into the coach and driving off, I turned to look back at our house. The sun was glinting off the window panes, the garden gate was open, and the heather seemed the brightest purple. I-I didn't want to leave it. Any of it. I felt I shouldn't leave. To tell the truth, I almost clutched your hand and begged you to let me stay home, Jack—even begged you to stay there at Arbor Gate with me."

Drawn out of his reverie, Jack smiled. "You're such a practical woman, Rosaline, I wouldn't have thought you prone to fancies."

"They weren't fancies," she argued, offended by his light treatment of her concern which had been so difficult to voice.

He looked at her curiously, as if her mood had finally affected his own. "Will you promise me something while we're here in Egypt?" he asked.

"Promise you what?"

''Simply that you won't step outside the house without one of the servants or me to escort you.''

''Are you concerned over the political unrest?''

''Not presently, no. But European women don't command a great deal of respect here. You've read about the customs, and I've told you much about the people and their attitudes myself. Based on that, surely you understand my concern?''

Rosaline nodded, thinking she understood very well. Jack had lost his lover here and he did not intend to lose his wife as well.

Even while such sentiment wounded her, Jack's show of protectiveness brought Rosaline comfort. Although her husband did not love her, he valued her in other ways.

Jack regarded her keenly for a moment, then said, ''I suspect you're eager to go out and shop. Shall we explore the bazaars together?''

Rosaline clapped her hands together. ''Oh, please, Jack! I could spend days and days wandering about and looking at everything.''

''No doubt. But we have an embassy dinner to attend tonight—you haven't forgotten?''

''Of course not. We'll need to be back by late afternoon to dress. But do let's take the boys with us to the bazaar. Hoseyn will surely appreciate the respite.''

Hoseyn was one of several house servants they had hired, his primary responsibility being to look after the boys, and escort them to and from their European school each day. Rosaline had worried that Antonio might try and escape the confines of the villa and roam the dangerous streets, but apparently even he was not bold enough to venture out into the exotic bedlam of traffic and noise.

They discovered the boys in the courtyard beneath a banyan tree, the young mahogany faced Hoseyn teaching them how to juggle a set of wooden cups and balls. For a moment, Jack and Rosaline watched the entertainment, applauding when Rajad managed the feat.

"Rajad, Antonio," Jack called, striding forward. "Follow me. I've decided to turn you loose on the citizens of Cairo."

Rajad giggled, Antonio looked hopeful, and as they all filed out the door and down the steps a moment later, a gaggle of wily salesmen offering donkeys for hire besieged them.

"They're called dragomen," Jack explained to Rosaline above the shouting. He tossed a few shillings to a pair of the dragomen, who eagerly, with much bowing and scraping, led forward a couple of shaggy beasts for the boys to ride. "You'll find them as numerous and persistent as beggars. If I let them, every last one will trail us with their string of animals, and plead with me continually to try another donkey at a lower price."

Amused, Rosaline regarded the herd of decorated donkeys, their stubby legs painted with zebra stripes, their flanks tinted purple or red.

The boys were put astride the shaggy beasts, which the servant Hoseyn led while Jack took hold of Rosaline's arm and forced a path through the noisy throng of pedestrians and camels. There was so much of interest that Rosaline scarcely knew where to look first, her attention claimed by the Moorish and Saracen buildings with their bright marble stripes and undecipherable inscriptions, then by the medieval arches and lacy, mysterious lattices through which cloistered concubines observed the outside world.

The sale items on display in the crowded booths intrigued as well, causing Rosaline either to stop and admire, or to grimace in distaste. Scorpions in glass, ivory fans, spears, red slippers, old coins, sabres, colocynth apples, pumpkin seeds, brass bells, tasselled bridles and cushioned saddles all gleamed and beckoned the eye. The whirl of exotic goods blended with the brown, blue, green and violet *kuftans* worn by the natives, costumes tied at the waist with tasseled sashes. Shabby policemen passed in blue frock coats and white pantaloons, and a few parading soldiers sporting uniforms of white cotton paraded past in perfect order.

All at once, while the Darlingtons looked on, one of the officers pointed at a man in the crowd, then shouted a command at him. When the fellow refused to halt, the officer ordered two soldiers to run him down in the street. After handcuffing the poor man, the soldiers threw him across the back of a horse, dispersed the crowd, and rode away with him.

In the resulting turmoil, Jack adroitly guided the boys and Rosaline in another direction, and remarked calmly, "Likely the handcuffed fellow was an enemy to the new regime. A little reminder of the unease here—an unease which most Europeans pretend doesn't exit."

"Why do they pretend?"

"Because they've grown comfortable and rich off of Egypt's resources. They don't like the thought of their lives being inconvenienced by a rebellion. It might interrupt afternoon tea."

Because Jack's tone was light, Rosaline relaxed again, secure on his arm, the beads and scarfs and gaudy jewelry recapturing her attention. The smells intrigued her too, pungent from thick black coffee and honey cakes, underlaid with the odors of sheep and coarse haired camels. There was no dearth of beggars. Rosaline would never have been able to forge a path through them if Jack had not cleared one for her, elbowing, cursing in Arabic whenever a dirty hand dared to reach out and pluck at her sleeve.

Feeling overwhelmed yet safe with her hand tucked beneath Jack's elbow, Rosaline turned around to glance at the boys. Antonio rode his donkey proudly, like a dark-eyed prince. She smiled at him, then turned to Rajad. Much to her chagrin, she saw large tears snaking down his cheeks.

"Rajad!" she exclaimed, pulling at Jack's arm to get his attention. "What is it? What's the matter?"

But the boy would say nothing to her. Without preamble, Jack lifted Rajad from the donkey's back and carried him out of the crowd to a quiet gallery where vines flowed down from an overhanging terrace. The boy clung to the man, his arms wrapped about Jack's neck while silent sobs shook his little frame.

Jack tightened his own arms about the lad, stroked his head, reassured him. His compassion, so tenderly displayed, moved Rosaline. She watched while her husband waylaid a sherbet seller on the street and bought orange flavored treats, giving one to Rajad in order to cheer him. When the boy was calm again, preoccupied with his ice, Jack returned to Rosaline's side and said, "I think the crisis has passed."

"What frightened him?" she asked.

"The streets, probably. No doubt they reminded him of those in Calcutta, where I found him."

His words reminded her of how little she knew of Jack Darlington, of how far he had traveled, the dangerous adventures he had experienced while she had led a sheltered, proper and spinsterish life in her father's house. She found herself glancing at him askance with a new sort of respect as they continued on their sightseeing tour, passing the perfume sellers, the henna sellers, the sellers of roses, lemons and cucumbers. The scents from the booths mingled with the odor of wool from the rug bazaar, where hundreds of gem-hued carpets hung from strung ropes, creating a maze of color through shadowy arcades. Vendors shouted out bargains while barefoot water sellers trotted up and down the avenues offering licorice water in red clay cups.

Noticing Rosaline's interest in the rugs, Jack paused and haggled shrewdly for a quarter hour over a beautiful carpet decorated with a pattern of vines and roses, coming away with it, laying it with satisfaction across the back of Rajad's donkey.

Rosaline realized how well Jack adapted to the customs, how fluently he spoke the language as he asked, *"Kam dee?"* for "How much is that?" Or, with a shake of his head, declared, *"Filoos ketir,"* for "Too much money." He was even more at ease in the chaos of brown skinned men and heavily draped ladies than he was in her father's Edinburgh drawing room, she thought with vague surprise. Except that his eyes continually hunted every corner, every shadowed archway, every pair of kohl rimmed lashes for a glimpse of a face—a face that had begun to haunt Rosaline, too.

When they returned to their villa, she bathed, then enjoyed a refreshment of mint flavored tea, oranges and almond cakes in her room. Jack entered, already dressed for their dinner outing in formal evening black and a starched white shirt, looking dark and wicked as he always did whenever he made up his mind to be charming.

"That's a never ending task, you know," he remarked, amused, nodding at her dust cloth. "The sand blows in from the desert day and night. Along with the fleas."

"Fleas won't be allowed to enter this house," Rosaline declared. "And the dust won't get the best of me either."

Jack observed her with humor as she continued to tidy her bottles of scent. She had already washed and coiled her hair and the braid was adorned with a coronet of silk roses and ribbons. He could smell the heliotrope she wore; it drifted from her floral dressing robe.

Making his way to the clothes press, an old French piece that had come with the house, he riffled through her gowns, found the one she had made from his gift of green silk and tossed it across the bed. "Wear this tonight," he said.

Gathering it up, Rosaline paused, for the gown was daring in its cut. But, she had saved it for a special occasion, and smiling in anticipation, nodded. "Very well, I'll wear it if you like. The quality of the silk should make all those London embassy wives that you hope to impress more than a little envious."

"Not too envious, I hope. We want them to invite us back."

"Don't worry. I'll make certain of that."

He grinned. "You don't lack confidence."

"I've been entertaining noblemen and their families since I

was thirteen. Why should I be daunted by a few old matrons with gout and outdated gowns?''

"Rosaline," Jack said with pretended shock. "I believe you're growing cynical."

She had the grace to look shamefaced, but needled him. "No doubt it's the company I've been keeping lately. Now, shall I dress?" She hesitated, waiting for Jack to leave the room and give her privacy.

"By all means. Dress." But he didn't leave, only took up the glass of brandy he had left on her vanity, raised it to her with a twinkle in his eye, and roamed out onto the terrace. Gazing out over the sea of minarets, he sipped wordlessly.

Uncomfortable with him nearby, Rosaline turned her back modestly and slid out of her dressing robe, then slipped the green gown over her corset, drawers, and white silk stockings. The garment was the new draped style with a bustle, the underskirt gold and trimmed in black lace, the hem festooned with silk rosettes. Rosaline had never bared her shoulders before and experienced a pang of self-consciousness. Hurriedly, she fastened the concealed hooks down the front and pivoted to study herself in the mirror.

Jack turned from the terrace just as she tugged at the neckline of the gown. When he grinned, she scowled, then fumbled in her jewel casket for the string of pearls her father had given her.

"I'm surprised you haven't hired yourself a lady's maid," her husband commented casually, his hands cool and impersonal on her neck as he moved to help her with the necklace. His gaze rested on her shoulders, which were rounded and smooth above the drape of silk.

Such scrutiny made Rosaline nervous. She stammered, "I-I've never kept a lady's maid."

"Really? Why not?"

"I suppose it's that I prefer to do things myself."

"Self-sufficient, as always." Jack straightened the pearls,

then roamed to an arm chair and eased down, leaning back to watch her put the final touches on her hair.

"I must say," Rosaline said, wanting to distract him from studying her, feeling more plain than ever when his worldly, measuring eyes roved over her face and figure. "I thought to find Cairo more unsettled than it is. Except for the soldiers we saw handcuffing that man on the street, I've seen nothing to indicate unrest."

"There's turmoil enough at the government level, believe me," Jack replied, swirling the brandy in his glass. "If one could even call it a government."

"Tell me about this rebel everyone calls Arabi. I've heard that he and his army banished Egypt's real leader—the khedive."

Jack reached to pick up a volume of poetry she had been reading, and idly riffled the pages. "Arabi forced him out without too much trouble. The khedive was a very weak leader, you see. So weak that Britain would desperately like to help put him back upon the throne."

"Why?"

"Because he makes a great puppet for our Parliament members to play with."

Rosaline selected a pair of pearl earrings from her case and screwed them on. "But didn't the khedive borrow vast sums of money and put Egypt terribly in debt?"

"Yes. And therein lies the problem. He borrowed the money from England, you see—from financiers like the Rothschilds who are now growing very nervous over their investments here. If Arabi's military rule continues, they may never see a shilling paid back."

"So what will happen, do you think?"

"I suspect that England, pushed by her richest citizens, will try and see Arabi defeated and the khedive returned to power—quietly, if possible," Jack added, stretching out his legs. "The trouble is, the natives here like Arabi. He's reported to be quite dashing."

Rosaline opened a drawer and selected gloves and a colorful fan of hand painted gauze. "Does your embassy maintain any sort of relationship with the fellow?"

"Hardly. The British government considers him little more than a brigand."

"So if the embassy has nothing to do with him and the khedive has been banished, what are your duties here as an attaché?" she asked.

Jack smiled insolently. "I'm simply to make myself socially agreeable at the embassy dinners and to amuse myself however I wish—decorously of course."

Rosaline waved a hand at his facetiousness. "Jack, be serious. You're surely here to do something more important than *amuse* yourself."

"No, it seems I'm not. Amazing, isn't it? I have no duties— at least not for the time being. The embassy staff are simply to be a presence here, a reminder to Arabi that we're watching him and thinking about our position."

"That sounds easy enough."

"For some men, perhaps. But I'll doubtless find it tedious before long. That's why I'm relying on you, my dear Rosaline," he said, coming up behind her again. "I'll need you to perform social pleasantries for me—host dinners, and entertain the gossipy wives of my supervisors who will try to ferret out every detail about my less than sterling character. Yes, I fear you shall have to put in a good word for your low born husband who will—inadvertently of course—be a bit rough around the edges now and then at balls and dinners. I'm sure you can convince them all that I'm a most respectable gentleman."

Rosaline paused and said, "I'll do my best. But what will you be doing while I'm complimenting you, Jack Darlington?"

He lifted an indolent shoulder. "Sauntering in and out, making my required appearances." His voice grew serious all at once. "I'm ambitious, Rosaline, as I told you. I'll do everything required of me in order to succeed."

She turned and gave him a searching look. "What do you really want for yourself, Jack?"

For a moment, he didn't reply, considering his answer. "I suppose I wouldn't mind being promoted. Wouldn't mind becoming the new British consul."

Rosaline regarded her husband's expression via the mirror. She suspected, not for the first time, that Jack Darlington's ambitions were not as casual as he made them out to be, but a driving, burning necessity.

Taking up her fan, she slipped the braided cord over her wrist and lowered her eyes, concealing a sudden, unexpected hurt. Jack had married her for no other reason than to advance his career. He intended to use her to accomplish his aspirations, and knew that she, with her inbred, dutiful good grace, would agree to be used without complaint.

Well then, she thought, smothering the hurt, she would help Jack Darlington climb the ladder he had chosen to climb. She would do what she could because, in spite of everything, she wanted him to succeed. They were bound together, after all. Husband and wife. Never mind her feelings. She was going to have to take them in hand before they caused her any more disappointment.

Her husband, so tall and formidable in his black silk and chevoit, took her hand, his fingers hard and resolved. He regarded her, seemed to read her thoughts, and with a new comradery in his tone, asked, "Well, Mrs. Darlington, shall we go and face the lions?"

"Why not?" she said, her chin set at its determined angle. "I'm certainly not cowed by any of them."

But for a moment, Rosaline felt her reserve slip. Jack expected much of her, she knew. And yet, as she studied his chiseled jaw, his merry eyes, Rosaline realized she was quite happy to be Jack Darlington's wife. Quite proud.

On impulse, she admitted, "I'll have many compliments to pay you tonight, Jack. And I'm sure the ladies will have no trouble at all believing every one of them."

"And the gentlemen?"

She tapped his arm in a playful gesture. "I shall tell them how much you admire them all, of course."

Jack grinned broadly. Then he kissed her—in gratitude of course, she thought—if not in passion.

Chapter Eleven

The dinner was no different than any dinner given by a high ranking host and hostess in England, the fashions being almost the same as those in a London dining room. The menu was a delectable twelve-course ritual, and every custom of genteel society was followed to the letter beneath the watchful eyes of Lady Duff-Sarton, whose Cairo home was filled with furnishings shipped from England. There were Sheraton sideboards, Chippendale tables, lemon damask sofas, Wedgwood plates, and windows so elaborately draped in velvet and lace that they might have been shutting out a London fog instead of a clear Egyptian night.

Twenty guests attended, all fitting comfortably around the long tables, the gentlemen's pocketwatches and mother-of-pearl buttons gleaming alongside the ladies' combs, heirloom jewelry, and silver lace. Champagne flowed freely along with French wines that complimented the cheese souffle, lobster and heavy cream sauces.

"I envy you," Rosaline murmured to Jack just after they entered the sumptuous villa and found ten pairs of female eyes assessing them.

"Why?" he said under his breath.

"Because your task is easier than mine. All you have to do is smile the right way at those old harridans and they're yours. I can tell by looking at them. I shall have to work much harder for their approval."

And yet she had no real trouble making a good impression. Rosaline knew precisely how much to eat and how much to leave on her plate, how to delicately consume the roast duck, wielding knife and fork as deftly as she wielded her gauze fan. She knew what topics of conversation to either introduce or avoid, having acted, as she had told Jack, as hostess to her father's formal diplomatic dinners.

Since her husband had explained—wryly or not—that his position of attaché required nothing more than an observance of social pleasantries, Rosaline set out to be socially pleasant, speaking of travel and poetry. It was as if the world outside the *faux* English dining room did not exist, as if a revolutionary army and a leader called Arabi Bey were no more than characters in a discarded book. She glanced often across the table at Jack, who, with great skill and more than one flashing, devilish grin, flattered the matron in black silk seated to his left. Once, catching Rosaline's glance, he winked across at her; he was rogue who possessed not one ounce of sincerity toward such pretentious people, a man who condescended to play their games because he wanted something from them—ironically, to be a member of their ranks. At some point in his life, had he felt himself cheated by them? Rosaline wondered.

Later, while the gentlemen enjoyed brandy and cigars, Lady Duff-Sarton led the ladies into her pale lemon drawing room and spoke to Rosaline.

"How are you finding Cairo, Mrs. Darlington? Settling in nicely?"

"Yes, thank you."

"The heat isn't bothering you?" The lady, who felt it her job to know everything about everybody connected with the embassy, glanced significantly at Rosaline's mid-section.

"Not yet," Rosaline answered with a sudden flush, understanding the woman's train of thought, not doubting that Lady Duff-Sarton had been as impressed with Jack's virility as all the other women.

The lady's sharp eyes, bred to notice every detail of appearance, every shortcoming, swept over Rosaline's gown and string of pearls, and, finding them acceptable if not outstanding, smiled. "I remember your mother, Rosaline. Such a kind woman, with eyes just like yours. She played the pianoforte beautifully, as I recall. Of course, she had the hands for it— long and slender—somewhat like yours. Your husband must have your portrait painted, you know. Brides have a glow in the first year of marriage that should always be captured on canvas."

The subject of portrait painting was not a comfortable one for Rosaline, bringing back memories of a conservatory, red petals, and a young, passionate artist. But she didn't let so much as a hint of her thoughts show, smiling cordially in agreement. She had already taken measure of her hostess and knew what was expected.

Lady Duff-Sarton leaned forward in her chair in order to get a view of the dining room, where the gentlemen sat sipping brandy and listening to Jack relate, with obvious wit, some amusing tale. "I must tell you, Mrs. Darlington," the matron said in a conspiratorial, good-natured whisper, "your husband has certainly caused a stir among the ladies here."

At first, Rosaline feared Jack had been too bold with his compliments, had allowed his eyes to tarry too long on a pair of bare powdered shoulders or a neatly corsetted waist. Prepared to defend him, she opened her mouth to reply, but it seemed her maddeningly attractive husband needed no defense, for Lady Duff-Sarton continued. "I must say, it's not often one sees a man with looks like that and a wit to match. You had better hold tight to him, my dear." She laughed throatily, put a hand on Rosaline's arm, teasing by all appearances, but really quite serious.

Rosaline's confidence wavered. Did her hostess mean to
suggest that she was plain? Did she doubt Rosaline's ability
to keep a man with Jack's charm interested in the marital bed?
The old nag. Rosaline straightened her spine and for her own
benefit as well as Jack's turned these thoughts aside. She knew
that embassy wives loved to gossip more than anything, felt
it their supreme duty to learn everything they could about
newcomers and whisper their knowledge around the afternoon
tea table. Very well. Rosaline would invent the story she wanted
told.

"Jack is very devoted to me," she said shyly, affecting the
air of an innocent. "We had a whirlwind courtship that lasted—
I'm embarrassed to say—only a few weeks. He's so terribly
charming and persuasive. Why, before I could catch my breath,
the rogue had convinced me that I must shorten our engagement
and marry him immediately."

Lady Duff-Sarton nodded sagely, her gray hair bobbing at
her neck. "Charm and persuasiveness make for a good husband,
as well as a diplomat. No doubt that is why the Foreign Office
hand-picked Mr. Darlington for this post in Cairo."

"I am sure of it," Rosaline said with a sweet smile, then
lowered her head as if to conceal a bride's blush. "Jack has a
rare talent for always knowing just what to say and when to
say it, especially in—" she broke off as if appalled at herself
for a nearly immodest blunder. "Forgive me if I seem indis-
creet . . ."

"Not at all, dear." The lady leaned toward Rosaline as if
hoping to hear her elaborate, then disappointed, directed a
disgruntled frown at her own overweight mate, whom she could
just glimpse through the door as he sat opposite Jack at the
table stuffing pistachio nuts in his mouth. "A wife should be
proud of her husband's attributes. And *your* husband, Mrs.
Darlington," she added in an almost resentful tone, "has no
lack of those."

"I'm so glad you think so, Lady Duff-Sarton. By the way,
Jack and I will be hosting a dinner ourselves soon—our first

since arriving here. I wonder if I might beg your advice concerning the menu—perhaps over tea some afternoon?''

''Why, of course, dear,'' came the satisfied reply. ''I make it my policy to take young brides new to Cairo under my wing. There's so much one must learn about entertaining the upper echelon, after all, and it would be a shame to get off on the wrong foot.''

''You're so gracious to understand.'' Knowing that she had successfully paved the way for a future ally should Jack ever have need of one, Rosaline smiled.

Indeed, her husband was vastly pleased that night.

Later, when they were alone in the bedchamber, Rosaline allowed Jack to persuade her to sip a glass of champagne in celebration of their successful first social evening together. She sat at her vanity, still dressed in the green gown. Jack stood behind her with his glass in hand, the light gleaming off the crystal rim, off the blackness of his hair as he lazily, with supreme satisfaction, recounted the details of the dinner.

By the glow of candlelight, she contemplated the attributes the other women must have earlier seen and admired. She studied every feature of Jack's face and form with as much objectivity as she could muster, and then, having assessed him, felt a trifle overwhelmed that she wore his wedding ring.

''You seemed in your element,'' he remarked. ''Did you enjoy yourself?''

''As a matter of fact, I did. I never thought of social occasions as particularly challenging before I met you.''

''You didn't tire yourself, did you?'' he asked, teasing.

''Actually I felt quite at home amongst them. Lady Duff-Sarton even spoke well of my mother.'' Rosaline lifted her lashes to meet the blue eyes reflected in the mirror, and her voice softened as she added, ''And of you.''

''Indeed? Well, I was quite proud of you, Rosaline,'' he said, his tone altering from light to serious. "There's no question that you're the sort of woman who can help a man."

When she lowered her head, Jack's gaze moved to her hair, to the pearl drops in her ears, then traveled slowly downward. "You have lovely shoulders, by the way," he commented, his voice deep, more than a little suggestive. "You should show them off more often."

Rosaline put a modest hand across her collarbone as if to cover herself, then, fearing she had been too obvious, acted as if she had only meant to unclasp her necklace.

"My pearls!" she exclaimed, finding the double strand gone. "Oh dear . . . have you seen them, Jack? I know they were around my neck only a moment ago. I remember noticing them when I sat down at the mirror."

"Your pearls, did you say?"

"Yes. My father gave them to me." She bent down to search the floor. "He bought them on my sixteenth birthday," she went on, distracted.

Jack held out his hand, waited until she straightened again, and with maddening innocence, asked, "These pearls, do you mean?"

Rosaline saw them dangling from his hand, his thumb and forefinger idly stroking each bead. For a few seconds, she stared at them in his palm. He seemed to be unconsciously evaluating the texture and weight of the pearls—as if he knew, simply by the casual touch, the difference between good and poor quality.

"Jack!"

With a rakish grin, he reached out and draped the lustrous strings across her shoulders, then leaned, very leisurely, to kiss the hollow beneath her ear.

Heady with champagne, softened by his charm, lured by his physique, Rosaline allowed her husband the liberty, wanting all at once to experience pleasure in his arms, to feel like a real wife. She leaned back against his body, forced herself to melt into him as the scent of jasmine floated in from the dark but warm terrace.

As the moments glided on and Jack's touch grew more intimate, Rosaline concentrated on nothing but his hands as he reached to unhook her gown, as he smoothly released the strings of her corset, freed the tabs of her white ruffled drawers, the garters of her stockings. And a moment later, when Jack pulled her to face him, his talented fingers trailed over the curves beneath her chemise and encountered the silver locket hanging there. He murmured no jealous words, nor did his touch become any less leisured, any less evocative than before.

He seemed determined to enjoy the sensual play between them, just as he had enjoyed the whole evening, including the French wines, and the sparkling social intercourse that he had helped manipulate to his own advantage. And Rosaline knew that Jack wanted her to enjoy the act, too, every bit as much as he intended to enjoy it, with no complicated entanglement of heart or mind.

Jack drew her to the bed, laid her down, and in an unhasty fashion, removed his own clothes—jacket, shirt, waistcoat, trousers—giving Rosaline an opportunity to peruse the attributes of his now roused body. Openly, for the first time, she allowed herself the liberty.

And then, as Jack made love to her, his palms running the length of her form, his mouth following the same path, Rosaline relaxed, contributing little to the process in her ignorance, but showing Jack her willingness. Just for a few moments, she wanted to be free, satiated. As if in a half-dream, she heard Jack's excited breaths, heard the soft friction of their intertwined limbs, the tender sound of his kisses, then the haunting, not-so-distant voice of a woman singing in the night.

Jack seemed to hear it too, for he paused, listened for several seconds before dipping his head once again to savor the warmth of Rosaline's neck. And although Rosaline willed her body to reach a culmination, her body would not, or could not comply, thwarting the desire that seemed to hover so close, with such trembling, expectant hope.

Or perhaps it was not her body's fault at all, Rosaline thought, but something in her own mind that prevented the joy, that resisted the release that Jack's body was so amply skilled to give. It was the part of her mind that still belonged to David, that still resented Jack's love for Julie.

Rosaline almost wept in disappointment, almost clutched the breadth of Jack Darlington's shoulders and voiced her frustration. Jack loved another, but was still able to find physical satisfaction with her. Why couldn't she do the same? He had tried his best to pleasure her, she knew. She wondered if he blamed himself; she hoped he didn't.

Unable to voice her thoughts, unable to explain such fragile and intimate feelings, Rosaline remained mute beside him.

Jack sighed and rolled to face her. He realized his wife's frustration; he was experienced enough to understand the meaning of her frenzied straining and empty moans. But he did not allow her to turn her back against him; instead he drew her into his arms and held her until the two of them quietly breathed together, unaccustomed to the familiarity, thinking similar thoughts, still strangers and yet bound by a marriage that both needed for different reasons.

"There will be other nights, you know," he told her finally in a low, gentle voice.

"Yes," she breathed.

"And other ways."

She nodded as the sounds of the strange city drifted in through the open terrace doors. She thought unwillingly of Lady Duff-Sarton's remarks, and wondered how long she could keep Jack Darlington interested in this net-hung bed, keep him interested in holding a woman who couldn't properly respond to him.

When she came down the next morning dressed in her cheeriest gown of sprigged muslin, she found Jack had ordered breakfast served in the courtyard. A table sat under the pink mimosas laden with all sorts of tempting foods.

There was sweet raisin bread drizzled with honey butter, as

well as figs, orange wedges, roasted lamb, and sugared dates, along with black coffee served from a silver samovar. The fountain splashed melodiously in its blue tiled basin and a white stork perched beside it, spreading graceful wings. Best of all— almost miraculously—she saw Antonio and Rajad dressed and seated at the table, their hair slicked into place, their faces carefully arranged as if Jack had threatened them with a thrashing if they behaved any way but as little gentlemen.

Jack himself was attired for a day of business in gray jacket and trousers, and when Rosaline entered the courtyard, he rose to greet her. "How do you like my picnic?" he asked.

"It's delightful, Jack. And very civilized." Glancing at the two boys in their gray Eton suits with the starched turndown collars she had bought in London, she whispered, *"They* are very civilized. What did you do?"

"Put the fear of God into them. I can be a tyrant when necessary. And they're going to school today," he said more loudly, pinning Antonio with a hard stare. "Rajad has copied out a poem for you. He said you taught it to him, made him memorize the spelling of the words aboard ship."

"See?" the boy said shyly, holding up a half crumpled paper.

Rosaline examined the effort. "Beautiful work. I'm sure your new headmaster will be most impressed."

The Darlington family enjoyed a lovely breakfast after that, and as Rosaline sampled the delicacies prepared by the Greek cook she had interviewed herself, she let her eyes sweep around the table, almost holding her breath as she realized that the four of them resembled any happily settled English clan. Though she had not yet had the opportunity to school Antonio in table etiquette, she noted with a private smile that Jack patiently corrected him each time he chewed noisily or slouched. Her husband also kept the conversation light and amusing, and when Rosaline's shawl slipped to the tiles, he bent to drape it about her shoulders.

And yet there was a look of guardedness in Jack's eyes today, she thought. The bright gleam of satisfaction he had worn home from the dinner was gone—chased away, no doubt, by what had happened between them in the darkness of last night.

After Hoseyn had been summoned to take the boys to school, Jack bade Rosaline goodbye. "I'll be at the embassy all day," he said, straightening his necktie in the vestibule. "There's trouble brewing, it seems."

"Trouble?"

"Yes. In Alexandria."

"Alexandria isn't far from Cairo," she said with concern. "What has happened?"

He shrugged. "A few of Arabi's followers are harassing the Europeans living there, threatening to burn their homes, run them out of town—that sort of thing. I suspect the embassy will take some sort of action shortly."

"Are we safe here?" Rosaline asked worriedly, thinking of the boys.

"For the time being. But remember what I told you. If you go out into the streets, take one of the houseboys as an escort."

"Of course, Jack."

Lance Cardew entered the courtyard, walked through the sunlight filtered through the palm leaves, and greeted them. His room was connected to a small book lined office and he spent most of his time either there or at the embassy offices, doing for Jack the tedious paperwork and reports required by the administration. "Are you ready to go, sir?" he asked Jack.

"Wait for me outside," Jack replied, turning back to Rosaline. Fishing about in his pocket, he produced a heavy gold bracelet. "I discovered this last night as we were leaving Lady Duff-Sarton's house. It was lying outside on the pavement, near the curb. Could it belong to one of the ladies who were at dinner, do you think?"

Rosaline took it from his fingers. "Why, yes. I believe I saw the wife of the undersecretary of state wearing it."

"Indeed? Then perhaps you would care to call on her this

morning and return it?'' Jack smiled and bent to touch his lips to her cheek. "Good day, Rosaline. I'll see you before dinner.''

He sauntered through the archway to join Cardew, leaving Rosaline to examine the bracelet with vague, unformed suspicion niggling at her memory. Strange that she didn't recall having seen Jack lean and pick up the piece of jewelry from the pavement last night as they departed. Odd that he hadn't immediately returned to Lady Duff-Sarton's house and left it with his hostess. The owner would have been most grateful, for the bracelet looked quite old, possibly an heirloom.

She dropped it in her pocket, stood listening for a moment to the tinkling of the fountain, watched as a mimosa blossom fell from the tree and landed in the water.

She remembered Jack's warm, clever hands last night as he produced her string of pearls from his pocket and draped them with a mischievous grin across the point of her shoulder. She recalled the scene in detail, going over it several times, putting a hand to her forehead as she thought. Why, she wondered, did the memory of such a playful, innocent gesture involving nothing more than a double string of pearls, plague her at all? And the acorns that had been lined upon the table at home in Orkney. . . .

Finally, telling herself she was fanciful, anxious over nothing, Rosaline went to plan the menu and inspect the kitchen stores.

Chapter Twelve

The young daughter of the undersecretary of state was thankful to the point of tears to have her bracelet returned that day, having slept poorly all night thinking that her great grandmother's heirloom had been lost to her forever.

"And my father will be so grateful too, knowing I shall not keep him up another night fretting about it. Did you say that your husband discovered the bracelet on the street? Please tell him that my father and I are greatly in his debt."

Rosaline smiled. Her young hostess could not have known that the smile was a rueful one prompted by Rosaline's realization of Jack's cleverness. "I'll tell him of your gratitude." Inventing an excuse to leave now that her mission had been accomplished, she set down her teacup and rose to go. But Honore Shapcott, obviously loathe to let her newfound friend escape, invited Rosaline to accompany her on a trip to the market. Rosaline hesitated, but only briefly. She felt a sudden yearning for a female friend, for a European companion in this hot, gold colored land so far from the green and mist of Scotland. Besides, she knew Jack would be pleased if she cultivated a friendship with the daughter of the undersecretary of state.

"I do so love the bazaar, don't you?" Honore said. She was a lovely girl with the silver blonde hair and china blue eyes so prized by Englishmen, the sort of girl whose dance card would never go unfilled, and who, had she stayed in London, would doubtless have received countless marriage offers. "I already have a whole trunkload of treasures from the bazaars to take back to England with me," she continued, looking a bit shame-faced. "Only, Keith says we won't be going back home for awhile."

"Keith?" Rosaline asked, stepping outside where Hoseyn awaited, raising her parasol against the sun.

"He's my betrothed."

"Oh? Is he with the embassy?"

Honore laughed. "Oh, no. I'm afraid Keith would never make a diplomat. He's a journalist for *The Times.*"

"The London newspaper? Really? I've never met a journalist before. You must bring him to dine at our house one evening so I can meet him."

"My father doesn't really approve of Keith, of course," Honore confided with a sigh. "In fact, he threatened to send me back home when Keith first proposed. But I argued that sending me back to London would only make me contrary. I told Father that I might even feel rebellious enough to elope with the first chap who drives a milk cart past."

Rosaline laughed. "I think Mr. Keith Grange had better be thankful he's managed to catch such a determined girl."

"Determined and jealous. I have forbidden him to go and watch those shameless Arabian dancing girls that so many European gentleman are inviting into their homes for entertainment. If he does, I'll break our engagement immediately, and I've told him so. Scandalous, those dancers are. Have you heard about them? Wearing practically nothing but veils, and beating tambourines against their thighs while they dance."

Rosaline smiled, then frowned, wondering if Jack had ever watched such a show.

The day was clear and warm. The ladies walked many blocks,

finally entering the Muskee of Cairo—the great native street packed with hawkers and exotic shops—escorted by Honore's servant and Hoseyn who, gesticulating wildly and shouting curses, cleared a path among the beggars.

Honore hastily dragged her skirts out of the way. "I am always a little afraid when I go into these streets," she whispered. "The men here stare at European women so rudely, and there is an air about them—oh, I don't know—a sort of dislike I can actually *feel.*"

Rosaline remembered Jack's warnings, but said reassuringly, "Even so, my husband says there is little crime here."

"That's because a person can be beaten half to death for nothing more than pilfering a pocketwatch. But white slavery still abounds." Honore shuddered even though the heat filtered through her parasol and touched her arms. "And then, there's that heathen rebel they call Arabi Bey. Who knows what sort of chaos *he'll* cause before it's over? My father told me that the Foreign Office plans to order him out of Egypt today."

"Arabi doesn't seem the sort of fellow who'd feel moved to oblige our Foreign Office."

"I'm afraid you're right. It's rumored that the Rothschilds have already offered the rascal L4,000 to simply disappear. He's a handsome devil, you know. I saw him riding his horse through the streets once, waving to the crowds. Yes, tension will doubtless be high tonight after Britain orders him to leave. That's why I wanted to get my shopping done this afternoon. It may not be safe to go out tomorrow."

Water sellers in tarbooshes accosted the ladies at every turn, thrusting out brimming clay cups. The ladies' skirts blended with the sea of colorful *kuftans* worn by native men, and occasionally a group of veiled women in black garments glided past, their eyes cast down, meeting the gaze of no one. To combat the dust, which rose in gritty clouds from sandaled feet and trotting hooves, the streets were watered down, and servants came out to sweep the stoops of shadowed, elegant villas, leaving piles of dust which would be carried away in carts.

Honore stopped at a booth which sold silver jewelry and amber, ignoring the toothless agent who bowed and lavished praise upon her, saying, ''O, Princess from Europe! Good day! These jewels are fit for a jin.''

Rosaline's attention was captured not by the baubles, but by the adjoining booth, where small wooden cages displayed assorted parakeets and doves.

''The Egyptians consider the dove a sort of sacred bird,'' Honore commented, coming to stand beside Rosaline. ''It's said Mohammed kept them as pets. All around the city you'll see dovecotes fashioned like miniature royal parapets—they're roosting places for the birds.'' Honore made a grimace of distaste and whispered, ''Believe it or not, even though they're sacred, the doves are sold for food. I'm told some natives eat them once or twice a day.''

''Eat them?'' Rosaline looked in horror at the gentle doves, then the bright flapping and squawking parakeets packed in the cages with them. Her skirts stirred feathers on the ground as she leaned closer to inspect the birds, and her interest prompted the stall keeper to begin his irksome sales pitch. Discreetly she counted the piastres in her velvet reticule, then asked the man, ''How much for the lot of birds?''

Honore's jaw dropped. The stall keeper stared at her as if he hadn't heard correctly. Hoseyn stepped forward, obviously feeling it his duty to interfere, but Rosaline straightened her posture and repeated herself succinctly. ''I asked how much for the lot—for all of the birds.''

''All? Oh, my lady, only two hundred piastres!'' the stall keeper cried. ''Birds fit for a sultan!''

''Too much money,'' she said automatically with a stern expression, having learned through Jack that haggling was a long and necessary process in Cairo. He had also warned her that every stall keeper considered cheating a fine art. And indeed, after a quarter hour of bartering in the hot sun, having walked away twice as if in earnest, only to be drawn back again, Rosaline purchased two dozen assorted birds to be delivered later to her address.

"Whatever will you *do* with them all?" Honore asked, squinting in her nearsighted way at the crude reed cages. "Good heavens, you're not going to *eat* them?"

Rosaline looked horrified. "Of course not. They'll be pets." She glanced at Honore, who was wilting in the heat. "Honore, you're as pale as a ghost. Are you well?"

"Drooping. I'm quite ready to return home and have tea. The heat and flies are becoming a terrible nuisance, and my feet ache." She looked at Rosaline fondly. "But I can't wait to tell Father how you haggled with the shopkeeper and bought two dozen birds for practically nothing. I shall have to take you with me every time I shop."

The woman exchanged fond goodbyes, parted, and with Hoseyn close beside her, Rosaline began a leisurely walk home, stopping here and there to admire a pair of earrings or an inlaid box, drinking in the whole spice scented world, the galleries, the mosques with their bright green tiles. She strolled through an arcade of perfume sellers, her parasol held high. Several vendors rushed forward, thrust bottles of scent beneath her nose, and implored her in Arabic, then French, then in any other language they knew to buy their wares. She shook her head, pushed away the tempting vials of sandalwood and musk, then forged on.

As she walked she began to notice groups of men milling about in restless knots, some speaking heatedly. A peculiar excitement, a tension, seemed to stretch itself upon the air all at once, and discomfitted, Rosaline increased her pace. The ancient red and white striped buildings suddenly took on a threatening air, and the lattices, usually concealing nothing but shy, veiled faces gazing wistfully at the world, seemed to hide malicious eyes. There seemed a change in mood throughout the crowd, a rippling of emotion that affected even the horses with their silk-clad riders.

Hoseyn seemed to sense it too, and the young man attempted

to clear a straighter path through the jostling mass of people for Rosaline, who was beginning to earn sullen, slanted glances and pointed stares. Disquieted, she began to trot along, her eyes searching for the rented villa, for any familiar sight. She began to wish that she had started for home earlier.

She thought she heard Jack's voice penetrate the din of the shifting throng.

"Rosaline! Rosaline!"

"Jack!" she cried, her alarm increasing, her breath becoming shallow.

She caught sight of him as he shoved aside a man who barred his way. Her husband appeared disheveled and slightly out of breath, as if he had run a great distance to find her, and his eyes were alertly watching the movements of the crowd.

Never having seen Jack even mildly perturbed before, Rosaline felt her own trepidation double. Damp, odiferous bodies pressed on all sides of them and the faces seemed to snarl at her as Jack dragged her forward by the waist. One or two Egyptians shouted at their backs, hurling a series of guttural Arabic words Rosaline couldn't understand. Grateful for Jack's hard, sure grip, she asked, "What is it, Jack? What's happening? What are they yelling?"

"They're cursing us."

"Wh . . ." Rosaline never completed the word, for a hand snaked out suddenly and yanked her parasol from her grip, while another hand tore at the flowered hat she wore. She screamed, and before she could veer out of the way, a man spat upon her skirts.

Jack released her long enough to deliver a punishing blow to the offender's jaw, and when retaliatory hands attempted to seize him, he jerked Rosaline forward, throwing punches along the way, eluding any who tried to throttle him.

When he and Rosaline were only a few yards from the carved cedar door of their villa, Jack shouted at Hoseyn to escort Rosaline inside. Before he could get over the threshold himself, three turbanned men from the crowd surrounded him, pounced and brought him down.

Rosaline screamed, battling Hoseyn as he attempted to force her inside the house, watching as Jack fought with savage skill, disappearing amid the melee even as he drew a revolver from his coat.

He fired. One attacker fell. The others froze, then ran in all directions. A clatter of hooves echoed off the buildings and Rosaline, standing upon the stoop in terror, saw a company of mounted Egyptian soldiers canter into the square. They yelled orders at the maddened crowd and aimed their guns at those who defaced the European residences. Women screamed in fright as the soldiers drew sabres to subdue the riotous destruction. Camels and mules ran loose in panic, overturning displays of melons, fruits and brass, the sounds of pots and bells crashing to the earth. The animals galloped around the smashed pots of hibiscus decorating the villa doorsteps, and looters scrambled to get out of the way as the army galloped through, issuing orders, subduing the insurrection.

Jack backed toward Rosaline, his revolver ready to target any molester who would dare come forward, the crumpled body of his victim evidence of his earnestness. His jacket hung off one shoulder and Rosaline saw that his lip bled.

"Jack!" she cried, running forward. "Are you wounded?"

"No. But you don't happen to be in possession of a handkerchief, do you? Mine seems to have disappeared along with my pocketwatch."

Rosaline fumbled in her pocket and, finding the scrap of silken lace, handed it over. "What was this all about, Jack?" she asked. "What prompted it? Why, one minute I was strolling home from a morning of shopping with only the perfume sellers paying any attention to me, and the next minute I felt as if I had every eye in all of Cairo fastened upon my face."

Before he answered, Jack scanned the streets, which stood almost empty now except for the soldiers who sat astride their horses with their pistols in hand. Vendors timidly stepped forward to collect scattered wares, dragomen rounded up donkeys, caravan agents beat stubborn camels into place so cargoes could be unloaded at shop doors. Gradually servants crept out of the neighboring European houses to inspect the damage, righting overturned vases of flowers. The atmosphere grew normal again, the skies as blue as they had been an hour past, the palm trees nodding in a lazy breeze.

"This morning the British government demanded that Arabi leave Egypt," Jack explained, answering Rosaline's question. "The people here didn't take kindly to the order. They don't think England has a right to tell their rebel leader what to do."

"One can scarcely blame them," Rosaline admitted. "Will Arabi go?"

Jack gave a short laugh. "I doubt it. Oddly enough, it was his army you saw a few minutes ago quelling the disturbance in order to protect Europeans."

"*Arabi's* army? Why would Arabi command his army to protect us when we're the ones who oppose him?"

Jack shrugged. "Perhaps as a reminder to Britain that he's the one in charge here and that he can either keep control or allow havoc, depending upon how charitable he feels."

They went inside, each to their own rooms where they bathed and dined quietly together. Still restless but tired from the day's activities, they sat on the terrace where a servant brought them wine. Rosaline did not want to speak of the horrible day, but of ordinary family matters. Sitting beside Jack in a wicker chair, looking down at the now calm street just touched by twilight, Rosaline felt a comfortable intimacy with Jack.

"You are doing very well with Antonio," she commented, looking askance at her husband. "I believe you are learning patience."

"Thank you, my dear," he said dryly, appreciating her compliment nonetheless.

"One could look at the two of you together and imagine Antonio as your natural born son."

He turned the wine glass in his hand and lowered his eyes.

"Would you like to have children, Rosaline, children of your own?"

Of course she would. Jack's children. But she wondered if her contrary body would cooperate.

"You hesitate," he said.

"I didn't mean to, I . . ." But before Rosaline could finish, her attention was captured by a procession in the streets. Gaily dressed musicians with pipes and tambourines headed a group of people, followed by finely garbed Egyptians surrounded by turbanned servants wearing red slippers and wide copper bracelets. In the center of the parade, a veiled woman in voluminous red robes glided along, four servants holding a canopy of scarlet silk above her head, which sparkled with an intricately carved diadem of gold.

"It's a wedding procession," Jack commented, noting Rosaline's interest. "The bride is the lady in red and the well-wishers are trailing behind."

Rosaline watched, intrigued, thinking of the enthralling contrasts of Cairo. She and Jack stood up and watched together, leaning over the rail as the bridal throng passed, its members dancing and singing with merry abandon. All at once, Rosaline noticed a figure standing motionless across the street, a feminine figure swathed in the native dress of white veil and black robes. Moslem women did not go alone on the streets; nor did they linger anywhere in public, moving always like shy, skittish specters toward their destinations, never pausing lest they call unseemly attention to themselves. But this woman was staring at them fixedly, standing on tiptoe, Rosaline realized, as if she were trying to catch a glimpse of Jack. More oddly still, the woman pulled aside her veil with a slender hand to reveal her face, a gesture forbidden in public. Her face was enchanting, Rosaline noted, her eyes slanted, exotic and brown.

"Jack," Rosaline breathed with a frown, for he was sipping his wine. "Look there—at the woman on the other side of the street. She's staring at us strangely."

Jack peered past the line of merrymakers while their cymbals and tambourines clashed. Then, when his gaze fastened upon the face of the lady, his body tensed. For several seconds he remained riveted, his eyes focused intently on the small, still figure. The woman did not see him look at her, and turned to go. He started forward, ran headlong down the wrought-iron steps, his hand upraised, his cry hoarse. *"Julie! Julie!"*

Rosaline watched him dart across the street, interrupt the line of the wedding procession, then disappear from her line of view. She waited, afraid, feeling ill, but an hour passed and still he did not return. She ordered more wine and, glass in hand, proceeded downstairs and paced the length of the blue tiled parlor with its Rabat wool rugs, its carved screens and high beamed ceilings. The chime of the ormolu clock caused her to start, and she crossed to the open window for the dozent time, peering through the darkness, searching the dusty foreign streets for the sight of a tall man in European dress.

Had he found her? Were they embracing in some shadowy arcade, Jack unable to let Julie go now that he had found her again?

Unable to settle, unable to sit down, Rosaline wandered the house. Jack's quiet entry startled her, caused her body to stiffen as he walked into the room. He looked dreadful, his eyes weary and his expression remote. He had not found Julie, she realized, he had been unable to call her back after her ghostly vanishing.

What should she say to him? What could she say that would not betray her pain? "Here's tea," she murmured, more cooly than she intended. With a wave of her hand, she indicated the silver samovar and cups.

"Thank you." He answered so quietly, so absently, that Rosaline was surprised he had even heard her words at all.

Jack made no move to accept the tea she poured for him, going instead to the sideboard and sloshing whiskey into a glass, downing it in one quick gulp.

Rosaline didn't know how to break the stretching gap that seemed to grow by the second between them. And yet, she was no coward, and in spite of her hurt and the delicate subject of

Jack's disappointment, she would not leave him alone. Not just yet. She would not run from the silence, nor would she avoid the question that must be asked and answered.

Jack hadn't yet looked at her, but leaned with his hands braced upon the sideboard, his eyes staring at the whiskey yet surely seeing something far more significant, far more dear than the crystal decanter and gold brown liquid. Rosaline wondered if her husband had forgotten her presence, forgotten her altogether.

After a few minutes he bestirred himself and went to sit down in a chair, leaned his head back and, for a second or two, closed his eyes.

And in that small, infinitesimal interim of time, Rosaline pitied him. She hated to feel pity for him, for his pain, but she did. Walking forward quietly, she took up the decanter and poured him another glass. He fixed his eyes upon her face for the first time, almost as if he were surprised to find her there at all. Bravely, she asked, "Was it Julie, then?"

Jack winced at the directness of her question. Then he swallowed. His gaze shifted to the window and after long moments he replied, "There are times when I think she no longer lives. That she no longer exists anywhere at all except in my own mind."

Rosaline sensed he had just revealed a great, inward part of himself, and because she always respected candor in anyone—especially when it was difficult to deliver—she answered in a soft tone. "But . . . I saw her, too."

"Did you?" He grimaced slightly and drank the whiskey. "It could have been anyone," he said, his voice deep from the drink. "Anyone at all."

And although Rosaline was grateful to hear the words, she suspected he didn't really believe them. "Will you tell me now? Will you tell me about her, Jack?"

"No, Rosaline. I won't."

But she was relieved, nonetheless, when he walked forward and took hold of her hand—in thankfulness perhaps for her intuitive understanding—and pressed it to his lips. "There may be a time to tell you," he said, "in the future. But not now, not tonight."

"I'm not sure that's wise, Jack."

But he would not be persuaded. His mouth firmed and he said, "I must change and go out again, Rosaline. It may be very late when I return. There's no need to wait up for me. Will you be all right here with only the servants about?"

She nodded, tried to smile, and wished suddenly that Jack would stay, that he would keep holding her hand just as he was now. "Yes," she said instead with her breath constricted. "Yes, I'll manage fine, Jack. Just fine."

"As you always do." Her husband smiled briefly and pressed her hand again, one final time, but Rosaline sensed his thoughts were already far from her.

And she sensed too that her relationship, her budding intimacy with Jack Darlington, had somehow just frozen itself, like a flower that had tried to blossom too soon, too imprudently, in early spring. And she sensed something else as well. With certainty. She had seen Julie.

Chapter Thirteen

Early the next morning, Rosaline stood with Jack in the little cedar beamed vestibule with its array of beaten copper vases and brass sconces. Jack, after having been home only long enough to bathe, change, and eat breakfast with her, was on his way back to the embassy, and paused at the door while Rosaline handed him his hat. She studied him, a tall, powerful man in well-cut clothes, a man to be reckoned with, a man who could hold his own inside the embassy offices as well as out. She tried to smother her wifely pride, reaching out to smooth his lapel. By mutual but unspoken agreement, the two of them pretended that nothing had happened on the street last night, that no shadowy figure had been seen or frantically pursued.

Jack gave her a smile. Then, finishing the conversation they had earlier begun, said soberly, "Arabi has refused to leave Egypt as he was ordered by our embassy—which should come as no surprise to anyone."

Rosaline watched him settle his hat upon his head. She frowned in consternation and asked, "So what will happen now?"

"The next move will be ours. At the embassy meeting last night, there were rumblings about the British government taking military action against Arabi in spite of the fact that he called in his army yesterday to quell the riot against the Europeans." He raised a brow. "Which you and I experienced firsthand. That little act of power was Arabi's gesture of good will toward us all—tongue in cheek, of course."

"You said military action," Rosaline repeated worriedly. "Do you mean British troops might be sent in to take control of Egypt simply because the Rothschilds are concerned about their investments in this country?"

Jack's lips curved. "Something like that."

"That's sheer madness."

"No. Just reality, Rosaline. The world is driven by greed." He bade her goodbye and stepped out the door, only to be accosted by the toothless bird seller from the bazaar. The old man had arrived with cages of birds tied on the back of a sway-backed donkey. Greeting Rosaline as if she were a Nile queen who had deigned to patronize his humble business, he bowed low, than began to unload the flapping, squawking merchandise which he placed with pride just inches from Jack's well-shod feet.

Jack raised his brows, cocked his head, and considered the assorted cages of doves. "Next week's menu, Rosaline?"

"As if I'd even consider such a notion! I've decided to make pets of them, Jack, keep them in the courtyard. They've been treated despicably, as you can see," she reported beneath a cupped hand so that the merchant couldn't hear. "Terribly cramped and dirty. I plan to keep some of them in cages—large ones of course—and let the rest fly free in the courtyard—that is, if a net can be stretched across the length from roof to roof. Do you think that can be managed?"

Regarding his wife with curiosity, Jack asked, "Do you intend to have all these birds flying around the courtyard?"

"Most of them, yes."

"I see. Won't breakfasting by the fountain become a rather risky proposition each morning?"

"Jack, for heaven's sake," she protested. "If you're that fastidious . . ."

"I'm not fastidious at all, as well you know," he said, knowing she had not forgotten her first sight of his untidy house in the Orkneys. He found himself entertained by her excitement over the project, her indignation over the treatment of the birds, and laughed. "Have fun with your endeavor, then. But don't go out to shop for any more of your feathered collection today. I suspect the atmosphere in the streets is still volatile. Oh, and by the way," he added, "the Chittleboroughs will be dining with us tonight. You didn't forget?"

"The Chittleboroughs, the Tylers, and the Duff-Sartons," she listed on her fingers. "How could I forget such impressive guests?"

"Could you set an extra place for a friend of mine as well? He happens to be Honore Shapcott's fiancé."

"Honore's fiancé—Keith Grange? By all means. I've been anxious to meet the gentleman."

Jack's eyes twinkled. "I don't know whether or not he could be termed a gentleman—but, one way or the other, he's a man you'll likely not forget." Tipping his hat on that cryptic note, Jack strolled away.

Before he had gone more than three paces, Rosaline saw his eyes shift to the place where, yesterday, Julie—or a woman with an extraordinary likeness to her—had stood gazing up at him. Rosaline had known he would look, be unable risk the temptation. She saw his gaze search the shadows of the arcade, sweep each niche, the broken, sun-splashed pavement. The sight of his tense hope caused Rosaline a stab of pain. She asked herself what would happen to the plain-faced Mrs. Darlington if the lovely and mysterious Julie were to reappear and enter Jack's life again. Would he leave his wife and go in search of new adventures with his old love? Would all his political ambitions evaporate, his sense of duty dissolve at the first touch of Julie's hand?

Taking her emotions in rein, knowing speculation over Jack's actions to be fruitless, Rosaline forced her mind to consider domestic matters. She dispatched Hoseyn to the bazaar to find some new birdcages, large fanciful metal ones with cupolas and towers and minarets, which she would fill with little doves the color of caramel and pearl. She would pair the parakeets together, putting turquoise with bright emerald. Smiling at the imagined sound of their bird song in the courtyard, she summoned the servants. She had discovered that Egyptian houseboys were quite different from English servants. They had a tendency to forget to lay out fresh towels every day, turn beds, and iron newspapers. She had to educate them entirely upon the way to set and wait upon a proper table. With Hoseyn translating, they were only just learning to dust under the rugs instead of around them. And then there was the Greek cook, who spoke English, and with whom she had already spent two hours the day before discussing in detail every dish to be included in this evening's important menu.

Donning an apron, she went about vanquishing the day's accumulation of dust herself, efficiently wiping every piece of bric-a-brac, climbing upon a stepstool to polish the top of each oak wardrobe. Not an hour after she had begun to polish the tiles around the courtyard fountain, a pair of men arrived with a huge net rolled up the back of a donkey. She laughed and threw up her hands. Jack, even with his own pressing embassy matters to attend, had not only remembered her request to enclose the courtyard but had wasted no time in sending workmen to see it done. Perhaps it was his gift of reconciliation.

Her busy day continued to proceed smoothly until, at mid-afternoon, an official from the European school pounded on the door. The headmaster himself stood on the steps, stern and displeased, his plump, freckled hand grasping the collar of a stony-faced Antonio who struggled to free himself of his captor.

Take advantage of this offer to enjoy Zebra's newest line of historical romance novels....Splendor Romances (formerly Lovegrams Historical Romances)- Take our introductory shipment of 4 romance novels -Absolutely Free! (a $19.96 value)

Now you'll be able to savor today's best romance novels without even leaving your home with our convenient and inexpensive home subscription service. Here's what you get for joining:

- 4 BRAND NEW bestselling Splendor Romances delivered to your doorstep every month
- 20% off every title (or almost $4.00 off) with your home subscription
- FREE home delivery
- A FREE monthly newsletter, *Zebra/Pinnacle Romance News* filled with author interviews, member benefits, book previews and more!
- No risks or obligations...you're free to cancel whenever you wish...no questions asked

To get started with your own home subscription, simply complete and return the card provided. You'll receive your FREE introductory shipment of 4 Splendor Romances and then you'll begin to receive monthly shipments of new Zebra Splendor titles. Each shipment will be yours to examine for 10 days and then if you decide to keep the books, you'll pay the preferred home subscriber's price of just $4.00 per title. That's $16 for all 4 books with FREE home delivery! And if you want us to stop sending books, just say the word...it's that simple.

4 Free BOOKS are waiting for you!
Just mail in the certificate below!

If the certificate is missing below, write to: Splendor Romances, Zebra Home Subscription Service, Inc., P.O. Box 5214, Clifton, New Jersey 07015-5214

FREE BOOK CERTIFICATE

Yes! Please send me 4 Splendor Romances (formerly Zebra Lovegram Historical Romances), ABSOLUTELY FREE! After my introductory shipment, I will be able to preview 4 new Splendor Romances each month FREE for 10 days. Then if I decide to keep them, I will pay the money-saving preferred publisher's price of just $4.00 each... a total of $16.00. That's 20% off the regular publisher's price and there's never any additional charge for shipping and handling. I may return any shipment within 10 days and owe nothing, and I may cancel my subscription at any time. The 4 FREE books will be mine to keep in any case.

Name _____

Address _____ Apt. _____

City _____ State _____ Zip _____

Telephone ( ) _____

Signature _____ SP1297
(If under 18, parent or guardian must sign.)

Terms and prices subject to change. Orders subject to acceptance by Zebra Home Subscription Service, Inc. . Zebra Home Subscription Service, Inc. reserves the right to reject or cancel any subscription.

AFFIX
STAMP
HERE

SPLENDOR ROMANCES
ZEBRA HOME SUBSCRIPTION SERVICE, INC.
120 BRIGHTON ROAD
P.O. BOX 5214
CLIFTON, NEW JERSEY 07015-5214

‖‖‖‖‖‖‖‖‖‖‖‖‖‖‖‖‖‖‖‖‖‖‖‖‖‖‖‖‖‖‖‖‖‖‖‖‖

"Mrs. Darlington," the portly, out of breath gentleman said in an officious tone. "Is your husband at home?"

"No, he isn't. He won't be returning until tonight. But if this is a matter concerning Antonio," she said with a touch of her inbred aristocratic arrogance, "I shall handle it. Won't you come in?"

Sending Antonio to his room with a firm command, she seated the headmaster in the courtyard beside the fountain, hoping the rhythmic splashing of the water would soothe his obviously flaring temper.

"Now, Mr. Whiffle," she said calmly. "What has Antonio done that has upset you so?"

"The boy is entirely ungovernable," the gentleman replied with a sniff. "Besides that, he's ten years old and doesn't even know his letters."

"That's because he has never attended school until now, Mr. Whiffle," Rosaline said with her serene air, serving tea. "Sugar or lemon?"

"Er—neither. I am aware of Antonio's rather. . . . unusual circumstances, but, Mrs. Darlington, surely you cannot expect our school to be responsible for a boy who is not only completely illiterate, but belligerent as well."

"Antonio is very bright, Mr. Whiffle. You cannot argue with that."

"No, but—"

"More tea, Mr. Whiffle? And will you have another of the almond cakes? They *are* delicious, aren't they? My cook is Greek, you know, and a positive wizard with pastries. Perhaps I might send some home with you . . . ?"

The gentleman, his bulk looking too considerable for the small wicker chair, glanced at the sugar dusting his fingers before discreetly wiping them on a napkin. He had already consumed an entire plate of the delicacies in less than a quarter hour, and seemed distracted by the promise of more. "I should like to take some home, ma'am, if you'd be so kind. I'm a bachelor and eat most of my meals out, you know. Abominable fare here in Cairo, for the most part—too much curry and garlic. Er—now, as I was saying, Antonio simply isn't a candidate for our kind of school. Perhaps a tutor—''

"I've been thinking, Mr. Whiffle . . .'' Rosaline said, interrupting him gently, frowning with a delicate indecision as she pushed the dish of honey butter toward her guest in a scarcely noticeable gesture. "Yes, I've been thinking about a collection of fine, rare books my father owns. By any chance, do you know my father, Mr. Whiffle? He's Lord Bardo of the Foreign Office.''

"Of course I've heard of Lord Bardo, but—''

"Well, you see, he has the most *marvelous* collection of volumes by Sir Walter Scott, and another of Swift,'' she interrupted. "And he owns an original unfinished manuscript, never published, by Gustave Flaubert himself. Father would like to donate all of these literary treasures to a worthy institution, and it occurs to me that—well,'' Rosaline said, giving her guest her slowest, sweetest smile. "Do you think your school might, just possibly, be interested in them, Mr. Whiffle . . . ?''

Ten minutes later, Rosaline escorted her suddenly smug, overfed guest to the door, the two of them having come to a mutual, if delicate, understanding that a bargain had been struck without any formal words exchanged.

Upon her return to the courtyard, Rosaline called out in a dry tone, "You may come out now, Antonio. Mr. Whiffle has gone back to his ink and primers.''

After a moment the boy appeared, his head popping up from the hibiscus bordering the outer wall. "He's a old toad.''

Rosaline ignored the comment, idly tossing sunflower seeds to a gray dove that had landed near her feet. She regarded Antonio askance. "Do you like my new birds?''

The boy's shoulders jerked in a sullen shrug, but when Rosaline laid the bag of seeds on the edge of the fountain in invitation, Antonio skulked forward and snatched them up.

"You placed me in a rather difficult position today, you know, young man,'' she told the lad, watching as he scattered the seeds over the sunny tiles with a careless hand. "I really thought you'd prefer staying in school here with Rajad instead of—"

"Rajad is a baby."

"Instead of going to a boarding school in England," she finished in an unruffled tone. "In the event that school here does not suit you, Mr. Darlington has suggested that an English boarding school will be the alternative."

"Humph."

In spite of his disdainful attitude, Rosaline could imagine the wheels turning in Antonio's head, his calculating, his weighing of the truth in her words. "Did I ever tell you about my cousins who went to a boarding school in Yorkshire?" she asked him casually. "A bleak, gray place, the school was, with canings and knuckle rappings and washing at stand pipes outside in the dead of winter. The walls of the school were so high that no one could possibly escape, even if they were prone to risk a good thrashing by the headmaster. My cousins were only allowed to go home during holidays, and those were never long. But, well," she concluded with an airy sigh, "if that is what you prefer, of course . . ."

The boy threw the bag of sunflower seeds on the ground, his gesture so violent the doves pecking near her feet winged their way back to the pink mimosa trees in alarm.

"I only want to be free!" he cried, his face ruddy and fierce, his wolf cub eyes a hard black, sparkling with unshed tears. "I hate it here! I hate being told what to do every moment, what to think, what clothes to put on . In the streets of Rome, Antonio did what Antonio wanted to do, slept where he wanted, ate when he wanted." Putting a small fist to his chest, the lad pounded it and added, "There, Antonio was free!"

"Antonio was free in Rome," Rosaline returned in a hard voice, her eyes level, "because no one cared for him there."

The boy kicked the bag of seed and then thrust his hands in his pockets, plopping down on the edge of the fountain, picking at the white begonia blooms before tossing the petals into the water.

In a soft swish of skirts, Rosaline came to sit beside him, seeing the confusion, the misery, the incompleteness in the eyes of a boy who had not yet been able to determine who he was and where he belonged. Not daring to touch him, breathing lightly so as not to make him bolt from his fear of human closeness, she said gently, "No one is ever entirely free, Antonio. Never free of duty and responsibility. That's what being a man is all about. A man can only really be free in here—" She put a hand to her heart. "Just as free as he desires to be."

Antonio leaned to scoop up a handful of seed and sprinkle it through the bars of the cage of brown finches that Jack had bought in Edinburgh. "I don't know what you mean," he told her moodily. "I only know that—that I feel like *them.*" He indicated the little birds. "Locked up in a cage, never able to sing."

"I have felt so at times, too," Rosaline told him softly, her eyes misting. "Especially in my father's house in Edinburgh. But now . . . well," she glanced at the sky through the nearly invisible net that kept her birds secure, "perhaps it's only a matter of finding one's wings."

A parakeet flew down then, one of brilliant green plumage, and landed upon Antonio's shoulder. After cocking its head, it pecked at his ear. In spite of himself, the boy smiled in delight, then laughed the barest laugh.

Rosaline couldn't recall ever having heard him laugh before, and the sound of it gladdened her heart, made her feel hopeful that Jack's little family would eventually find their road to happiness. It would be a difficult and complicated road to follow at times, perhaps, but well worth the journey.

During the course of the day, Rosaline realized how much she loved to entertain, to prepare, to decorate, to dress when it was her own home and her own guests rather than those of her father. She draped the long teakwood dining table in her good Irish linen, before collecting sprays of oleander and jasmine to twine around the candelabra and the centerpiece of gladioli. With a frown, she looked over her shoulder at her houseboy as he set each place. She had vigilantly supervised the cook and his two Egyptian assistants earlier, carrying her well-worn cookbook, *The Gastronomic Regenerator* in hand, making certain that the roast mutton, the jelly molds, the Capon à la Godard, the wild duck, iced pudding and neapolitan cake à la Chantilly were properly prepared.

She set up a table for card playing in the small book-lined room Jack had commandeered for a library, then rearranged the parlor furniture to facilitate conversation before setting out porcelain dishes of mint bonbons and lemon candies Hoseyn had found in the bazaar. As a final touch, she sprinkled rose petals in the splashing courtyard fountain.

Finally, after seeing to every last detail, making certain each met her standards, Rosaline went up to dress.

She had already laid out her cream and apricot striped silk, its bodice molded to the bust, its draperies tight about the hips, and the pleated overpetticoat trailing behind from bustle to floor. The embroidered satin slippers matched the apricot ribbons threaded through her braided coil of hair, and she chose earrings and a necklace of topaz set in filigree. Stealing a moment to peer at her image in the mirror, Rosaline realized with vague surprise that she was not as plain as usual, but radiant.

With a fanciful turn of mind, she recalled her words to Antonio about finding one's wings, and wondered at her own belief in this. Had marriage given her complexion its rare color? Tonight, as she prepared to host her first dinner that might help her husband fulfill his ambitions, the specter of Julie began to recede just a little, pushed aside by a sudden surge of self-confidence—and by the promise of a special bond that Rosaline was determined to forge with Jack. She had decided that in order to seal their marriage, protect it, she must become indispensable to him. Every woman had her own special talents, after all, her own gift.

Jack arrived only a bare fifteen minutes before the guests, looking preoccupied but expectant, grinning when Rosaline floated toward him and pressed an aperitif to his hand. His smile widened as he saw his well-bred wife in her fashionable clothes, saw the graciously inviting villa she had transformed, its rooms ablaze with candles, its doors open to the warmth of the exotically scented air, the table sparkling.

"Rosaline," he declared, laughing, pleased beyond expectation. "You are a marvel."

His compliment delighted Rosaline and she tried not to flush in her annoying way, turning her sleekly coiffed head instead to inspect the flowers she had heaped in copper containers. "Thank you."

"You are too formal with me Rosaline. I wish you would take a glass of wine with me and relax. No? Then come upstairs with me while I dress," he said with a wave of his hand as he started up. "I'll tell you about Honore Shapcott's fiancé—that friend of mine I mentioned this morning."

"He's still coming to dine with us tonight, isn't he?" Rosaline asked, joining him on the stairs as if it were natural to follow him to his bedroom and watch him dress.

"Wild horses couldn't drag him away. Keith Grange is someone I've known for years—he's been almost as much of a vagabond as I have."

"Honore told me he's a correspondent for *The Times*. It must be an exciting profession."

Jack entered his bedroom, one that adjoined Rosaline's, and shrugged out of his frock coat before removing his already loosened tie. "The newspaper assigns him to cover stories all over the world," he told her, "especially Africa and the Mediterranean. We've crossed paths frequently over the years." Jack gave her a rueful grin over his shoulder. "He's brash and ill-mannered. But—" Jack raised a brow, "I think you'll like him, despite his rather coarse faults."

"He hardly sounds like a good match for Honore. She's so refined and naive."

Jack proceeded to the washstand, where he splashed water on his face before taking up a towel to dab it dry. "The marriage isn't a wise one, I'm afraid. Keith will try to drag her all over the globe with him."

"Then she'll have to become a deal more adventurous in order to survive. The morning we went out to shop in the bazaar, she was like a mouse in a street full of cats, poor dear. Jumping at her shadow at every turn. And that was before signs of the riot began."

Jack glanced at her by way of the mirror while he doffed his shirt. "You, on the other hand, probably took the shopkeepers by storm. How much did you pay for those birds?"

Rosaline lifted her chin. "Ten piastres."

Jack laughed. "A hard bargain, indeed."

"Do you forget I'm used to dealing with the butchers and coal sellers in the streets of Edinburgh? People aren't so different here, trying to cheat an honest body at every turn." Rosaline opened the leather box where her husband kept his cuff links, removed his best gold pair and handed them to him as he slipped an arm through a starched shirt, its whiteness a contrast to the smooth hard flesh of his chest.

He took them from her hand and, regarding her through good-humored but serious eyes, commented, "How quickly you've adapted, Rosie, especially coming as you did straight from your father's drawing room. A man would have to consider himself fortunate to have a wife like you. Don't you think so?" He gave her a slow smile and waited for an answer. The smile seemed to sweep away, for the moment at least, the shadow of the previous night. That, combined with his use of an endearing nickname and—most of all—the curious, wonderfully flattering seriousness that underlaid his voice, made Rosaline's heart soar, and she found she could not meet his eyes during the next few seconds.

"I can hardly compliment myself," she murmured in confusion, busying her hands by wiping a smudge of dust from his bureau. ''But I'm happy that you seem to appreciate my accomplishments.''

''Oh, Rosaline, Rosaline,'' he laughed, seizing her hand to stop her efforts at tidying, an occupation he knew she sought whenever she grew nervous. ''We're going to have to find a way to loosen your stays.''

''Jack!''

He laughed again and looped a strong arm around her waist to quell her temper over his indelicacy. ''Don't get those modest feathers of yours ruffled. Let's go down now. Remember, this is an important night for me. I need those serene, good manners of yours to charm old Lord Duff-Sarton. Come here. You seem flushed and a wee bit flustered. Will it help if I kiss you once or twice?''

Full of good humor, his vitality heightened over his powerful optimism that ambition was within reasonable reach, that the dream he had fashioned for himself might soon be grasped, Jack put his lips on Rosaline's. Roughly playful, he kissed her quickly, almost impersonally, as if she were a partner rather than a lover, a co-conspirator instead of a wife who all at once, wanted desperately to make Jack Darlington fall in love with her.

Chapter Fourteen

Keith Grange proved every bit as brash and ill-mannered as Jack had described, and yet, inexplicably, Rosaline liked him, even found him charming in an unconventional way.

A huge bear of a man with a brass-colored mustache and side whiskers, shrewd brown eyes and a voice that was too loud and crass for genteel company, Grange left an immediate impression of high adventure mixed with ruthlessness. He was a man to like, Rosaline decided after several minutes in his presence, even a man to enjoy, but never a man to trust.

She had always loved to analyze character, to study people and try to decide what motivated them. She had read none of Grange's newspaper articles, but intended to research them in order to better glean the nature of this man Jack considered a long-time friend—this man who was, she suspected, nothing if not self-serving and opportunistic. But then, she thought, her gaze shifting across the table to fasten upon the handsome face that was growing frighteningly more dear to her by the day, so was Jack Darlington.

Her husband wore a look of pride tonight. Well on his way to success, he seemed to be satisfied with the aura that his well-

bred, well-selected wife had created for his guests, those people
who had the power to help him rise to the level he had chosen
for himself. Rosaline could sense his exuberance; it underlaid
his every movement, animated his expression, made his startling
smile more affecting than ever, and gleamed intensely in the
blue eyes that stayed aware of everything that occurred around
him. Like the other men at the table, he was dressed in formal
black, a gardenia boutonniere finishing the debonair effect. And
yet, he stood out from them all, splendidly so. He was popular
with the men, Rosaline realized, and an irresistible visual delight
to feminine eyes; the ladies' gazes flitted to him often, discreetly
but instinctively, the way they would to anything pleasing to
the senses. To her own dismay, Rosaline also found it difficult
to keep her gaze from the remarkable figure of Jack Darlington.

The servants she had so assiduously trained in the art of
decorum waited upon the table almost as well as any English
footmen, refilling glasses, removing plates, ladling soup, standing expressionless and ready to serve. Two dozen blazing candles lit the room. Rosaline kept an eye on each of her guests,
making certain all were well-fed and engaged in conversation,
and she was ready, when the time came, to usher them into
her tastefully decorated parlor to play whist, chat, and drink
cordials.

After a while, Jack encouraged the ladies to stroll in the
courtyard. The air hung fragrant with jasmine. The cooing of
doves perched in the limbs of the pink mimosas delighted the
ears, and when the matrons in their silk and gauze gowns
exclaimed over the delightful atmosphere, Jack winked at Rosaline. In a gesture meant for her eyes only, he then raised his
glass in a discreet salute—the same sort of salute one officer
might give to another after a cleverly plotted coup.

A while later, as Rosaline sat watching Lady Duff-Sarton
play whist with Honore, Keith Grange joined her. ''If it weren't
for the heat,'' he said, giving her his wide, uneven smile, ''I
might believe I was lounging in a London brownstone instead
of a mud villa in Egypt.''

"Since you're English, Mr. Grange," Rosaline replied with a nod of her head, "I'll consider your remark a compliment."

"As it was intended to be, Mrs. Darlington."

"Are you to be on assignment here in Egypt long?"

"As long as there's excitement—and I don't believe there'll be any lack of that for some time to come. Indeed, if Britain sails her warships to Alexandria to glower down upon Arabi and his troops, I can count on a lengthy sojourn in the land of pyramids and sand."

"What sort of articles have you been sending home to England?"

He crossed his legs at the ankles, leaned his hip against the back of the sofa and idly examined his fingernails. "Oh, I and my fellows have been fanning the fires a trifle, giving the wealthy folks in London something to fret about. Nothing alarms rich people like the fear of losing money, you know."

"Mr. Grange," Rosaline said with an admonishing arch of her brow, "surely you're not a journalist who's guilty of sensationalism?"

"Why, no, Mrs. Darlington," he said in feigned abashment. "I'm not guilty of anything."

The corner of her mouth lifted in a doubtful smile, and she asked, "Where did you meet Jack?"

"In Athens."

"How long ago?"

"Oh, I suppose it's been about seven years now." Grange chuckled and leaned his head back to reminisce. "Good lord, I'm not likely to forget that night. We were total strangers, Jack and I, standing outside an inn waiting for our horses to be brought round. All of a sudden, after I'd made a slightly off-color remark—not intending to offend anyone of course— Jack hauled back one of those deadly fists of his and knocked me senseless. But then, he was always deucedly protective of—" Grange broke off, hesitating. Then his eyes twinkled as he finished in a whisper, "Well, no doubt your husband would appreciate my being discreet at this point. I'll keep the particulars of our first encounter to myself.''

Julie. The name came rushing on taunting wings to Rosaline's mind. It had surely been hovering on Keith Grange's lips before his male instinct had warned him not to mention a woman whom Jack's wife might, just possibly, consider: . . . what? A threat for his affection?

Gathering her wits, refusing to allow Julie's ever-looming specter to ruin her important evening, or to permit Keith Grange the satisfaction of witnessing her discomfort, Rosaline smoothly changed the subject. ''When are you to be married, Mr. Grange? Honore hasn't mentioned the date.''

''Two weeks from tomorrow. Our wedding will be quite small and private.''

''So soon? I had no idea. I shall have to offer her my help in preparing for the ceremony. Will Honore stay here in Egypt with you, or will you have her return to England?''

''Why would I marry a woman only to send her away?'' Keith Grange adopted a superior male air and smiled. ''No, Mrs. Darlington, Honore will have to accustom herself to traveling in foreign places. She'll have to view it as an exciting way to live, just as I do. Egypt, Afghanistan, India—my work will take me to all those places and many more.''

''I hope you'll be considerate of her fragile nerves, Mr. Grange,'' Rosaline said, undaunted by his slightly condescending manner. ''Her constitution is not as strong as that of some women.''

Assessingly, with his usual lack of social delicacy, Grange eyed Rosaline's straight frame and level brown eyes, her resolute expression and capable hands. ''You speak your mind, don't you?'' he asked, tilting his head. ''I think Jack did rather well, after all. Better than he might have done—well, I shall leave it at that, for even I know there are some boundaries that should not be overstepped.''

Had he, once again, alluded to Julie? As a journalist, Grange's instincts were quite well-honed, Rosaline suspected. She was beginning to think he enjoyed the game of dropping hints through suspended sentences, enjoyed watching her confused reaction—hoping, perhaps, that he could prick her smooth exterior and discover the vulnerable creature just beneath it. Why was she suspicious of him?

Suddenly, Rajad came marching down the corridor, his nightgown flapping against his pipestem ankles. Excusing herself, Rosaline rushed to intercept the boy, noting that Antonio lurked just behind with the usual puckish smile on his face.

"Antonio stole my tiger's tooth!" Rajad complained, the seriousness of the situation prompting him to wail.

Through the parlor door, Rosaline noted the turned heads of her guests, their curiosity, Jack's quick, sharp glance of concern as his conversation with Lord Duff-Sarton was interrupted. He started to excuse himself, but Rosaline exchanged a glance with him, letting him know she would handle the disturbance, smooth it over so that he could resume his exchange with the aristocrat.

Jack understood her wordless message, and with a smile and apology to Lord Duff-Sarton, ushered the old man through the parlor door and into the private, book-lined study.

"What's happened, Rajad?" Rosaline whispered then, leaning down to gather him up, carry him back down the corridor. "Did you say Antonio had taken your tiger's tooth?"

He nodded, and Rosaline gestured to Antonio, who still skulked in the gloom. She took the Italian lad in hand and told him sternly that he would not be allowed the collection of Roman coins he had been coveting in the bazaar if he didn't promptly return Rajad's treasure.

With no grace at all, the boy obeyed, casting the tiger's tooth onto the floor in a fit of pique.

When her wards were once again tucked in bed, both sullen and sleepy enough to stay beneath the covers, Rosaline opened their shuttered windows so that they might gaze out at the candlelit courtyard and the ladies who milled there. Then she slipped away to rejoin her guests. As she passed the study door, she heard Jack's voice and that of Lord Duff-Sarton, heard the conversational exchange between them, and unable to help herself—paused to eavesdrop.

"Ah, yes, Darlington," the aristocrat said with a chuckle in his voice, "I vividly recall the first time I clapped eyes on you—ragged, despicable little devil you were, slinking about, awaiting an easy prey in the East End. And, God help me, along I came."

Jack laughed softly, his long brown fingers toying with the paperweight on his desk, his manner suggesting no offense at the unflattering recollection described by the noble old man. "And what were you doing there in the East End, may I ask, my lord? A social call, was it?"

At the suggestiveness in Jack's drawling tone, the aristocrat laughed with hearty enjoyment. "What else? I kept a beautiful, quite talented actress at a discreet little address there. I'd spent the evening with her, drunk a quantity of good wine. As a matter of fact, I was relieving myself on the side of the road when you happened along and with no hesitation at all, stole my ivory-handled cane right out of the carriage. What happened to it, by the way? It was one of my favorites, given to me by my grandfather."

"Pawned within the hour," Jack said without an ounce of shame. "The handful of quid I got in exchange kept me fed a month or more."

"I still fail to understand how you managed it. My coachman caught you before you ran a block."

"I remember," came the wry answer. "Bad luck. A drunken sailor tripped me up. But the cane had already been safely transferred to other hands."

"Ah, you had a partner then?"

A brief silence ensued, which caused Rosaline to lean forward and listen more intently.

"Yes," Jack admitted, the tone of his voice altered to one of quiet detachment. "I had a partner."

"Ah, even then . . . ?" Lord Duff-Sarton's voice came quietly. "How could I have forgotten? At any rate, I was much taken by your intelligence when you were thrust into my coach by the disgruntled coachman, whose shins showed bruises for weeks to come, I might add. Usefully charming, you were, even then, Jack. Knew just how to talk your way around my angry accusations, how to negotiate, when to speak and when to listen with that perfectly false but convincing grin of yours. In case you're wondering, it was the grin that caused me to consider you for the occupation that has suited you—*and* our Foreign Office—so well over the years.''

''You flatter me, my Lord. And I'm glad to know you don't hold a grudge over the loss of the cane.''

''Oh, but I do, my boy. I do.'' The old man chuckled, almost with maliciousness, then leaned back in his chair, stretched out his short legs and said more soberly, ''Did you ever learn what happened to Julie?''

Outside the door, Rosaline held her breath. Through the crack between the jamb and the portal, she could just glimpse Jack's arrow straight form as he moved from his desk to the window, stood with his back to his guest, his head lowered, his hands balled at his thighs.

''No,'' he said shortly. ''I never knew.''

''Dreadful shame. How it must have worried you.''

''It worries me still.'' The reply was immediate, swift with unconcealed emotion.

Rosaline could not bear to hear more of the conversation. Taking up her skirts, her color pale, she quickly swept through the corridor and into the parlor to rejoin her guests. But somehow the evening was spoiled.

Later that night, when the guests had all left and she and her husband stood together, seeing the last couple out, Jack's manner was the easy, negligent one that always disarmed Rosaline. She could detect no vestige of the emotion that she had earlier heard in his voice while she had eavesdropped—the emotion that had shattered her own composure. Touching her cheek in a teasing manner, his fingers light and lazy, Jack spoke with a smile. ''Why so glum, Rosie? Didn't you enjoy our success tonight? You should have. I believe I overheard Lady Duff-Sarton touting you as Cairo's newest and most gracious hostess. You managed to make everyone feel as if they were back in England, which is precisely where all of them—except Keith Grange, perhaps—long to be.''

''I'm glad they felt at home,'' Rosaline murmured, reaching toward the huntboard to pick up a half-empty glass of wine that the servants had failed to notice. ''Are you happy with the way the evening went?''

''Need you ask?'' In spite of her slight resistance, Jack took her arm and pulled her toward him, his face close to hers, his mouth only inches away, near enough that she caught the aroma of the after-dinner brandy he had drunk. ''You're a credit to me, Rosaline. Do you know that?''

She knew she should have been satisfied with that, content to know that he valued her, admired her domestic abilities, her grace. But she was not. For those were merely skills she had been trained to do, been bred for. Jack could just as easily admire a fine horse for its bloodlines, or a new carriage its luxury furnishings. The appreciation of a woman's good qualities was not the same as loving her heart, her soul—even if she was too tall and plain and cool.

''You're going to spoil me with your compliments, Jack,'' she said lightly, covering all the chaotic, contradictory emotions that threatened to surface at any moment. Why did she feel the need to throw her arms around his neck and beg him to look more deeply into her eyes, to find the feelings there, to discover what sort of woman really lay beneath the surface of her calm?

''Then spoil you I will,'' he declared. ''For we're going to Alexandria tomorrow, where you'll have a new European enclave to charm. The English consul and his wife will be hosting a dinner for us, and if you can do as well with them as you've done with the Duff-Sartons and the Chittleboroughs and everyone else you've met in Cairo, you may soon find yourself married to a man with an enviable position in the Foreign Office—not to mention a husband who treasures you.''

He kissed her then, in the same conspiratorial manner he had done earlier in the evening, his lips practiced at seduction, and yet not gaspingly passionate as she knew they could be, in other circumstances.

Still, Rosaline's response was warm and desperate. She clung to the fine, black fabric of his jacket, and hoped Jack would take her to bed and allow her another chance to give him pleasure, a chance to find pleasure herself. Only then, she felt, could she really begin to compete with Julie, vie for that hard won, not easily opened space in Jack Darlington's heart.

But Jack only smiled as she kissed him in her breathless, inexperienced way; he was pleased with her demonstrativeness, but not tempted to take more.

"I've got to go out," he said, reaching for his hat and giving her another smile that, at the moment, almost broke her heart. "A late briefing at the Foreign Office—God, they're boring. Likely I'll be gone until morning."

Rosaline managed to hide her disappointment, and then, for one excruciating moment, hide the sudden fear that he had found Julie again and was going to meet her. "Very well, then," she said, forcing the words to come out without a falter. "I'll see you at breakfast."

As he turned to enter the dark street, its dusty pavement still warm from the day's sun, Rosaline lingered with the front door slightly cracked, peering out, watching him, remembering Lord Duff-Sarton's comments. Her handsome, so charming husband, it seemed, had been nothing more than a common cutpurse plucked from the filthy streets of London before he was put to work by the Foreign Office. She closed her eyes briefly and remembered his fine, long-fingered hands; she thought of them picking pockets, she thought of them pawning pocketwatches, deftly sliding into fashionable silk purses and withdrawing money, passing it on to another hand—more slender but just as nimble.

With a new and profound disquiet, Rosaline wondered at the

darkness of Jack's secrets, at the cleverness of his deceit, and how those things would affect her life—their life together.

Her eyes opened, fastened upon the street, upon the black space where a motionless woman, just yesterday, had stood and let down her veil. She was no phantom, no ghost. Rosaline knew it for a certainty, even if Jack did not.

Yes, God help her, Julie was real.

Chapter Fifteen

To Rosaline, the train trip from Cairo to Alexandria proved as intriguing as the first time when she had traveled in the opposite direction, a newcomer to an enchantingly ancient land.

But beside her, Jack gazed with no interest at the scenery, having seen too many times the long ribbons of plodding camels in their desert-bound caravans, the bowing palm trees that dotted flat tan sands, the tiny villages with their mud and thatched homes that resembled swallows' nests. The finer homes and mosques along the way displayed the horizontal lines of Saracenic architecture, and in the fields the scarecrows wore a strange assortment of fluttering blue *kuftans* instead of the woolen trousers and straw hats one saw in Britain.

He leaned back against the worn leather upholstery of the first class compartment, and through narrowed eyes, studied his wife, finding her face far more interesting, far more perplexing than anything in the exotic landscape. Her gaze was fixed pensively on the passing sights, the lines of her profile clean and aristocratic, the chin firm, the nose straight, the length of the throat accentuated by the high neck of a gray traveling gown. Her lace fichu was impeccably arranged, and nestled within its folds, catching the gold Egyptian light, winked a brooch that matched the earrings which dangled from her lobes.

Unlike other females he had encountered in his life, Rosaline was a woman Jack failed to understand. She was no simpering coquette, no helpless ingenue, no sensual courtesan. She was not emotional like the others either, not prone to tears or sulkiness or hysteria when circumstances did not go her way. Instead, she kept to herself whatever tender or tumultuous feelings she harbored, maintained her independence, went efficiently about her duties as his wife and the chatelaine of his house, while playing mother to a pair of difficult boys.

Rosaline had made progress with Antonio and Rajad, Jack admitted, handling them with such steadiness and caring consistency that much of their rebelliousness and social backwardness had disappeared. She had even been confident enough to leave them temporarily under Hoseyn's direction in Cairo. Rajad was doing well in school, apparently responding to its structured atmosphere, and Antonio .... well, Antonio was attending school at least. Jack hid a smile. In a circuitous way, he had learned that the school had acquired a donation of rare books from none other than Lord Bardo himself, and Jack had little doubt that the gift had been Rosaline's very clever solution— or bribe—to keep the headmaster agreeable to Antonio's continued presence there.

Suddenly, the subject of Jack's close perusal turned slightly, provided a view of her nape and her tightly coiled hair beneath a small blue feathered hat. He liked the texture of Rosaline's hair, wished she would unbind it for him at night—just once— let it fall to her hips and invite him to touch it. . . .

Speculatively, his eyes shifted from her hair to her body, to the long line of the straightly held spine, to the breasts beneath the molded jacket, then to the corseted waist. It pained Jack, angered him, that he was able derive so much pleasure from her long, cool body when she refused to find complete pleasure in his. And he believed that Rosaline *did* indeed refuse herself pleasure—although *why* he didn't know. But she held herself back, fulfilled, but not passionately fulfilled.

And yet, aside from that, Jack admired his wife a great deal, held her in high esteem. He had decided that Rosaline Darlington was a woman he could rely on for anything; he had even started to let down his guard around her, and experienced a rare, unaccustomed trust whose very novelty disquieted him.

Frowning, Jack shifted his sprawled legs, pondered his wife's cameo-like profile with new consternation. Perhaps he should speak to her, express a few of his sentiments so that she might begin to trust him too, to open herself up to him the next time he risked disappointment and made love to her.

Taking a quick breath, he leaned forward and said, "Rosaline—"

At the urgent sound of her husband's voice, Rosaline turned, startled, her lips parted and her eyes wide.

The expression on her face suggested to Jack that she had been deep in thought, daydreaming perhaps. He sensed that his interruption had in some way caused her to feel a pang of guilt. He couldn't help but wonder whom she had been dreaming about, and with a wry smile shook his head. As so often seemed to be the case in their unlikely relationship, the proper moment for sharing sentiment had fled, irretrievably lost.

"Did I pull you away from your woolgathering?" Jack asked, switching his mood from soberness to an amused curiosity in order to conceal his thoughts. "You seemed far away—riding on one of those caravan camels heading for the desert, were you?"

Laughter crept into Rosaline's voice as she answered, "I hardly think I'm suited for such an adventure, Jack. It would be rather tiresome holding my parasol upright all day to shade my complexion from the sun, don't you think?"

Jack smiled at the picture of his wife's proper carriage in the camel's rocking saddle, a feather hat bobbing atop her head, and above it a flimsy parasol turned inside out from the searing desert winds.

"I don't think you'd be holding it long," he commented with a chuckle. "Some Bedouin woman would fancy it and insist that her husband steal it from you."

At his words, Rosaline unwillingly recalled that Jack himself was no stranger to thievery, and she wondered how many gewgaws Julie had fancied long ago, and how many he had stolen to please her. All of them, no doubt. Jack's gaze sharpened, fastened upon her eyes, and Rosaline felt the hot, unbecoming color creep up her neck. Fearing that he would somehow read her thoughts and know that she had begun to dwell on his unsavory past with an alarming frequency, Rosaline jerked her head away. For some inexplicable reason, she was loath to let Jack know she had overheard his conversation with Lord Duff-Sarton, had overheard the details about the stolen cane, and about his clever partner—the increasingly mysterious Julie. She had come to realize, ironically, that whenever she experienced jealousy over Julie, David came to mind. She had been thinking about the artist only a few moments ago, in fact, dreaming about him, remembering his hands upon her on the red velvet chaise lounge. Were thoughts of him a refuge of sorts, a retaliation?

Reaching out all at once, Jack took hold of her chin and pulled her face around until she was forced to meet his eyes again. "Is there something about the subject of thievery that makes you uncomfortable, my dear?"

After an initial moment of panic over the possible significance of his words, Rosaline recovered her courage, raised her lashes and locked her gaze with his. "Should there be, Jack?"

"I'm asking you, Rosie."

Drawing free of his hand, Rosaline stood as the train braked and slid to a rattling halt. She wondered if Jack sensed she had discovered his low beginnings, knew that he had been a thief in the most desperate part of East London. If so, did he understand that she trusted him anyway, even while her intellect warned her to beware? Most of all, did Jack Darlington know that his wife loved him, despite the fact that he was not free—would likely never be free—to love her in return?

Rosaline continued to meet his gaze, hoping, in the evasive game of words they played, that he would glean the meaning behind her statement as she said, "I would never associate with anyone I felt to be the least untrustworthy, Jack. And I believe myself to be a very good judge of character."

After giving her a long, measuring regard, Jack's face grew solemn. "Come to think of it," he said with deliberate lightness, "perhaps you're wise to keep up your guard—even around me. I've made a point of it myself. One survives that way. Come, we've arrived at the station. Lance Cardew should be meeting us. I sent him ahead.

He reached out for her arm stiffly, and she accepted his escort with equal discomfort. Leading her out then, he slipped an arm about her waist as they stepped into the jumbled mass of humanity at the station. All around, blue *kuftans* mingled with black European broadcloth suits, a few French silk gowns, and the baggy white trousers and red caps of the dragomen who swarmed around hoping to wheedle piastres from tourists.

Indeed, so many of the bothersome dragomen circled with their painted donkeys that Rosaline could scarcely see any of Alexandria—the graceful acacia trees, the Italian architecture, and the tall Pillar of Pompey, that ancient red granite obelisk that overlooked the desert beyond the fringe of the city.

With the hot dust from the train stinging her eyes, Rosaline glanced around. Swathed in bright colored clothes, a dervish danced in the street, chanting in a whining voice that pierced the general din. A singing juggler in colorful rags pulled a cigar from a donkey's nose, then drew three eggs from beneath a Frenchwoman's hat, causing her to squeal in indignation and slap him with her parasol. And yet, amid the seemingly normal activity, a tension seemed to coil itself around the foreign crowd, a heightened anticipation much like the one Rosaline had experienced in Cairo before the riot there.

"Jack . . ." she said, glancing about, worried. "I . . ."

''Hold on to my arm, Rosaline,'' he ordered, his eyes vigilant too, as if he also sensed the underlying menace. ''Don't let go.''

A few rickety carriages lined up to take passengers to local hotels, the dragomen insinuating themselves between drivers and tourists, offering to arrange transportation for a token fee. With a curt order, Jack dismissed the annoying fellows, directing Lance Cardew, who had only just joined them, to secure a carriage.

When the three were seated in the interior of a mule drawn conveyance, the driver snapped his whip and ventured with a reckless confidence into the press of heavy traffic. Lance Cardew sat opposite Rosaline, his attaché tucked between his feet, his expression more pinched than usual, his usual glib tongue silent. She wondered at the change she had lately noticed in Jack's aide. Often he had joined them for Sunday dinner, and she had detected a subtle strain in his expression, noted his nervous starts whenever something caught him unawares. Lance Cardew was fastidious, of course, used to the more polished society found in London and Paris. No doubt he found the threat of rebellion unnerving, the dust and donkeys and strange customs of Egypt something to despise.

Askance, Rosaline observed Jack. Very little ever disconcerted her self-possessed husband, and nothing at all seemed to rob him of his confidence in life's most frightening and awkward moments. She yearned to know what he was thinking. His sudden coolness toward her on the train brought her a sadness she could not shake. When the vehicle halted before the colonnaded Hotel d' Europe, she was still in a vaguely fretful state, and clung to Jack's arm as he handed her down the coach steps. Besieged by a ragged army of beggar children, she handed out coins while Jack paid the driver.

She stood staring out at the crowd, then paused, and froze. Blood drained from her face. She stood on tiptoe to better glimpse the slender, long-limbed gentleman who wended his way through the masses. The sun burnished his long hair to bright gold, and his finely featured, pale complexion seemed incongruous amid the countless bronzed visages who surrounded him. "My God," she breathed. *David!*

Forgetting herself, even forgetting that Jack stood just behind her, she opened her mouth to call out the artist's name, ready to take flight and run after him. How did David come to be in Alexandria just when she arrived? How could such an unlikely coincidence occur? Had fate, always capricious and sometimes cruel, brought them together here in this country of warm, white walls and green tiled mosques? Were they destined to meet again, after all?

Just in time, Rosaline checked her mad impulse to lift her skirts and follow after him. But she promised herself one more glimpse of his face. *Just one more.* Then she would turn away, compose her features, never let on to Jack that she had seen the artist.

Once more, she fixed her eyes on David, held her breath when his eyes found hers and fastened upon them. He halted in mid-stride, smiled broadly, then raised one of his long, slender hands before a train of camels passed and obscured his view.

Unable to help herself, Rosaline held out a hand to beckon, her action unconscious, too eager.

Then hearing Jack's footsteps, she whirled in sudden guilt, her gaze flickering upward to meet her husband's steady regard.

Jack's eyes swept over her face, noting its high color beneath the shade of her hat brim. Then he glanced down at her hands, which wadded the lace edge of her parasol. Taking her arm, his touch smooth but firm, he asked in a quiet voice, "Shall we go into the hotel, Rosaline? I believe the streets have grown too dangerous for loitering. Don't you agree?"

She allowed him to pull her away, resisted the temptation, the terrible need, to look back one last time and find the artist. She still felt a glow inside her breast, felt it suffuse her cheeks again as she remembered her glimpse of David. Lance Cardew seemed to notice her high color, too. He had been standing close, and with dismay Rosaline realized he had witnessed her joyous smile at the sight of her former lover. Had Jack seen it, too?

All at once, on the opposite street corner, a group of Egyptians began to shout at a pair of Greek water sellers. No love lost between the nationalities, the men spat at one another in typical fashion, then exchanged verbal insults before trading punches. Others on the street joined in, abandoning camels and donkeys in order to jab and shove and increase the general confusion. A group of well-dressed European businessmen stopped to watch, and failing to realize the danger, found themselves sudden targets.

Concerned over the trouble, Jack pulled Rosaline through the open doors of the hotel and into the lobby, and ordered her to stay inside, out of sight. Then he threw open his portmanteau and removed a pair of loaded revolvers from a case, scarcely glancing up when a disheveled gentleman dashed in from the street. "There will be a riot, surely!" he exclaimed in a heavy French accent, breathing hard, obviously frightened. He gesticulated, wild-eyed. "I just came from the direction of the Custom House. Three Europeans have been shot by a gang of natives."

"What has caused this tension?" Rosaline cried, distraught as she watched Jack with the pistols. "Is it the trouble with Arabi?"

"Yes, tempers are high, Madam. The native bankers and moneylenders are at each other's throats because the economy is failing, and the British stock exchange is in an uproar over this crisis with Arabi." The Frenchman looked at Rosaline, then at Jack, who was removing the Colt revolvers. "Monsieur! Surely you don't intend to go back out on the streets?"

Jack spared him little more than one contemptuous glance. "For God's sake, man, there are Europeans being attacked out there—your countrymen as well as mine." Turning away, he thrust a revolver at Lance Cardew. "You know how to use this, I trust."

Cardew, his usual sanguine complexion pale, shook his head

in shame. "No, sir. I-I'm afraid I never felt the need to learn. . . ."

Jack threw him an irritable glance. "Then maybe you and the Frenchman should go back to Paris together."

"Give me the revolver," Rosaline said, stepping forward and holding out her hand. "I know how to use it—very well, as a matter of fact."

Jack looked at her and hesitated only a second before he intrusted the revolver to her. "Next you'll tell me you know how to roll cartridges."

"I know how to roll cartridges." She gripped the weapon and stared out at the frightening, deadly melee intensifying in the street. "Good lord, Jack, must you go out there?"

"Would you consign me to the ranks of Cardew and the Frenchman?" he asked over his shoulder, running out the door, his coattails flying.

In trepidation, Rosaline watched, an icy dread gripping her heart as she watched the violence from the hotel lobby. She feared not only for her husband, but for David. He was not bold and resourceful like Jack, not meant for danger and tumult and fury.

She saw Jack throw himself into the fray, fire at a native who straddled a fallen European gentleman before backhanding another who flew at him from behind. The noise of the disturbance increased. Screams sounded and the footsteps of horrified Europeans as they ran for their lives mingled with the pounding slippers of native women as they darted through herds of squealing animals. The smells of dust and sweat were strong. Chaos reigned in the streets, but Rosaline felt eerily calm as she readied the revolver and prepared to fire as the fighting grew closer to the hotel steps.

Several hotel employees rushed to close and bar the doors, yelled at her to go upstairs and lock herself in one of the rooms. She paused and glanced around for Lance Cardew just as he hurried forward and gripped her arm.

"Come with me!" he exclaimed. "I'll escort you upstairs."

Cardew's usual composure had left him; the affable, urbane aide had been replaced by a perspiring youth whose lack of experience was apparent.

Just as they turned to go upstairs, a stone struck the glass of the front door and shattered it. Rosaline stared in terror as several turbanned natives sprinted toward the hotel, wielding knives, obviously intending to demolish the decorative portal made of glass and cedar. To give him credit, Lance Cardew waited long enough for Rosaline to gather her skirts and run up the carpeted stairway to the upper story, where he threw open the door of a room and all but pushed her inside, his damp hand crumpling the sleeve of her blouse.

While he shoved a heavy chiffonier across the space to barricade the threshold, Rosaline rushed to the window and looked down, watched in horror as natives dragged screaming Europeans from shops and residences. Frantically she searched the confusion for Jack, hunted in vain for his tall form. At the same time she looked for David and saw no fair head, no thin frame dressed in fashionable clothes.

Before she could contemplate the possible fate of the artist, she caught sight of a rented coach careening through the bedlam, its driver snapping a whip over the team of lathered horses, managing with sheer determination to force a passage to the front drive of the hotel. Through the open windows of the coach, Rosaline could see a woman in European dress, her flowered bonnet askew, her face drawn in lines of terror. Lady Duff-Sarton! The poor woman managed to wrench open the door and stumble out, breathlessly clutching her reticule while standing amid the whirl of dust and turmoil. Bedazed and disoriented, she appeared too paralyzed with fear to take another step.

Catching sight of her rich gown and glittering jewels, an opportunistic native in blood spattered white darted through the throng toward her, his knife upraised and a grimace of hatred twisting his face.

Rosaline gripped her revolver and rushed out onto the balcony, aiming to fire until she saw Jack materialize all at once in the haze. He leapt forward, grabbed the attacker by the throat, and used his knife upon him. Then jumping to his feet, Jack seized Lady Duff-Sarton by the arm and dragged her toward the now dubious safety of the hotel.

The aristocrat stumbled and lost a shoe, and when Jack turned to lift her, another native hurtled toward him with a pistol leveled.

Rosaline raised her revolver and pulled the trigger, watching with a strange dispassion as the turbanned man fell to the ground.

Jack glanced up and spied her on the balcony; in that instant, fear, surprise and pride all marked the features of his face.

"Go back inside, Rosaline!" he shouted, still guiding Lady Duff-Sarton through the danger, half carrying the swooning woman to the hotel steps where several slain Europeans lay sprawled.

But Rosaline disobeyed her husband's command. In that moment, near the cascading central fountain of the square, she glimpsed a bright golden head and an ivory-colored coat. Penned in the deadly embrace of an Egyptian in a blue *kuftan,* David fought, landing several ineffectual blows while struggling for his life.

Giving no thought to her own safety, Rosaline descended the balcony steps two at a time, tripped in her kid boots, and dashed onto the street. A galloping horse nearly knocked her to the ground, but she managed to keep sight of David, watching in alarm as his attacker dragged him to the fountain and shoved his head beneath the water.

Rosaline did not dare use her revolver for fear of injuring David; she knew only that she must save the artist, and hurled her body at the attacker's back, clawing his face, his eyes, screaming like a madwoman for the mercy of God.

Jack had seen his wife flee from the terrace, and now as he witnessed her danger, saw her in the grip of the Egyptian, he let out a cry, and thrust Lady Duff-Sarton toward a hotel employee as he tore across the avenue.

"Rosaline!" he cried. *"Rosaline!"* Charging at the native who clutched Rosaline by the hair, Jack flew at him, plunging a hard, furious fist into his side. Doubling over, the savage collapsed, his hold on Rosaline broken. She leaned to grasp David, who lay half submerged in the fountain basin, drowning.

Feeling the hot air on his face, the artist gasped and tried to draw air into his lungs. Jack stood aside, momentarily ignoring the brutality raging all around as he watched his wife encircle the artist with her arms, cradle his drooping frame, fiercely hold onto his thin, narrow shoulders as if she intended never to let them go. For several seconds, as Jack fixed his gaze on Rosaline's loving face, the sound of screams receded to a cottony silence.

Then, cold-eyed, feeling an odd repugnance, he stepped forward and took upon himself the other man's frail weight, supporting him so that David could stagger across an avenue now littered with the bodies of both Europeans and Egyptians. With a jerk of his head and a brusque command, Jack ordered Rosaline to walk close beside him. "Stay on my left," he said. "And if you can manage it, reload my revolver."

A few minutes later, when he brought her and David Mellon through the sagging hotel doors, he turned on his heel, and without a word to either, went out again. He felt better able to confront killing and death than the writhing jealousy that had so unexpectedly jarred him. Battle, at least, was more familiar.

"Mrs. Darlington!" Lady Duff-Sarton shrilled, crouching in a corner behind a potted palm, hysterical as she came forward to clutch at Rosaline's arm. "Shall we all be *murdered?* I don't know what has happened to my husband! Lost in that madness, he is, after being pulled from our coach! There was no one to help, nothing but savages swarming around us like jackals!"

Her nerves frayed but still steady, Rosaline took the lady's

trembling hand in its soiled knitted gloves. Even though she
was scarcely able to tear her eyes from David's ashen face and
dripping gold hair, she said with gentle urgency, "When Jack
returns, Lady Duff-Sarton, I'll send him out to search. Now,
come along, hurry, go upstairs with Mr. Mellon and me.
David . . . ?"

Holding out her other hand, Rosaline gripped the artist's
cold wrist and squeezed it, and was rewarded with a weak but
valiant smile. Together, the three of them wended through a
mass of European refugees huddled on the stairs. All the rooms
had been claimed by those seeking safety, and it was only
because Lance Cardew had remained securely in the same suite,
refusing to venture so much as one well-shod foot out the door,
that Rosaline and her friends were able to claim a private and—
for the moment, at least—safe haven.

After seeing Lady Duff-Sarton seated in a chair and intrusted
to Lance Cardew's smooth care, Rosaline hastened onto the
balcony, blinked against both the sting of dust and the sight of
destruction, feeling caught in a sense of unreality as she glanced
at the sky with its serenely circling sea birds and bright coin
of sun. The fighting had decreased, and only a few lone natives
moved about robbing the bodies of fallen Europeans or searching out new victims in the bank across the street. Gripping the
iron railing, Rosaline leaned out to look for Jack, afraid for
him, yet knowing that his survival skills were extraordinary,
that he was adept and cool at watching his back. As she removed
the revolver from her deep skirt pocket, prepared to use it again
if necessary, David came up behind her.

"Madness!" he hissed. His voice was odd. He sounded
vaguely taken aback, offended, as if the world were obliged to
hide its ugliness from his painter's eyes. He looked at Rosaline.
"For God's sake, Rosaline, at least crouch down behind the
vines so you don't make a target."

She did as bade, regarding David with concern as he joined
her. His hair trickled water over the features of his face, which
were drawn and pale. A smear of blood stained his jacket, and

his eyes, so accustomed to reinterpreting the harshness of the world to dreamy paintings, stared at her in exhaustion.

"Are you well, David?"

"I'll mend. But, dear God, what horror I saw out there. I'd be floating in that fountain now but for you and that fierce-eyed gentleman who appeared in the nick of time."

Rosaline turned her eyes away. "That gentleman is my husband."

"Your husband?" David looked at her, stunned. Then he shook his head. "Lord, but destiny is strange, isn't it? I suppose I should be grateful that you chose someone so . . . resourceful. He slit the throat of that Egyptian with all the skill of a savage."

Rosaline's gaze swept the now quiet street again. "Jack is the sort of man daunted by little," she murmured, half to herself. "I think he relishes danger."

"And you, a woman of such keen sensibilities, considered him a suitable match?"

"My father did." Rosaline regretted the words immediately, but they were too late to retract.

David contemplated her for several seconds, replying with a hint of sullenness. "Ah . . . so it was a wedding expediently arranged after your—what shall I call it—your tryst with me?"

She made no reply, felt his own hurt, watching as a regiment of Egyptian soldiers entered the dust-cloaked square. Their caparisoned horses pounded the baked earth, snorting as the smell of death met their nostrils.

"It appears the army has finally come to the rescue," David observed with a dry hatred. "Deliberately late no doubt, now that so many Europeans have been gotten out of the way."

"Many natives are dead, too."

"Their lives are worth less—at least, that's what we've been taught to believe by the British press."

"How did you come to be here in Alexandria, David?" Rosaline asked, her eyes still searching for a glimpse of Jack in the now eerie square.

"I came to paint, of course. And you? Is that half savage husband of yours a financier looking after his golden interests?"

"He's with the Foreign Office. An attaché."

David pushed his hair from his brow. "So you are in *that* set? Then perhaps I can prevail upon your good nature—and our past relationship—and ask you to recommend me as a portraitist. British aristocrats always want their wives immortalized on canvas, regardless of their looks." He raised a brow in Lady Duff-Sarton's direction. "Even *she* could be made to look dignified with a little shadowing beneath the chin and jowls."

His flippancy at such a time annoyed her, but Rosaline said, "You know I'll recommend you, that I think highly of your work."

David studied the woman beside him for a moment, his eyes turned from the world's ugliness to the face he had always found fascinatingly unusual, to the eyes that reflected inward depth, to the mink-colored hair which hung heavily, half-unmoored now, from its braided coils. In a quiet voice he asked, "Have you found with your husband what you once found with me?"

She refused to answer, could not answer. She just stood still and waited until she caught a glimpse of Jack, safe for now, speaking with an officer of the army. Dusk descended, and Lady Duff-Sarton dozed exhaustedly in a chair while David poured red wine.

"I shall ask you again," he said, handing her a glass. "Have you found with your husband what you found with me?"

Rosaline glanced at him, uncomfortable with the directness of the question. Her gaze slid away, shaded by lowered dark lashes. "That's hardly an appropriate question, David, especially now, at a time like this."

"Why? Why isn't it appropriate? Crises are the best time for confidences, for confessions. We meant something to one another in Edinburgh, didn't we?"

"You never came back for me, David," she said, turning

suddenly, accusing him. All the emotion of the past suddenly flooded back.

"As if your father would have allowed it! For God's sake, Rosaline, I needed a chance to plan carefully, to find a way to arrange an elopement. You might have given me time."

She stared at him. Then, growing agitated, dismayed that she had underestimated David's devotion and had failed to trust him, Rosaline faltered. "I-I thought you'd given up, gone on to paint somewhere. I thought you didn't love me enough to—"

"Didn't *love* you enough?"

At the wounded tone in his voice, which increased her own remorse and confusion, Rosaline turned in an abrupt way. She was married now, and it was wrong, dangerous to feel such emotion for another man. "It's pointless to speak of it now. I don't want to speak of it. P-Perhaps you should sit down and rest, David," she stammered, "while I go down to help tend the wounded—"

"Rosaline—"

She hesitated.

"I really did love you."

"David—"

"It's true, I swear it's true," he said with feeling. He knew that something about Rosaline—something unique—had drawn him. What was it? Not beauty. Not the coquettish charm he usually sought. What then? Was it the way she looked out through her steady, brown eyes? Was it the way she so calmly accepted life just as it was, believing the world a good place even if she felt cheated by it? He knew that she wanted passion and that at one time she had wanted to experience the passion with him. Did she still? With sudden urgency he took hold of her arm. "Do you love your husband, Rosaline?" he asked. "Do you love him?"

She pulled away, unable to meet his eyes, and said in distress, "For mercy's sake, David, don't ask me such things."

"I should not have left without you," he declared, feeling

an impulsive, loin-stirring desire. "What a fool I was! I should have taken you from your father's home by stealth if necessary."

"And what would you have done with me then, David?" she demanded. "What would you have done with me then?"

"I would have loved you, pampered you, of course," he shot back. "What a marvelous partner you'd make in foreign places! Few women bred in drawing rooms could endure it as you seem to do, few could see the beauty lying just beneath its savagery. But you can, I wager. It's what I'm trying to paint, to capture, Rosaline," he said in excitement, gripped suddenly by a creative urge. "You could help me see it."

Rosaline lowered her head, her pained eyes fixed upon his leather shoes filmed with dust. "It does no good to speak of such things now," she whispered.

With a sigh of deflation, the artist removed his damp, ruined jacket and draped it with deliberate care across the railing. "Perhaps not. But I am an unconventional sort." He waited until Rosaline met his eyes. He felt his belly tighten, knowing himself to be addicted to anything that was both sensual and forbidden. In a low voice he said, "Even respectable British wives take lovers, you know."

Below, unseen by either, Jack strode through the hush of the riot's aftermath, weary with having defended himself and countless other men against the earlier storm of insanity. His eyes scanned the curved balconies of the hotel, seeking Rosaline, needing her, desperate to see that she was safe. Squinting against the sun, he discovered her standing motionless amid the tracery of vines that twined over the balustrade, the bright white of the limewashed wall at her back. She did not stand alone. Her head was lowered in a way he knew, as if she were hiding the color that sometimes rose so tellingly to her face. Lamplight sparked off one of her earrings, and her left hand, with Jack's own gold ring set upon it, tenderly smoothed a man's jacket draped across the rail. David Mellon stood close to her. Reaching out, he put a hand on Rosaline's arm.

With the killing instinct still flowing through his veins, Jack watched as the artist leaned closer, too close, to Rosaline. In reaction, Jack balled his fists and cursed aloud. He was taken aback by the viciousness he felt seeing his wife with another man.

Chapter Sixteen

"Mr. Darlington!" Lady Duff-Sarton exclaimed, awakening as Jack stepped into the room. Still disheveled from her awful ordeal, her bonnet lopsided upon her gray ringletted head, she squeezed his sleeve and cried, "Did you find my husband? Please God, do not tell me that he's been harmed or worse."

"Injured, my lady, but only slightly," Jack answered in a gentle tone. "He's at the home of a British physician. He's instructed me to send you to him as soon as I judge the streets safe enough."

Standing in the presence of a man who exuded such steadiness and presence of mind, Lady Duff-Sarton wilted in relief, then made an effort to reclaim a measure of her own self-possession. Straightening, she removed her hand from Jack's sleeve and said with aplomb, "You can be certain, Mr. Darlington, that I will tell my husband all about your act of courage today—yours and Mrs. Darlington's. My heavens, she is handy with a revolver! I would surely have been a casualty of this foreign madness had you both not been so near and ready to defend me."

Despite his weariness and grim mood, Jack did not fail to

realize the opportunity he had gained by his importune rescue of the British consul's wife. His smile was humble, but, as usual, still devastating in its effect. "You needn't mention my part in it, my lady. Any man would have done the same."

"But it was not what any man *could* have done, Mr. Darlington," she argued, charmed in spite of herself, unconsciously lifting a hand to set her bonnet aright, trying without success to ignore the gruesome array of crimson splatters on her rescuer's clothes. "I didn't realize English diplomats could fight quite so fiercely."

"Scottish," he said with another disarming grin, almost hating to lie, but possessing the presence of mind to recall that he was supposed to be a vicar's son from Golspie.

"Oh, indeed." She laughed softly, traces of girlishness shining through her matronly age. "That explains it. No doubt you're a descendent of some hero of Culloden." She said the words hopefully, having already investigated his background and found him, disappointingly, only the son of a vicar from Northern Scotland. Surely there was more, a noble or brave predecessor somewhere in his family tree . . . ?

David Mellon strolled forward from the balcony then, and as his eyes locked with Jack's narrowed gaze, a swift, palpable enmity sparked between the two men, a mutual hatred that both intuitively sensed would set a tone for all future encounters.

"Yes," the artist said with a flattery not meant to be sincere. He touched his damp hair in salute and drawled, "It seems the Scotsman must be hailed by both of us, Lady Duff-Sarton. More than once today he proved himself a hero."

"Have we met?" Jack asked with deliberate contrariness.

"David Mellon. Your wife and I," the artist lifted a brow, "knew each other before your marriage to her. And if you don't mind my seconding Lady Duff-Sarton, Rosaline's quite courageous herself. She threw herself upon the man who attacked me. I believe she would have killed him with her bare hands if you hadn't arrived. How fortunate that she and I are old friends and that she holds such a fondness for my life."

"Where is my wife?" Jack asked, keeping his voice neutral for the benefit of the influential woman standing behind him, but allowing rancor to darken his eyes. He had hated Mellon on sight, was contemptuous of his subtly taunting repartee, and had no intention of been drawn any further into it.

David's mouth curved. With a sudden satisfaction, he knew that Darlington had witnessed the tete d'tete on the balcony. How secure was the brash, overconfident Darlington in his new marriage, the artist wondered. Familiar with the stringent rules of embassy society, he knew Darlington, as an attaché, must watch himself in the presence of Lady Duff-Sarton, must measure every word he uttered in front of her.

Hoping to pique the other man's temper, test the waters of their enmity, he said, "Your wife went down to tend the wounded—I understand they're being lined up in the hotel courtyard for treatment. I tried to stop her, warn her that the work was too gruesome for a lady, but she insisted upon going. She's a remarkable woman, isn't she?" David said with a slow, meaningful smile. "I feel fortunate that she's agreed to let me paint her portrait."

Jack's eyes glinted. "I believe you have painted it already, sir. Odd, that you should have forgotten."

"Oh, I haven't forgotten, not at all. But you see, the portrait was never finished."

Despite his intention to maintain a cool head for Lady Duff-Sarton's benefit, Jack could not stem the words which burst through his teeth with hard, swift violence. "Nor shall it ever be."

Taken aback, the lady drew in an audible breath.

Jack didn't know precisely why he had reacted in such a way, except that the recent vision of Rosaline's hand stroking the artist's coat upon the balcony had stayed fixed in his mind, along with the memory of the locket that always lay between his wife's breasts whenever he made love to her.

Beside him, Lady Duff-Sarton stood stiffly. He knew that she would repeat his words with relish to her friends. "Mr.

Darlington was positively *harsh* with that poor young artist,"
she would whisper at her tea parties. "Of course, he *did* come
from common beginnings—nothing more than a vicar's son.
You never can trust that sort to maintain their civility, can you?
But, did you know? It seems David Mellon once began a portrait
of Rosaline, although whether he started the painting *before* or
after her marriage to Jack Darlington is anyone's guess. Could
there—just possibly—be some scandal, do you think?"

Jack clamped his jaw. With a stubborn will, he resisted the
temptation to apologize for his outburst and smooth over the
incident, to blame his temper on the events of the day. By God,
he decided with the recklessness he had sought so carefully to
curb over the last weeks, let the old woman talk then, let her
undermine all the careful, costly work of his ambition if she
chose. Yes, by God, let her. It was worth the price.

Lance Cardew had entered the room just behind Jack. Knowing himself already in a state of disgrace for his show of
cowardice earlier in the day, hoping to appease, he hastily
poured a glass of whiskey and brought it, together with a
clean towel and water, for Jack's use. Disregarding all but the
whiskey, downing it in one violent gulp, Jack spoke to the aide
with a jerk of his head. "Make yourself useful and escort Lady
Duff-Sarton to her husband. He's here in the square at the
house of a physician named Tadridge. Someone in the lobby
will know the address."

"Yes, sir. Will that be all, sir?"

"You can escort Mr. Mellon out, as well." Jack's tone was
inimical. "He looks sufficiently recovered to make his way
home on his own." Turning, Jack managed to bid an appropriately deferential goodbye to the lady, who now had the power
as she chose, to either hinder or secure the promise of his
future.

So be it. Wishing he had another shot of whiskey, Jack
proceeded downstairs, pushed through the confusion of the
lobby and outside into the soft, ephemeral atmosphere of early
evening. It was that time in Egypt when light and shadow

sharpen until, in one quivering, unexpected shimmer, they merge like liquid gold over canvas. In the hot, breezeless court-yard with its green jasmine scents, Rosaline's face was sheened with moisture, flushed with warmth and fatigue. In her hands she held a cup of water, which she tilted toward the dry lips of a wounded Englishman lying upon the flagstones.

Jack wended through exhausted victims, kneeling close to his wife, gratified to see relief flood her face at the sight of him.

"You're safe," she said simply, her eyes scanning his face and body for reassurance. "But, Jack ..." she said with a sudden frown, "you've been injured. There's blood on your chin."

She reached to dab it with her handkerchief, but in mid-air, he clasped her wrist and spoke to her with an impatience born of a lingering and jealous irritation. "It's nothing. Leave it. You needn't tend me."

"Has the fighting we saw here spread on to Cairo?" she asked. "Have you heard?"

"Cairo is calm, or so I was told by Lord Duff-Sarton, who sent a messenger to the train station for news."

"Thank God. I've been fretting about Antonio and Rajad for hours, wondering if they were safe. That's one worry off my mind. But can you help me here? There are so few who are willing to do what's necessary, and so many injured." She lifted the head of the man she tended, helped him drink, then set down the cup and pushed hair from her brow with a tired hand. "There's a young man over there, wounded, who keeps calling for me. The physician told me his hand is shattered and he will lose it. I-I find I don't know quite what to say to the boy—"

"I'll go to him—"

"No. I want to go. I want to comfort him like a mother would. I've been reassuring him that he'll be fine, that he'll be going back to Wales soon to join his family. I—"

"How old is he?"

"Sixteen or so."

"Then he's a man. Tell him that he's to lose his hand."

Rosaline glanced with dread in the direction of the suffering boy. Slowly then, she stood and brushed the sand from her gown. "Very well. If you think it's best." She bent to retrieve the cup, and asked, "And Lady Duff-Sarton's husband? You were able to find him, then?"

"Only a little while ago. He's wounded slightly and staying in a house nearby. As a matter of fact, Lance Cardew is escorting the lady there now." Jack saw another question hovered on Rosaline's lips, one she would not ask and, knowing precisely who it concerned, said with challenge in his tone, "I sent David Mellon on his way, as well."

She glanced up at him sharply but remained mute.

He regarded her. "Are you disappointed?"

Looking at the ground, Rosaline affected a cool tone. "Would it matter?"

"No. I daresay it would not, given past circumstances."

At the hardness of Jack's tone, Rosaline met his eyes again, and accused sharply, "You have a past, too."

"But one that is little more than a ghost, that doesn't stand with me upon hotel balconies."

"You were watching us?" she asked with indignation.

"There was no need to watch. It only took a glance."

Rosaline turned her head, and Jack knew immediately, as if it were a visible thing of mortar and brick, that the artist's appearance had built a new wall between them, perhaps a wall even more solid that the one Julie's spirit had made. Mellon's ill-timed presence would make their difficult marriage even more complex, and reawaken emotions within Rosaline's heart that would occupy her thoughts, make her wonder over the wisdom of her marriage.

Finding himself angry and retaliatory at once, Jack repressed the impulse to continue the conversation, knowing it would only increase the discord between them. "Go and speak with that young man over there about his hand," he told Rosaline

in a quiet voice, indicating the boy whose fevered eyes were
fixed with beseechment upon her face. "I'll see what else is
to be done here."

Welcoming the distraction, relieved not to have to argue
anymore, Rosaline hurried away from her husband. They both
labored long into the evening, until cool blue shadows washed
the tiles of the courtyard, obscuring the banana trees and olean-
ders, accentuating sounds of murmuring voices and splashing
water.

One by one, the wounded were carried home on makeshift
stretchers. Jack worked without pause, transported British businessmen, recruited the ever-opportunistic dragomen to help,
while keeping an eye on Rosaline as she smoothed blankets
and whispered prayers, as she lent her own brand of courage
to fearful hearts. Finally, when he saw her shoulders droop,
her tall, stoic frame sag, he took her by the arm.

"You've had enough."

She protested. "There's still so much to do and—"

"Go upstairs and get us both a change of clothes," he interrupted. "I'm taking you on an adventure."

"An adventure? For heaven's sake, Jack, this hardly an
appropriate time—"

"It's a highly appropriate time, actually. Now go. Go," he
said with more softness than she had heard him use in days.

Awhile later, he still would not confide their destination as
they ventured into the quiet streets patrolled by Arabi's army.
The officers silently smoked *kief* in the blue darkness and said
nothing as Jack and Rosaline walked briskly past. The two of
them came to a lovely dark gate, whose inner path was lined
with vine covered trellises and white begonias, and which ended
at a decaying but magnificent set of Pompiean archways. Jack
led her through the shadowed canopy, his shoes clicking upon
blue and white tiles made violet with night.

"Through here," he said, guiding Rosaline toward a closed
cedar door. "Go inside and take as much time as you like. In
a little while I'll meet you out here again."

"But, Jack, what is this place? What's inside?"

"What's inside is one of the few pleasures Egypt holds for me. Go in and see." With a sudden, all forgiving grin that showed white within the darkness of his day-old beard, he turned and strolled away toward another door, leaving Rosaline alone.

Perplexed but intrigued, she hesitated, and opened the cedar door. Her breath caught. Before her eyes, she saw a vaulted place of marble and stone wreathed in warm steam, and in the midst of the space, glistening baths that reflected amber lamplight. An attendant in black robes glided forward, and without speaking, offered Rosaline a muslin robe, a piece of rough soap, and a roll of palm leaves, which she later realized were used to scrub the body.

Rosaline saw no one about but the attendant and, overcoming modesty, crept to a corner, undressed herself, and eager to sink into the water, left her clothes on a cushioned divan and walked to the puddled steps. With a sigh she eased her body into the warmth and, leaning her head against the cold tiles, relaxed, allowing her limbs to float, feeling anonymous and isolated in the cloaking, incense-scented steam.

As she luxuriated, Rosaline shut out thoughts of the savage day, thought of Jack, the smile he'd flashed her just a moment ago at the door. Then she pushed away the vision of the smile, permitting images of David to drift into her thoughts instead. She remembered every word of the artist's proposal on the balcony, his suggestion that she become his lover. David had been the first man—the only man—who had ever noticed her, who had told a plain, tall spinster that she was lovely. Did she still want to make love with him? Rosaline asked herself. Did she want to finish what the two of them had begun amid a pool of red petals in Edinburgh?

Closing her eyes and letting water lap over her breasts, Rosaline allowed herself, in a rare moment of inhibition, to entertain forbidden thoughts. Yes, she believed she might like to experience love with David Mellon, for she believed she shared a sort of spiritual passion with him, a kind of romantic sensitivity which she thought might allow her—if she tried, if she dared—to grasp the complete, abandoned fulfillment that had so far eluded her in Jack's arms.

Jack. Rosaline opened her eyes. What did she feel for Jack? Something stronger, rougher, more elemental than that which she experienced with David. She loved Jack in a painful sort of way, and she knew the pain stemmed from the quiet, sober words he had said to her on the day he'd presented her with the finches. What had he said? *"I'll demand much and give little in the way of affection."* And she believed that he was capable of that, of loving her carnally, stealing pleasure from her inexperienced flesh while keeping his feelings at bay—feelings claimed, long ago, it seemed, by another woman.

Yes, ironically, it was easier to love David, even from afar, than Jack, with whom she must forever share a bed, share two children, share a life. Jack was too often remote, unreadable, a charming opportunist who would use her, good-naturedly and without conscience, to seize his ambitions and his pleasures. Loving Jack was dangerous. It left her ripe for heartache, a pain she had already felt, still felt. Someday soon he would find Julie again. Her intuition warned her of it. And what if he went off with that mysterious lady, left his marriage, his ambitions, his hastily secured roots? What then? What would Rosaline have left but regret? She would be a fool to love him, to count upon him to fulfil that part of her that wanted . . . what? Sheer, selfish pleasure, the sort of utter joy—if only in moments—that made risk of pain and loss worth the sacrifice.

Rosaline knew all of these things. And yet, as she arose from the water, warm and langourous with every sense reawakened and ready to be heightened, it was Jack for whom her body yearned.

Chapter Seventeen

They walked back to the hotel through streets hushed with night, the only sounds a strumming gimbrey, a whining dog, and a trotting soldier's horse, all invisible but near. Smells of warm sand, oleander and jasmine blended gently with sea salt, and a horned moon dangled in a sky netted with stars.

"It seems unreal," Rosaline commented to Jack, her hand, still warm and soap-scented, nestled in the crook of his arm. "It seems impossible that only hours ago, such horror took place here, just exactly where we walk. Isn't it strange . . . " she mused, "the way men can murder in one moment, and in the next, sit down and enjoy dinner with pretty wives and laughing children?"

"Blood sport makes the enjoyment of such things sweeter."

Rosaline glanced at her husband, at the night-shaded planes of his face. Jack had spoken with a shrug of simple matter-of-factness, whereas her own voice had been full of a quiet tragedy. David, she thought, would never have answered in such a way as Jack—the artist was too sensitive, too reflective. But then of course, he had never experienced the curiously wicked exhilaration of battle as Jack had done.

With a tinge of condemnation, she said to her husband, "Why do you treat the tragedies of life as if they are inconsequential?"

He laughed at her observation. But he laughed at himself, not at her. "I'm accustomed to taking nothing too seriously except my own interests. And besides that, I suppose I picture the world in a different way than you do."

"What sort of way?"

Jack smiled in the darkness at the gravity in her tone, and pondered for a moment. His strides were lazy as they crossed the now quiet square. "Well, my dear wife," he said at last, "you seem to believe that the world has been created to produce some sort of civilized order, that it's obliged to be good."

She accepted that, and prompted, "And what do you believe?"

"I believe the world is obliged to be nothing at all."

"Cynicism at its best."

"As you say." He chuckled, the sound throaty and rich in the eastern night. "Those taught in the school of hard knocks make the world's greatest cynics, don't you know?"

"I suppose you resent people like me who grew up pampered and well-heeled."

"No. As I've said before, I simply envy them. Cynical, ruthless, whatever my faults may be, I should think you would at least credit me for being honest."

Rosaline cast him a glance. "Yes, well, I'll concede that you're honest—but only when you're forced to be."

"Ah, Rosie, Rosie," he said with pretended hurt, "I can see that you intend to keep me in line."

"As the wife of a potential gentleman, that's my duty, at least, as I understand it."

He laughed aloud. "So, to your mind, I have not yet reached that exalted pinnacle, eh?"

She preceded him up the hotel steps, suddenly enjoying their banter, her tiredness evaporated, her body exhilarated from the bath and the dry, scented night. "No. But I believe that there's still a ray or two of hope."

"I'm glad to hear it."

He escorted her to their room, which was dark, the lamp having run out of oil during their absence, the moon hidden now behind a scrap of cloud. Night gave an intimacy to the space, a dreaminess which transformed it into a still-life of faded color. Jack closed the door and at the same time, moved forward to touch Rosaline's arm.

She turned in surprise, and in an impulse of urgency, he took her face between his hands, then bent to kiss her with the ardor of a virile man who has had his senses roused by the aphrodisiacs of both war and the flesh of a woman.

Rosaline did not resist, but succumbed willingly, stirred too by the turbulence of the day, by her need for Jack—unwilling or not—and by a desperation to smother thoughts of David. Her hands were just as eager, just as restless as Jack's, her lips as greedy. As his fingers slid beneath the silk of her blouse, they prompted soft sighs from both joined lips, followed by a shiver from Rosaline as the garment slipped from her shoulders, leaving them bare to the coolness of the breeze curling past the open balcony doors.

Through half-closed eyes, Rosaline pulled back and gazed at her husband's taut face, at his brown chest beneath her flattened palms, at his hands on her waist. Jack backed her toward the bed, intent and inflamed. To please him, Rosaline began to loosen her still damp hair, letting it fall while her fingers trailed through the short length of his own, dried now by the heat.

And with a great wonder she began to believe that, within the moments to come, she would discover in full measure the gratification she had, with great effort, tried and failed to find with Jack. He seemed to know it too, touching her ready flesh with all the mastery of his experience—until, outside, the breeze gusted in a sudden nervous, impish start and lifted a forgotten jacket from the rail.

The garment drifted, then floated down toward the flagstones in a langourous slide, as if to delay its descent as long as possible in order to make fevered minds remember. David's jacket. . . .

Momentarily, for a brief but telling fraction, Rosaline stiffened, and her melting body grew rigid within the circle of her husband's hold.

Panting fast, his voice harsh, Jack breathed against her ear, "You're thinking of him, aren't you? Do you love him, Rosaline? Do you love the artist still?"

Oddly, Rosaline could think of no reason to lie. With a degree of defiance, and with the need to punish him for his own love of Julie, she whispered in soft misery, "Perhaps . . . I don't know, I don't know. . . ."

She thought that her words startled Jack, for he paused in his loving of her, took his rough cheek away from hers. Then his arms tightened on her shoulders, and with curt ferocity he breathed, "Good, then. It's simpler between us when I'm not burdened by your affection. We can have a more straightforward understanding that way, a marriage made up mostly of this," He bent to kiss her neck, his teeth scraping the tender rise of her collar bone as he added, "And of this."

He took her then, laid her back against the bed upon the coverlet. With no further delay, with a kind of painful but harsh tenderness she knew sprang from the confusion pounding inside his own heart, Jack thrust his body into hers.

Outside, the white jacket lay almost still, fluttering with life only once or twice. Rosaline's eyes fastened on it while she held Jack's splendid body, clutched it, trying to shut out of her mind the complicated net that held both her and Jack, the artist and Julie all together.

In Alexandria they rented a house by the sea, a lovely house, so white and clean it dazzled the eyes on days when the sun shone particularly gold. Often Rosaline found herself gazing at the water, watching it lap at the yellow shoreline, its liquid beauty not even dimmed by the dark, gathering warships that sailed one by one into the harbor.

"Jack," she said in surprise, calling him to the balcony one morning. "Those are British warships, aren't they?" Faintly frightened, she squinted her eyes to see better. "Why are they here?"

Her husband came to stand behind her, sliding into his frockcoat, freshly shaven, smelling clean and male. He hadn't come home until very late the previous night—his habit since the evening when he had so fiercely made love to her while she lay with David in her mind. Now, beyond an occasionally good-natured kiss or an obligatory embrace when they danced at embassy balls, he rarely touched her. Nor did he come often to her bedroom.

"The British government has become a laughingstock here in Alexandria," he told her. "Parliament has blown its top and has decided to let its collection of warships ride in the harbor for awhile—cannons poised of course—hoping that it will wipe the smile off of Arabi's face."

"Will there be war?"

"Probably, if British financiers have anything to say about it. They've invested heavily in Egyptian railroads, telegraphs and steamer lines, and they want England to annex this country so their fortunes will be kept safe and sound. And just as important, Disraeli has shares in the Suez Canal. He wouldn't want to see Arabi blow it up."

"And what do you think about that, about British policy?"

Jack's mouth tilted, giving his handsome face a disrespectful insolence. "I care nothing for Britain's politics beyond what they can do for my position in the Foreign Office."

Jack, Rosaline thought, was becoming more hard-edged than ever, more brashly determined to achieve the power and status he had set out to seize for himself. And although he always treated her with the utmost respect, even with a husbandly playfulness at times, she wondered if his recklessness had anything to do with her relationship with him and the underlying tension it caused.

She looked at Jack now, knowing she probably did so with the same longing that stayed always in her heart, and which she did not completely understand despite countless hours of pondering. She felt clearly, though, as if she and Jack stood upon a precipice together, as if something momentous were about to happen over which she had no control and which would decide their future for them.

She absently touched the potted violets on the balcony wall and forced her thoughts to other matters. "It seems Arabi is becoming more and more a national hero."

"That he is. And as a show of his popular support, he's manning the old stone fort near the harbor, arming it with thousands of men. If British ships fire on his fort, he says he'll start a holy war."

"Do you believe him?"

"I never underestimate the fanaticism of the East," Jack said. "The idea of a holy war is already being preached in the mosques here."

"And your role? What is the Foreign Office doing with you?"

"Ostensibly?" Jack laughed with short, scornful humor. "Ordering me to smile at Arabi's representatives. We're all supposedly working for peace, but we're really just playing a game. It doesn't matter a damn what we manage to negotiate with Arabi here. Ultimately, the gentlemen with the heaviest purses in London will decide what's to be done in Egypt. Monetary power is everything. It always has been. And one day I intend to wield some of that power myself. One way or the other."

With sudden, inexplicable concern, Rosaline studied her husband. He was standing beside her now, gazing out at the water. His eyes, she noted, were filled with a gleam, the sort of faraway gleam sparked by something that remains just out of reach. And Rosaline surmised that Jack saw something far beyond the ocean and the warships. She suspected he saw in his mind a ragged, hungry-eyed boy on the East side of London with a stolen pocketwatch in his hand.

"Are you happy, Jack?" she asked all at once, knowing he wasn't, fearing intuitively he would push his ambition to the limit and grow reckless to the point of danger. She knew ambitious men often drove themselves to ruin, and she was afraid of such a fate for Jack. "After all," she said a bit too intently, "Lord Duff-Sarton has commended you for saving his wife's life, and promoted you to an enviable level. Now we're accepted in every circle here—besides being quite popular, if I must say so myself." She said this last in an almost playful way, hoping to lighten his mood.

"All true."

"Then can't you be happy with that, Jack?" she said in a soft voice. "For awhile at least?"

He turned to look at her, his eyes shimmering just faintly with a moisture that indicated the degree of his passion. "No, Rosaline," he said roughly. "It is not enough."

"I wish . . . " She broke off, almost having said, "I wish that *I* could be enough, that the two of us together could be enough."

His eyes stayed fastened upon her face for several seconds, and she feared that he guessed what had just crossed her mind, for suddenly he looked away, almost as if he pitied her.

She too turned, retreating into the shadows of the room, mortified and nonplussed. Her eyes fastened upon the drawer to her vanity. A few days ago, David had sent her a note asking for a rendezvous. She hadn't answered, unable to bring herself to decline his offer, yet not brave enough to set a day and time to schedule her act of infidelity. The letter still rested, waiting, in the top drawer below her bottle of French perfume.

Rajad and Antonio ran into the room then, having breakfasted already. They begged permission to go out and play. Last week Jack had sent a message to Hoseyn and asked him to bring them from Cairo, preferring to have the boys close now that political tensions had increased.

"Antonio," Jack said with a frown, noting the cage that swung negligently from the boy's hand. "What are you doing with Rosaline's finches?"

Defensiveness crossed the lad's face and he declared, "She said I could take them out into the garden, let them sit in the sunshine."

It wasn't true, but Rosaline interfered to prevent contention. "Antonio knows I trust him with the finches." She smiled at the boy, leaning to ruffle his tangled hair, disappointed when he dodged her affectionate gesture in his usual and apparently instinctive way. "I've given him permission to take care of my little feathered treasures."

The boy's chest puffed out in smugness, and sensing a conspiracy, Jack grumbled, "Take good care of them, then. Show us that you can be trusted."

Rosaline glanced at Jack, sensing that he attached some special significance to the finches, considered them . . . what? Mementos of a misty day in Edinburgh? Whatever his thoughts regarding the birds, she wished her husband would show more faith in the boy, even though Antonio gave repeated cause to break even the most steadfast faith. Yet Antonio craved Jack's approval and had begun to grow jealous of Rajad. Now that school and family life had coaxed him out of his shell, Rashad received a great deal of fatherly attention from his ward.

For a moment, Rosaline observed her trio of males, and her eyes came to rest upon the Italian boy's rebellious face. She knew Antonio would never be the sort to follow rules, would always fend for himself, and would take whatever he wanted from the world if he could. Like Jack. She suspected that Jack knew it as well and recognized too much of himself in Antonio; and therein lay the problem between them.

"You young hellions run on out and play," Jack told his adopted sons. "But stay in the garden. If I see so much as one disobedient toe inched past the gate, I'll skin you alive. Come with me," he said then to Rosaline, smiling the smile she had never quite learned to resist. "Let's have breakfast in the bazaar. I have a sudden yearning for those honey cakes sold on the corner—you know the ones? Those with the nutmeg sprinkled on top?"

They went out together into the brilliant sunshine and heard the cries of the hawkers, particularly the seller of *chusaf*—or fruit juice—and the fellow who peddled butter cakes and pretzels. A beggar in multi-colored rags and a red turban threw himself at their feet, and in a prayerful attitude whined, "I'm the guest of God, and have not yet breakfasted!"

"Neither have we," Jack drawled, but tossed him a coin.

He took Rosaline's arm and led her through the bazaar and its countless, crowded booths of scarabari, dried fruits, Moroccan slippers, spears, peanuts, and long strings of dried okra called *bamie*. The smells of curry and cinnamon and incense were strong, and the air was dry and warm, fraught with the cries of hungry gulls, braying donkeys, and chattering, half-naked children.

When they passed the jewelry exhibit, Rosaline paused, her eye caught by a tiny silver box heavily engraved and mounted upon a plinth of velvet as if it were an object of honor.

"Do you like it?" Jack asked, noticing the direction of her gaze.

"Oh, yes, Jack! It's quiet beautiful, engraved all over with birds. Did you notice?"

"Those are crows. There's a legend about them here."

"Really? Now that you mention it, I don't believe I've noticed any crows in Alexandria."

"That's because once upon a time an Egyptian magician conjured up a talisman to ban them."

"To ban them?" Rosaline said through a smile.

"Um. The magician buried the talisman right here in Alexandria, and since then, not a single crow has dared to fly over the city."

"Jack," she laughed, but he held up a finger and continued. "It's said that if the talisman is ever found, the spell will be broken and the birds will be at liberty to return."

With mischievousness not normal to her nature, Rosaline slanted her gaze and said, "Perhaps the talisman is in that box there."

Raising a brow, then grinning, Jack turned to the stall keeper and asked in Arabic, "How much for the box?"

The monkey-faced old man shook his head and began to speak vociferously, gesticulating and pointing to the heavens.

"He says the box is not for sale," Jack interpreted, while drawing money from his pocket and adding in an undertone, "Let's see how bright the glitter of gold must be for the fellow to sell."

But, surprisingly, the owner of the item was not tempted by the generous offer, and held out his knotty hands as if to ward off temptation, even when Jack offered yet more money.

"What does he say?" Rosaline asked, amazed that the man could resist the lure of so much coin.

"He says the box is magic."

"Of course," she said with a knowing smile. "He wants you to offer him even a higher amount."

"No, I think we have just witnessed the impossible in an Arab bazaar. The fellow genuinely seems to treasure the box too much to sell. And it has nothing to do with the crows," Jack confided. "It has to do with happiness. The fellow claims that anyone who opens the lid will be instantly transported to a happy, faraway island."

"Orkney perhaps?" Rosaline said with the raise of a teasing brow, prompting Jack to grin.

Intrigued in spite of herself, Rosaline touched the engraving on the box, gave it one last, longing look before throwing off its enchantment, and took hold of Jack's arm in her properly decorous way. "Leave the old man his treasure, then. Let's get breakfast. I'm starving."

Awhile later, when they returned to the steps of their house by the sea, Jack paused at the door where the sun glossed his hair blue-black. "You have sugar on your mouth," he told Rosaline, fishing in his pocket for a handkerchief. Frowning, he paused, then drew out something other than a handkerchief while he pretended to be surprised at finding it there. Sunlight sparkled off the polished silver in his hand, and Rosaline gasped.

"Jack!"

With a flourish, he took her palm and laid the box of magic in it, and she laughed at him in happiness, cradling the prize, not daring to open it. "But—it wasn't for sale!"

"My dear Rosaline," Jack said with his slow, secret smile, "don't you know there are ways of acquiring things you want without paying for them?"

His words caused Rosaline pause and her face fell. But she forced a smile, loath to spoil the rare, special moments of cheer between them. She turned away and entered the house with the little treasure nestled in her hands, feeling cold all at once, chagrined. Had Jack, out of habit and without conscience, stolen the box for her just because she had fancied it? Would he have dared to do such a thing?

Rosaline didn't know, and couldn't bring herself to ask; but the carefree mood was suddenly gone from the day.

Perhaps the incident was a presage. For all at once, just as she made her way toward the kitchen, a child's thin, high cry pierced the air. Alarmed, Rosaline rushed to the garden to find Hoseyn chastising Antonio, who knelt upon the grass in a tragic posture with something nestled in his palms.

"What's going on here?" Jack demanded, striding forward as well, addressing Hoseyn. The servant, in agitation, began to explain in Arabic.

While the two men conversed, Rosaline ran to Antonio, bent down, her full muslin skirts billowing over the lawn. In the boy's trembling hand, she saw one of the brown finches Jack had given her.

"I wanted to let them fly!" Antonio cried. "I wanted to let them go for a few minutes so they would know what it was like to be free! I carried them into the house and opened the cage. This one," he said, holding out the bird, "he hopped out, he flew."

"He flew into the window glass!" Rajad wailed, his hands covering his eyes as if he couldn't bear to glimpse the tiny ball of feathers. "The bird wanted to go out into the sunshine, to go up into the clouds and fly. Antonio let him be killed. His neck is broken!"

"Antonio, for God's sake." Jack said, coming forward.

But Rosaline stayed him with a sharp look, her maternal instincts surging.

Antonio threw himself into her arms, buried his face against the lace at her bosom, his long pent-up feelings dissolving in a wretched torrent of grief as he sobbed. "You shall hate me now! You shall hate me like *he* does!"

"No, no!" she soothed, and tightened her arms about him in a fierce denial. "I shall love you even more. It was not your fault, not really, not really."

Jack observed Rosaline and the boy as they rocked together in each other's arms, Rosaline's dark head bent over the youngster's quivering form. As he watched, he experienced a sudden, sharp prick of shame, and turned away just as a thunderous boom rent the air and rattled the windows of the house.

Rajad screamed in fright and clapped his hand over his ears. "What is it? What is it?"

Sprinting to the garden wall, peering over the top toward the sea, Jack sighted the row of British warships, saw a curl of black smoke wend up from one poised cannon.

"Damn it!" he swore, scanning the shoreline, finding the ancient, battlemented fort of Arabi's ablaze with fire. "Damn those fools in Parliament!"

"What is it, Jack?" Rosaline cried, gathering both children to her arms. "What's happened?"

"One of our battleships has fired on Arabi's fort," he explained, already running toward the gate that led out onto the street. "Stay in the house with Hoseyn, Rosaline!" he shouted over his shoulder. "Don't open the door for anyone until I return."

But when Jack saw the condition of the streets, already chaotic, and heard another deafening boom delivered by the warship, he paused in indecision. A messenger from the embassy riding a lathered horse clattered to the gate and yelled, "Get your family out, sir! The admiral has given orders for our forces to bombard Arabi's garrison!"

"Damn his eyes! Why weren't we warned? There's no time to get my family on the train. It's too far, for God's sake, it'll be packed before we can push through this madness."

"Yes, no doubt, sir."

"Is the embassy secured? My aide is there."

"Yes, sir. For now, at least."

In the streets, people panicked as they heard the repeated thunder of the cannon and the resultant fiery explosions. Running wildly to find shelter, people gathered children close and abandoned parcels of food or water jugs just filled at the fountain. Prepared and eager to retaliate, Arabi's patrols wasted no time. Within minutes, mounted calvary swooped vengefully through the square, knowing the seaside villas housed families of financiers and diplomats who threatened to overrun their country. Several of the Egyptian soldiers tossed flaming torches atop the flat wooden roofs used as terraces, setting alight the wicker chaise lounges, the fringed silk cushions, the baskets of flowers so enjoyed by the fair-skinned invaders.

"Bloody hell! They're wasting no time," Jack growled as the messenger whipped up his wild-eyed horse and galloped away. Sprinting into the house, Jack seized a rifle from its case, shattered a window pane in the parlor and targeted a mounted Egyptian soldier, killing him just as the dark-faced man rose in the stirrups and hurled a torch at the roof. It sailed to the ground and lay smoldering near the front steps.

"Hoseyn!" Jack yelled over his shoulder, stopping long

enough to sight another charging soldier and fire. "Run up to the terrace with some water buckets and wet it down. Rosaline," he continued, glancing around to assure himself that she and the children were safe, "go upstairs and look in my trunk—you'll find sets of native clothes both for yourself and the boys. Dress in them quickly. Then stay near the garden doors in case one of these soldiers manages to escape my aim and set the house afire."

"Yes, Jack!" she yelled, terrified, grabbing hold of the boys.

"And Rosaline," he added, leveling the rifle again through the broken pane, "if something happens to me, hide in the garden until Hoseyn can get you and the children to the train. Do you understand?"

"Yes." She did as he had bade, trying to maintain her composure for the boys' sake, as she grasped their hands and drew them toward the stairs, only to falter in her progress when Antonio jerked free.

"I'm staying with *him!*" the boy cried, his face twisted with both anxiety and bravado. "I'm staying to help him kill the soldiers!"

"Antonio!" Rosaline grappled with him, but he eluded her hold, scampering to Jack's side and crouching down.

Jack had no time to argue with Antonio, urgently reloading his rifle, trying to see through the haze, and cursed when a cannon shot, louder than the rest, rattled the windows of the house. Rajad screamed and clutched Rosaline's skirts as she battled to yank Antonio to his feet. Just then, the front door shuddered with a sudden battering force.

Jack left his post at the window, running while he raised his rifle to his shoulder and aimed at the portal just when it gave way against a mighty assault.

Rosaline seized the two boys and dragged them up the stairs, tripping, breathing hard, catching only a horrifying glimpse of three turbanned invaders as they stormed across the threshold. Fleeing, literally carrying the boys, one under each arm as she clambered up to reach the landing, she cried out when shots rang below. With icy hands, she yanked the clothes from Jack's trunk and bundled them under one arm. Shouting at the children to stay close and follow, she made for the door again, glancing down first to see what had happened below. Jack had slain the intruders; they lay dead upon the tiles just inside the house, but Jack was not in sight.

Rajad sobbed and gripped her skirts, impeding her as she tried to carry him down the stairs. Antonio jerked from her grasp again and darted to the window just as Hoseyn ran into the room. "Mr. Darlington says to come hide in the garden!" he exclaimed. "House next door on fire. Come! Come!"

Rosaline pulled the children to the lower story and guided them to the garden where drifting layers of smoke overlaid the flowers. On the streets, churning hooves and crackling blazes pierced the once peaceful air, and cannon blasts shook the earth itself as Rosaline herded the children to the corner of the garden where the hydrangeas formed a dense growth. Hurriedly she sorted the clothes in her arms, pulled the wide trousers over the boys' European clothes, then quickly stepped into the black drapes worn by native women. Wrapping a veil haphazardly about her shoulders and head, she stooped down as Hoseyn parted the foliage and waited for her and the children to creep through and burrow into a hiding place.

As the servant sprinted off to join Jack, Rosaline eyed his retreating back through the branches, and contemplated for the first time the extent of the Egyptian servant's loyalty, conjuring possible scenes of his betrayal. She shuddered, then jumped as another cannon shot boomed. Putting the children behind her in the deepest part of the green sanctuary, she agonized, yearned to go and assure herself of Jack's safety, to help him defend the house if she could.

Earlier Antonio had grabbed the bird cage containing its single finch, and the creature huddled on the bottom now, quivering. For a moment, as she breathed the acrid smoke mingled with the sweet smell of leaves, Rosaline stared at the bird, remembered in a vivid flash the day Jack had bought it for her in the cool Scottish rain.

"It's a sign," Antonio said in a quiet, earnest voice beside her, his eyes, too, fixed upon the finch.

"What is a sign, Antonio?"

"The other bird's death. It's a sign of bad fortune."

"Hush!" Rosaline snapped, disturbed because the boy had echoed aloud her own deep thoughts. Antonio turned his head away from her sullenly, and, wanting to distract both him and the other child half buried in her skirts, she felt in her pocket and withdrew the silver box Jack had given her.

"It's a magic box," she whispered, her voice trembling as she heard Jack's rifle crack somewhere in the house. "See how fine it is. If I open it, the magic will whisk us away home."

"Then let's go now! Let's go home now!" Rajad wailed, reaching out to prize the box away from her hands.

"No. We can't leave Mr. Jack. We'll stay just where we are, safe and warm for now. Alright? Now, come closer and I shall tell you a story."

After that, Rosaline was never certain how many hours passed, she only recalled them as hours of terror filled with choking smoke, wisps of ash, and the damp gritty sand beneath her hips. The ear-splitting fury of battle seemed to rage on and on, making Rajad cringe and Antonio restless to jump up on the garden wall and watch the burning city.

Rosaline could scarcely imagine the destruction, the fate of Europeans if the British attack failed to subdue Arabi and he launched his promised war. More than once she thought of David, wondered if he had managed to survive the turmoil, tried to remember the quiet, passionate interlude with him in her father's rose-scented conservatory. And Jack. She thought of Jack ceaselessly, and touched the magic box now tucked inside her pocket.

She grew numb with weariness after awhile, not even hearing at first the thud of hurried male footsteps pounding the garden path. Gathering the children close, she peeked fearfully through the hydrangeas to see who approached.

"Jack!" Shooing the children out, then following them, she threw herself at her husband's solid form while he shifted his rifle to the crook of one arm and pressed her waist.

"The worst seems to be over," he said, "at least for now. Much of the city is in flames and will likely burn for days. But the streets are almost quiet. It seems most of the natives have fled to seek safety in the country villages."

"And the Europeans?"

Jack's expression tightened. "It's anyone's guess how many of them were able to escape."

"What of Arabi's fort?"

"Practically demolished."

"And Arabi himself?"

"He's a wily fellow. My guess is that he and most of his army retreated hours ago, leaving Alexandria to the mercy of fanatics and looters. I have already shot a number of them. The rest have apparently been driven away by the fires and heat."

"What are we to do now?"

Jack looked out over the garden wall toward the sea, which that morning had been so clear, visible for miles, sequined with the sun's reflection. Now its waves and warships lay shrouded in shreds of dark gray smoke. There were no sounds except the lapping of the water and the fast roar of distant flames. "We'll have to keep the roof wet through the night to keep the blaze next door from igniting it," he said. "I've assigned Hoseyn the chore for now, but he'll have to be sent to the railway station soon to see if the train to Cairo is still running. Can you find us some food? The kitchen servants took to their heels at the sound of the first cannon blast this morning. I suppose we should thank God they didn't take the opportunity to bash us over the head on the way out."

"Can Hoseyn be trusted?" Rosaline asked, voicing her earlier fear.

Jack shrugged as a brief, wry grin crossed his shadowed face. "Who knows? I have to keep my eye on him—but not too closely. Loyalty, like anything else, can be bought." His eyes held a hint of mischief. "For good measure, I promised to finance his next pilgrimage to Mecca."

Incredibly, Rosaline felt a smile tug at her mouth. "What will you do now, Jack?"

"Go out on the streets and see what's left, what needs to be done. If possible, I'll find someone to take a message to the embassy—let's hope it still stands. I'll not be gone more than a quarter hour or so. Keep this revolver close."

"Take care of yourself." She pocketed the weapon and touched his sleeve.

After he had gone, she gathered the boys close and made her way to the kitchens. The cool, tiled place had been abruptly abandoned by the servants, who had left a meal in a suspended state of preparation, as evidenced by an assortment of half sliced vegetables, loaves of bread rising in baskets, and a mold of orange butter melting in its dish.

"Rajad, pour us all a glass of water," Rosaline said tensely, glancing out the window at the shadowy smoke. "Then rummage through that crate over there and pick out the best oranges—a half dozen of them, please. Antonio, finish peeling these cucumbers—I know you're handy with a knife and . . ." She paused. "Antonio?" she repeated, turning impatiently to Rajad. "Rajad, where is your brother?"

Preoccupied with the oranges, the boy shoved a slice in his mouth thirstily, shrugged and murmured, "I dunno. Gone to fight soldiers with Mr. Jack, maybe."

Irritated, her nerves frazzled, Rosaline ran along the corridor calling the recalcitrant boy, found the house empty and silent, haze floating in through the battered front door.

"Antonio!" she called. When he failed to answer, she went to the door and shouted for Jack in alarm, then for Hoseyn, but no reply came.

Lifting her soiled skirts, she jogged back to the hot kitchen, and in a firm voice instructed Rajad to stay where he was. "Antonio has been naughty and slipped away, my pet. I have to go and find him. Hide here, beneath the table—like a bunny, that's a good lad. Eat all the oranges you want till I return. Remember—*don't move.* Do you understand?"

He nodded and Rosaline hurried back to the front of the house, pausing at the porch step to stare into the eerily smoldering air. Although a blue twilight had fallen, so many fires blazed around the city that their flares filtered a bright yellow glow through the haze. With a hand over her mouth, Rosaline stepped over the soldiers Jack had earlier slain. She ventured tentatively forward, and experienced a pang of anxiety no less strong than that of a natural mother as she imagined Antonio roaming lost through the dangerous streets.

"Antonio!" she cried, feeling the heat of the pavement burn through the thin kid soles of her boots. "Jack!"

No answer came from either, and she traversed the smoke-wrapped avenue with its scattering of slain, closed her eyes momentarily against the sight, and tried to gain direction by the faint, muffled sound of the fountain at the center of the square.

"Antonio!" she called again, frantic now. *"Antonio!"*

Through the smoke veils a few tattered, sooty-faced European men moved, helping wounded victims or rushing to and from the fountain in order to fill up pails of water which would be tossed at the roaring conflagration. The heat caused perspiration to roll down Rosaline's face; cinders floated through the air, causing her to cough. She fumbled in her pocket for a handkerchief to put over her nose, then shrieked Antonio's name again and again.

A moment later she thought she heard an answering echo, dim and faraway, coming from the direction of the marketplace, and hurriedly made her way through the strewn remains of vegetables, broken trinkets and Nubian fans, seeing a small shape in native dress, his familiar gait almost a swagger. Antonio, surely, for no other child would display a lack of fear amid such chaos.

"Are you safe?" she cried, holding out her arms, running to gather him up.

He did not pull away; it seemed that the death of the little finch had somehow, quite miraculously, broken through a barricade and softened him toward receiving her affection. "Come!" he commanded in a manlike voice. "Follow me. I take you to *him.*"

"To Jack?"

Antonio pulled Rosaline's arm, and after hesitating a fraction, she followed through the vaporous maze of the ruined marketplace, broken beads crunching beneath her soles, the sound of burning wood loud. She had trouble breathing and her eyes stung. After several blocks, the boy halted abruptly and stood motionless, saying nothing. He seemed to be waiting until Rosaline's eyes, too, found what his had already sighted.

Two figures stood together beside the half-charred booth of a bellmaker, embracing like lost lovers, their two molded bodies backlit by fitful flames. The couple was not still, but touched frenziedly, deliriously, as they reassured themselves of the reality of the other, their hands clutching, their faces pressed together. The woman, her movements desperate, began to kiss Jack Darlington.

A searing breeze blew, and the brass bells jingled, making a jarring melody.

Antonio threw himself against her suddenly, almost as if defending her from hurt. The silver box lay heavy in her pocket, and when Antonio pressed against her, the edge of it cut into her thigh. Fumbling, half dazed by the sight of her husband in the arms of the woman she had grown to fear, Rosaline absently drew it out and would have dropped it on the ground.

"No!" Antonio cried, wrenching it from her hand, his bravery gone now and replaced by all the fears of childhood. ''Open it so we can go home—just you and me and Rajad. Let *him* stay here with *her!* She does not belong with us!''

Rosaline thought how intuitively and accurately children understood.

Chapter Eighteen

Rosaline did not remember the walk home. She remembered only that Antonio stayed close beside her, in a protective manner, clutching her hand, his strides those of an angry and secretly uncertain child. Once inside the house, Rosaline directed him in a dull tone to light the lamps while she, like some bedazed but purposeful sleepwalker, went to the kitchens to assure herself that Rajad was safe. Seeing him happily playing marbles in a corner, she began in a mechanical way to slice a loaf of bread and arrange it on a clean blue platter. The children needed to eat. They all would need to eat. They all would need refreshment. Think of nothing but the necessary, she told herself, think only of the elemental tasks of life, of doing what must be done. *Do not think of him, of them.*

After the oranges were finished, she retrieved a basket of fresh lemons and limes, and systemically, thinking of nothing but the fragrant juice that ran stickily through her fingers, squeezed them into a pitcher. Too soon, as she knew he would, Antonio appeared, and in a quiet but very level little voice said, "*He* asked to see you now."

The time had come. She must face her husband and the woman that surely he had brought home with him.

"Yes, Antonio," she said, wiping her hands slowly on a linen cloth, her face stiff and drawn, "I'll go. I'll be there presently."

Walking along the corridor, her shoes leaving marks through the film of cinders and sand, Rosaline paused at the entrance to the parlor door. Taking a breath, mustering all the emotional resources she possessed in order to endure the sight of her husband beside the woman he loved, Rosaline entered the room.

Julie. For a moment, Rosaline did nothing but take in the look of her, every nuance, every detail of face and dress and expression. She was most unusual. Her features suggested foreignness, yet did not claim the look of a particular race, so that if she chose, if it were necessary, Rosaline thought, she could doubtless pass for a member of almost any land. She resembled a small dark fox, alert, exceedingly self-possessed. Wild, insubstantial, able to melt in and out of places, able to give an impression of vulnerability; and yet, she probably was not vulnerable at all. Black hair, tangled, thick and long, deep black eyes, skin the color of dusky, unflawed amber.

She stood in Rosaline's ravaged parlor in her trailing Egyptian dress, the fabric half swallowing her diminutive figure. She was a creature created for shadowy places and nighttime, Rosaline thought. A man, all men, would consider her an enchantment.

Jack?

He stood close beside Julie. His eyes, briefly meeting Rosaline's, communicated everything, nothing at all, before they turned once again to Julie, devouring, and drowning in her. Rosaline didn't blame him then, in those first few tumultuous minutes, for she knew he simply couldn't help himself after so many years, after so much worry and wonder. To his credit, he kept his hands from Julie, but, oh dear God, how Rosaline's heart writhed, sliced through with envy, gasping with a deep, silently struggling rage.

And yet, with the grace, the pride that so often kept her spine straight and her eyes brightly dry, Lord Bardo's daughter took matters in hand, functioning in the way that was necessary, doing what must be done.

"I shall bring us food and something to drink," she said with a nod of her head, not faltering over a single syllable. "I've been preparing refreshments in the kitchen. The staff are all gone, you see," she added formally, unnecessarily. And then, her whole body feeling numb, she turned her back upon the pair, left her husband alone with Julie in a room made so terribly, so romantically dangerous with the reflection of flames in its windows.

Her kitchen tasks kept her hands occupied, thank God, even while her mind flashed with pictures of a man and woman just down the corridor, in each other's arms, hands joined together, lips whispering . . .

"Rajad," she said in a steady voice, "bring the cheese and fruit. Antonio, pour lemonade for five—no six. Hoseyn should be returning from the embassy soon with news. We'll eat in the parlor. Can you help carry the trays?"

"Yes, of course, we can," Antonio answered, understanding, doing what he could, his child's heart experienced enough to sense her pain and respond to it with maturity. "I will help you carry everything up. But Rajad and I will eat here in the kitchen. Not with *her*."

When Rosaline returned to the little room at the front of the house, she was breathing shallowly, knowing her life with Jack was altered now. As she stepped across the threshold, she saw her husband and Julie draw quickly apart—in guilt perhaps?

Setting down the tray of food and in a stilted voice, Rosaline invited them to be seated and eat, just as if they were guests who had dropped in for tea.

No one spoke, all silently ate, nourishing themselves because they were famished and thirsty, and because eating was an excuse not to speak. Rosaline watched askance and noticed Julie's hands, the narrow palms, the thin deft fingers as they quickly peeled an orange, then tore a piece of bread apart with a greediness not quite concealed. Jack ate little but drank a great deal of brandy.

Later, after Rosaline had tucked both exhausted boys beneath their quilts, passed the closed door of the room she assumed Jack had offered to Julie, she went along to her own bed, only to find her husband awaiting her.

The room was lit by nothing more than a half-consumed white taper, its flicker casting shadows over the thick white walls, over the glazed blue tiles, over the bed. Because she was too wounded, too bruised and numb, gripped by an undefinable fear to speak, Rosaline moved to stand before the mirror of her vanity, and, with her back turned, removed the ruby earrings she had put in that morning—how many hours ago? It seemed odd to her that so much had happened in such a short space of time, only a few moments really, each of them of terrible import to her life. It seemed odd to be doing nothing now but removing her earrings.

"This is one of the few times that you don't know what to say to me, do you, Rosaline?" Jack remarked in a quiet voice, not unkindly, behind her. "You can't even mutter something ordinary and mundane. How shaken you must be."

Yes, the subject of Julie hung heavily between them, separated them like some impenetrable sheet of gauze and, taking a breath, unable to voice the syllables of Julie's name lest she falter over them, Rosaline asked, "What are her circumstances?"

As if reluctant to let words about Julie flow, Jack moved to the washstand and without haste leaned to wash the soot from his face before he took up a towel. After he had dried and delayed his answer as long as possible, he spoke to Rosaline in a sober voice. "The house where she was living is half burned and no longer habitable. She was staying with friends, and can't manage to find them now."

"So she will be staying with us." The words were flat, with no charity in them at all.

"Yes. Until I can decide what she must do."

"Why? She cannot decide for herself?"

Jack turned to face Rosaline, sensing his wife was on the verge of saying something she felt must be said, something significant. He said evenly, "I will not turn her out."

"I did not think you would." Then, in a straight forward manner, as if she were hurling an arrow at him, she said, "I am in your way."

"I have never known you to be self-effacing, Rosaline."

"Nor am I now."

"I believe you are. I believe you pity yourself because Julie has reappeared."

"It's not pity that I feel. But I'd be a fool not to know that I am in the way. And I will not be a fool."

"Rosaline . . ."

"No!" she cried, whirling to face him, her fists clenched at her sides. "I'm inconveniently in the way now, aren't I, Jack? Aren't I?"

"For God's sake, you're my wife," he said through his teeth."

"But I wouldn't be, would I, if you'd found *her* a few months earlier? If you'd postponed my father's arrangement, delayed the marriage until after your trip to Egypt."

Jack moved toward the window, presenting a hostile back to Rosaline's demanding, tragic eyes. After several long moments, he shook his head and said in a burst of frustration, "I don't know. I don't know."

"Was I such a good bargain, then? Did you really believe I could do that much for the advancement of your career?"

Her tone was sarcastic, and Jack had never known her to use sarcasm before. "Rosaline."

But she refused to respond to the condescending patience of his tone. "Was your ambition for power and position just as strong as what you felt for Julie—still feel for her, Jack? Or doesn't the sort of relationship you have with Julie *require* marriage?"

"It hasn't, over the years." He pinned her with hard eyes.

"I'm surprised you dare admit it to me."

"Why? You'd come to your own conclusions regardless of what I admitted."

"Such conclusions are not difficult."

Jack waited until Rosaline had locked her gaze with his, then with a slow, brutal honesty, said, "Perhaps you would do well to remember why your father arranged your marriage with me. You see, we have been on equal footing from the beginning."

"But you have brought your lover into our *house.*"

"We are in the midst of a war, for God's sake."

"Yes. On more than one front."

"So it seems."

Their conversation had escalated close to a dangerous and angry point of no return. Afraid of the precipice all at once, Rosaline stepped back, clasped her hands tightly together, and tried to smother the jealous bitterness on her tongue as she looked into Jack's penetrating blue eyes. "Where has she been all this time? Why were you not able to find her?"

"She was captured on the streets of Cairo when we were together in Egypt last. Sold into slavery—a common fate for beautiful and unprotected women. A few months ago, she managed to escape—although she hasn't yet told me the particulars."

"I'm surprised she hasn't contacted you."

"She sent letters through the Foreign Office. They never caught up with me."

"And tomorrow?" Rosaline asked very quietly, her head lowered. "What about tomorrow?"

Although unsure whether she referred to the matters of the next twenty-four hours or to their future together—and Julie's part in it—Jack chose to address the immediate concerns, for he himself did not have the answers to the more complicated issue. "Hoseyn has returned from the embassy with a message. The embassy still stands intact—the admiral made certain he didn't fire in *that* direction—and Lance Cardew is safe. I'm to report there at first light. I'm not certain whether the Foreign Office will keep me here in Alexandria or order me back to Cairo."

Rosaline felt the need to be reassured, and at the same time, was afraid of blurting out a drastic option she hoped she didn't have to take. She opened her mouth to say, "Perhaps the children and I should sail back to Scotland. Perhaps we should leave Egypt just as soon as passage can be arranged." A part of her yearned to say just that—the cowardly part, the part that knew there was nothing ahead of her in Egypt but pain as Julie sought to take Jack from her. But Rosaline resisted. Her pride, her heart, prevented her from surrendering her husband so easily, so quickly, to the woman who had, doubtless, reappeared with hopes of claiming him again.

"Very well," she said tightly, rearranging the objects on her vanity with a shaky hand. "I'll be prepared to stay or go at a moment's notice, whatever is required of me. Now, I'd like to lie down, if you don't mind, and try to get some rest."

Rosaline waited wordlessly then, dismissed him, having made it plain that she did not want to speak further on the subject of his lover.

Jack turned and regarded her via the mirror, his gaze meeting hers, noting the strained paleness in her face, the darkness of her eyes and the hollowness below them. Some vital element seemed to have drained out of Rosaline during the trials of the day, leaving her fragile, remote, her usual courage gone. Oddly, sadly, in that moment, Jack felt as if he were observing a stranger, one who needed him but would not allow his touch or even the comfort of a gentle word. "Good night, then, Rosaline," he said in a regretful voice, turning away.

And Rosaline wondered, once Jack had closed her door, if he would walk straight down the corridor and, relieved to have his duty with his wife done, open another door. She feared that, for many nights to come, she would wonder precisely the same thing over and over.

* * *

Jack stayed up most of the night, sitting by the window downstairs with his rifle poised as he watched for looters who might still hope to find an unguarded house. Early, before dawn, Rosaline descended the stairs dressed for the day but looking very tired. She handed Jack a cup of tea in silence.

"I'll watch in your place for awhile," she offered softly, with none of the bitter edge born of the previous night. "Go and get some sleep before you have to leave for the embassy."

Jack looked up, his eyes boring into hers, and he wondered what conclusions his wife had drawn during the night, what attitude she had decided to take. He shook his head. "Sleep can wait. I'll go to the embassy now that it's almost light and see what sort of plots are being hatched there. I don't intend to get caught in another round of cannon fire today."

"Jack . . ." Rosaline broke off, looking away, unable to voice what she felt all at once, finding it too difficult to sort through her feelings, to articulate her fears at the risk that he would have no solace to give her, no promise that all would be well between them.

"Yes?"

She went to the patch of sunshine shimmering on the floor, and stood with her head bowed. After a moment, she said in a quiet voice, "Remember when we spoke about taking wrong paths, Jack? On the night of our marriage, remember?"

"I do."

"You said a path could not be a wrong one if you made a decision to take it. Do you believe that still?"

Jack read his wife's thoughts, understood what she was really asking. The last few hours, a part of him had thought endlessly of Julie lying just down the hall in her bed; the other part had dwelled on Rosaline. He was a man caught in a trap of his own making, and therefore could blame neither fate nor any living soul but himself. He said with a ghost of a smile, "I would stand to lose rather a lot of integrity if I said otherwise now, don't you think?"

"I suppose you would."

He held out a hand, the firm well-shaped hand that Rosaline loved. "Truce?" he asked.

The weariness in his voice revealed a beleaguered man, and sent a pang of yearning sadness through her, so that Rosaline wanted to reach out and stroke not just his hand but his face; she wanted to lay her palm alongside his rough cheek and caress it, break down, beg him to reassure her, even if it required a lie.

But Julie appeared just then, materialized upon the threshold of the parlor in that way she had of melting in and out of places.

At the sight of her, Jack's face changed. Rosaline could not describe the change, except to liken it to sunlight reflecting off cold still water.

Julie stood motionless, waiting for him. He went to her, looked into her eyes for a moment, and said softly, "Stay by the window with Rosaline."

He spoke as one speaks to an intimate, his voice low, carrying a deeper communication than words. And suddenly, Rosaline could imagine the two of them together as waifs in East London, and later as vagabonds sharing adventures, Jack giving orders, Julie obeying because she trusted his judgment, knew he would keep her safe. And then, she could imagine them as lovers, laughing together on the dim evening shores of exotic oceans, lying abed with pewter goblets of shared red wine.

Giving no farewell, Jack left for the embassy then, and for the first time Julie and Rosaline were alone together, the two women connected to him, one by the bonds of marriage, one by the strings of the past, both by the heart. Because the silence between them begged to be broken, and because her nerves were stretched to a point of breaking, Rosaline said for no reason other than to speak, "The fires are still smoldering outside, but the street seems to be quiet."

"Nothing here is as it seems."

They were the first words Rosaline had ever heard Julie utter, and they were spoken soberly, and yet underpinned with the faintest tinge of condescension. As Rosaline stared into the other woman's long black eyes, she had the oddest notion that laughter was behind them, as well as judgment. Julie was taking the measure of Jack's wife.

With a cool directness, Rosaline met the clever stare. "I daresay you're right."

Julie laughed then, a fairy bell sound that was natural and free. "You aren't as naive as some women of your kind, are you? Jack told me you weren't; don't worry, every word he said about you was a gentlemanly one. Yes, Mrs. Darlington, you've left your mark upon my Jackdaw, but he's not changed. He'll never change—at least, I hope he won't. It would be a shame to spoil such a man."

"I don't intend either to alter or to spoil him."

"Jack wouldn't allow you to unless he decided it would be to his own benefit."

"No doubt that it true." Rosaline studied the other woman, and asked with cold abruptness, "What are your plans?"

Julie smiled at the obvious ill-will in Rosaline's tone, and without haste to answer, she regarded the disordered objects on the table beside her—the stack of books, Jack's untouched teacup, the extra cartridges. One by one she picked them up, her hands as if out of habit judging the texture of each, the weight, the value. Magpie hands, Rosaline thought, acquisitive, always ready to take whatever might be taken.

"Plans?" Julie echoed, tasting Jack's cold tea. "I never have any plans beyond the day." Askance, she looked at Rosaline, as if daring her to question, or to believe the sincerity of the statement. "You would like me to say I'm off to the ends of the earth tomorrow, no doubt. I can't blame you, really. I suppose it's inconvenient for a wife to have her husband's . . . well, for the sake of peace we shall not put a name to what I am to him."

Refusing to be drawn into some sort of verbal sparring,

Rosaline tidied the little table to keep her numbed hands busy and her voice calm. "Do you intend to return to England?"

Julie lifted a narrow shoulder. "As I said, I never plan. I wait and see what opportunities present themselves each morning, then decide what course to take. I'm a creature of impulse, of whim, of fancy. And you," she said, regarding Rosaline with a quick, measuring eye, "I imagine you're the sort of woman who plots your life very carefully, one who lives by rules, by some book of etiquette, rarely giving in to spontaneity. I haven't yet decided how that rubs with Jack, but I suspect he finds it different, maybe even entertaining. Although, when we were growing up he talked constantly about becoming a gentleman. Back then he held gentlemen in top hats and silk waistcoats in high esteem—and contempt." Her eyes slanted in their shimmering, inquisitive way. "Has Jack ever told you about our times growing up?"

"No."

Julie smiled. "I thought not. Dear Jack. For the most part, he doesn't give a damn about anyone's opinion—he's too sure of himself for that. Except when it comes to his beginnings . . . well, but no one can change the conditions of his birth, can he? No matter how high he climbs."

"And how high have you climbed?" Rosaline asked shrewdly, thinking Julie too well-spoken, too bright to have spent all her life in the streets, never brushing shoulders with those in higher circumstances. Julie had watched and listened to the well-to-do until she was able to mimic them.

Julie smiled in her blithe, secretive way, but her eyes were brightly hard. "Quite high, once. But it wasn't a perch I wanted to keep."

Sensing she would be unable to glean more, Rosaline turned her gaze to the street and saw a figure wind through the debris of the ruined market. The haze of slow burning fires made it difficult to identify the person for a few moments, but as the form approached, the glimmer of dawn allowed Rosaline to recognize the mincing gait.

"Lance Cardew," she said aloud. "Jack's aide."

Julie said nothing, remained quiet as the young man entered the house looking haggard and nervous, his usually pressed clothes wrinkled and stained with soot.

"Mrs. Darlington," he said in a weary greeting before his eyes fixed upon Julie's slight, compelling, still figure.

Rosaline performed the introductions. "Mr. Cardew, this is Julie . . ." she broke off, realizing she had never heard a last name.

"Just Julie," came the unabashed, amused reply. "If I were to give you a last name, it would only be made-up."

Although the aide murmured an appropriate reply, his eyes flickered strangely, and Rosaline had the oddest notion that he had met Julie before, that it was not the first time he had seen or spoken with her. And yet, he simply bowed over her hand in a formal way and said, "So pleased to meet you."

Was there a mischievous twinkle in Julie's eyes?

It was not long after, while the three of them sat sipping hot black coffee, that Jack returned from the embassy, striding in at an energetic pace that made Rosaline marvel over his stamina after days without sleep or proper food.

"Do you have news, Jack?" she asked anxiously, going to his side. She saw that there was a greater than normal spark about him, that his eyes were agleam with some excitement he was about to share.

"We are to leave Alexandria in the morning and travel back to Cairo," he announced, his voice scarcely able to restrain its exuberance. "From there I'll be going to a place called Luxor—you've been given permission to go too, Rosaline—if you care to brave the journey and its inconveniences."

"What is in Luxor that is of such importance?"

"Arabi Bey's army—and Arabi himself. I've been chosen by the British government to go and meet with him and try to negotiate a truce."

Rosaline stood staring at her husband, trying to take in the news, understand the significance of it. Jack has reached that pinnacle he fought so hard to reach, she thought. She observed the tangible air of victory about him, the energy of achievement. And felt his triumph. I have stood by his side, helped him, she thought with an anxious pride, even if in a small way. I am his wife.

His wife.

But would he remember that now, with Julie giving him her smile?

Chapter Nineteen

"They say it's a hundred degrees on the Nile some days. And they say there are winds—winds so terribly damp and fierce they keep one from sleeping all night. Flies and sand. And the mosquitos!"

Honore shook her head, pitying Rosaline as she folded a crisp white chemise and laid it amid a pile of others in a brass bound trunk. "You really should have brought a lady's maid, Rosaline. I don't know how you keep everything straight without one. I'd be at sixes and sevens trying to decide what I needed to pack on such a journey. And how awful that you must wear a *native* costume—except that this blue silk *is* pretty." With a sigh, the near-sighted girl held up the voluminous garment, which was fitted with loops at the wrists. Beside it there was a white halter-like piece for the head, to which a white veil could be fastened, and atop that, a large black scarf.

Rosaline laughed. "Honore, this is a pleasure trip for me, not some dreadful duty. How many wives have the honor of being part of a diplomatic mission that will float down the Nile and see all the wondrous sights along the way? There are even

resorts south of Cairo that European scholars and writers flock
to enjoy. I feel privileged to go.''

''I wish you didn't have such an enthusiastic attitude,'' Honore pouted prettily. ''Keith is put out with me for refusing to
accompany him on this madcap party. Can you believe he
suggested it as a honeymoon? Appalling.''

''But *The Times* has sent him on the trip to report.''

Honore raised her chin at a stubborn angle. ''Nevertheless,
he shall have to go without his bride.''

''A disappointment, I'm sure. He's very much in love with
you.''

At Rosaline's softly spoken, mollifying words, Honore lowered her head, her profile with its wreath of spiral curls a picture
of demure Victorian womanhood. ''And I with him,'' she said.
''But I don't know how we shall get on together as time passes.
He's so confoundingly brash, and I'm so headstrong—dare I
say spoiled? I'm afraid I'm rather prone to fits of petulance
when he doesn't give me my way.''

''That keeps him on his toes.''

''Will you watch out for him, Rosaline?''

Rosaline laughed at the sudden wifely distress in Honore's
tone. ''You have the overstrung nerves of any bride,'' she said,
laying a hand comfortingly on her friend's lacy sleeve. ''But,
yes, I promise to do my best to keep Keith Grange out of
trouble on the Nile.''

The other woman smiled, abandoned the packing to which
her pampered hands were so delicately unaccustomed, and
floated to the French doors which viewed Rosaline's delightful,
bird-filled courtyard.

''There's a woman sitting by the fountain,'' Honore
exclaimed, pointing. ''A woman I've never seen before. Who
is she, Rosaline?''

Rosaline had not intended to speak of Julie to anyone, not
wanting to explain the other woman's presence, to explain her
identity, her relationship to Jack, almost as if by not uttering
Julie's name, she could make her less real. She glanced through

the glass at the small, vixen figure whose feet were tucked under her hips, and who reclined beside the fountain as if it were some isolated woodland pond. Rosaline had noted that Julie rarely sat still long. As usual, she seemed unable to settle; her restless fingers trailed back and forth through the cool water, testing it in a sensual way, just as they seemed to test everything.

"She's a woman Jack rescued from the fire in Alexandria," Rosaline explained with a careful tonelessness. "An Englishwoman who was staying with friends. During the catastrophe she became separated from them."

"Really?" Her curiosity, as well as her romanticism aroused, Honore mused, "She looks so . . . so exotic, even in her English clothes. She's lovely in an odd way, don't you think? But she seems unconventional somehow, out of place, faintly bored. And . . . well, a bit *tragic*."

"Tragic?"

"Yes. You know, she has an air about her, an air of something being not quite right. Don't you see it?"

"No."

At the crispness in Rosaline's voice, Honore turned and asked, "Will she be sailing back to England?"

"I don't know. We—Jack and I, that is—don't know precisely what to do with her." How easily the lie came, smooth and steady off her lips.

"But you're leaving on your Nile journey tomorrow," Honore said. "Is she to stay here with the two little boys and the servants?"

Rosaline took up the packing again, folded the linen, the stockings, and the soft kid gloves with meticulous care. Her voice came as cool as the water splashing in the fountain. "No. She's to accompany us on the trip." Julie had asked to go, and Jack had agreed to let her.

"Well, it's a perfectly practical idea, don't you think?" Honore sensed no undercurrents in Rosaline's placid reply. "Now you'll have a woman with you in the midst of all those adventurous, rough and tumble men. I'd consider her a godsend, Rosaline, a most convenient companion.''

Rosaline snapped the lid of the trunk shut, her mouth dry with thoughts of what the journey could bring. ''A convenient companion.'' Strange to think of Julie as such.

After sharing heartrending farewells with Antonio and Rajad, who both, much to Rosaline's astonished pleasure, clung to her hands as she bade them goodbye, the British party—Rosaline, Jack, Keith Grange, Lance Cardew and Julie—departed from Cairo in the early morning. As they made their way through the city, all wore native dress so as not to offend, so as not to draw undue attention in a land that hovered precariously on the brink of rebellion.

Rosaline, swathed in her uncorseted, shapeless blue drapes and long white veil, shifted uncomfortably in the high bowed saddle and looked with envy at Julie, who appeared so at ease in her own garb, her small animated body natural and quick and unencumbered, as if it were accustomed to wearing the loose-fitting costume, even savored the freedom of it. Did that ease come from her ability to adapt, to slink in her foxlike way through alleyways and colonnades and woodlets in order to go unnoticed, or had her ordeal of captivity—for surely it *had* been an ordeal—only enhanced her sense of freedom, giving Julie her blitheness and energy?

Regardless, Rosaline suddenly felt herself more plain than ever beside Julie, more staid and matronly. Resenting the feeling, she turned her eyes to watch Jack as he rode a pace ahead. Not for the first time, she realized that where Lance Cardew and Keith Grange made discrepant figures in their native clothes, Jack, like Julie, wore his native garb with an easy and dashing negligence, his dark skin and black hair lending a further impression of congruity.

She shifted her gaze away from the tall, straight body that had lain with hers—how many weeks ago now?—and attempted to

concentrate upon the Cairo landscape: the two hundred minarets, the single citadel, the three distant pyramids that lent such
timeless mystery to the scene. But, maddeningly, she could
think only of the number of days that had passed since Julie
had insinuated herself into their lives.

Although the black-haired woman had, for the most part,
kept herself out of the way, disappearing in the bazaars by day
or wandering alone about the villa by night, she had managed
by the essence of her very presence, to keep a wall between
Rosaline and Jack. Since Julie had reappeared, Jack now wore
a tense, kind of fine-strung intensity like a man torn. If it hadn't
been for the mission to Arabi's camp, the all consuming and
golden opportunity which would secure a future for him, if
successful, Rosaline suspected Jack would have squarely faced
and summarily dealt with the problem of his marriage, rather
than allow the tension to go on. He was not a man to put off
confrontation. Eventually, he would have to make a choice.

But his marriage *was* a problem. For Rosaline had no doubt
at all that Jack loved Julie; she had seen them together in the
courtyard at night when everyone else had gone to bed; she
had seen them with their heads bent close in the parlor just
before they had become aware of her proximity; she had seen
them talking quietly beside the fountain in the apricot light of
dawn. Julie had a hold on Jack, physically as well as spiritually,
a hold that had been forged over years, through common experience, through a complete and intimate understanding of mutual
instincts. They were alike, connected, attuned in an essential
way, weren't they? Surely. For Julie was the sort of girl-woman,
the sort of skittish, half-wild creature who could, if she chose,
drive a man mad with the impossible need to tame her. And
knowing that, sensing it, Rosaline had, over the last few days,
lived in a state of despair, even though she did not think her
husband had yet broken his marriage vows.

She gazed out at the Nile, trying to think only of the journey,
of the sights she would see, her eyes focused on the harbor
ahead, on the shimmering, wide green ribbon of water crowded

with short masted sailboats. When they arrived at the edge of the shore, she halted her horse and surveyed the flat reedy land of gold and brown, the tall date palms, the distant muddy fields and the strewn villages with flat roofs.

Interrupting her reverie, Keith Grange guided his horse beside her, crossed his forearms over the high pommel, and commented idly, "Quite a difference from Edinburgh, eh?"

"But just look at the Nile, Mr. Grange!" Rosaline said breathlessly, awed. "Look at the scenery. It's Biblical, isn't it?" An excitement quivered through her suddenly, an anticipation she had never thought to feel so strongly.

"Biblical, yes. And have you read the Old Testament, Mrs. Darlington? Full of brutal tales."

"Are you trying to daunt me, Mr. Grange?" she asked with a raised brow, wondering why the two of them always fell into a game of words.

"Only trying to find out if such a thing is possible, Ma'am."

"Perhaps Scotswomen are made of sterner stuff than you think."

"One in particular, at any rate." He smiled, pulled his forelock as he nudged his horse ahead. Rosaline's mouth curved in amusement. She was beginning to believe that the brash Mr. Grange rather admired her.

"Saba'hak bil-ch'er," Jack called out, greeting the crew of the sailboat. Dismounting, he conversed with the brown-faced men for several minutes while Rosaline stole a glance at Julie.

She had reined her mount to a nearby vantage point in order to gaze at the panorama, to breathe in, perhaps, the ancient green smell of Egypt. The woman sat in her saddle, still for once, her eyes above the veil revealing no excitement at the prospect of sailing the Nile, no dread, no hint of anything at all. But then, Julie would be used to adventure, Rosaline thought, even danger. Perhaps, like Jack, she felt undeterred by it.

"I've ordered the men to unload the stores." Jack had come to stand beside Rosaline. Pointing toward the river, he said,

"We've rented two *dahabiehs*—those boats there. You and I and Julie will be sailing on the first. It has a crew of nine, including a sort of cook/houseboy who speaks a smattering of English. He's a willful fellow—not the best at obeying orders— and I thought you might want to take him in hand." Jack's eyes twinkled at her look of wide-eyed chagrin. "You might get across to him when we'd like to have our meals served. Oh, and make sure he's not planning to serve us some regional favorite, like roast dove—not that I would have any particular objection, having eaten it before, but I daresay you would find digestion difficult."

"Jack," Rosaline admonished, unable to hide a smile. She knew by his light-hearted conversation that he was trying to smooth over the rift in their relationship, to make it easier to carry on; and even though she knew it would never be easy to carry on now, she accepted the olive branch because her heart yearned for Jack's affection. She disregarded the brightness of his blue eyes in the gold sun, unable to meet them, wondering if they were bright only from the good-natured banter and the prospect of his mission, or bright because he had found Julie again.

"You see," he said, his voice a trace more serious, his eyes holding hers, "even on a rented boat at the end of the world, I need your domestic talents."

He could have said anything other than that to appease her, anything at all. Looking down, gripping the reins fiercely as if to transfer the hurt of her heart into her hands, Rosaline said with perfect aplomb, "And I shall be faithful to my duty, of course." She was surprised that her voice held no hint of the silent rage in her heart.

"I never doubted you would."

She saw his slow, secret smile and because it made her ache, said with stiffness, "I should think the Arab cook would be offended by a woman's interference."

"I'm paying him too well for that. Come aboard. I'll give you a tour of your quarters."

After helping her dismount, he escorted her onboard the boat, which was seventy feet long with two short masts. The area around the foremast housed the crew.

"This is the cook's oven," Jack explained, pointing out a small brick furnace on deck. "And the cabin is through here— the two divans are used for sleeping. You'll find a table and washroom through there. I'll bunk on deck with the crew. Cardew and Grange will sail on the other boat. They'll join us when we stop each night."

"Will we camp ashore?" Rosaline asked, her eyes, trained for spotting inefficiency in all domestic arrangements, skimming the narrow cabin windows, the five-foot ceilings, the wooden slatted blinds and rickety campstools.

"Some nights. On others we'll just moor the boat close to shore and extinguish the lamps so we don't attract attention."

"Attention? What sort of attention?"

"Water thieves." Jack grinned in such a way that Rosaline couldn't tell whether he teased or not. "Mostly just ragtag groups of Bedouins out to relieve travelers of a few trinkets or sacks of sugar."

Although her husband seemed unconcerned about any danger, a shiver of anxiety raised the flesh on Rosaline's arms, and she started when the boat jerked suddenly, its sails catching wind and propelling the craft forward as the shouting, energetic crew unmoored it.

Jack steadied her and smiled. "We're on our way. Look there," he pointed. "It's a barge of camels being ferried from the desert to Cairo."

Rosaline glanced at the fantastic scene while the white veil fluttered around her face, and all at once she felt a part of the scene as she surveyed the distant sugar cane fields soaked with river water, the buffalo plodding before crude plows, the palm groves dotting the flat brown loam. "What are those odd-shaped domes?" she asked with a nod. "They look like curious little mud cupboards."

"Those are homes. They're made of mud bricks and so small

the villagers literally have to crawl in and out of them. Believe it or not, the residents house their hens and goats in there as well—it keeps the animals safe from foxes.''

"Whole families sleep inside those places?" Rosaline asked appalled.

"So I'm told."

"So different from the way we live," she mused aloud. "Strange, I don't believe I'll ever be able to sit in an English drawing room again, and sip tea and lemon without thinking of some other poor woman crouched down amid her hens and goats.''

"Don't feel too ashamed. If given the opportunity, she'd probably pity you for having to wear corsets and crinolines to please the social code.''

Rosaline smiled, and for a moment, gloried in the simple pleasure of Jack's presence beside her, in the timbre of his voice and the scent of his skin, in his mere breathing, which gave her a sense of comfort and well-being despite the circumstances of their relationship.

Suddenly Julie appeared near the prow, gazing out too, and although she neither looked at Jack nor spoke, she seemed to call to him. And he seemed to hear the siren's song.

Without knowing why she made it easy for them, Rosaline excused herself, left her husband free. "I'll go speak with the cook now," she said tersely, turning on her heel, "see what can be put together for a noon meal." Ducking quickly into the cabin, Rosaline very carefully—restraining an impulse to hurl the silverware and copper cups across the room—began to plan a meal, her first of many luncheons on the Nile, shared with the woman Jack loved.

The evening's sunset proved the most dazzling, the most mysterious Rosaline had ever witnessed, the golden tones of Egypt's sun blending with the corals of evaporating clouds, with the fragile glaze of a lapis lazuli sky.

A merry natured, lackadaisical lot, the crew perched on the gunwhale singing and beating drums, letting the wind tug the craft along while Osman, the cook, sat on deck and ground coffee in a mortar with the same stick he used to walk with. It was his habit to give advice to everyone regarding everything, and when he wasn't talking, he was humming. He was a temperamental fellow with whom Rosaline had already, on their first day out, learned to compromise. She liked him even if his careless habits horrified her sense of hygiene. Before the trip was out, she vowed, she would have him scrubbing vegetables and washing his hands with all the alacrity of an English scullery maid in disgrace.

The pilot of the boat sat atop the cabin maneuvering the arm of the rudder. Since the wind kept the vessel at an even pace, one of the crew members took out a Persian waterpipe and lazily assembled the amber tube and glass vase, which was filled with rose water. As he smoked, the pipe made a bubbling sound which blended with the lapping of the river. The scent of old rose clouded the deck, mingled with the smell of the ripe dates Julie sat eating, alone on the weathered deck.

Rosaline studied the other woman. Her smooth skin was almost as dark as Jack's, her hair glossy and thick under the white veil, which she had lowered in order to taste the dates. She had been quiet all day, her attentive eyes gazing out with an unreadable expression at the barges filled with elephant tusks and ostrich feathers or the camels. But they never lingered long on the passing river sights; they always slid back, devotedly, to Jack. Rosaline wondered if it were a habit long ingrained— a little tangle-haired girl watching and staying close to her resourceful protector, adoring him, observing his fearlessness and ingenuity until she had learned the tricks of survival as well as he.

Rosaline thought the two might have quarreled earlier. She had seen them speaking together, their voices so low as to be inaudible, but Julie had been very quiet after the encounter, sullen. Rosaline suspected she could punish a man with her sullenness, her practiced petulance, the flash of her slanted eyes.

Jack sat with the pilot now, speaking in Arabic, but as the gold sun hovered upon the gilded horizon, he moved to Rosaline's side. If Julie's mood affected him, he did not show it.

"See the procession coming there?" he asked, pointing to an approaching line of gaily painted vessels adorned with bright banners.

Rosaline nodded. "Yes, how lovely and graceful the boats are."

"It's a celebration. In ancient times, the Egyptians used to sacrifice virgins in the hope that the Nile would rise and flood the fields for a good harvest. The poor girl went to her death in a boat like one of those you see ahead—the Bride of the Nile she was called. Now when the water rises, the natives simply sail their boats and fire guns to celebrate. There are no more virgins."

Rosaline gazed out, overcome with a sense of enormity, of remoteness, and yet a connection with times past as her silk robe, caught by the gentle warm wind, rippled about her body. For a moment, she hardly felt like Rosaline Cheevers from Edinburgh, keeper of drawing rooms and silver tea services, but like a true bride ready for the passion and pain of a woman's destiny—she felt not twenty-six years of age but sixteen.

Jack placed his hand next to hers on the wooden rail and she stared down at it, at the complicated architecture of sinew and bone, thinking she wanted to slide her fingers beneath its hard warmth, wanted to feel it enclose her hand and hold on. She acutely felt Julie's eyes on her back, watching somewhat condescendingly, with curiosity but little concern. Was the other woman so confident of Jack's devotion that she experienced no envy, no burning, bitter jealousy as Rosaline did?

"Do you still wish we'd never left the Orkneys?" Jack asked quietly, his eyes on her face.

Rosaline was warmed by his remembrance of the fanciful sentiment she had shared on their first day in Cairo, the premonition that had caused her to feel a melancholy yearning to remain at Arbor Gate. And even while she felt softened by his mention of it, she couldn't help but wonder now if the wiser option would have been for both of them to have stayed home.

No, she told herself firmly. Jack would always have harbored his memories of Julie, wondered about her, kept her enshrined in his heart's locket. Julie, Rosaline realized, had been just as real to Jack in Scotland as she was here now in Egypt. It was better that Jack had found her now, so he could decide what he must do with her; better to let the slippery hand of cards play itself out.

"I still think of Arbor Gate often," she breathed softly in reply. "Especially in the middle of the day, when the sun seems the hottest. I think of the heather and the cliffs and the misty clouds at Arbor Gate, the way the butterflies float up out of the scrub. And I wonder if the acorns have sprouted."

Jack smiled. She saw his mouth curve slowly, saw the dark rough angle of his jaw, the hollow at his throat as the wind ruffled the loose white shirt around it. All at once, with a longing almost too great to bear, she yearned for the heat of his mouth, the power in his arms. She felt Julie's eyes, still watching; and knew Jack felt them, too. And suddenly afraid of the pain of loving Jack too much, Rosaline took a breath and closed her eyes, willed her heart to distance itself, to find another flame, to think and dream of David.

Jack looked at his wife, at the clean classic profile, the long neck; he smelled the heliotrope and thought of Scotland, of the home she had made for him there. For some reason, it annoyed him to see her dressed as a native. He longed suddenly to have her in pale, well-molded if prim English gowns, a pink and ivory cameo at her throat, the intricately coiled hair uncovered instead of hidden by a scrap of Eastern silk. He clenched his jaw. Even filled as he was now with tender thoughts of his Rosaline, he *felt* Julie.

She had asked him to make love to her, had offered herself once in a shadowy corner of the Cairo courtyard, and then, later, the night before their journey, had flitted along the dark corridor to his bed. With the kind of complete lack of inhibition that had driven his maleness mad since the early age of twelve, she had presented herself to him. But holding on to a perverse sense of duty foreign to his nature, to a scrap of fidelity he would have disdained only months ago, Jack had refused her offer.

And yet a part of him still longed to know Julie again, to know the taste of her wildness, the unchasteness of her abandonment, to try and tame the danger that burned in her always. He could please Julie, bring her to the height of passion until her insatiability returned once more to make her clutch at him again. His body understood hers, just as his intellect understood the workings of her mind.

Rosaline was different sort of woman, fashioned of other elements, a cool Scottish April far removed in seasons from Julie's vivid, burning summer. In his innermost mind, he knew which woman was best for him. And yet, did a man always have the wisdom to chose what was best?

The sun had gone, and with it the heat. Beside him, Rosaline shivered. Jack suddenly felt her remoteness, her willful detachment from him. Reluctant to experience the loss of her attention even while understanding it, he took hold of her shoulders. As he had begun to do more and more often in his dilemma, he felt the sudden need to force her to respond to him, to give herself wholeheartedly despite his own unreliable heart; he felt the need to make Rosaline love him. Seizing his wife's face between his hands, he leaned down, and put his mouth on hers.

Rosaline resisted, then relented, despite the fact that Jack's unexpected kiss was roughly and inconsiderately given, deeply intimate, indecent. The crew watched, smiled, but he gave no care, as he thrust his tongue past her teeth, crushed her to his chest, his hands pulling her hips into his. Did he kiss her to punish Julie now that they had quarreled? Rosaline wondered. The possibility prompted her to pull away abruptly, to hang on to her dignity. She hissed, "Let me go, Jack. I'll not be used in this way."

"You're my wife."

"Am I, Jack?" she said beneath her breath. "Am I *really?* Look at us, standing here together with the woman you love looking on. Do you not expect me to feel even a little outraged?"

Everyone in the boat had grown silent, unable to hear the words exchanged but able to see the tension between husband and wife. Mortified that she had contributed to such a display, feeling the tears of hopelessness prickle behind her lids, Rosaline ducked into the dark little cabin and sat rigidly down on the divan. She wished she were back in Scotland; she wished she were anywhere else at all; she wished she were wearing petticoats, a muslin gown and corset.

After a moment, she felt the boat anchor, heard the warm stillness, smelled the rose scents of the waterpipe and the musky odor of fertile earth. The mosquitos buzzed and she yanked the net around the divan, then heard Julie enter and remove her veil with a soft slither of silk.

"I don't suppose you'll get much sleep tonight," the black haired woman remarked, just as if there should be no strain between them. She curled up on her divan, leaned back and commented, "Sleeping on the river always takes several nights. You must get used to the movement of the boat, the sounds of the water, all things unusual."

"You speak as if you've traveled on the Nile before," Rosaline said, her voice hard with bitterness.

"I've traveled by many means these last few years."

The reply held an obliqueness, a quiet intriguing inflection, and risking a rebuff, Rosaline ventured unsparingly, "Jack told me you were a captive here once."

Julie made no reply for several minutes, and by the dim shaft of moonlight slashing through the window, Rosaline could see her restless hands stroke the tassels on the pillow, relishing the rich slick texture. There were moments, Rosaline thought, when the impression of vulnerability seemed strong in Julie, when she resembled a young kit fox hiding from the hounds, slightly out of breath and rumpled while her clever mind worked. The impression was fleeting, but provocative.

"Yes," she said at last.

"A terrible ordeal, surely."

"An ordeal?" Julie echoed. "What you consider an ordeal would surely be less of one for me."

Rosaline huffed. "I have no doubt of that."

Julie remained silent for a spell, then admitted, "It was the loss of my freedom that I resented most, not the things I was forced to do. I'm adaptable, you see. It matters little to me how or where I live—even with whom for a short term—as long as I'm at liberty to come and go when I like. I wasn't free. Not for a very long time."

"Were you . . . owned by a man?" Rosaline asked, discretion and sensitivity so ingrained in her upbringing that she found the words difficult, even while knowing Julie cared little for the finer points of propriety.

Julie laughed. "Are women ever slaves to anything other than men?"

Rosaline contemplated the question and said, "I believe they are."

"Really? To what?"

Rosaline had been lying upon her back; she turned now to face the cabin wall, her mind filled with thoughts of her own life, her own circumstances. She was weary of the mystery of it, of not knowing what the outcome was to be, of always feeling she must say and do the "right" thing, present the best side lest the world condemn her as being less than gracious.

"Duty makes us slaves," she murmured to herself, resentful for the first time. "It is a very firm-handed master in my world."

"Duty to what?"

Of course Julie would ask, Rosaline thought. She would be sincere in her ignorance of the sort of life other women had been brought up to lead. Sighing, weary all at once, Rosaline said, "Duty to family, to society, to our home and servants, to all the things that require a woman's attention. It keeps us bound just as securely as any captor."

Julie laughed, not maliciously, but in a soft, pitying way. "But who creates those conventions, my dear Mrs. Darlington? Men, of course. They set the path of a woman's life—if she allows them to, if she doesn't chose her own path and take it. If we have to be burdened with any sort of duty at all, it should be to ourselves."

Rosaline's mouth tightened. "What sort of existence is there outside of convention?"

"An existence like the one I have had."

Unable to resist a smile at Julie's proud, blithely delivered answer, Rosaline knew her reply would not be taken as offense. "I would wager that your existence has been nothing but one long, wandering adventure."

"And what's wrong with adventure?"

"Nothing. But surely everyone should feel they serve a purpose, that they have a place, some sort of *structure*."

"It sounds as if you've talked yourself into liking boundaries. You speak of purpose—well, mine is simply to live, to experience as much of life as I can."

She is like Jack, Rosaline thought, and the notion rankled so greatly that she snapped, "Don't you ever feel as if you'd like to accomplish something? Something meaningful, enduring?"

"No. Never."

"We are very different, then."

"But we knew that from the beginning, didn't we? We knew it the moment our eyes met—perhaps even before." Julie paused. "Did you know about me before I appeared in your house in Alexandria? Did Jack mention me?"

Julie's doubt pleased Rosaline, and although the admission chafed her, she admitted, "Yes. He spoke of you. A little."

"Don't blame him. He couldn't help himself. If Jack has one weakness, it is me. Our lives are interwoven, you see, they've been interwoven for as long as either one of us can remember.''

Rosaline wanted to shut out Julie's voice and remain silent; she almost had to hold her breath, almost ready to pray that Julie would not say anything more about her life with Jack. But she did, and the words were soft, exceedingly troublesome.

''What do you think he'll do now—Jack I mean? What will our dear Jack decide to do about us, Rosaline?''

Rosaline lay very still. The river had grown quiet, the motion of the *dahabieh* had gentled as if to listen, and Rosaline imagined Jack on deck, stretched out and able to view the stars. She wondered what he thought as he gazed up at their bright remoteness; did he think about the two women in the cabin— did he think about one more than the other?

Perhaps he did not think of either. Perhaps his mind was filled only with thoughts of Arabi, of the mission that would make his name famous in every London street.

''Perhaps I will not wait for him to decide,'' Rosaline breathed at last against her pillow, so that Julie could not hear.

Chapter Twenty

One night they moored close to a village and the next morning went ashore to get supplies and "judge the mood of the natives," as Jack said, since the British party was nearing Arabi's camp.

Rosaline could scarcely contain her excitement as she walked with Jack and the others through a village comprised of a curious arrangement of mud huts and cone-shaped dovecotes and a series of walled enclosures called a *khan* which was set aside for travelers and their beasts of burden. Camels lay tethered all around, chewing cuds while barefoot women strolled past with water jugs balanced on their heads. The women's black hair was braided into long plaits, the ends daubed with yellow clay and swaying rhythmically against their deep bronze-colored skin. Their simply gathered clothes—tied over one shoulder—and their aquiline noses gave them the look of the ancient ladies painted on the walls of Egyptian tombs.

Enthralled by their British visitors, the villagers sidled shyly up to offer eggs and jars of milk, but when Rosaline held out coins for the ragged children, the mothers politely declined with a shake of their noble heads.

Merchants milled around the environs of the coffee shop, which was little more than a hut built of maize stalks fitted with wooden benches. Some of the tradesmen had journeyed from far desert villages; they offered beads, amber, ivory, and camels for sale as well as slaves, who proved to be a collection of a half dozen Nubian women and two Greek boys, all tied together by the wrists and standing in the heat.

Rosaline stared at them in pitying horror; she knew well that slavery existed in Egypt, but this was her first encounter with its ugliness. Askance, unable to help herself, she looked at Julie, wondering if such a sight would cause her to blanch and turn away, but the other woman regarded the captives with no expression in her eyes at all.

Beside her, Keith Grange made hasty sketches of the group for his journal, while Lance Cardew's fastidious nostrils flared in disgust over the scene.

"Can nothing be done for them?" Rosaline whispered to Jack.

"Slavery has been a way of life here for thousands of years, Rosaline. Five British citizens do not march into a village and try to change its culture within a day—at least not without the risk of ending up slaves themselves."

"Nevertheless, something should be done."

He put a hand on her arm in warning and guided her past the huddle of wretches just as a group of wizened merchants approached and invited the Britons to join them in the midday meal, which was laid down on mats beneath a palm grove in the *khan*. Winking at Rosaline when she gave him a less than enthusiastic glance, Jack accepted the merchant's wares, not wishing to incur any ill-will from the natives by refusing their offering of dates, yeastless bread spread with goat cheese, and sherbet made mostly of brown sugar and water served in little leather cups.

Jack spoke with the fellows in Arabic and translated now and then for Rosaline and the others, explaining that the merchants held little malice toward Westerners, mistrustful of their infidel Christian religion of course, but indifferent to their political views and unconcerned over the recent battle in Alexandria. One camel driver made an odd comment which Jack interpreted for Rosaline with a smile. "They say they know little of what the British are about, but swear that our queen plans to murder Arabi."

At the picture of plump and dignified Queen Victoria wrapped in a black cloak bent upon tracking down and murdering some Arab rebel, even Rosaline could not conceal a smile and a droll reply. "I wonder if she will commit the act alone, or bring Prince Albert as an accomplice?"

Jack leaned close and murmured, "I don't believe poor Albert's been trained to hunt anything but hand-fed grouse."

Rosaline laughed, and yet, oddly, as she glanced at the shrewd, leathery faces of the turbanned merchants, a chill raised the flesh upon her arms.

They finished the unpalatable meal with thimblefuls of rich black coffee—a ritual, Jack explained, practiced throughout Egypt. Rosaline's refined senses were so offended that she found herself amazed she could swallow at all, but she refused to show her squeamishness, partly because Julie watched her with amused, expectant eyes, waiting for her to swoon no doubt, to make a fuss, to leave her meal unfinished. Rosaline chewed and swallowed, and privately congratulated herself on being able to drink the bitter coffee with no grimace at all.

"What are those women doing there?" she asked Jack awhile later when they strolled through the dusty market. Although there remained a tension between them, a discord that would only be solved when the mission came to an end and the issue of Julie and their marriage was resolved, they spoke easily enough about ordinary matters.

"They're churning butter," Jack answered, watching the woman tie goatskin bags to the trunk of a palm tree.

"Churning butter?"

"Yes. Watch. See how they swing the goatskin bag back and forth—it's full of milk."

"Ingenious. But surely not so fast as a churn."

"They've been doing it like this for centuries and likely see no reason to change. They aren't like Westerners who are always looking for ways to make work easier. What would they do with their free time anyway?" he teased. "There aren't any masked balls or carriage jaunts to Hyde Park here."

"You never pity other people for the kind of life they lead, do you, Jack?"

"Not often. I've lived the other side of life myself, and I never cared for anyone's pity."

She remained silent a moment, allowed the warm wind to bring in the smell of apricots and sand, and tilted her parasol a degree to permit the sun to touch her shoulders. She felt drowsy, compelled to lean toward Jack, compelled to brush her sleeve against his as she said, "Tell me about your mission to Arabi, Jack. You've said little about it. What do you hope to accomplish?"

"A truce, Rosaline. A truce that will hold. Nothing more. It will buy me the approval of all of London."

She shivered in the sun.

Just before evening fell, a caravan of Bedouins rode into the village astride beautiful, long-tailed horses. The weathered riders were swathed in white, wearing goatskin boots, their rifles slung across their saddles. A large group of women accompanied them, and after camel hide tents were speedily erected, the ladies sequestered themselves inside. They were not veiled as the women of the cities had been, Rosaline noted, nor did they seem as timid as their urban counterparts. They exhibited a certain haughtiness instead, a few of them even remaining outside to work with the men.

Knowing that Bedouins were unpredictable in character, renowned as petty robbers and often little more than savages, Rosaline looked at Jack anxiously, wondering if he would order the party back to the boat for safety, but he seemed imperturbed, even relaxed while he and Keith Grange waited for the Bedouin leader to approach.

"I thought Bedouins were thieves," Rosaline murmured under her breath to Julie, who had come to stand close and watch the proceedings. "Oughtn't we to keep away from them?"

"If they wanted anything from us, they would have taken it already. It's too late to escape. Jack is wise to show no fear."

Rosaline uneasily observed his exchange with the turbanned, rough-clad man, surprised when Jack joined her a moment later with a smile on his face. "It seems we are to be entertained."

"Entertained?"

"Yes. The rascals have invited us to watch their dancing girls."

"Dancing girls?" Recalling Honore's description of such indecent performances—related in whispers by her aunt—Rosaline folded her arms across her chest. "Then I suppose I had better be escorted back to the boat."

He smiled. "They'll be offended if you don't stay."

"It's hardly appropriate . . ."

"There's no place for appropriate behavior here, Rosaline. Besides, in Cairo, wealthy European gentlemen regularly host such entertainments—their wives are often invited to attend. Just think, Mrs. Darlington, you can enliven every afternoon tea party back home with your stories of the Bedouin soiree. You'll be a guest much in demand."

His humor failed to mollify her. "The ladies I know would likely cover their ears rather than hear details."

"I'd put a wager on the opposite—they'll be agog to hear and only pretend to be shocked."

Still eyeing the rough dress and hard, weather beaten visages with distrust, Rosaline ignored her husband's facetiousness and touched his arm. "Aren't you fearful of them, Jack? They hardly look trustworthy."

"Nevertheless, they're a prosperous bunch with a harem of women, not a fast hungry looking rabble you sometimes find wandering up and down the Nile."

"You can tell the difference?"

"I've learned to recognize scoundrels in whatever country I happen to be visiting," he said wryly. "Just as you can spot a gentleman at first glance, my dear, I can spot a thief."

"I'm beginning to think yours is the more useful skill."

"It is, even in English drawing rooms."

She slanted a glance at him. "Thieves in English drawing rooms?"

"More there than anywhere else."

"Oh, Jack. One of these days you're going to realize I don't believe everything you say."

"Would you believe me if I told you I particularly enjoy your company this way?"

"What way is that?"

"Giving back the same measure that I give."

She waved a hand airily. "I don't understand you."

"Yes, you do. You understand me very well." He studied her, his gaze sweeping over her eyes, her mouth. "Which is probably to my great misfortune."

Darkness enshrouded the village and the little walled *khan* and the mud dovecots aflutter with pale birds. Smells of maize, hot blooded horses, and the flowing water of the Nile began to weave a magic spell, and the Bedouins built a fire, their laughter low and easy. Rosaline watched as they prepared the meal that the Britons were to share, carefully seating herself on a woven mat at Jack's invitation while he lounged beside her, his legs stretched out in their fine English leather boots, his attitude relaxed even with Julie sitting so near—watchful and restless, her eyes unreadably bright in the fire-light.

Next to her, Keith Grange sat busily scratching lines in his notebook, and Lance Cardew stood alone in the shadows, perpetually ill at ease and out of place. Earlier Rosaline had seen him speak with Julie, who had appeared to dismiss him without so much as a nod, walking away even while he spoke. Rosaline wondered if she were spurning his amorous attentions, wondered if the young aide had fallen beneath her spell; if so, she pitied him.

The air had grown heavy and very hot, making the simple act of breathing difficult, and the clouds were so low they seemed to hang over the landscape like a blanket. Perspiration began to bead on Rosaline's brow and she pulled a handkerchief from her pocket while a group of Bedouins invited Jack to admire their string of horses. Keith Grange, seeing Rosaline alone, ambled to her side to chat.

"You look as if you're not entirely comfortable, Mrs. Darlington," he commented with his usual underlying attempt to needle her, to test her well-bred composure.

"I confess I've been longing for my wing back chair and footstool this last hour, Mr. Grange."

He chuckled. "If Honore were here, I daresay she'd be longing for the same things."

"No doubt you miss your bride."

"I do. I'm sure you know that I wanted her here with me rather badly."

Rosaline could sense by the way in which he bit off the words that the subject was a sore one, and she suspected the couple had quarreled bitterly before Grange's departure. He seemed the sort of husband who believed he should have complete authority over his wife, just as if she were a child or an ornament.

"And yet," Rosaline said, defending Honore with a subtleness she hoped would not be lost, "it must be nice for you to envision your bride safely in Cairo, embroidering your pillowcases, waiting for you to come home."

"Aye," he mused. "Some women are exceedingly good at making a home. Honore is one of those. Others . . ." He paused, glanced at Julie, whose small figure was lined in orange firelight. "Well, they are made for other things."

"One hopes that a man's wisdom can be relied upon to know which is which."

"I beg your pardon?"

"Which qualities are important, and which are not."

"And do you believe Jack is wise, Mrs. Darlington?" Grange asked all at once, pinning her with his eyes.

"Wise?" she repeated, her own eyes searching for and finding Jack where he stood assessing the Arabian horses. "I don't know, Mr. Grange. What do you think?"

"I believe Jack always looks out for his own best interests."

"You're telling me nothing that I don't already know."

"Really? I wondered. I'm curious to see how you handle it."

He was referring to Julie, of course, but Rosaline intended to say no more beyond, "No doubt you are curious, Mr. Grange. No doubt you are."

The dancing girls appeared then, filing out of a large tent, their bodies draped in gauzy layered skirts and striped tunics that left their bronze stomachs bare; silver girdles strung with bells jingled as they walked. Their hair fell to their waists in braided ropes and they sported silken caps of red. None wore shoes and the firelight caught the gleam of oil on their legs as they raised their arms and played castanets, swaying in slow, langourous steps.

Bowls of food were passed round to the spectators. Jack returned from the horses, and Rosaline noted that his hands were just as deft and knowledgeable as Julie's while he managed to eat in the traditional way without utensils, consuming the mutton, watermelon, stewed apricots mixed with nuts and raisins, and cucumbers. The rice was formed in little balls and sprinkled with the juice of sliced lime. Much to her surprise, Rosaline found the food tasty, the seasoning exotic and strong, complemented by the drink called *arakee,* which was flavored with dates and the closest thing to alcohol Muslims ever drank.

At first, in her struggle to overcome her strict sense of decorum, Rosaline had difficulty looking directly at the dancing girls. As the beat of the tambourines increased, the girls escalated their seductive gyrations, raised their braceletted arms and leapt across the space of sand in a manner Rosaline could only compare to wild ballerinas. Leaning back on his elbows, Jack watched with appreciation while Keith Grange observed avidly, a wide and sensual smile on his whiskered face. Lance Cardew had finally deigned to join the circle of spectators, creeping up to sit tailor fashion on a mat to get a better view. Julie appeared breathless, her eyes bright, her body restless as if seized by a longing to leap up and join the dancers, who continued as the gold coins hanging from their necklaces quivered. The air grew hotter, damper, heavier, so that Rosaline's breathing became shallow and her clothes clung to her skin. Fitful gusts of wind rife with sand gusted across the flat landscape.

A few of the Bedouins nodded toward the low sky and murmured, and Rosaline was relieved when the dancing finally concluded and the lithe young girls trotted away like gazelles, their bodies flushed and drenched with perspiration.

Just as Jack rose and inquired if she were ready to return to the boat, a Bedouin man approached. He spoke with both Jack and Keith, gesticulating as if making some offer.

Jack smiled and shook his head, declining, but Grange hesitated and glanced in the direction of the retreating dancers.

"What was that all about?" Rosaline asked Jack when he escorted her to the *dahabieh.* "Was the Bedouin offering something to you and Keith Grange?"

"That he was." Jack strolled along beside her, following a shadowy path through bullrushes, while the campfire cast its lemon glow over his back, accentuating the width of his shoulders. "The Arabs have strict customs concerning hospitality, just as we do in Britain. Only here, a host believes it's his duty to invite travelers into the tent of his concubines."

"What?"

"The guest is bathed by the women and afterwards well, anything is allowed for the night so long as the guest, upon his honor, vows never to speak of it to anyone."

"Do you mean those men offered to share their women with strangers?"

"Accommodating fellows, the Bedouins, aren't they?"

Rosaline's lips thinned. "I'd chose quite another term."

"Don't worry," he said with a laugh, not bothering to hide his amusement as he helped her onboard the boat where the crew had already settled in for the night. "I declined the offer."

"So good of you," she said dryly.

Jack laughed, saying nothing else, and as her husband left her, Rosaline privately wondered if he had declined the offer of pleasurable debauchery out of faithfulness to his marriage, or out of faithfulness to Julie.

As the evening wore on, the air grew increasingly hot and smothering, and Rosaline knew any attempt to sleep in the confines of the tiny cabin would be fruitless. So she eased down on the deck, loosened her clothing, and used a palm leaf for a fan, reluctantly waiting for Julie, assuming the woman would follow on her heels at any moment. She looked out the window and saw that the black haired woman still sat beside the camp-fire, oblivious to the wind, her posture almost sphinx-like. Lance Cardew appeared out of the shadows and approached her, and after exchanging only a few words with the aide, Julie got up and walked away alone. Cardew, Rosaline thought, was persistent if nothing else.

Despite the clamminess of the air, Rosaline began to doze at last, her eyelids heavy and gritty with sand, her ears only faintly able to hear the voices outside until she recognized them as her husband's and Julie's.

Focusing her eyes in the darkness, Rosaline spotted the pair standing close together on the path, and although she could not distinguish their words, she could tell that Julie's were urgent while Jack answered in a short and forceful manner. For a long time, Rosaline watched, knowing she should not, knowing that she would only suffer—which she did, excruciatingly—when Julie suddenly threw her arms around Jack and began to kiss him.

Sickened, wondering if, in the next few weeks, she would be abandoned, sent back to Scotland married but husbandless, Rosaline turned from the window and put her hands over her face. She loved Jack—dear God, why had she allowed herself to love him? It had been so unwise, so foolish to expect the affection of such a man. He had tried to tell her in the beginning that the best course for their marriage would be one of indifferent passion.

Standing upon the shore, Jack was unaware that his wife had observed him. He had not intended to be alone with Julie tonight; his blood had been running high and the dancing had assaulted his senses in such a way that left him hungry for the feel of a woman. His wife. He kept thinking of Rosaline standing in a white nightgown, barefoot, her hair hanging down her back as he had seen her once, the morning after their marriage in Scotland. He kept thinking of her long, cool body . . .

But Julie was putting her hands on his chest, the small clever hands that knew so well how to tempt him, how to boldly trail down the length of his belly, how to touch every inch of his body in order to rouse it.

With sudden, inexplicable impatience, he pushed her hands away, his jaw throbbing, his mind still absorbed with a picture of Rosaline standing in the garden in her nightgown, the soil of the Orkneys on her hands as she planted acorns. He remembered her in lilac dresses and flowered hats, wearing knitted gloves. A lady, the sort of lady he had always wanted for himself.

"Jack," Julie said, her voice husky, hurt, urgent. Her hands seized his shirt. "After you've been to Luxor and seen Arabi, let's go away together. We'll travel to Istanbul again, or India if you like—just the two of us, free as we used to be."

He answered tightly, grasping her wrists and holding them together so that she would not touch him any more. "I have a career, Julie. I have a family.'' He found he liked saying the words.

''And you'll tire of them all within the year, Jack! You know that this—this career as you call it, will only bore you after awhile. Where can it lead? To a desk, my love. Sitting with a lot of stuffy old men in some London office planning silly wars. And your family,'' she said, throwing up a thin brown hand. ''Two boys who'll go off to English boarding schools before long and a wife who's as cold and plain as a . . .''

''That's enough!'' Jack said through his teeth. He took hold of her arms and shook her. ''That's enough.''

But Julie refused to be silenced, knowing she had too much at stake, feeling him slipping away from her. ''She's not for you, Jack! She's not *like* you. She's an overbred prig who thinks that convention and properly polished silver are the stuff of life. She can never understand you, never be the other part of you like I can—like I've always *been*. You're a vagabond, Jack, just like me. You're a thief and an adventurer and an opportunist who doesn't give a damn about soirees and charity balls and donating stained glass windows to the village church—or to anything else that might tie you down. You belong with *me!*'' she said, her voice gentle, placating, ''I thought I wouldn't survive without you these last long years. And I know you must have been crazy with worry over me, looking for me until you believed I might be dead. Things can be just as they were between us. This ambition, this dream that you've always held onto is of no more substance than the sweetmeats and the feather beds we dreamed about when we were children shivering under bridges in winter.''

Jack walked a pace of two away from her, wanting to separate himself from her words, from the possible truth of them, a truth that seemed to be gradually growing dimmer each day he was married to Rosaline. But when Julie put her hands upon him again, when she put her mouth hard against his mouth, Jack seized the love of his youth, his teeth bringing blood to her full red lips, his body arcing suddenly even while his mind envisioned Rosaline—Rosaline kissing him this way, opening, demanding . . .

"Come away with me after you've seen Arabi," Julie panted, ignoring the wind that whined about them, her thin, eager body only fueled by its wildness.

But Jack pushed her away from him, shrugging off her hands, and ignored the beseechment of her voice as she shouted out at him one last time. "Come with me after you've seen Arabi, Jack! Come away with me! Everything will be just as it was. You can't escape the past. It'll catch up with you, it always does. Come away with me. You'll regret it if you don't!"

Inside the boat, Rosaline lay huddled on the floor away from the window, for the wind rocked the boat violently, making it creak and tug at is moorings. Sand swirled in the air and Rosaline clamped a hand over her eyes to keep them from burning as she heard the crew struggling to batten down the hatches and secure the lines. Apprehensive, she opened the cabin door to look for Jack, but the sand was so thick she could not see a foot beyond her face. She called out for him again and again.

"Rosaline!"

She heard his voice and cried out in reply, trying to see through the whirling sand, just able to make out her husband's figure as he sprinted toward the boat and jumped aboard. A moment later she felt his arms go around her, felt the hard security of his body, his urgency as he pulled her back inside the cabin.

"Get inside!" he said. "It's not the safest place to be, but it's too late to go ashore now and find shelter. You're good at saying prayers—pray that the ropes hold!"

Rosaline stumbled as the craft pitched and groaned, its wooden sides pounded both by wind driven waves and sand. Jack called to her to bolt the window, and when she had it secured, told her to crouch down with a blanket over her head. Then he made for the door again.

"Jack!" she shouted, tugging at his sleeve. "Jack! Where are you going?"

"I've got to help the crew. Stay put!"

And he was gone, leaving her to face the savage terror of nature as she huddled with the veil shielding her face while the wind made an unholy noise outside, screaming around the cabin. Rosaline grew disoriented with the motion of the boat, feeling as if it were capsized and turned upside down, all the while fearful for Jack's well-being, wondering how he could possibly remain aboard without being torn from the unprotected deck.

Just as the storm's fury peaked and ripped the shutter from the window, Jack burst into the cabin again, coughing, his clothes full of sand. Rosaline pulled him down beside her and put a damp cloth she'd soaked in water to his nose and mouth. As the wind howled through the window, he shielded her with his body, taking the brunt of the hard rain, remaining protectively draped over her until, finally, the fury abated. After awhile, the sand was replaced by the patter of warm, soft raindrops that smelled of desert flowers.

The air calmed, and the *dahabieh* ceased its violent rocking, swaying as gently as a cradle. Jack, his body still sheltering Rosaline's, began to move against her, stirred by the closeness of her, by the wetness of the warm raindrops. He kissed her neck, her cheek, pushed a hand beyond the softness of her temples to touch the full fall of her mink colored hair.

But Rosaline, her mind still crowded with visions of Julie kissing Jack, recoiled at the idea that he could so easily and with such utter lack of conscience, go from one woman's arms into another's.

She stiffened and inched away, avoiding his rousing mouth, his searching hands, knowing Jack wanted to make love to her, knowing that had she not seen him with Julie only a few hours past, she would have opened to him gladly. But theirs was not a marriage now, Rosaline told herself. And until it could be— if ever—giving herself to Jack seemed wrong, impossible.

When she stood up and straightened her clothes, brushed the sand from them, Jack didn't require an explanation for her rejection. He didn't demand that she behave like a wife, nor did he pin her with his eyes, which could slice through her like a knife. He understood the reasons for her rebuff and could not find it in himself to condemn her for it.

Chapter Twenty-One

"Osman has never seen wind like that—only in March, April. Devil wind, she is, sent to punish Christian sinners." Spouting his wisdom, the loquacious little cook, Osman, chattered on and on as he clucked over the butter crock the next morning. The butter crock had been overturned in the storm and was now filled with sand. As he complained, Osman kneaded a huge batch of *dourra* dough with his bare feet, which were tough and brown, by stomping round and round in a large flat pan.

Rosaline had already told him with utter disdain in no uncertain terms that he could feed the cake to the crew, but that the Britons would not eat a bite of it.

"Jack, he eat! He like it!" the cook insisted defiantly, marching with more energy than ever in the dough-filled pan.

"Jack's stomach is not as delicate as mine, but he does have *some* sensibilities," Rosaline declared, adding under her breath, "Mrs. Wiggins would swoon dead away if she were here to witness this."

Rosaline had been moving about the cabin with a dampened rag, cleaning up the sand, and when she saw the condition of the butter, offered to go and buy more from the village women, even though the thought of eating anything out of a goatskin bag was nearly as distasteful as the uncleanliness of Osman's bread. After enduring the cook's lecture on the amount she should pay for the butter, she walked ashore, using her veil in place of a parasol to protect her complexion from the sun, which, as if to apologize for nature's temper of yesterday, glittered bright in a glazed blue sky.

As Rosaline passed the Bedouin encampment, she saw the fringed flap of one of the concubine tents flutter, and unable to smother a pang of feminine curiosity, slowed, hoping to glimpse some exotic face with sleepy, kohl-lined eyes.

To her astonishment, she saw instead Keith Grange's whiskered visage. He stuck his head through the flap, yawned, then sauntered out with his thumbs hooked in his belt, displaying all the swagger of a cockerel round a hen house. His eyes met Rosaline's immediately, read the accusation in them, and, having been caught and possessing no possible excuse, simply shrugged and walked out to greet her.

"Fine morning after such a tempestuous night, isn't it, Mrs. Darlington?"

"Appropriately put, Mr. Grange." She gave him a disdainful glance, then forged ahead of him.

But he was not to be so easily dismissed; he needed to cajole her, to secure her promise not to reveal to Honore his infidelity. "You seem to have survived the storm well," he commented, just to open conversation.

"Not as comfortably as you did, no doubt. Don't you have something to do, some reporting, some journal keeping or fact finding?"

He allowed her the barb, attempted a shamed expression and ventured as humbly as he could, "It is a night we would all do well to forget, eh?"

Rosaline stopped and turned to face him. "You are asking me to keep a secret, Mr. Grange. Well, I'm afraid this is one of those rather delicate secrets that is at the mercy of everyone's good judgment. Don't you agree?''

''Mrs. Darlington . . .''

''Good day, Mr. Grange,'' she interrupted, giving him a cool nod, having no intention of allaying his concerns. Let him stew for Honore's sake. ''I shall leave you to continue your . . .'' She glanced distastefully at the gilt spangle that clung to his sleeve, an accidental memento of the night. ''Fact finding.''

The party sailed onward that morning, gliding past laden barges and *dahabiehs,* heading for Luxor where Jack planned to install Rosaline in a rented house until his business with Arabi was complete. Many Europeans idled there, especially writers and artists and scholars who considered the village a resort, one where they might enjoy climbing over the crumbled stone ruins, pondering the spectacular Nile view and contemplating its timelessness. Jack had told her about Luxor the night before the storm; they had scarcely spoken since. If she derived any satisfaction from the strained situation at all, it stemmed from the fact that Julie had apparently decided not to speak to him either; indeed, *she* had, in an earlier act of obvious pique, gone to sail on the other boat with Lance Cardew and Keith Grange.

That night they anchored in the middle of the river, at a distance far from shore, for the stretch of the Nile they sailed was known for its roving bands of thieves who sometimes attempted to swim out and rob boats moored too close to land. The crew had all gone to sleep—Jack too, Rosaline assumed—but Rosaline remained unaccountably restless, her body hot and damp with the languid air, the noise of the buzzing mosquitos more annoying than usual.

Lying still with her hands behind her head, the shutters of the cabin windows propped open for air, she listened to the sounds of eddying water and night birds, imagining after a moment that she heard a faint scraping thud against the hull of the boat. She strained her ears, grew still, and listened until she heard the sound again, this time louder. The craft jolted slightly.

Edgy, she sat up and peered out the window, but saw nothing. Another thud prompted her to get up and creep to the cabin door to investigate. She turned the latch, opened her mouth to call Jack, who always slept nearby, and suddenly froze in the very act of yelling out to him, her eyes focused upon the sinister figures, who, like shadowy monkeys, leapt out of the darkness one by one to board the *dahabieh.*

Jack had seen them too, perhaps only a second or two before Rosaline, for he had already sprung to his feet and drawn a knife while shouting to alert the sleeping crew.

In the next few moments, Rosaline stood transfixed, terrorized, watching as five turbanned men swooped noiselessly down to the deck, and with brutal speed, using quick gleaming knives, murdered half the groggy, disoriented crew before any of them could do much more than stagger to their feet.

Jack plunged his knife into the chest of one of the invaders, fended off another with his fists, his reflexes as accustomed as theirs to savagery and the tricks of survival. He parried first one attack then another with a back alley skill that seemed to come as naturally to him as breathing. Suddenly energized, Rosaline scrambled back into the cabin to seize the little pistol Jack had given her in Cairo. But when she emerged ready to use it, Jack lunged at her, knocked her backward with such deliberate force that she lost her footing and tumbled over the side of the boat.

She did not even have time to cry out as she hit the water. She struggled mightily, fearing she would drown, dragged down by her weighty clothing as water enveloped her body and closed above her head. Having no breath, disoriented in the liquid darkness, she frantically fought to find the surface before she was suddenly lifted and pushed forward. Desperate for air, she drew quick vital breaths as Jack's arms held her afloat, and towed her toward the distant, uncertain shore.

"I've got you," he said, keeping her head just above water. "Don't fight me. Relax . . . that's a girl. I'll get you ashore."

After a few minutes, she could feel him slowing down, tiring, needing to pause once or twice to catch his breath before continuing as he pulled the burden of her dragging weight. Squelching the desperate need to grab him around the neck as water lapped over her nose, Rosaline forced her muscles to relax, allowing him to maneuver as freely as he could. She wondered how he could see the shore; all was purple darkness, even the sky above her stinging eyes appeared low and heavy, devoid of any stars.

She felt the sandy bottom of the river beneath her feet suddenly, and staggered, landing with Jack in the inch deep fringe of the river, the bitter taste of algae in her mouth, her hair plastered over her eyes, her body leaden with fear and the unwieldiness of her sodden clothes.

"Forgive me for tossing you in," Jack croaked beside her, lying on his back with his knees up, catching his breath. "But I was outnumbered four to one."

Rosaline was still too breathless and stunned to reply; she simply lay with her cheek against the mossy sand, feeling the water lap around her legs, marveling that after such gruesome pandemonium aboard the boat, the world dared be so still, so gently and irreverently quiet. Pictures of the horror flashed in red and black before her eyes, and she kept envisioning Osman and his jaunty smile, the merry, lackadaisical crew and their happy songs.

"The pilot was supposed to be on watch," Jack said beside her. "He must've fallen asleep. Bloody hell, I should have kept watch with him."

"What about the other boat?" Rosaline managed to gasp.

"They're anchored a good distance upstream. We can't possibly get close enough to get their attention in the darkness. Doubtless they're safe. The thieves won't bother with them now that they've captured and made off with our perfectly good boat and all the stores on it."

"What will we do?"

"Wait here. At first light we'll walk along the shore until we sight Grange's boat. They'll notice that our boat hasn't joined them and begin to search for us. We'll be able to flag them." Jack sat up and leaned over Rosaline, who still lay like a saturated rag doll, her arms outflung and her cheek pressed against the warm, soft shore. "Can you stand?" he asked, his arm already circling her waist. "No? Then hold on. I'm going to carry you to a drier place."

As she was lifted, held against the hard wet heat of Jack's body, she heard his still uneven breathing and the sucking sound his boots made as he traversed the frothy edge of the shore. He tramped through the pungent green bullrushes, then to a little rise flanked by a field of sugar cane.

He set her down, and as the warm dry air began to lend life again to her body, as the shock began to subside, aided by Jack's protective presence, Rosaline felt herself able to sit up and establish her bearings.

"If only I had stepped out of the cabin sooner," she wailed, overcome with remorse. "I heard a noise, but lay there on my divan a minute or two, just listening. I should have jumped up right away. I should have called for you then."

"And I should not have trusted the pilot to watch alone," Jack returned, taking the burden of responsibility from Rosaline's shoulders. "I've grown lax in my habits lately, letting others watch my back for me. Damn fool, I am, especially now when I need my senses more finely honed than ever in order to face Arabi Bey."

"Osman," Rosaline breathed, staring at the dark river, her thoughts still with the men on the little *dahabieh* with its gay yellow sails.

"A good fellow," Jack admitted, tightening his arm around Rosaline, holding her close until her body ceased quivering. "I had grown to like him, too. He, and all the others."

They spoke no more for a spell, staring together into the violet night, their thoughts with the men who had died and with the knowledge that they themselves had come close to death. Jack pulled Rosaline's head to his shoulders so that she could rest, so that he could feel the life of her body, her wet soft hair.

After awhile Rosaline whispered, "I shall surely remember this night—and the horrors I witnessed in Cairo and Alexandria—forever. I shall surely relive it all in nightmares over and over again."

"I have my nightmares, too, Rosaline," he returned quietly, "but not often. There used to be so many that they simply crowded each other out after awhile, I suppose, by the time I was ten or eleven."

"Why have you never told me about your life, Jack?" she asked, pushing the wet strands of hair from her eyes. David was right, she thought. Confession was best at times of crises. "Why have you never told me about your past? Surely now, after the last few weeks, when it seems there is nothing more to lose between us, you would feel a need to reveal it all, to simply put it on the table so there will be no more cause for secrets. Besides, I should think you're hardly the sort of man to feel ashamed of anything."

"Ashamed? No." Rosaline's words had wounded Jack. Why had she said that there was nothing more to lose between them? He would have thought she would be steadfast in her loyalty toward their marriage, for Rosaline was that manner of woman—loyal and staunch and reliable to a fault, regardless of the state of her own emotions, which he knew she could squelch, if not entirely hide.

"I know a little about your past," Rosaline pushed on, when he didn't respond. "I discovered it some time ago—surely you're astute enough to have sensed it."

"Yes." He smile was wan. "I sensed it. You changed toward me a bit. And every now and then you'd drop a hint, as if you wanted to make certain that I recognized your cleverness in finding me out."

Rosaline bristled. "You're suggesting that it was a matter

of pride, which it wasn't. I simply wanted you to talk about it with me. To give up your secrets.''

"Why? Because you believe you already know the worst of them?''

"Yes.''

"Well, you don't,'' he said, leaning back on his elbows and raising one knee.

"And yet, I don't believe there's anything at all you could tell me about yourself now that would shock me.''

Yes, there would be, Jack thought. *If I were to tell you that I love you, Rosaline, that would shock you.* And you wouldn't believe me. You'd add lying to my list of vices—if you haven't already—because, for some reason, you think I cannot love you. Why? In my own stupid and clumsy way, did I make it seem impossibly unwise for a virgin spinster to love an unscrupulous man like Jack Darlington? The words I said to you in Edinburgh on the day I bought the finches have proved untrue and have come to haunt me, as precipitous words so often do. Aye. Or was it Julie's fault? Yes, I love Julie still, but not in the way you think I do. I love her as any man would love a woman who had visited and survived the dragons of hell with him. But Julie, God help her, is a reflection of who I was. I see her so now, and perhaps I have begun, unfairly and with self-loathing, to despise her for it. I've only just now realized it, understood it fully. It's difficult to let go of the past now, after all. It is an admission that what I was wasn't all I could have been, and such a confession is difficult for a proud man such as I.

Jack turned his head to regard his wife, felt a current of emotion flow strongly through his mind. He could not tell her of such thoughts; he held them back, judging the moment unwise.

"Tell me about your life as a boy,'' she prompted again. "It is time, now, don't you think? When there is nothing but the water and the sky and the night between us.''

He turned his eyes from her face to the river. "I did not

know my father, or his father. Doubtless my mother did not know them either.''

"Your mother. What was she like?''

"Carefree, irresponsible. Full of laughter when she should not have been. My legacy from her, I guess. During her finer moments she was a tavern maid by trade, and during her worst—well, you might imagine. Unfortunately she was at her worst most of the time. She allowed me to run loose, and when there were no scraps from the tavern kitchen, I learned to find them elsewhere. You'd be amazed at how many ragged children there used to be wandering about the East End of London, how clever they were at eluding the workhouse beadles, how resourceful they were at finding ways to survive. At the age of eight I joined the Mud Larks on the Thames. Have you ever heard the term?''

"Mud Larks?''

"Aye. They're the poorest of the poor who dig through the mud on the banks and see what the tide has washed in—bits of metal or wood to sell, a coin if they're lucky. I met Julie there. She was only five or six, but very clever for her age. And bold, too.''

Rosaline had grown still in order to concentrate upon every word he said, upon the timbre of his voice, the way it had altered, not grown bitter as one might expect recounting such tales, but containing, oddly, a note of near nostalgia.

"And Julie's parents?" she asked.

"Both of them had a fondness for gin and an aversion to work—not that there were many jobs anyway for people like them. At any rate, if Julie wanted to eat, she learned that she had to forage for herself. I taught her ways, and together we invented new schemes—which became more elaborate as we grew older. I became a 'toy-getter' of some repute—a collector of gentlemen's pocketwatches, and Julie had a penchant for ladies' purses. We lived in alleyways and shabby parks in the summer, and under bridges in the winter. I think Julie might have died that first winter without me—her parents had been consigned to Marshalsea Prison for debt, and she had no place to go. My mother had disappeared as well—run off to Paris with a French sailor, or so I heard.'' Jack smiled wryly, without pain.

Julie became my constant companion, my accomplice, my family. Later, much later, the Foreign Office discovered me and decided that I could be useful to them—they need the services of thieves and cutthroats from time to time, you know, to infiltrate the kitchens and stables of palaces, to learn the secrets of kings and generals—if there are any to learn. Julie proved just as useful as I. She's quite good at mimicking accents and manners, of insinuating herself into other people's lives when it suits her. She did it because it was an adventure, because it stirred her blood, and because I asked her to. The Foreign Office came to be grateful after awhile. There were benefits, you see. Rewards.''

Of which I am one, just possibly, Rosaline silently finished.

Jack continued, his voice mingling with the exotic Eastern sounds, his clothes and hair drying with hers in the warm date scented air. Rosaline began to understand his relationship with Julie as never before, the bond they had shared, and strangely, even to feel as if it would be somehow unnatural, even selfish to break it.

Jack's arm was pressed to hers and she felt the vital heat of it, its hard bulging strength. While she yearned to be a part of him, like Julie, with all the shared experiences and adventures, with the familiarity it takes half a lifetime to build, she purposefully detached herself. Somehow, through relating his tales of survival and adventure, Jack seemed less a thief and more a man to be admired. He was handsome and intelligent and unashamed of what he had done, and he had come far from the ragged urchin in the East End. He had a right to be proud of his achievements, the respect he had earned from his government. And Rosaline, as his wife—beloved or not, bargained for or not—felt pride in his accomplishments, too.

She wished suddenly that they could plan a life together, a

smooth, uncomplicated one filled with embassy balls and London fetes, Rosaline in her well-bred steady manner helping to pave the way for Jack's winning charm and talents. They would experience the normal passages of a marriage, of course, the domestic quarrels, the occasional storms, but also the companionable nights sitting beside a crackling fire with their feet propped upon her fringed footstools, the hope of love between them at least possible, if not assured.

And perhaps because such a picture *was* so bright and because she wanted to punish herself for her foolishness in dreaming it, Rosaline asked, ''And so you loved Julie from the start. At first as a childhood companion, and then later as . . .''

''Does it serve a purpose to ask such questions?'' he asked, disappointed. ''But, yes,'' he finally admitted, knowing it wiser, better to have it out. ''In every way a man can love a woman, I loved Julie.''

Except that he no longer felt that way, for he had stepped from one world into another, and where once Julie had been the passion of his youth, Rosaline had become the love of his maturity. He wanted to tell her so all at once, but he knew she did not love him, was afraid to love him for a reason he could not quite grasp. If he could discover why. . . .

''It is right that you should be with her then.'' Rosaline's unexpected, solemn and sincere words surprised Jack, and he turned his head to look at her. ''What did you say?''

''I said that it is right that you should be with Julie. You belong together, just as you always have.'' With that, Rosaline struggled to her feet and began to walk away, toward the shore.

Jack had always considered himself a practical man, but as he had heard Rosaline speak the words, as he saw her move away in her pale gown, looking like a retreating ghost, he felt as if all he had ever wanted was evaporating. If he did not seize it now and manage to hold onto it, it would forever drift out of his reach, like a bird on the wing leaving not even a feather behind. He felt as if his life had reached some point of crisis all at once, as if he were about to be swallowed by a

destiny of which he had lost command. His only redemption
was to seize Rosaline. If he did not, he would again become
what he had been before he had seen her walk into the drafty
Edinburgh drawing room with her long, calm hands and heavy
coil of hair.

He jumped up, slipped in the yellow mud, shouted, reached
out a hand to catch Rosaline's arm. But she evaded him, fleeing
from emotions as she ran headlong through the purple bullrushes, her head scarcely visible, her passage a violent rustling
of silk. Jack pursued, afraid for the first time in his life, not of
mortality but of the loss of a dream, the one he had held for
as long as he could remember. He could hardly see Rosaline's
flying figure, and chased her blindly, calling, shouting, cursing
her because she had made him feel afraid.

Rosaline ran toward the shore, where the way was clear of
the reeds, and the slope downward grew so steep she lost her
footing and tumbled, staggered to her knees before she jogged
on, not able to heed Jack's hoarse commands to stop, not ever
slowing, not yielding even when his fingers finally seized her
arm, bruising it. She fought, struggled, batted away his hands,
slapped his face when he cursed her yet again.

"I want nothing more to do with you!" she cried, wrenching
away, afraid of him, of herself. "I'll go back to Scotland if
you like, but you'll live your life elsewhere, apart from me.
I'll not live with you, with Julie always between us, watching,
waiting in the wings. It's undignified, *unclean.* At least allow
me to live as I was brought up to live—in the way that you
value so much. Give me the right to my decency. After all, I
sacrificed my own love for you—I kept myself away from
David when he asked me to be his lover. At least I made
a decision, Jack, I maintained a sense of honor where you
cannot!"

"Don't throw your righteous brand of morality at me, Rosaline," Jack said through his teeth.

"Why not? Morality is what this is all about—what our

marriage is all about! Two different lives, two different standards.''

"You knew the score from the very beginning, didn't you,
Rosaline? You knew I was no well-mannered gentleman, but
you took me anyway—you took me because you needed me
to save you from your spinsterhood, from your virginity!''

Rosaline raised a hand to slap his face, but Jack caught her
against his body, and suddenly he forced her to the ground,
pinned her beneath his weight, and his mouth found hers in
the blackness, invading it even while she fought against the
wonder of his flesh, her own need of it.

Just once, she told herself, feeling the warm air brush her
throat, feeling the heat of Jack's breaths against her cheek. Just
once I'll take from Jack Darlington what he so casually takes
from me. Perhaps it is now *my* prerogative. Rosaline felt the
fire of necessity build rapidly within her and knew that she
would not let it burn itself out slowly as before, would not let
it smother beneath the ashes of her will. Now she would simply
take, assuage herself with the man she loved because it seemed
right, only fair in the mad order of things to steal this moment
of pleasure that suddenly was more important to her than any
previous act of her life.

And so when Jack put his lips upon her neck and his hand
upon the curve of her breast where the yellow silk strained,
still damp from the Nile, she did not resist, but arched, grasped
his head, his shoulders, and urged him to do what he was driven
to do.

By the time he had pulled the hem of her garment up in a
long urgent slide, she had pushed his shirt aside, found his bare
flesh and put her palms to it. As his movement grew rhythmic
and resolute, she helped him to enter her body, casting aside
the last remnants of her inhibition, the armor that had kept her
inwardly chaste.

Beneath her, she felt the wet sand at her hips; inside, she
felt Jack's heat. And the thing she had denied herself grew,
then blossomed, and burst.

Atop her Jack spent himself with a long, tormented groan, possessing her in a way somehow more complete, more possessive than any other time, as he held her face in his hands, said her name, not once but many times.

She lay still in his arms, throbbing, her body feeling perfect, entire, her whole being light. She heard the night birds, the tiny rustle of things unknown, saw the shift of the shadows, and knew that time would progress until she would forget these things of the Nile, regardless of her desire to hold onto them. But she would never forget the feel of Jack's body pressed into her, the tranquility it brought.

She knew that Jack was deeply satisfied too. Just now Jack had triumphed in a sense, and doubtless felt secure because she had at last experienced the kind of pleasure in his arms that he had sought for her. But Rosaline's practical heart told her that nothing had really changed between them, for Julie still slept on a boat somewhere out in the darkness, serene with the confidence that no matter what, she would always have Jack's devotion. He would not, could not, abandon her.

Rosaline remembered the moment she had first seen Jack, remembered exactly her first impression and the quick, sharp pang of dismay that had come swiftly on its heels. *He is too much for me,* she had thought. *Too much.* Jack Darlington was a young girl's romance, not really substance, not a man made for hearth and home, too handsome, too self-assured, too splendid by half for a plain, twenty-six year old spinster from Edinburgh. And, after all, Rosaline told herself, I have known since the age of sixteen that I would have to settle for less. Indeed, I would have felt more comfortable, more at ease, with less. Jack belonged with Julie. They were a pair, and Rosaline Cheevers needed a gentleman, someone tame and quiet who understood her nature, who understood the rules.

Nevertheless, for a moment more, she lay still, nestled exactly in the place where she wanted most to be, her head cradled on Jack's magnificent shoulder, her half-clothed body pressed desperately into the length of his. She savored every texture, smell and sound: the roughness of his jaw where her upraised arm brushed against it, the scent of his skin mingled with that of the sugar cane field, the wind-rippled bullrushes, the slow green slide of the Nile. And it seemed to her that the world in that single, borrowed instant was precisely as it should be.

Pity that the moment could never be coaxed to come again.

Chapter Twenty-Two

She would never forget her first glimpse of Luxor. The village would remain in her memory as a place of warm and mysterious beauty, rendered in every shade of gold. The sunlight touched her hands and warmed them as she grasped the rail of the boat and contemplated the ancient temple ruins that stood so regally along the Nile, their sandstone columns crumbling but still resplendent with past glory. Tombs nestled in the group of obelisks reflected the sun's glaze, and if she looked closely, she could see the ravaged hieroglyphics still deeply etched on the grand monuments.

She and Jack were safe. Just as he had predicted, the thieves had not bothered the boat that Cardew, Grange and Julie sailed on. At daylight their crew had noticed Jack signaling from shore and rescued them.

Now Rosaline stood near Jack at the prow, absorbing the scenery. "Luxor," she breathed to Jack, entranced. "They say it was once the capital of Upper Egypt. The Greeks called it Thebes. Did you know Homer mentioned it in the *Iliad?*"

"Yes. You may be surprised to know that I've read the *Iliad* twice,'' he answered with a wry smile. ''The natives call the city el-Ukser—Arabic for 'the castles.' ''

''The castles. How romantic. I shall use that name when I refer to the village in my journal.''

''Your journal? Is Keith Grange to have competition then?''

''Hardly. But I've decided to begin recording my impressions during our stay here, to document all the wonders I see, so that years from now, when I'm sitting in my rocking chair looking out at the cold Scottish mist, I shall be able to remember the wonders of Egypt.''

Jack's mouth curved. ''Will you let me read over your shoulder while you write it?''

''If you like,'' Rosaline said, her eyes still fixed upon the ruins.

Her voice was cool, distant, Jack noted, and he wondered at it. Since their fierce lovemaking the previous night, her manner had puzzled him. While he had expected her to be affectionate and warm, she kept herself apart, and her behavior filled him with slow-burning anger.

He regarded her in the pale yellow dress she had worn since yesterday, the same one that had been christened by the water of the Nile and then, later, crumpled by the roughness of his impatient hands. Jack marveled that she still managed to look fresh and neat in the soiled garment, and that her composure, despite the horror of last night's massacre, remained intact. She had borrowed a large straw hat from one of the crew, which she used to shade her complexion now, and its brim threw a long blue shadow across the lower half of her face, hiding her eyes from his speculative view. He had told her she could safely dress as an Englishwoman now that they had neared the resort patronized by so many Europeans.

''During our time in Luxor, you'll be staying in a house staffed by two servants,'' he told her. ''I hope you'll find it acceptable. Unfortunately, I won't be around to enjoy it much. Tomorrow I'll leave for Arabi's camp, which is about a two or three hour ride south.''

"How long will you be there?"

"As long as I'm welcome."

"Will Mr. Cardew and Mr. Grange accompany you?"

"I don't yet know. I plan to send a messenger ahead to see if Arabi will agree to have them. Frankly, I think Cardew is hoping to be spared the excitement, while Grange, on the other hand, is champing at the bit to go."

"He'll have fascinating stories to send back to London."

"Sensationalized, I imagine."

She watched a honeybee alight on the rail, fold its wings, then fly away again. "Sensationalism could be to your benefit, of course," she said. "Especially considering that Mr. Grange is a good friend of yours. No doubt you'll be the subject of every drawing room conversation in England once his articles appear."

"No doubt—especially if I fail to accomplish anything and the Foreign Office declares the whole mission a waste of time."

She regarded him curiously. "I've never known you to lack confidence in what you set out to do."

"My lack of confidence is due, perhaps, to one or two failures I've recently experienced here."

Jack let the words hang significantly between them; Rosaline could not continue to meet his gaze, knowing that he referred to her behavior toward him today, to what seemed to be a continual failure to make the marriage real.

Out of the corner of her eye she saw Julie move to the rail, and Rosaline thought that, more than ever, the black-haired woman looked like a little fox alert to the first scent of danger, her senses fine-tuned and wary, her movements quick with the nervousness of a creature unused to confinement. Keith Grange could not settle either, and his heavy footsteps thudded against the weathered deck as he paced with an eagerness to depart. Lance Cardew appeared agitated too, and Rosaline almost pitied him his anxiety over the possible journey to the camp of the infamous Arabi and his barbarous army. The aide was not meant for anything more adventurous than an evening stroll

through Hyde Park, was suited better for a post in London or
Paris, far removed from sand and fleas and hostile weathered
faces.

At last they arrived on shore. The house where Rosaline was
to live was delightful in its pink rambling length, its untended
garden of marigolds, its countless open windows and the balcony which overlooked the gold pylons of the temple and the
lazy flowing Nile. As she climbed the trail at Jack's side, she
absorbed every sight and sound around her, eyeing the brown
lizards with wide toes who sunned themselves in the sand along
the meandering path, smelling the jasmine that cloaked half of
the white shuttered house.

The sun was hot, but the arid breeze that skipped off the
river rippled Rosaline's clothes and cooled her as she hurried,
scarcely able to keep up with Jack's long stride, eager to explore
the house perched so charmingly on the shore. Nearby she
noticed several people wandering through the ancient temple,
men of scholarly appearance scribbling thoughtfully in note-
books, tilting their heads to study hieroglyphics shaded by the
feathered tops of palms.

"Oh, Jack," she gasped, unable to contain her excitement.
"I see why so many Londoners consider Luxor an ideal place
to winter. It's surely one of the loveliest spots on earth."

"Then you'll be able to enjoy yourself here for several days
in my absence? I've been told that the servants of the house
are accustomed to serving Europeans and that they speak
English well enough."

"I could live in one of those little mud cupboards if it were
situated as well as this. But, Jack," Rosaline said, plucking her
gown, the only one she owned now that their *dahabieh* had
been stolen. "Will there be clothes for sale in the village—
gowns?"

"You can be sure that the natives are enterprising enough
to know that Britons have heavy purses. I daresay you'll find
something suitable."

As they stepped into the cool, thick walled space of the

house, three slippered servants rushed forward to greet them, performing greetings before scurrying to bring a tray laden with dates, apricots and a roast chicken stuffed with wheat. The usual samovar filled with mint tea accompanied the meal, served amid colorful Rabat rugs and copper urns filled with fresh flowers.

Rosaline glanced over a shoulder toward the door. Jack noticed the direction of her gaze and commented, ''The others will be quartered elsewhere.''

Although the news pleased Rosaline, she deigned not to reply as she crossed the spacious low ceilinged room with its scarred pieces of English furniture that had doubtless been ferried down from Cairo. The scent of incense filled the air, combining itself with the smell of the barley fields which stretched beyond the temple. The view from the balcony was magnificent. Rosaline roamed outside, feeling Jack's eyes upon her back, knowing he was both mystified and angered by her aloofness.

''It's safe here in Luxor, I'm told,'' he remarked casually as he walked up behind her and set his hands beside hers upon the warm rail. ''You can wander about the ruins all you want. There's shopping in the village and plenty of Europeans around if you'd like company for tea.''

''I'll make the most of my time. You needn't worry about me while you're away.

''It seems that I needn't worry about you while I'm present.''

''I don't intend to quarrel with you, Jack.''

''It would be better than your silence, Rosaline.''

''We'll speak about it tonight. There are things that need to be said. But not now.''

''Very well,'' he said curtly, regarding her through narrowed eyes, feeling put off. ''I'll leave you, then. I've business to attend to and a message that must be dispatched to Arabi. Don't expect me back until evening.''

Rosaline nodded. ''I'll see that there's a meal prepared.''

He left, irritated and uneasy over her manner and determined to get to the bottom of its cause when he returned. His disquiet was hardly lessened when, after grabbing a handful of apricots from the untouched tray on his way out, he stepped into the yard and saw a painter's easel angled near the edge of the market. The artist himself was busy at work with his brushes, daubing in images of the colorful displays of rugs and silks. For several seconds Jack observed the artist—his rival—then in a scathing voice said aloud to himself, "I'll be damned. The four of us here. Fate could not have planned it better."

He returned to the house an hour before sunset after having made preparations for his impending mission to Arabi's camp, invigorated by all it would mean to his career. His nerves were taut with anticipation even while his mind was crowded with thoughts of Rosaline. He wondered if she had seen David Mellon yet; if not, she soon would, for the village was small, and the artist had surely heard of the arrival of the diplomatic mission. He would seek her out the moment Jack departed— if not before—the son-of-a-bitch. If Jack didn't have to watch his behavior so closely, now that London had its eye upon him, he might have paid Mellon a visit and punched him in the nose to discourage any ideas of a dalliance.

He had spoken briefly with Julie earlier; she had pleaded with him again to leave with her after the mission was complete, but he had staunchly refused. Instead he had raised the subject of her future, had asked her what she planned to do, what she would like to do with herself.

"I'd like to take up the life the two of us shared before," she had declared simply, clasping his hand, drawing him close. He had tried to explain why such a life could never again be possible, felt his belly tense as he spoke, for despite his deep, committed love for Rosaline, he still loved Julie in a fundamental way that he suspected would never cease.

As he entered his house, a servant greeted and ushered him to the room set aside for dining, where he searched the cool shadows for Rosaline in her pale lemon dress, eager to seal their relationship in some way, to make love with her, to know that when he rode away tomorrow on a perilous mission, she would be anxious for his return, anxious to sail back to Britain with him and build a life together. And Jack wanted to feel assured that, in his absence, she would not invite David Mellon to have tea—or anything else.

Jack discovered her on the adjoining balcony, just where he had left her, and if she hadn't been wearing a different gown, he might have thought she had spent the whole day lingering in the same spot, gazing out with museful eyes at the intriguing landscape.

"You went shopping today," he commented, flashing her a smile meant to be complimentary, meant to be seductive, meant to remind her of the pleasure she'd found in his arms last night.

"Yes," she answered, not pivoting to his welcome arms, turning only her well-coiffed head, her manner no warmer than it had been earlier.

"Did you visit the ruins, as well?"

"Yes. I was fortunate to meet a party of German archaeologists who told me all about the Temple of Der-el-Bahri. Did you know that it was built by Queen Hatshepset? The Germans said she was the first woman to become a pharoah. I bought some books about her in the market. Perhaps you'd care to look at them. They're quite interesting."

"I care nothing for Queen Hatshepset."

She turned at last, struck by the odd timbre of his voice, by the harshness of it. "Why do you speak to me in such an uncivilized tone?" she demanded.

"Because I'm weary of your avoidance, Rosaline, and have little time to understand it. And because I want to make love with you again."

He ran his hands over the gown that was a delicate shade of green gathered and draped in folds that slithered over the tiles as she moved away from him.

She smelled sweet, like a fine English spring, and her hair was secured in its shining, complicated twists. Recalling the feel of her flesh, her abandonment and the unconcealed pleasure she had found beneath his body last night, Jack seized her again and, ignoring her stiffening protest, kissed her hungrily, with determination, waiting until she relaxed, felt the beginnings of what he knew he could stir and satisfy.

Surrendering her resolve, Rosaline opened her mouth, let him invade it, allowed his hands to explore her silk-covered waist, her skin above the scooped neckline, and the nakedness of her breasts beyond lace and linen.

For a moment, because she couldn't help herself, she laid back her head so that he could kiss the curve of her neck, a frown of distress between her brows and her eyes closed, her senses and her mind at odds with one another. She let her hand trail down his back, to his hips, then over the front of his breeches so that he drew in a sharp breath of desire.

But then, as Jack pulled Rosaline from the balcony, took her inside for privacy, pressed her shoulders against the cool inner wall, she turned her head aside to avoid his mouth. "No, Jack. I'll not allow this. I meant every word I said to you last night."

Her tone was grave, her eyes direct and sober, devoid of the soft, promising passion he had glimpsed only a moment before. "What damned words?" he snapped, angry, afraid. "Remind me of what you said last night—all of it. I fear it was overshadowed by what came after," he added with cutting sarcasm.

She turned her back, waited until she could speak with calm. "I've decided to sail to Scotland," she said in a low, quiet voice. "Just as soon as we return to Cairo and can make arrangements."

Behind her, Jack simply stared, unable to comprehend her words. Without realizing it, he held out a hand of appeal. "Of course. We'll go back together. I doubt I'll be detained in Cairo long."

Her back stiffened with resolve. "I mean that I shall go back alone. You'll be free to do exactly as you like."

"Exactly as I like?" He laughed, the sound short and bitter. "What in the hell is that supposed to mean?"

"It means exactly as it sounds."

"I fail to understand why you bring this up after last night. What's the point in . . ."

"The point is that last night changed nothing between us, Jack!" Rosaline cried, turning to face him. "Why can't you understand? Our situation is no different than it was yesterday, or the day before, or last week. Can you not see that?"

"No, I cannot."

"Why? Is it because you believe that women who are conquered sexually are conquered emotionally as well?"

"That's the general understanding men are given by women of your breed," he returned, still sarcastic, still furious and hurt.

"Women of my breed?"

"Aye. You don't usually submit to a man's lovemaking with any particular enthusiasm unless you care for him—or care for what he can give you."

"And how many women of my 'breed' have you bedded, Jack, to make you such an expert at understanding them?"

"Not nearly enough, it would seem," he drawled, feeling a sudden dread of what was to come. He knew he needed to tell her quickly that he loved her, before anything else—something dreadfully regrettable—was blurted out. "Rosaline . . ."

She cut him off and demanded, "What do you intend to do about Julie?"

Jack regarded the pale outline of his wife's face, the long neck, the intelligent eyes, and felt all at once as if he were losing a battle, a battle of the kind in which a man had no weapons.

"Will you send her away after all the years she's spent loving you—after all the years you've spent loving her? I don't believe so, Jack. So what *will* you do with her? Will she come to live with us in the Orkneys, wander about the moors, eat at our table—or be set up in some little cottage conveniently close?"

And Jack knew that he had to provide an answer, had to

admit that he'd not decided what course to take. He wanted, needed, Rosaline more than he needed anything in the world, but could he simply cast Julie off like a worn overcoat and tell her to disappear? In a sense it would be casting off a part of himself. And it would be cruel to Julie, too, for she had trusted him, depended upon him, been ready to suffer for him countless times in the years since she had been barely five years old. And even if he told her to go—demanded it—would she? Or would she linger near as Rosaline had suggested, waiting for him, for any scrap of attention he might deign to throw her way? She was too clever to be passive, she would cause endless trouble if she were near.

Jack stepped back, released a weary breath, and said with an honesty he rather despised, "I don't know, Rosaline. I don't know what's to be done. "I cannot give you an answer now."

"Don't mistake my own intentions regarding our marriage," she said. "I'm not stupid. I've been thinking about it quite hard for weeks. I have a solution."

"What solution?" he asked, deflated, hating the biting mockery in her tone.

"I'm concerned about appearances, about what the gossips will say. It's another of my inbred preoccupations. I'll still be your wife, of course, ensconced in our Orkney estate, patching linen, arranging flowers, and tending to two small boys of whom I've grown inordinately fond. Doing all the things I'm supposed to do. You shall have the wife you bargained for. But you shall have your mistress, too."

He stared at her.

"It's perfectly acceptable, you know. You've always aspired to reach the rank of a gentleman," she finished with a light and bitter sarcasm, "and fornicating, after all, is what gentlemen *do*."

Jack regarded her with smoldering eyes, his voice coming from low in his throat. "By God, I can scarcely credit it."

"Credit what? My giving you permission to sleep with Julie or my speaking so bluntly?"

"Rosaline, damn it . . ."

"No, Jack!" she cried, throwing off his hands, her face twisted into lines of heartbreak. "You determined the course of our marriage the very day we met, remember? And you've determined it every day since! You've not changed its course. You've not!"

"It's not as simple as you would make it out to be. Julie's not some casual whore I happened to fancy last week."

"I know that." Rosaline swallowed, took a step away from him, her voice softening. "I know that, Jack. And I'm practical, not naive. I know how things will likely end, how matters will likely evolve between the three of us."

"No, you don't, Rosaline. No you don't."

"Let it be for now, Jack. We had our moment to remember last night. You have other concerns today."

She turned from him and walked out onto the balcony and down the stairs, managing to look steady and dignified even as her body trembled and her heart ached.

Jack started to follow, but she put up a hand as if to ward him off, and he checked the impulse, just watching, knowing he had lost a great deal—a prize—all in the space of a moment. In a burst of frustration, he realized that he did not know what he could have said or done to prevent the tragedy that had happened between them. "I'm in love with you, Rosaline," he breathed to himself, watching her tall, straight figure as she went to stand beside the Nile. "Would it have made a difference if I had told you so?"

Chapter Twenty-Three

When Rosaline awoke the next morning, she looked at the bright patch of sunshine on the green tiles of the floor, her eyes sore from tears.

She had wept half the night with the knowledge that she might have had Jack beside her through the dark lonely hours, the two of them entwined, listening together to the owl who had come to nest on the roof. Now Jack was preparing to leave, or perhaps he had left already, too angry and frustrated with her to say farewell.

Feeling old, Rosaline pushed back the light coverlet and padded to the window and, squinting against the early dawn light, looked in the direction of the village where a huddle of people gathered, including Keith Grange and Lance Cardew. They were speaking with Jack, who sat astride a grey horse. No one else was mounted, nor were any other horses in sight. Apparently, Arabi had sent word that he wanted no one in his camp but Jack.

Suddenly Rosaline could scarcely bear the thought of allowing him to go from her without a goodbye, but she knew if she threw on her clothes and ran down to him that, she might weaken, beg to take back all she had said last night. Such an action would not be wise.

So she remained at the window, strong with the confidence that what she had done was best, that certainly the suffering of this heartache was inevitable and better to be gotten over with now, rather than endured when they returned to Scotland. But she wished her husband well, nonetheless, was proud of him, and fervently hoped his mission would be successful and safe.

"Goodspeed, Jack," she breathed aloud, and felt a small measure of satisfaction that Julie was not in evidence, not able to bid him goodbye. Perhaps she had done so already, privately with her hair let down over the pillows. For Rosaline did not know where Jack had slept last night.

Turning from the window with great sorrow, Rosaline then washed and dressed. As she walked through the corridor to find breakfast, a servant beckoned her to the front door, where a gentleman stood waiting with his hat in his hand. He was dressed as he often was, in light colored trousers and a coat, his hair pomaded, his hands stained with paint.

Rosaline drew in a breath, feeling as if her poor bruised heart had been sent a ray of light from heaven. "David!" she cried, rushing forward with her hands outstretched. *"David!"*

"I find that the colors of the landscape here are actually softer than those in Italy. The light and shadow are less sharp too. You must come to my house and see what I've painted."

"How long do you plan to stay in Luxor?" Rosaline asked, strolling beside the artist through the garden, full of marigolds and bees, behind her rented house.

"At least another fortnight. I don't feel I've quite captured the mystery of the place, its oldness."

"I know what you mean. I told Keith Grange once that the whole of Egypt seemed Biblical to me—women still going about with water jugs balanced on their heads, donkeys carrying bundles of wheat.''

David regarded Rosaline in the amber sunlight, her pale skirts flanked by flowers, her floppy brimmed hat deepening the shade of her eyes. ''When is your husband due to return from this famous mission of his?''

''He expects the negotiations to take several days.''

''I was up at dawn sketching a scene of the river and saw him depart.'' David gave her a glance from beneath his brows. ''I didn't notice you in the little crowd of well-wishers.''

Rosaline walked a few steps forward, her head lowered, the trail of her ivory skirts startling a dove from the flower beds. ''I watched him from my window.''

David reached to pluck a marigold, twirl it between his fingers, his artist's eye noting the exact arrangement of the petals. ''It's not a marriage of the spirit, is it?''

She smiled sadly, staring out across the Nile and the empty expanse beyond. ''I don't know what sort of marriage it is, David. At first I . . . I was sure it was no more than a marriage of mutual convenience. I needed a husband to save me from my spinsterhood.'' She glanced askance at David and gave him another wan smile. ''And Jack needed . . . well, Jack needed a wife who could further his career.''

''And that has changed now?''

''No. It's just that certain feelings have developed between us—unexpectedly, inconveniently. Matters have become complicated.''

''Aren't they always when two people live together?''

She sighed, wanting very much to confide her heartache all at once, and to have someone explain it to her, make sense of it where she could not. Rosaline blurted, ''We quarreled. I told Jack we would have the usual sort of upper class marriage. I would have my children and my pretty house, and Jack would have his gentlemen's club, his horses . . . and his mistress.''

''Ah,'' David said slowly, watching her, a finger to his chin. ''There is already a mistress, then?''

"A lover, yes. She was with Jack long before our marriage. I don't believe he will be able to give her up."

Being a man with no particular appreciation for monogamy, David lifted an indolent shoulder and drawled sagely, "It is the way of things, Rosaline. Very few men I know can keep themselves to one woman over a lifetime."

"But Jack could," she argued, suddenly fierce, surprised that such vehement words in Jack's defense had come out of her mouth. "He could if he made up his mind to do it. He's the sort of man who is firm in his convictions."

"I believe you have fallen in love with him, dear Rosaline."

"And why must it be so difficult to love one's own husband?"

"Because you did it backward, darling, don't you see? You wed him first, simply for what marriage could provide, then found yourself falling in love. Now, had you married *me* instead . . ."

David let the sentence trail, smiling at Rosaline in such a way that she laughed all at once, happy to be able to share her burden with someone willing to listen. He said flirtatiously, "Of course, you *could* have a marriage of equality, if you cared to, Rosaline. As I've said before, there's no reason why wives cannot have lovers, too."

He had made the same offer once before and, looking at his tall narrow body, Rosaline considered the idea of trying to recapture the spark of passion that had briefly flared among red petals. Her thoughts horrified her, for she was not the sort of woman to cross moral boundaries. And besides, having known in Jack's arms the sort of completeness rarely found, she knew any dalliance with David would be pale and tarnished by comparison.

And yet, she would enjoy David's company for awhile, for a few suspended days in this hot, melted gold place, she would let him think that she might, just possibly, succumb to his seductions. She would permit him to sip wine with her and eat sugared almonds, she would watch him paint. And then she

would pack away her girlish daydreams and prepare to return
to the marriage made of practicality, the marriage that required
a cool head and a cooler heart, as a defense against Jack's love
for Julie.

On the fourth day of her husband's absence, Rosaline began
to fret, watching the horizon for signs of him, sending one of
the servants to the market to inquire of any news. Lance Cardew
took tea with her that afternoon and spoke absently, superfi-
cially, seemingly preoccupied with some weighty concern.
Keith Grange, who called to pass the time and to read aloud
to her the latest story he was sending back to London, dismissed
her worries and assured her that Jack Darlington could take
care of himself.

Julie did not show herself at all.

David called on her daily. Determined to be circumspect,
Rosaline brought along a servant and accompanied the artist
to the ruins, to the marketplace, and to all the hot desert-scented
vantage points he insisted she see. One evening, he persuaded
her to go to his house. She agreed to go after dark against her
better judgment. Feeling wicked, she hurried along with David
over the rocky sand, the scent of the marigolds strong, the air
warm and sticky despite the lateness of the hour.

While they sat in his house surrounded by vivid, still wet
canvases, turpentine and linseed oil making her sneeze, David
entertained Rosaline with stories of his travels. Later—much
later—when a supper of mutton, sweet cream sauce, hon-
eycakes, tangerines and pistachios was served, Rosaline savored
every bite, drinking far too much red wine to assuage her thirst,
which had been made great by the heat.

She felt as if this was the last night of her young womanhood,
the last night she could ever feel daring and beautiful and
slightly intoxicated with the idea of girlish flirtation. She had
worn her most daring gown, red with ecru lace, and had tightened her corset so that her waist seemed trimmer and her breasts

higher. A blush colored her cheeks. Her hair was piled high in ringlets and a gold filigree comb nestled in its dark, scented curls. She wished, dolefully, that Jack could see her.

Jack rode toward Luxor in darkness, the stars brighter against an ink-black sky so that, with the moon's help, his way was at least discernible. His mission to Arabi had not been a great success, but neither had it been a failure; no agreements had been reached, no sure peace, but Jack felt as if a truce might soon be negotiated. At least the Foreign Office would not be displeased, especially since Arabi had given him a letter, whose lines they had both labored over, listing suggestions for a more stable treaty.

As soon as the talks in the rebel's tent had ended, Jack had departed, declining to spend another night in the camp, restless and eager to return to Luxor—to Rosaline. He had been angry with her when he'd left. But he now understood that she had delivered an ultimatum, one he not only understood, but gradually grew to respect, and he would bid farewell to Julie in order to reassure Rosaline of his love.

He longed to share with his wife the details of his mission, the events of the last few days that seemed to be the pinnacle of his life. He would be promoted again, no doubt, and would be able to rent a townhouse in London, where he and Rosaline could spend the season, dividing their time between the diversions of the city and the heathered fields of Arbor Gate. He imagined the two of them living their clean, orderly lives filled with intimacy and laughter. He imagined them dancing together, riding together, making love. The boys would attend a good boarding school and when the time came, he would see that they had profitable careers.

And Julie . . . well, he would not see Julie again once he left Cairo. He had made his decision concerning the course of his life and the woman he wanted in it, and Julie would have to find her own way without him. To his dismay, she had followed him to Arabi's camp and waylaid him there one last time in an attempt to persuade him again to go away with her. But there would be no more Jackdaw. He told her that in no uncertain terms. Julie was a survivor and would land on her feet wherever she went; he had taught her how.

Jack spurred his horse into a faster canter, uneasy all at once, thinking of the artist David Mellon, of Rosaline's affection for him. The village was quiet when he arrived, as was the rambling pink house by the shore, with only a single candle left burning as he opened the door. In several long strides he reached Rosaline's bedroom, saw that she was not behind the gauzy white netting, and with sudden dread, strode briskly through all the other rooms, then through the garden, even onto the shore beyond the lawn. Jack called for her in a voice that grew sharper by the minute, but could find her nowhere. Then, after suffering an initial fear that she had already left him, packed up and sailed for Scotland, Jack knew—suddenly and without question—where he would find his wife.

Sprinting alongside the Nile a moment later, negotiating a rocky path, he saw that the house he sought was not dark. The French doors stood open to catch the breeze. Jack did not pause in his step, but walked through them, his heels ringing sharply on the tiles. A sleepy servant rushed forward only to be shoved aside.

He saw them then, his wife and David Mellon, sitting together at a low table lit by candles, the remains of a midnight meal and an empty bottle of wine crowded haphazardly between them.

Startled by the sudden sound of footsteps, Rosaline glanced up, and Jack saw that her face was flushed, the collar of her scarlet gown was loose in a way it had never been for him, and her hair was down in ringlets.

David Mellon jumped up, the laughter on his lips dying, his eyes fearful as they fixed upon the grim faced man striding forward to confront him with fists clenched.

"You bastard!" Jack said in a low, savage voice. He heard blood roaring in his ears, pictured the two of them as lovers, writhing together in bed before languidly enjoying a meal. The images tore at his heart.

"Jack!" Rosaline came quickly to her feet and rushed to put herself between the pair of men, terrorized over what might happen.

But Jack pushed her aside. Then, clenching the artist's collar, he hauled back a fist and delivered a blow to the man's belly. David doubled over, gasping, backing away. He knew he was no match for the other man.

"Jack, for God's sake!" Rosaline cried as David stumbled against a chair and fell to his knees. "I beg you to stop!"

"Do you beg me, Rosaline? Really? You shall beg me harder before this night is done. But you needn't beg on his behalf, because I'm done with the rutting bastard. If I were to touch him again, I'd kill him."

Giving Mellon a contemptuous look, he kicked aside the wine bottle that had fallen from the table, then pivoted on a heel and stalked toward the door, saying to Rosaline over his shoulder, "Come home or not, as you please. But give my temper time to cool, else you will face me in a way that you never have before."

When the ringing sound of Jack's furious exit had faded, and all hung quiet on the air, David stirred. "I pity you," he muttered. He clutched his middle and remained on the floor where he had fallen.

Rosaline's eyes fixed unseeing on the blackness outside. "Don't pity me. For I have done nothing more than *he* has— and probably a great deal less."

David snorted. "He'll never believe that."

She leaned to retrieve the wine bottle, drops of red Burgundy still dripping from its lip, falling to the floor like petals. "He doesn't have to," she said with iron in her voice. "He doesn't have to."

* * *

An hour later, Rosaline tarried in the garden behind the pink house, chilled despite the air's lazy warmth, collecting herself and her thoughts, prepared to meet Jack's wrath, his indifference or whatever attitude he chose to take. A part of·her ached, for she had not wanted her husband's return to be this way; she had wanted to greet him civilly, quietly, eager to hear his news. Even now she wished to know if all had gone well, if he had accomplished what he had hoped with Arabi.

She realized that the first fringes of dawn had smudged themselves across the horizon. Rosaline was calm, her spine straight as she walked into the house to meet Jack. She found him sitting beside a window, one leg draped over the arm of the chair, his posture pensive, tired, his eyes turned toward the river. He heard her approach, of course, his senses alert as they always were, but he said nothing for awhile, waiting, then turned his head to speak at last. "We'll be leaving for Cairo tomorrow."

She stopped and, needing to busy her hands, moved to pour tea from the samovar. "Very well. I shall be ready."

He slanted a wintry glance in her direction. "Are you sure?"

Rosaline ignored the inference, the cutting sarcasm, and asked, "Did all go well with Arabi?"

"Ah, so you have remembered that I was gone."

She did not reply and a silence fell, lasting several moments. "Is that all you have to say to me?" she murmured at last.

"Yes. For now." His blue eyes flicked over her with utter disdain. "Perhaps you'll care to change. A party from the Foreign Office is on its way to meet us here, including a regiment of British soldiers who will camp in Luxor and keep an eye on Arabi as long as he stays quartered nearby."

"Jack . . ."

"Do not test my temper by speaking about a subject I'm not ready to discuss."

Rosaline stared at him, her shoulders drooping suddenly with a weary sadness, just as his were. She found herself longing to go and touch his shoulder, lay her cheek against the top of his head, to make things better, right, but not knowing how. She sipped the fragrant tea but did not taste it, and finally, after she carefully set down the cup and turned to go from the room to change, she heard Jack shift in his chair.

She looked at him, met his eyes bravely.

"Did you make love with him, Rosaline?"

The words fell coldly like stones between them, and Rosaline felt the pain in them too, the certainty in Jack's mind that only needed confirmation. She would tell him the truth, of course, for it had not been her intention to make him jealous through David. She had only wanted—for some mad, childish reason she could not even remember now—to have the artist's attention and flattery tonight. One last time before she told him goodbye.

She walked toward Jack, heard every sound her slippers made, the sound of the owl outside, and the sound of dry leaves skittering across the balcony. But a commotion sounded outside, and Jack came to his feet when a loud rap sounded against the door.

He flung it open and discovered a group of men flanked by two British calvary officers standing outside, their faces sober, tense. "Jack Darlington?" one of them inquired.

"I'm Darlington."

"I'm Sir Roger Blakely with the Foreign Office. You've recently returned from the camp of Arabi Bey, is that correct, sir?"

"I have. But I didn't expect to see you until this afternoon."

"We've got word of a most distressing accusation. A messenger met us on the Nile and we hastened here with all speed. You, Mr. Darlington, have been accused of the attempted assassination of Arabi Bey."

Silence followed. Rosaline stood stunned, staring at Jack, then at the man who had accused him.

The sudden sound of Jack's laughter broke the terrible hush.

"I can assure you, Sir Roger, that when I left Arabi Bey he was quite the picture of health."

"No doubt. It was his aide who was murdered. Stabbed to death. The fellow was sleeping on Arabi's cot—which he often does upon Arabi's orders. To foil assassination attempts such as this."

Jack's eyes narrowed. "You can't seriously believe I'd commit such a crime. I was sent to Arabi's camp with specific orders to negotiate peace, for God's sake, to try and talk the fellow out of blowing up the Suez Canal in order to save Disraeli's money."

"Nevertheless, we've been ordered to apprehend you, to search you and the house, if necessary."

Jack stepped back, coldly, and with a flourish of his arm, invited them to do whatever they needed. A soldier walked forward to search his clothing.

Julie appeared, breathless and pushing roughly through the huddle of men, her eyes level, black, fastened upon Jack's face. Her hem was muddied, and her dark face was streaked with dust. "You should have gone with me, Jack," she cried. "I told you that you should have gone away with me!"

Jack studied her. Then, his eyes darkened with sudden realization as the soldier, searching Jack's own saddlebags tossed on the floor, retrieved a heavy gold ring known to belong to Arabi Bey.

Chapter Twenty-Four

London was veiled in fog, its silver fairy spires disappearing into moisture, the chimes of its bells muffled but still sweet. Rosaline heard them faintly as she peered out of the window of the Grange townhouse, where she was staying until the Foreign Office decided Jack's fate.

For the past two days, the government had been conducting an inquiry into the Arabi matter. Keith Grange's sensational story had reached *The Times* last month and had outraged most of Britain and all of Europe. It was one thing, people said, to make war against a country, to overthrow and annex her government to secure investments, but quite another to send a former thief in the guise of a diplomat and try to assassinate the enemy's leader.

Oh, yes, every detail of Jack's past life that could possibly have been ferreted out had been published and duly discussed in every drawing room. Of course, the government denied involvement in what they called a deplorable crime, insisting that Jack—or persons unknown—had acted alone in the treachery, and that there had been no plot masterminded by the Foreign Office.

Now, as Honore offered her tea and biscuits, Rosaline commented quietly, "Regardless of the outcome, Jack's future with the government is ruined."

"But will they put him in jail?" Honore fretted. "Can they? The very idea makes me shudder, makes me question our government's notion of justice."

"My father says they won't go as far as that."

"The whole thing is perfectly outrageous. As if Jack would commit such a crime, plunge a knife into a fellow's back while he slept. Can your father do nothing to help, Rosaline?"

"He should be arriving at any moment, and I intend to demand that he take some action. We can't simply sit by and allow Jack to be convicted of the murder of Arabi's top aide—which boils down to an attempted assassination, since the aide was sleeping on Arabi's cot in his place."

"Has Lord Bardo been at the inquiry today?"

"Yes. And the minute he arrives here, I'll make him tell me every detail."

"Pity that you weren't allowed to attend yourself."

"Those pompous old goats," Rosaline said hotly. "Had I been allowed to go to the hearing, I would have stood up and—oh, look, Honore, there's father now, getting out of the hansom."

Not waiting for the butler, Rosaline rushed to open the door, throwing it wide, welcoming the sight of Sir Bardo's portly frame in his Bond Street suit, greeting him gratefully. She took his hat and cane and ushered him into the vestibule where, without preamble, she launched into the subject of her husband's predicament. "What happened today, Father? What did they determine about Jack's involvement? Are they still holding him responsible?"

"Calm yourself, daughter. I shall tell you all in good time, just as soon as I've had some of Mrs. Grange's tea. I'm parched and cold."

Rosaline herself went to the trolley and poured, her hands unsteady, her heart racing in dread despite the fact that her father's tone had given no hint, positive or negative, as to Jack's fate.

While she handed him a plate of cinnamon cakes, Honore rushed forward to offer her guest a seat beside the fire. "Did it go unpleasantly for Mr. Darlington?" she asked in a breathless voice.

Lord Bardo shook his head, then sipped the steaming tea and swallowed. "The Foreign Office is still insisting that Jack attempted the assassination. They claim that he met with Arabi as planned, conducted the series of talks, then pretended to leave the camp before doubling back to Arabi's tent and stabbing the aide by mistake. The aide, as you know, was sleeping in the rebel's bed. Such an arrangement is one of Arabi's precautions. He also makes his servants sample his food in case it's been poisoned. Well, his caution paid off the night that Jack visited his camp."

"But what motive could Jack have possibly had to murder anyone?" Rosaline demanded.

Lord Bardo met her eyes, uncomfortable. "Thievery, of course," he said, letting out a breath. "Arabi was known to wear a ring—one of those Cheops pieces the Egyptians hold in such high esteem. Worth a fortune. Apparently Arabi had taken the thing off his finger and left it in the tent. At any rate, it was found in Jack's possession, as you know, and well, with his record . . ."

"Yes," Rosaline said, cutting him off, unable to bear hearing it, despite the fact they every detail of her husband's sordid beginnings had already been discovered, published and bandied about the whole of England.

"They set the time of the servant's murder just before midnight when the sound of hooves were heard—those of a retreating horse. The body was discovered shortly after. Of course, Arabi was enraged at what he considered a plot by the British government to kill him. Europe and our own countrymen half suspect that Parliament really did plot the whole shameful thing. If the attempt *had* been planned and successfully carried out with no suspicion attached to the government, no doubt they would have applauded Arabi's demise. And Jack.''

Rosaline had moved to the hearth, where she stared at the orange coals with a frown of concentration. Some thought niggled at the back of her mind, some persistent, vital clue that eluded her as she recalled the events of that night in Luxor, recalled Jack's angry entrance into David's candlelit house; the sand on his boots, the way he clenched one riding glove and wore the other. She recalled the smell of Burgundy wine, the color, the taste of the figs in the blue glazed bowl on David's table . . .

"Father," she said suddenly, turning to face him. "What did you say about the time?"

"The time, my dear?"

"Yes. When did you say Arabi's servant was reportedly killed?"

"They claim midnight."

"And it's a two hour ride from Arabi's camp to Luxor—maybe three hours in darkness?"

"Yes. What is it, Rosaline? Why do you ask?"

She did not reply but grabbed her paisley shawl from the arm of the sofa and said to Honore, "Can you ring for the carriage, please? I must make a call."

"Of course, dear. But what on earth . . . ? You act as if you have a bee in your bonnet."

"Yes, Rosaline," Lord Bardo said with a frown of misgiving. He quickly came to his feet. "What do you intend to do?"

"Whatever I must to help Jack."

Her first call was to an address on Bleinham Lane, a visit which lasted, the coachman later whispered to the staff, a bare quarter of an hour. The second visit was to the address of the Foreign Office, where Mrs. Darlington vanished for twenty minutes before reappearing in the company of a gentleman of slight build and fastidious dress who strolled with her an hour in a nearby park.

The gentleman was Lance Cardew. Rosaline, having remembered his brief conversation with Julie, had decided to confront him about what he knew. Despite his obvious reluctance, she persuaded Cardew to walk with her in the green privacy of the park, and after a few minutes of chitchat and a brief discussion of Jack's still pending fate, she stopped. "My husband was made a scapegoat, wasn't he, Mr. Cardew?"

The aide's eyes slid away to the sculptures bordering the privet. "I'm sure I don't know what you're talking about, Mrs. Darlington."

"Don't you?" she intoned. She strolled forward, letting her gloved hand trail over the head of a stone cherub situated near the path. "Then let's speak of other things first. I heard that you've recently become betrothed to a very lovely girl—Miss Merriweather, isn't it?"

With wariness, the young man nodded. "I met her during my stay in Paris. And we renewed our acquaintanceship here in London."

"I'm delighted to hear it. It must have been a whirlwind courtship. So romantic. Do send us an invitation to the wedding, won't you?"

"Of course," he murmured, polite but distant, shifting his feet in such a way as to suggest that he was ready to end the interview.

"I was wondering," Rosaline continued, ignoring his unease. "Does your betrothed—I'm sorry, I don't recall your mentioning her Christian name?"

"Priscilla, Ma'am."

"Lovely. Does Priscilla know of—well . . . is she aware of your *beginnings,* Mr. Cardew? Not that she would be put off by them in any way, of course, if she loves you," Rosaline rushed on to say, as if she found talking about such delicate matters difficult. "But sometimes fathers can be an altogether different matter. Her father is a prominent banker, is he not?"

Rosaline's tactic had been a shot in the dark, but she was intuitive when it came to judging people and, being of gentle blood herself, recognized the veneer of one who is not well-born but who has acquired the manners of the genteel through observation.

The aide blanched. "Mrs. Darlington," he said, stammering over the words, drawing out a handkerchief to dab nervously at his nose. "I really don't see how . . ."

"Don't you, Mr. Cardew? I am surprised, for I know you to be an intelligent man. Perhaps if I were to repeat the question—you remember it—the question concerning my husband, the man you were hired to serve? Was he made a scapegoat by the Foreign Office?"

A sparrow flew out of the shrubbery, sunlight sparkling off its wings, and Lance Cardew started, his eyes darting all around as if witnesses might be watching. "Mrs. Darlington," he hissed. "I beg you to have mercy. I shall lose my position if I so much as . . ."

"No, you won't. I am discreet, Mr. Cardew, and I will never breathe your name to a soul. If someone suspects, I'll make certain my father protects your career. It's the least he can do," she added testily. "The very least."

The aide ran his tongue over his lips, weighing the situation against her determination to carry through with her threat regarding his fiancée, a girl whose influence and money could buy him any number of plum positions at her father's bank. "Very well," he said finally, expelling a breath through his white, pinched mouth. "I'll tell you what I know. Truthfully, I never thought it right, and whether you believe me or not, I tried to change the course of the plot."

"Father, I want you to see to it that I have entrance into the inquiry tomorrow," Rosaline stated flatly an hour later when she arrived at the Grange townhouse amid a whirl of damp taffeta skirts. Removing her hat, she pinned her sire with a determined eye.

Having long recognized not only Rosaline's intelligence but her will—which could match a man's at times—Lord Bardo did not dismiss the demand, but observed the set of his daughter's mouth. "Go on," he said.

"Not only do I want you to get me entrance," she continued. "I want you to see to it that I have an opportunity to speak to the inquiry officials. I and a gentleman."

"A gentleman? What gentleman?"

"You will know his name when the time comes."

Lord Bardo stepped forward, his pale blue eyes sharp, his hands reaching nervously for the pipe in his pocket. "Now look here, Rosaline. I don't know what sort of scheme you have planned, but this is not some drawing room game. It's serious government business and . . ."

"I beg to differ with you, Father, as always. But having been the daughter of a government man and now the wife of one, it's my opinion that government business is little more *than* a drawing room game."

"Rosaline . . ."

"Father, you arranged my marriage to Jack. God forgive you if you knew what the Foreign Office really intended for him, for *I* know, and it's unconscionable. But I'm not naive enough to believe it doesn't occur every day, that men aren't sacrificed for some political aim considered to be of greater price than a life."

"Rosaline, I beg you to lower your voice. You don't know what you're saying."

"Or who might hear? Don't worry, Father. I hardly consider myself influential enough to bring down an entire system of Parliamentary intrigue. But I will tell you this." Rosaline paused, looked hard at her father. "I will do anything to salvage Jack's name. *Anything,* do you hear?"

Lord Bardo grumbled at the fierceness of her words, walked to the hearth and contemplated the flames. He lit his pipe and with a shaky hand put it to his lips. When the moment had calmed, when he heard the soft swish of Rosaline's skirts as she seated herself, he asked quietly, "You have come to love Jack Darlington?"

Rosaline had no reason to prevaricate. "Yes," she said simply. "I do. Unfortunately, despite the fact that I love him, the marriage is not a good one."

"Not a good one?"

"No. Indeed, I plan to return to Edinburgh after this is over. Jack will go where he will. It's my hope that we will be able to keep up appearances. Of course, it's doubtful that we'll be accepted company in higher circles. But I intend to smooth that over by degrees."

"Rosaline," Lord Bardo said, puffing on his pipe, letting the smoke curl about his whiskers. His eyes were suddenly pained. "I want you to understand that I didn't know any of this beforehand. I believe that I was duped, too, although not to such a damaging degree as Jack, of course. I knew he was to be involved in a plot, but we have used him in many ways before and he has never complained—indeed, he has relished the adventure in his reckless way. I knew he was ambitious, of course, and there's certainly nothing wrong with ambition in a man. But for heaven's sake, I wouldn't have turned my own daughter over to him if I had thought he'd come to *this*. I wanted you to have a good man."

"And I do, Father, I do. It's just that . . ." She paused and took a breath. "Jack is too much for me."

"Too much for you?"

"He is made for a different sort of woman." Rosaline walked to the tea trolley, neatly reordered the sugar tongs and silver spoons on their doilies of lace.

Her father remained silent a moment, regarding her with wise, softened eyes. "I believe you're wrong about that, Rosaline," he said with gentleness. "Yes. I believe you're wrong."

"And yet," she sighed, "I must act upon my own instincts. The worst part is, I fear that what I plan to do tomorrow will drive a wedge between Jack and me that will truly be the end of us.''

The next morning, Rosaline was escorted into a great panelled chamber filled with dour faced men who all bore the stamp of nobility, their long thin noses and heavy lidded eyes proclaiming some of the bluest blood in all of England. They seemed to disapprove of her presence, despite their respectful hush as she seated herself, gloved, bonneted, and attired in the most demurely fashionable way, her own lineage not one to be frowned upon.

Rosaline had not seen Jack since he had been apprehended in Luxor, and her eyes immediately sought and found him. She admired his sober black coat and white shirt, noticing the black hair perfectly brushed back from a brow made bronze by the sun. His blue eyes held both a gladness and a grave concern over her presence. He seemed to know that she was about to do something imprudent, something which he would disapprove of that would shatter the last shred of trust that remained between them.

Indeed, Jack curbed an impulse to stand up and call out to her, command that she not to say a word. The sight of her made the place below his breastbone ache. To him she seemed to be something very fine, of great value, like the most fragile piece of porcelain, although he had come to know that she wasn't fragile at all. At the same time, she seemed untouchable, unreachable, as if the short space of several feet that lay between them could not be breached by either a word or by the reach of a hand.

He had been so distracted by her appearance that he had scarcely listened to what was being said by his inquisitors. But he saw Rosaline rise suddenly, stand very tall and straight, her expression set as she stated to Lord Percy, ''I am here to say that my husband could not possibly have killed Arabi Bey's servant as you would like to prove. He was not in Arabi's camp at that time, nor could he have been there in the hours just before or just after midnight.''

A silence followed her declaration, then a few discreet coughs before Lord Percy said, ''Mrs. Darlington, we are aware that any wife would want to defend the honor of her husband in any way she could. Therein lies the reason why such a statement as yours cannot be admissible, cannot be a deciding factor in a situation such as this. The charges are quite serious and we could never dismiss them on the simple plea—however well-intended—of a dutiful wife.''

Rosaline sensed it did not suit Lord Percy's agenda to make her statement admissible. ''I am not the only one who can testify to my husband's whereabouts on the night in question.''

Across the room, Jack clenched his hands, sickened with dread and disbelief over what Rosaline intended to do.

''Very well, Mrs. Darlington,'' Lord Percy said reluctantly, realizing that there was no way to put her off now. ''Perhaps you should tell us where you were at midnight on the night in question. Were you with this—er—other witness?''

Rosaline glanced for one telling second at Jack's taut face, at his blue eyes, which demanded, beseeched her not to go on. She straightened herself, steadied her voice, and stated, ''I was in the company of an English gentleman by the name of David Mellon, an artist of some renown. I was in his Luxor home on the evening in question. I was there from shortly after nightfall until shortly after my husband's arrival at midnight. I remember it was midnight because Mr. Mellon owns a little clock, a clock specially made in Switzerland, and it chimed only minutes before Mr. Darlington entered the house and found us together.''

For a moment, Lord Percy said nothing at all, stunned as were his peers, at a loss as to how to proceed. Lord Bardo, seated beside his daughter, stared at her in what could only be termed as horror. Jack, who had the look of a man barely in command of himself, rose to his feet as if his very will, his powerful size alone, could prevent his wife from speaking more.

"Who else was in Mr. Mellon's house?" Lord Percy asked at last, very quietly. "Who else was with you, Mrs. Darlington?"

She kept her eyes fixed to the blank space of panelling at the front of the room, then looked directly at Jack and answered, "No one. No one was with us. We were entirely alone in his home until my husband arrived."

The words fell like stones upon a granite floor, resounding, revealing, utterly ruinous. A woman, a decent woman—a married woman—did not go alone to a bachelor's establishment. It did not matter whether she had made love with him or not— although it was assumed that she had. The sin of shared and unchaperoned company, especially with a man of Mellon's repute, was great enough to condemn her as a woman without principles, an adulteress.

"This David Mellon," Lord Percy said grimly, his manner strained, "where is he now? Can he be contacted, do you know?"

A rustle sounded from the rear of the chamber as the artist stirred and stood up. "I am David Mellon, Milord. And I am prepared to verify everything Mrs. Darlington has just told you."

After a few seconds of shocked silence and deep rumblings, Lord Bardo stood and begged the inquiry to adjourn, a request which Lord Percy gratefully obliged.

Not wanting to face her father's outrage, unable to bear Jack's eyes, Rosaline slipped out, clutching her reticule and umbrella with icy fingers, and pushed open a door to step into the maze of grey London streets. She wasn't sure of her direction and didn't care, but breathlessly ran forward in her thin kid shoes, rounding the corner of a cathedral soaring with spires and gargoyles. Before she had gone more than another step, a hand gripped her arm and hauled her backward, caused her to cry out, to struggle, not in surprise, but because she knew who it was who held her.

"Why did you do it, Rosaline? Why did you do it?"

She looked into the face above hers, the face of the man she loved so much, twisted now with pain and disbelief. Shaking her head, she cried, "I did it because *you* would not!"

"I had a *reason!*"

"A reason with which I didn't agree, Jack! Julie betrayed you, set you up with the full cooperation of the Foreign Office. She followed you to Arabi's camp, kept out of sight, then stabbed the aide, believing him to be Arabi. Afterwards, she stole Arabi's ring and slipped it in your saddlebags. Why would you protect her?"

"Because I always have," he said through his teeth. "I always have. And because Arabi Bey was her master for seven years. She was his captive. By God, she had a right to kill him. That's why the Foreign Office chose her for the job. Pity that she did not succeed!"

Rosaline stood still, staring at Jack, absorbing the truth of his words as rain began to drift in veils over their faces. He had left hastily and had forgotten his hat. He looked tired, Rosaline thought, more weary than she had ever seen him. A guard stood nearby, having followed him, discreet or compassionate enough to allow him a few moments alone with her.

"You would have accepted the blame, Jack," she said quietly. "You would have been maligned, forever accused. Your name would have been ruined."

"And now *yours* is."

"Yes," she said bitterly. "And with it goes all the value I once represented to you, doesn't it, Jack? What is my value to you now?"

"Why must you punish me with that sort of talk, Rosaline? It's as if you blame me for marrying you as part of your father's arrangement. What did you expect from me? What did you expect? After all, you wed me without anyone holding a pistol to your back. You must have had *your* reasons to accept a man you believed to be beneath you. Or was it only because your father told you to do it?"

"I married you because no one else asked!" she cried. "Because no one else asked me."

"Not even David Mellon?"

"No. But he wooed me just the same," she said in defense of her pride. "He told me I was lovely, seduced me, wooed me in order to win my affection instead of simply *taking* what he wanted as you always seem to do."

"I might have accommodated you in that way if you'd mentioned it earlier," he said with sarcasm.

"Having to *ask* a man to woo you takes away all the meaning of it."

A silence fell between them, accentuated by the patter of the rain which floated over them as they stood motionless. Jack's mouth tightened. "You believed me guilty of Arabi's murder, didn't you? You believed I stole his ring."

"No, Jack," she said with vehemence. "I never did. I never believed you guilty of that. I had my suspicions of others from the start, and then, yesterday, I pressed Lance Cardew for information. He told me Julie had stolen the ring and planted it in your saddlebags."

"I taught her well, after all."

Rosaline shook her head. "I can scarcely believe she betrayed you. I would have thought that her loyalty to you was unshakable, in a way sacred."

Jack's mouth curved with private self-mockery. "Perhaps she thought the same of my own loyalty to her." When Rosaline did not reply, he released a sigh and shrugged. "Truth to tell, I suspected deception from the first. There was a look in your father's eye when I met with him in Edinburgh before our marriage. Upon reflection, I think he knew that I was to be used in some way. I didn't want to suspect, I was too proud, too flattered that I'd been promoted, and thought myself clever enough to have brought it about on my own merit." He turned to contemplate the London traffic, the carriages and the drays and the sellers of second-hand clothing with their pushcarts and broken umbrellas, all so far removed from the other world he had recently left. "Julie was the one person in the world I believed I could turn my back upon even after I hurt her by marrying you.

"But she had a plan of sorts. She tried to persuade me to go way with her immediately after the mission. She must have known then what was to happen, what she intended to do. She thought we'd simply disappear together, melt into Africa or Turkey or India as we'd done before."

"She didn't realize the strength of your ambition. She didn't count on that."

Jack's eyes met Rosaline's, held them. "She didn't count on a lot of things that were more important even than that."

"Where is she now?"

"Here. In London." He hadn't meant for Julie to come, he had hoped she would stay in Egypt, or take up wandering again, make parting easy for him, to allow him to get on with his life with Rosaline. But she had not, her tie with him too strong, too instinctual—as well as her love. And perhaps she was afraid of being alone without him. She had no direction but his own— never had, being a creature of air and danger and freedom, a being who, having come from poverty, did not know what it was to own—or even to want—a place to call home.

"There's no point to our marriage now, is there, Jack?" Rosaline asked quietly. "The reasons that caused us both to wed simply exist no more. Your career with the government is over, regardless of your innocence or guilt. And I . . . well, my reputation no longer needs to be saved from the artist, does it?"

"What are you saying, Rosaline?"

"That we should part, just as I told you weeks ago in Luxor."

The words devastated Jack and for a moment, he groped for words. "We could at least make an attempt . . ."

"I don't think your heart is in it," Rosaline interrupted, turning her eyes from him. "Nor is mine. There doesn't even seem to be any point in keeping up appearances after today," she added, giving him a wry, sad smile. "I'll return to my aunts' home on the pretense of caring for them while you . . .

well, while you do whatever you will. I suppose there will be new adventures, new places to see."

He wanted Rosaline to go back to Orkney with him, to the place she called Arbor Gate, to the place she had made home. "What of Rajad and Antonio?" he said harshly, looking down at the wet cobblestones so she would not be able to see his eyes.

"They'll come and visit me, of course. I'd like that. But they're old enough now to attend a boarding school in Scotland. I know of several fine ones."

Jack could scarcely believe that she had determined the paths of their lives, compartmentalized them with such seeming dispassion. It angered him. Wounded him. "What am I supposed to do?" he asked, the words bursting from his lips. "Since you're arranging things so damned neatly, what is my role as your husband supposed to be?"

She took an unconscious step back as if to protect herself from his anger. "I don't want to see you, Jack. At least, not for awhile."

"Not for awhile? Rosaline, if this is about Julie, I intend . . ."

"It's not about Julie. Not anymore."

"Then what *is* it about?"

"I don't know. I'm not sure. The truth is, I haven't yet sorted it all out."

Jack made a sound of disgust and dashed the rain off his brow. Then, looking up at the sky, he said more calmly, "Hell of a thing. Hell of a thing to happen. Oh, Rosie, Rosie, how did we come to this pass?"

She made no reply for a moment. Then, as if to shift their conversation to one of more mundane matters, she said through a rush of warm tears, "You have a cold, Jack. You should take care of it. I'd like it if we could write, now and then."

Write? For God's sake, he thought. Is that all there is left of us? He spoke through his teeth. "Very well. If that's the way you want it."

No, that is not the way I want it, Rosaline cried inwardly.

But that's the way it must be. It is the best way for us now. The safest.

A few seconds passed. "The last time we stood in the rain like this," she said quietly, "we spoke about dreams. Do you remember, Jack?"

He turned away, rested his hand on the gate. "I remember a great deal about that day."

"You said it's rare that we get what we really want, what we dream of having."

"I remember."

"Did you get your dream in Egypt, Jack?" Rosaline asked with a sorrowful frown. "Even a tiny piece of it during the embassy balls and dinners? Were you ever happy there?"

He didn't answer immediately, turning his eyes to the grey skies and blinking, afraid that he would break down and make a fool of himself in front of her, that he would plead, throw his pride away and get down upon his knees.

"There was a moment," he breathed at last, his eyes returning to her face. "A moment on the Nile when I held you in my arms. I felt it then, knew that I had what I wanted—or almost—as close as any of us ever come. But it's all gone now, I guess." And then he reached into the pocket of his coat and withdrew a little silver box—the magic one she had seen and coveted in the marketplace in Alexandria. Had he stolen it after all?

He held it out, invited her to open it. "I need you now, Rosaline," he said, the dam of his despair breaking. "I *need* you."

Her throat tightened, she could scarcely speak. "You have Arbor Gate. Go back to it."

"No. It's empty now."

Unable to keep herself from touching him, Rosaline grasped Jack's bare, cold hand in her warm gloved one, then put his fingers to her lips, to her cheek, and for a few, long seconds pressed them there. Jack's eyes closed and his brow furrowed.

"Goodbye," she said, squeezing his hand.

He watched her walk away. At the sight of her abandonment of him, Jack experienced such a raw sense of loss that for a moment, he could do nothing more than stand with his head tilted back and stare at his surroundings. The rain pattered his face, obscured the moisture streaming from his lashes.

"So you lost her, too. After all. Didn't you?"

The voice came from behind, but Jack did not bother to turn around and face the speaker, saying only, "I suppose you got a great deal of satisfaction from your confession today."

With a shrug, the artist dismissed the insult. "Not particularly. It damaged her, tarnished her good name. That gives me no pleasure."

"Decent of you to have some compassion."

"I never took her to my bed, you know. I wanted to, but she's not the sort of woman to allow a dalliance. I'm only telling you for her sake. On second thought, Darlington, perhaps I'm doing it for your sake as well. I find that I actually feel sorry for you."

Jack smiled without mirth and, pulling up his coat collar, walked away.

Chapter Twenty-Five

The leaves fell early in her garden that autumn, sprinkling a light carpet of colors over the rows of dying herbs. The birds, tame and melodious, kept her company, but gave her less comfort than usual, causing her to remember the wild, raucous cries of the sea birds on an island far away. She thought often of that island, too often, during every task she performed during every day.

Drawing the hood of her cloak over her head, she stared up at the blue sky, imagining the skating white clouds over Orkney, imagining Rajad sitting cross-legged at his fishing stream and Antonio wandering boldly over mossy rocks splashed with foam.

And Jack.

He had written, more than once, and she had read the scrawled lines countless times, holding the pages carefully with a trembling hand before folding them, even more carefully, and tucking them away unanswered.

She had spent an inordinate amount of time thinking about her relationship with him, about how she felt, what she really wanted. And in the end, after tormented nights and long, exhausting days, she had decided, quite simply, that she wanted Jack Darlington to value her. She did not want to be valued for anything save herself—a tall, rather plain lady who liked to wear roses in her hair and read philosophy, who liked to use her brain and exercise her will with rather more alacrity than most women of her time.

Yes, in the twenty-seventh year of her life, Rosaline Cheevers Darlington wanted to be courted by the man with whom she had fallen in love. She would never admit it, of course. Not to her father, or to her aunts, and certainly not to Jack. It would sound, well . . . unreasonable, ingenuous, not at all practical.

He had sent Julie away. One of his letters had made mention of the fact, bluntly and without elaboration. "Julie is no longer in England," he had written, "nor will she return. I asked her to go. She didn't argue. She simply disappeared in the way she has of disappearing."

And yet, it was not enough for Rosaline.

In march, Aunt Columbine caught cold, sneezing while her curly haired spaniels wheezed all around her, their tails stirring the potted palms, their pointed noses sniffing for dropped crumbs of lemon cake on the rose-patterned carpet.

"Please, dear Rosaline," Aunt Columbine whimpered, her handkerchief fluttering above the balloon of her purple skirts. "Go to the apothecary and get me an elixir—or perhaps a box of Dr. Mayhew's Universal Pills. This augue! And oh, my head positively *throbs* with the megrem. I recall having an illness like this last year, just before your marriage to that divinely handsome man. I feared I'd be ill for the wedding. Where is he, did you say, dear? So inconvenient for you that he never has the time to come round. If you ask me, you need the moral support, after that dreadful affair concerning the Foreign Office. Thank heaven that journalist for *The Times* set the story straight. What *was* his name? I can never seem to recall—it sounds so *American*."

Rosaline watched the maid in her starched black uniform wend through the maze of upholstered chairs and ottomans to the hearth, where she shoveled more coal on the roaring fire. "Keith Grange, Aunt Columbine," Rosaline murmured. "His name is Keith Grange." She reached to insert another pillow behind the old lady's back, recalling the events immediately following her parting with Jack, when she had walked away in the rain, had proceeded to the Grange residence, then waited for an opportunity to speak with the journalist alone.

In no uncertain terms, she had told Grange that she wanted him to write the truth about Jack so that it could be printed in *The Times*. No blame need be placed upon anyone for the murder, she said, but Jack's name must be cleared. When Grange had smiled and protested that such a story would be impossibly delicate, and that his editor was a rather good friend of the government, Rosaline had given him a look that left him in no doubt that his night of pleasure in the Bedouin tent would be used against him. "We must use our knowledge—our secrets—wisely, mustn't we, Mr. Grange?" she had intoned.

And so, not long after, the story had been both written and published. It had rocked Britain, and ironically had helped rather than destroy Jack Darlington's reputation. His photographs in the papers and penny newsheets had done nothing to harm him, neither had his frequent appearances—always touchingly alone—on the promenade in Hyde Park astride a chestnut thoroughbred.

Rosaline had read the accounts, saved every one, pursing her lips when she came across unflattering mentions of her own name connected with a reportedly licentious artist. Odd. She felt as if she had stepped back into her spinsterhood again, as if she weren't married at all, had never been.

She recalled the passionate night on the Nile with the same painful longing as an adult who looks back on a particularly rapturous memory of childhood, wondering if it had really occurred at all, or had only become a blurred myth whose edges of truth and falseness could no longer be distinguished. She missed Jack. Missed him grievously.

"Yes, Aunt," Rosaline said now, mechanically patting the old lady's well-fed arm. "I'll go to the apothecary for you. It'll take me no more than an hour to get back with your elixir. See if you can doze until then."

She trailed downstairs, glad to leave the stifling room with its peacock feathers and palms, throwing her cloak over her shoulders and, hoping to lighten her mood, donning a new spring bonnet festooned with cherry colored ribbons. Since the day was fair, she declined to take her parasol and stepped outside to find the traffic on the streets light. The smells of coffee from the nearby shops traveled her way, along with the scent of flowers for sale in the corner marketplace.

Rosaline stepped across the street and turned. Every time she passed the old crone selling finches, she experienced a distressful tightening of her throat; today she walked briskly past, telling herself not to look. She had kept the solitary finch, brought it back to Scotland with her, and placed its cage on the velvet window seat of her room overlooking the garden. The bird never sang. Rosaline, with a degree of wry self-mockery, had begun to compare it to herself.

After she had purchased Aunt Columbine's pills, she stopped at a flower stall and, on impulse, bought a posey—not roses or gardenias, but a halfpenny sprig of heather which reminded her of Arbor Gate. And Jack.

She walked home at a slow pace, oppressively sad all at once, glancing at the lace-hung windows of each red brick house that she passed along the way, and it seemed to her that in each, there must surely reside a contented family, a man and a woman who were in love and comfortable, the routine of their lives crowded with people and parties—not lonely like hers, not empty. Rosaline knew that she suffered from a longing that could not be voiced, much less fulfilled, and with the hindsight that allows solid judgment to be questioned, she began to believe she had made a grave mistake in keeping Jack away.

She dabbed at the corner of her eye, telling herself it was only the wind that made it tear, then blinked, her gaze automatically shifting to the place where the old woman usually huddled with her birds. But no stooped and tattered figure loitered on that corner today beneath the flapping laundry hanging from upper story windows, only a man, a tall man in a black top hat and a fine wool greatcoat. He held a birdcage in his hand, a fancy gilded cage like the ones she had seen for sale in Haymarket.

She knew the gentleman, of course, and slowly walked toward him, almost afraid, as if somehow, through poor judgment, she might do or say something to risk the moment. Her eyes sprang with tears again. The sight of him was glorious. He seemed taller, younger, more anxious than any man with such self-possession should ever look.

She approached and came to stand before him.

He held out the cage and said, ''I thought the little finch might be ready for company.''

His voice was deep with a huskiness that might have come from emotion, or only from uncertainty. Rosaline looked at the gift and stammered, ''It's a lovely creature.'' She wanted to say much more, all in a rush; but she held back, waiting, letting him proceed.

''It's not brown like its predecessor,'' he commented. ''But rather a gaudy gold. Perhaps he'll get the other's attention a bit faster this way.''

Rosaline lowered her lashes. ''I don't know. My finch is rather a contrary little creature. I'm afraid it might take a good deal of effort to get her attention, to get her to sing again.''

''No matter. The effort will be worth it.''

Rosaline did not know what to say next, how to respond, feeling a faint blush of color mount her cheeks. The wind tugged at her hat, and she could feel Jack's warmth, his solidity, she could almost smell it too, mixed with the good Scottish wool of his coat. Askance, unable to help herself, she looked at his face, at his blue eyes beneath the black brows, at the jaw that was smooth—shaven only an hour ago for her?

Jack's gaze consumed her in turn, took in the ivory complexion beneath the short brim of the chip hat, the heavy mink-colored hair in its perfect coil, which allowed only a few tendrils to escape and dance about her cheeks. She seemed girlish, shy; indeed, he thought, the two of them might have been adolescents encountering a member of the opposite sex unchaperoned for the first time. His stomach tightened with the fear that she would send him away, that he would have to go back to Orkney without her, listen alone to the wind blow across the heather at night when the fire lay dying, surrounded by all the creature comforts she had chosen in order to create a home for them.

"Shall I carry the cage for you?" he asked, giving her his smile.

"Oh, yes. Yes, of course," she stammered, turning, leading the way, her neat, buttoned boots moving lightly over the pavement.

They spoke not a word during the short trip, and when they arrived at the front door, Rosaline hesitated, behaving as if she were a girl out with her first beau.

Jack began to wonder if she would refuse to invite him in. Well, he wouldn't let it end this way, he wouldn't let her shut him out, and keep shutting him out.

"May I join you for dinner tonight?" he asked, his voice firm, but still somewhere between a plea and a command.

Rosaline heard the firmness, took the cage from his hand, and put in her voice an equal measure of self-assertion, as well as a coquettishness Jack had not heard her use before. "Tomorrow night. We dine at eight."

"Tomorrow night?" Jack repeated, trying to smother the testiness in his tone, the impatience, before he understood his wife all at once, realized precisely what it was Rosaline Cheevers needed. She needed courting. He was unaccustomed to having to do it, but he thought he could manage very well.

"Tomorrow night, then," he said, bowing, gifting her again with his slow, white smile. "Shall I bring roses? Big hothouse blooms the color of red wine? I recall that you wore that color in your hair the first time we met. I remember thinking how well it went with the bloom in your cheeks.''

"Oh, Jack," she said, flattered, unable to keep from laughing. "What sort of blarney is that?''

"It's not blarney at all. You're a beautiful woman, Rosaline. Haven't I ever told you so before?''

"Yes, but I never believed you. Tomorrow night, then?''

"At seven.''

"Eight.''

He sighed. "Very well. As you wish, Mrs. Darlington. As you wish.''

"And, Jack?''

"Yes, my love?''

"Bring white roses, not red.''

And when he came the next night they dined and talked, and he was the most attentive of men, as he was all the following nights for a fortnight. As they shared wine before a fire in the drawing room, she finally permitted him to take her in his arms.

"Shall I be a gentleman about this?" he murmured against her mouth.

"Yes, Jack. Yes. Just this once.''

And he was just as she wanted him to be; he allowed Rosaline to take his hand and lead him up the stairs to her bed, allowed her to divest him of his jacket and waistcoat which she folded and laid aside. In a sensually and leisurely fashion, he relieved her of her gown, shoes, stockings and petticoats, then the corset and camisole, until all of her fine, scented skin lay bare to him. And then he bowed down on the old rose patterned carpet and kissed her feet, her ankles, touched her as if she were made of porcelain instead of flesh, told her sincerely that she was beautiful, that he loved her.

And then he led her to the bed and laid her down upon the embroidered pillows and lace sheets with their sweet herb scents, loosened her hair pin by pin, and waited until she drew his head down before he came into her, gently and with reverence.

"You *are* beautiful, Rosaline. Do you believe me now?"

She smiled. "Yes, Jack. Yes. I really do believe you now."

ROMANCE FROM JO BEVERLY

DANGEROUS JOY   (0-8217-5129-8, $5.99)

FORBIDDEN   (0-8217-4488-7, $4.99)

THE SHATTERED ROSE   (0-8217-5310-X, $5.99)

TEMPTING FORTUNE   (0-8217-4858-0, $4.99)

ROMANCE FROM JANELLE TAYLOR

ANYTHING FOR LOVE   (0-8217-4992-7, $5.99)

DESTINY MINE   (0-8217-5185-9, $5.99)

CHASE THE WIND   (0-8217-4740-1, $5.99)

MIDNIGHT SECRETS   (0-8217-5280-4, $5.99)

MOONBEAMS AND MAGIC (0-8217-0184-4, $5.99)

SWEET SAVAGE HEART   (0-8217-5276-6, $5.99)